AS THE
SHADOW
RISES

"You're right," Ephyra said at last. "I don't just want to know why my father was looking for the Chalice. I want to find it, too. I *need to find it*."

"And you want my help?" Shara asked, crossing one foot over the other on the desk. "Even after everything I just told you?"

"You're the Thief King now, aren't you?"

"I am," Shara replied. "But I told you only fools go looking for the Chalice."

Ephyra's heart thudded in her ears, desperation clawing at her throat.

Abruptly, Shara pushed her feet off the desk and stood, folding Ephyra's father's letter in her hands. "Luckily for you, I am a fool."

By Katy Rose Pool

Age of Darkness

There Will Come a Darkness

As the Shadow Rises

AS THE SHADOW RISES

AN AGE OF DARKNESS NOVEL

KATY ROSE POOL

www.orbitbooks.net

ORBIT

First published in Great Britain in 2020 by Orbit

1 3 5 7 9 10 8 6 4 2

Copyright © 2020 by Katy Pool

Map illustration by Maxime Plasse

Excerpt of *We Ride the Storm* by Devin Madson
Copyright © 2018 by Devin Madson

The moral right of the author has been asserted.

A CIP catalogue record for this book is available from the British Library.

ISBN 978-0-356-51354-6

Printed and bound in Great Britain by Clays Ltd, Elcograf S.p.A.

Papers used by Orbit are from well-managed forests
and other responsible sources.

Orbit
An imprint of
Little, Brown Book Group
Carmelite House
50 Victoria Embankment
London EC4Y 0DZ

An Hachette UK Company
www.hachette.co.uk

www.orbitbooks.net

For Lucy, who said love is the message

I

GRACE AND FIRE

1

EPHYRA

NO ONE IN THE SMOKE-FILLED GAMBLING HALL KNEW THAT A KILLER WALKED among them. Ephyra eyed the crowds of sailors and hustlers bellowing and brawling over tables strewn with dice, coin, and cards, their teeth and gold flashing in the dim light. None of them paid her any mind, and if she'd come here for a kill, she would have had an easy time of it.

But Ephyra wasn't hunting for a victim tonight. She was hunting for answers.

She'd spent over a week chasing down rumors about the Thief King in every gambling hall and slyhouse in Tel Amot before finally pinning down a lead thanks to a woman who'd sold her wine at the Night Market. It wasn't much, just a place and a name—Shara at the Laughing Jackal.

Ephyra picked her way across the sticky floor toward the bar, dodging a brawl that had broken out over cards.

"Have you seen my friend Shara?" Ephyra asked as a server drew up to the bar with an expectant look. "I'm supposed to meet her here. She been in tonight?"

The server gave her a flat look. "Do I look like a messenger to you? Order a drink or leave."

Ephyra gritted her teeth and placed two copper virtues on the table. "Fine. Palm wine."

The server scooped the coins off the table and disappeared into the back room. Ephyra watched him go, reaching into her bag and brushing a finger along the spine of her father's journal. She'd spent days poring over the pages, looking for clues beyond the short letter addressed to her father on the back of a map that, presumably, showed all the places he had gone in search of Eleazar's Chalice.

It was the same thing Ephyra was looking for now. The only thing capable of saving her sister.

She'd studied her father's drawings and the few short lines he'd scrawled on the corners of pages. There was only one thing that stood out. Six words beneath a sketch of a handsome man's face.

The Thief King has the key.

In the past week, she'd learned that the Thief King was a disgraced scholar of the Great Library of Nazirah who'd abandoned his studies to search for a legendary artefact called the White Shield of Pendaros. He'd realized he had a knack for hunting down treasures and legends, and styled himself the Thief King. Along with the White Shield, his crew was rumored to have stolen a whole host of other legendary artefacts—the Ruby Veil, Lyriah's Flame-tailed Arrows, the Eye of the Desert.

But according to the note tucked into her father's journal, not Eleazar's Chalice.

Ephyra jumped in surprise as the server thunked down a chipped glass of wine.

He jerked his chin over Ephyra's shoulder. "That'll be your friend."

The crack of breaking wood sounded, and Ephyra whipped around. Not ten feet away, a girl stood with her back to one of the card tables. A menagerie of bangles and rings clanked around her wrists, and a dark, loose braid lay coiled over her shoulder. Two men flanked her, the remains of a splintered chair scattered at their feet.

"I should have known a whiny cretin like you wasn't good for his word," the girl shouted. "Give me my money or I'll—"

"You'll what?" the man said, grinning. "Annoy us until we—"

The girl cracked a punch across his face. She got a fistful of his shirt and dragged him closer. "Give. Me. My. Money."

"You'll pay for that," the man growled. He raised a hand and smacked it across the girl's face. She reeled back as the other man advanced.

Ephyra cursed under her breath. Of *course* her lead had to be an absolute idiot. Slinging her bag across her chest, Ephyra slipped between Shara and the two men, pushing her back.

"It's time to go home," Ephyra said to the men.

"Who in Behezda's name are you?" one of them growled.

"Yeah, what are you doing?" the girl demanded. "This is a negotiation!"

"I'm currently saving you from possible dismemberment," Ephyra replied. "So I would shut up if I were you."

"Stay out of our way." The man moved to shove Ephyra with a meaty fist.

Ephyra twisted away and had her knife at his throat before he could so much as blink. "I suggest you stay out of *my* way."

Ephyra held the man's stunned gaze, waiting to see what he would do. If he would call what probably seemed like a bluff, or if the knife would scare him off.

Of course, the knife wasn't what he should be afraid of. But he didn't know that.

He held his hands up. "Fine." He jabbed a finger at Shara. "This isn't over."

Ephyra waited a beat and then reached back to grab Shara's arm, ushering her away from the men.

After a few steps, Shara suddenly shoved her into a nearby card table. It caught her hard in the hip and Ephyra stumbled to regain her footing.

"What is your *problem*—" Ephyra's protest died in her throat when she took in the scene. The man she'd threatened was holding a splintered chair leg. Shara had just pushed Ephyra out of the way of his intended blow.

"Should've known you'd fight dirty," Shara snarled. "Once a cheater always a cheater. You can keep the money. You're not worth my time."

She backed away from them, waiting until she was a good ten paces away before she turned and fled through the cardroom.

Ephyra scrambled after her, catching up to her near the back doors.

"Word of advice," Shara said. "Never turn your back on lowlifes."

With every step, her bracelets clinked against one another. Ephyra now also saw the polished rings on her fingers and the beaded necklaces coiled around her neck.

"Is that how your negotiations usually go?"

"You're obviously new here," Shara replied. "There something you want?"

Might as well cut to it. "I'm looking for the Thief King. Someone said you might be able to help."

Shara's eyebrows climbed up her forehead. "Is that right?"

"Can you?"

Shara frowned. "There's only two reasons you could be looking for the Thief King." She raised a finger. "One, you're searching for something." She put up a second. "Or two, you had something stolen from you. So which is it?"

"So you do know him."

"I didn't say that."

"But you do," Ephyra countered. "Can you take me to him?"

She appraised Ephyra, eyes scanning over her worn boots and threadbare cloak, lingering on the scar on Ephyra's face. The scar that had been Hector Navarro's parting gift, right before Ephyra had killed him. "That depends."

"On?"

"Whether you're willing to pay the price."

A chill slid down Ephyra's spine. "What kind of price?"

"What any thief wants."

Ephyra's heart sank. "I don't have much coin."

"Not money," Shara said. "Treasure."

"Well, I don't have that, either."

"Sure you do," Shara replied. "Everyone does. Treasure just needs to be valuable to the person giving it up."

Ephyra thought about what she had. Her belongings were few. She couldn't part with her father's journal, as it might contain more undiscovered clues. She definitely didn't want to give up her dagger. Tel Amot had already proved to be an untrustworthy city, and if she was to get out of there unscathed and without leaving any new victims of the Pale Hand, she needed something to defend herself with. That left only one option, though Ephyra's chest clenched at the thought of parting with it.

"Here," she said, slipping the bracelet off her wrist. It was the last thing Beru had made before she'd left Pallas Athos, stringing together bits of broken pottery and a glass bottle stopper Ephyra had brought her. Ephyra had found the bracelet among their scattered things in the burned-down shrine. She could still remember the panic rising in her throat when she'd realized Beru was gone. She pushed down that same panic now as Shara took the bracelet and spun it around one of her slender fingers.

"What?" Ephyra asked impatiently. "Do you need a sob story to go with it?"

She looked up. "Nope. As long as there *is* a sob story. Come with me."

She opened the back doors to a courtyard lined with date palms. A few people milled about, some of them clearly too drunk to stand. Shara led her past the courtyard, down a walkway.

"What did you do?" Shara asked casually. She drew a line down her cheek, indicating the scar on Ephyra's. "That's the mark of a criminal in Behezda."

"I'm not from Behezda," Ephyra replied. This question suddenly clarified a lot of the strange and wary glances she'd been getting. No one else had had the guts to ask, though.

They reached the end of the walkway, which tapered down to a set of stairs that descended into the cool earth.

"Here we are," Shara said, motioning Ephyra down the stairs.

Ephyra hesitated.

"Oh, come on," Shara said, rolling her eyes. "You're the one with the knife."

Ephyra descended and Shara followed. At the bottom of the stairs, a creaky door hung open to a long, rectangular room with a low ceiling. A desk and a leather chair sat in the middle of the room, surrounded by numerous shelves stacked with books and other trinkets.

No one else was in the room.

Ephyra glanced around as Shara closed the door behind them. "How long do we have to wait?"

"Wait for what?" Shara asked, circling around the desk and pouring herself a cup of palm wine from a crystal decanter.

"You said you were taking me to the Thief King."

"Oh, right," Shara replied, sounding bored. She folded herself into the leather chair, propping her thick boots on the desk. "Pleased to meet you."

Ephyra planted her hands on the desk, leaning toward Shara menacingly. "Don't waste my time. I know you're not the Thief King. The Thief King is a man, an ex-scholar from the Library of Nazirah."

"The Thief King *was* a man," Shara said, holding her wrist up to the light as if to admire Ephyra's bracelet. "He's dead now."

"No," Ephyra said, more forcefully than she meant to. "That can't be. I need to speak with him. It's important."

"Oh, it's *important*," Shara said. "Why didn't you say so? I'll just go dig him up and we can resurrect him, then."

Ephyra sucked in a startled breath. For a moment, she wondered if Shara somehow knew what Ephyra was. That she could raise the dead and had done it before. But that was impossible.

"If the Thief King is dead, then why are you calling yourself that?" Ephyra asked, recovering.

Shara shrugged. "Couldn't think of a better name."

Ephyra raised an eyebrow.

"Truthfully?" Shara asked. "The Thief King has a sort of reputation. Which I'm sure you're well aware of, if you're trying so hard to find him. When he croaked, I figured it would be a shame to let that reputation die with him. It comes with major perks—useful contacts, intimidation, things like that."

"You've been working as the Thief King?" Ephyra asked. "Stealing legendary artefacts in his name?"

"Pretty much."

"Did you know him?"

Shara's expression suddenly hardened. "Yeah. I knew him."

Ephyra knew that look well—the face of someone trying desperately not to let their grief show.

"Then maybe you can help me after all," Ephyra said, reaching into her bag for her father's journal. "Your predecessor sent a letter to my father."

She flipped through the journal and slid the letter from its pages. Shara took it warily.

Ephyra knew its contents by heart now. *Aran, I'm afraid we can't help you with this one. If the Chalice exists, you don't want to go looking for it. The only thing you'll find is a quick death.*

"So, did he?" Shara asked, eyes flicking up from the letter.

"What?"

"Your father," Shara clarified. "Did he find a quick death?"

"No," Ephyra replied. "He did die sometime after receiving this letter. But he was sick. It was a slow death." She didn't want to talk about this with Shara. "Can you tell if that letter really is from the Thief King?"

Shara frowned at the paper. "Looks like his writing to me. This Chalice he's talking about—that's Eleazar's Chalice?"

"You've heard of it?"

Shara's smile glinted like the edge of a knife. "Every treasure thief in the world has heard of Eleazar's Chalice."

"And have any of them ever found it?"

Shara laughed. "You read the letter. My predecessor was the boldest, ballsiest thief of them all. And he didn't want to set foot near

8

that thing. So what does that say to you?" She didn't wait for Ephyra's answer. "Now, what was your father doing looking for something like that?"

"That's what I'm here to find out," Ephyra said. "I think my father must have known your predecessor—maybe even quite well. He never mentioned him to me, but the letter makes it sound as though they'd worked together before. My father was a trader."

Shara nodded. "We work with traders often—they're our go-betweens, finding the right buyers for artefacts."

"Then you think my father was asking for the Chalice on behalf of someone else?"

"Could be," Shara replied. "Although I doubt it. I don't think there's a fence in the eastern Pelagos crazy enough to try to make that sale."

Ephyra shivered. She couldn't shake the thought that her father *had* been looking for the Chalice on behalf of someone else—her. But she didn't know what that meant. Her mother and father had always forbade her from using her Grace—it didn't seem likely that they would be looking for the very thing that would make her stronger.

Maybe . . . maybe somehow her father had known that Ephyra's Grace was tainted. *Wrong.* Maybe he'd known what she was capable of, and maybe he thought the Chalice could *fix* her.

You'll have to finish what your father started. That was what Mrs. Tappan had said to Ephyra in Medea. If she had any hope of saving Beru, she had to find the Chalice.

Shara interrupted her thoughts. "You aren't the first person to come asking about Eleazar's Chalice. Every so often, some fool comes poking around for it."

"My father wasn't a fool," Ephyra snapped.

"I'm just saying," Shara said, holding up her hands placatingly.

"It's not the first time someone looking for the Chalice has wound up dead."

"I told you, my father was sick," Ephyra said.

Shara raised an eyebrow. "There's lots of ways to kill someone."

"You think someone's trying to stop anyone from finding the Chalice?"

"I have my theories," Shara replied. "Come to think of it, there's been quite a bit of chatter about this Chalice as of late. More than usual."

That startled Ephyra. Besides Mrs. Tappan, who else could be asking about Eleazar's Chalice? It couldn't be a coincidence.

Shara eyed her. "There's more to this than you're telling me. Isn't there?"

Ephyra met her gaze evenly. She couldn't tell this girl the true reason she was asking about the Chalice. That it was her only hope of saving Beru. That for years Ephyra had killed to keep her sister alive, until finally she'd gone too far—she'd killed Hector Navarro, and Beru hadn't been able to forgive her. She'd walked away, ready to let herself die rather than let Ephyra keep killing. And now the Chalice was Ephyra's only chance to stop that from happening.

"You're right," Ephyra said at last. "I don't just want to know why my father was looking for the Chalice. I want to find it, too. I *need* to find it."

"And you want my help?" Shara asked, crossing one foot over the other on the desk. "Even after everything I just told you?"

"You're the Thief King now, aren't you?"

"I am," Shara replied. "But I told you only fools go looking for the Chalice."

Ephyra's heart thudded in her ears, desperation clawing at her throat.

Abruptly, Shara pushed her feet off the desk and stood, folding Ephyra's father's letter in her hands. "Luckily for you, I *am* a fool."

Ephyra blinked as Shara stepped up to her, her hand held out. "I'll take your job."

"Job?" Ephyra echoed. "I told you—I don't have much coin."

Shara shrugged. "We'll work all that out later. So, are you in or not?"

Ephyra's eyes narrowed. "Why would you want to help me after everything you've just said?"

Shara waved a hand. "I've a taste for glory and a penchant for ignoring consequences. And you caught me at a slow time. I get bored easily. Did you want to stand here and argue, or do you want to find that Chalice?"

Ephyra clasped Shara's hand, heart soaring in her chest. This morning, all she'd had was a name, a place, and her dwindling hope. Now she had a bona fide treasure thief on her side and her first, real belief that she could do this. *Hold on, Beru*, she thought fervently. *Just stay alive a little longer.*

Shara smiled as they shook hands. "Glad to be doing business with you."

2

JUDE

FOR THE FIRST TIME IN JUDE'S NINETEEN YEARS, A TRIBUNAL WAS CONVENED at Kerameikos Fort.

The last time a Tribunal had been assembled was before Jude was born, though he didn't know what had occasioned it. It was the practice of the Tribunal to keep all records of their proceedings sealed. The only person who had access to those records aside from the Tribunal itself was the Keeper of the Word—though Jude had hardly had time to exercise that right.

Two statues flanked the Tribunal Chambers' entrance—one of Tarseis the Just, and the other of Temara, the first Keeper of the Word who'd sworn herself in service to the Prophets almost two thousand years ago. Jude paused for a moment beside the statue of his ancestor. She was luminous in the morning light, her fierce gaze overlooking the fortress. She was a warrior, a soldier like Jude. Devoted to a cause greater than herself. He wondered if it was easy for her, to give up everything quiet and warm for cold armor and steel.

"Jude." His father's voice sounded from behind him.

The former Captain Weatherbourne stood in the center of the walkway, the span of his shoulders taking up its full width. His thick beard had begun to gray, and though his throat was no longer adorned with the golden torc of the Keeper, he still looked every inch the part.

"You're not supposed to be here," Jude blurted. "Unless they've allowed you to attend?"

His father shook his head. "I only came to see you beforehand. Whatever transpires is between you and the Tribunal." He set a hand on Jude's shoulder. "And I am not worried about you, my son. There are simply lingering questions around what happened to Navarro, what led him to desert."

Jude had heard some of the rumors. Some made him angrier than he thought possible, like the one that said Hector had deserted the Order to raise a child he'd fathered before he took his oath. And some of them—some of them hit much too close to home.

"If they decide that Hector is guilty of desertion—" Jude broke off. He didn't want to think about what would happen. Jude still remembered the grim look in his father's eyes when he'd explained to Jude that part of his duty as Keeper of the Word was to be the one to enforce the Paladin's oath and to administer—swiftly, irrevocably—punishment for breaking it.

His father gripped Jude's shoulder a little more tightly, his face drawn and solemn. Jude knew what he was thinking—that Hector's conviction was inevitable.

"No one even knows where he is," Jude said quietly. That day in Pallas Athos, when he had fought Hector in the ruins of a priest's shrine, had been the last time he'd seen his friend. "He could be half-way across the world."

"The Tribunal will decide what action to take," his father replied. "Just tell them everything you know."

Jude nodded, nerves buzzing in his stomach. His father didn't know exactly what had happened in Pallas Athos, beyond the fact that it had led to Jude finding the Last Prophet.

"When the Tribunal is over, I will be here for you. And for the Prophet," his father said. "That is what we must focus on."

Anton. Jude still had trouble thinking of him as the Prophet. When he'd first met him in Pallas Athos, he'd seen him only as a thief and a gambler—one who'd saved Jude's life. Jude had been avoiding him since their return to Kerameikos. He'd read Jude with such ease and Jude feared that if they were alone together now, Anton would take one look at him and know every wretched thought crowding inside Jude's head. He couldn't afford that, not with the Tribunal looming over him.

Jude's father withdrew his hand and then let him go alone through the doors of the Tribunal Chambers.

The Chambers were composed of stone platforms around a central circle, in which blue and gray tile formed the seven-pointed star of the Order. The members of the Tribunal were arranged on the platforms in a half circle, facing Jude as he entered. They were a mix of Paladin and stewards, although all wore gray cloaks on this occasion. Each also wore a pin with the scales of Tarseis the Just, and their faces were veiled to maintain secrecy. Anyone could be under those veils—Jude's old teachers, the other wards who had resented him, even his father, had Jude not seen him two minutes ago.

Jude bowed his head as he reached the center of the circle. To his left, Penrose and the rest of the Guard sat on stone benches at the perimeter.

The magistrate, nominated to conduct the Tribunal's questioning, stepped forward from the rest of the group. Unlike the others, he did not wear a mask, and Jude vaguely recognized him—not a swordsman, but a steward, involved in maintaining the fort's defenses.

"This eighty-first session of the Tribunal of Kerameikos has been called to order," the magistrate said. "The Tribunal would first like to acknowledge the unusual circumstance in which we find ourselves assembling. Never before has a Keeper of the Word been questioned in our proceedings."

"I am here of my own volition and will cooperate in any way the Tribunal requires," Jude said.

The magistrate nodded, satisfied. "The goal of these proceedings is to determine whether the Paladin oaths of the Order of the Last Light were broken, what circumstances led to the alleged oath-breaking, and what steps must be taken to resolve these matters. We will be speaking with all those who have immediate knowledge of these circumstances. The Tribunal first calls Jude Adlai Weatherbourne to speak."

Jude took a seat on the stone bench that sat atop a black marble dais.

"Captain Weatherbourne, please tell us the events that preceded Hector Navarro's departure from Pallas Athos."

Jude took a breath. Maybe he could convince them that Hector had left the Guard in service of the Order. Maybe then, Hector could return one day. He began to speak, telling them how he and Hector had gone together to the citadel of Pallas Athos. How they'd discovered the Pale Hand there.

"And how did you know it was the Pale Hand?" the magistrate asked.

Jude hesitated. The truth would count against Hector and make it appear that he had been acting out of revenge. It was exactly what Jude had accused him of, after all.

"He recognized her," he said at last. "He had seen her kill before. Knew what she was capable of."

The same fury and heartbreak that had wrenched at Jude's chest that day seemed to clog his throat now. He swallowed it down, forging on to explain how Hector had returned to the citadel the next morning, and Jude's own decision to follow him.

"And when you left the villa that morning, what were you intending to do?" the magistrate asked.

It wasn't the question Jude had anticipated. He wondered what the magistrate hoped to learn from his answer. "My aim was to find Hector. I thought I could persuade him to return with me."

He paused again. This was the most critical part of the story. For the Tribunal but also for himself. The moment when the two of them had fought and Hector had left him bleeding on the floor of the ruined shrine. Even now, in retelling it, Jude felt sick.

"And you couldn't?" the magistrate prompted.

"He . . . he felt he needed to see his mission through. To find the revenant he believed to be the last harbinger," Jude hedged. Like the rest of the Paladin, the Tribunal could all sense whether someone was lying by the minute changes in their pulse, their scent, and their breath. This wasn't a lie—it just wasn't the whole truth. "If he was right, then his actions might have stopped the Age of Darkness."

"Is that so?" the magistrate said. "Captain Weatherbourne, the question is not whether Hector's actions were wrong. What we are here to determine is not what he did but why. The breach of the covenant always starts in the same place—the heart."

"Only Hector can tell you exactly what was in his heart when he left." But Jude knew some of it. The words Hector had thrown at Jude—that he never should have accepted a place in his Guard—rang through his head.

"And if he were here, I would be asking him," the magistrate said pointedly.

Jude looked down at his clenched hands. The magistrate was right. No matter what Jude said to defend him, the simple truth was that Hector wasn't here. And yet Jude was still twisting himself into knots for the faintest hope that Hector would return one day. But deep in his heart, he knew it didn't matter if the Tribunal named Hector an oathbreaker. He was never coming back.

"Very well," the magistrate said softly. "On behalf of the Tribunal, we thank you for your participation today."

Jude felt numb as he stood from the bench and retreated from the circle.

"The Tribunal next calls Moria Penrose to speak," the magistrate said.

Penrose stepped into the circle, pausing for a moment when she was shoulder to shoulder with Jude. She didn't look at him, but he could hear the hitch in her breath as she passed him to step up onto the dais.

"Paladin Penrose, would you agree with Captain Weatherbourne's version of the events leading up to Hector Navarro's departure?" the magistrate asked.

"Yes, I would."

"Have you anything to add on your own account?"

Jude looked at Penrose. There were things Jude had left out, chief among them how desperately Penrose had tried to stop him from leaving. But when she met the magistrate's gaze, she simply shook her head. "It happened as Jude said."

"Very good," the magistrate said cheerfully. "Now, I'd like to go back, to the day that Hector Navarro returned to the Order. Do you remember speaking to anyone about Navarro's return that day?"

"I spoke with Captain Weatherbourne," Penrose said. "Theron Weatherbourne, that is."

"And what did he say?"

"He had concerns about Hector returning to us and taking his oaths."

Jude dug his nails into his palms. He'd known of his father's concerns about Hector being named to the Paladin Guard—he hadn't realized that his father's concern had extended to Hector returning at all.

"Did you share those concerns?"

Penrose seemed to choose her words carefully. "It's rare for a member of the Order to leave Kerameikos of their own will. It's even rarer for them to return once they've left. We all had questions."

"How did you respond to the former Captain Weatherbourne's concerns?" the magistrate asked.

"I told him I thought Jude might choose Navarro as a member of his Guard." Penrose paused. "And that I didn't think it was a good idea."

The magistrate latched onto Penrose's hesitation like a hound catching the scent of blood. "Are those the words you used?"

"No," Penrose said.

"Then what did you say?"

Penrose glanced toward Jude. "I said I thought it would be the worst mistake of Jude's life."

Her words cracked over Jude like a blow. He had known Penrose was worried when Hector came back, but he hadn't realized the depth of it. Even more shocking was that she'd spoken to his father in such a way. It bordered on insubordination to her future Keeper. Penrose would have known that, which meant her distrust of Hector was important enough to risk it.

"You felt it would be a mistake because of the questions surrounding

Hector Navarro?" the magistrate asked, almost gently. "Because you feared Navarro would not be committed to his oath?"

Penrose looked down. This was it. Despite Jude's attempts to protect Hector, Penrose's suspicion of him meant Hector would be deemed an oathbreaker. Sentenced to die.

Penrose took a deep breath, closing her eyes. "No."

Hope fluttered in Jude's chest.

"What was the reason for your objection?" the magistrate asked.

"I was afraid," Penrose said, her voice shaking ever so slightly, "that Jude was in love with Hector. And that as much as I knew Jude to be committed and true to his duty, I also feared that if Hector was with him, Jude's feelings would compromise him."

Jude's whole body went hot and then ice-cold, as though he'd been burned by Godfire. Ash coated his lungs, the pit of his stomach. This was the moment he'd feared since he was sixteen years old and realized that his commitment to his destiny was not as unshakable as he once thought. The moment when all Jude's shortcomings, his failures, his unworthiness was laid bare to the rest of the Order. When they all saw that instead of a staunch heart, inside Jude's chest beat a wild and tender thing.

"In your opinion, did Jude Weatherbourne's feelings compromise him?" the magistrate asked softly.

Penrose looked down at her lap and didn't answer. The magistrate let the silence hang.

Finally, in a tiny voice, Penrose said, "Yes."

"It's as I said," the magistrate said, almost pitying. "The breach of the covenant starts in the heart. Paladin Penrose, can you please speak the oath of the Paladin Guard?"

Penrose swallowed as if fighting back tears, but when she spoke her voice was as hard as steel. "'I swear to fulfill the duties of my office, to uphold the virtues of chastity, poverty, obedience, and devote myself, my Grace, and my life to the Order of the Last Light.'"

"By chasing after Hector Navarro, by putting his feelings for him above his sworn duty as Keeper of the Word, did Jude Weatherbourne uphold this oath?"

Jude sucked in a sharp breath. Even without looking into her eyes, Jude knew Penrose's answer. He knew, too, how much it hurt her to say it. The sentence for a Paladin who broke their oaths was death. But Jude also knew that when he'd decided to go after Hector, he understood exactly what it had meant.

"No," Penrose said, her voice hollow. "I don't believe he did."

"And this was your gravest concern, wasn't it?" the magistrate asked. "Not that Hector Navarro would break his oath—but that Jude Weatherbourne would."

3

BERU

THE WHOLE PLACE STANK OF PISS.

Beru pulled her blue linen scarf over her nose as she ducked through the crowd. It helped with the smell only slightly.

The air roiled with the jeers of the crowd as they huddled like vultures over the blood-soaked sandpits. Below, fighters brawled fist to fist—sometimes to the vicious end. Some were prisoners carted in from neighboring villages, for whom a good showing in the pits might mean early release. Some were desperate wanderers who'd blown in on a desert wind, looking for a handful of coin or a thrill.

This was what passed for entertainment in this dust-filled nothing of a town. People flocked here to attend matches and bet on their outcomes. Beru didn't much see the appeal of watching someone get their face smashed in or collecting broken teeth at the bottom of a pit, but she wasn't here to watch.

She'd left Medea over a week ago, walking away from her sister and the only life she'd ever known. She'd had no destination in mind, just a voice in her head that whispered, *Atone.*

It had led her east, to an outpost along the trade route between Tel Amot and Behezda. A town so small it didn't even really deserve the label, consisting of a single caravanserai, a watering hole, and the fighting pits. The owner of the caravanserai and her wife, Kala, had taken pity on Beru and allowed her to stay there in exchange for helping out with their various jobs in town.

"You missed the first few fights," Kala said when Beru reached the medic station on the sidelines.

"Medic station" was generous—it was more like a patch of dirt cordoned off from the crowd with a few benches in it. The pit fights were brutal and bloody, and there were no healers in the town, so a few of the townspeople doubled as medics, patching up wounds in exchange for a handful of the fighters' winnings. Beru had talked to enough of the fighters to know that they wouldn't get their injuries treated otherwise. The owner of the fighting pits didn't even *feed* them unless they won.

"I'm sorry I'm late," Beru replied. Already she could see a few fighters sprawled out on the benches, worse for the wear.

"What kept you?"

Beru gave her the answer she'd been practicing on the walk into town. "I was cleaning stalls and lost track of time."

But the real reason for Beru's lateness had nothing to do with mucking stalls and everything to do with the sudden, sharp pains that had been plaguing her for the past few days. She knew and feared what they meant. She didn't know how much time she had left before her life faded, but she thought—hoped—she would have more. Time enough to do what that voice in her head demanded.

Atone.

It was Hector's voice, she knew now. She could still recall the sound of it, low and rough, when he'd said that word to her in an abandoned crypt in Pallas Athos. He'd wanted her to confess that her sister was the Pale Hand. But Beru simply couldn't betray her like that, no matter what Ephyra had done.

And now Hector's words haunted her. His death haunted her. It was his life that Ephyra had taken to heal Beru. The last life Beru would ever live. This one, she promised herself, would be different. She would spend it trying to follow Hector's words.

Atone.

I'm trying. This job was a start. Healing, for the first time in her life, instead of harming. But it was so small in the face of everything she'd done. She knew what Hector would say. She wasn't trying. She wasn't doing anything. She was just waiting to die.

The ringing of the gong jolted Beru from her thoughts. The next fight was starting. Another gong followed the first. Two meant a fighter had defeated two challengers. Most fighters would quit at that point, taking their hard-won earnings. But there were a few who chose to keep fighting—for their third win was worth twice as much as the first two combined. It was rare that any fighter won their third match, but they were always the most popular to watch.

The announcer, who was also the owner of the pits, swaggered onto a platform, holding a small metal disk in front of his mouth.

"Our next contender is the fighter we all know and love!" his voice boomed, magnified by artificery. "Give it up for the Bonecrusher!"

The crowd cheered as the Bonecrusher stomped into the ring, sweat and oil dripping down his barrel-like chest. The low sunlight glinted off his shaved head, and the scar down his face made his sneer look particularly menacing. Beru had seen him fight before and knew his nickname had been more than earned. She might as well start prepping the splints for whatever poor soul had to face him.

"And our brand-new fighter, already vying for the title of

undefeated after winning his first two matches of the day—it's the Sandstorm!"

A smattering of applause welcomed the other fighter, much smaller than the Bonecrusher, as he stepped into the other side of the ring, his back to Beru.

The Bonecrusher spat into the dirt. "Playtime's over, kid."

He stomped down hard, and the whole pit shook with the force of it. The crowd roared its approval.

The other fighter did not reply to the Bonecrusher's taunt, his stance almost relaxed as the Bonecrusher prowled toward him.

The Bonecrusher attacked. The smaller fighter dodged. Dodged again as the attacks rained down. He seemed to be almost taunting him, dipping into the Bonecrusher's reach and then quickly dancing out of it. But Beru knew it wouldn't last long—eventually the Bonecrusher would land a blow, and one hit could knock out a man the Sandstorm's size.

The Bonecrusher swung a fist. The smaller fighter didn't dodge this time but deflected the blow with one hand, driving the other into the Bonecrusher's side with deadly precision.

The giant grunted and coughed. Blood dribbled from the side of his mouth.

Beru heard the collective gasp from the crowd, who weren't used to seeing anyone get the drop on the Bonecrusher.

The Bonecrusher snarled, charging. The other fighter leapt, flipping over the Bonecrusher with ease, landing in a crouch at the edge of the pit beneath the medic station.

Beru's breath caught in her throat as she saw the fighter's face for the first time. She knew those dark eyes. They haunted her dreams. And it was impossible that she was seeing them now.

Hector Navarro was dead.

Yet he was also right in front of her.

His eyes flickered up to the cheering crowd and then caught on Beru's. Satisfaction transformed into cold shock.

Beru could not look away. Their gazes held, impervious to the chaos blaring around them. Beru couldn't help but think of the last time he'd looked at her like this, his sword raised to bring her to her end.

Then the clasped fists of the Bonecrusher crashed down on Hector, pummeling him into the sand.

A jolt of sudden pain reverberated through Beru. She cried out, collapsing to the ground as though she were the one who'd been struck.

"Are you all right?" Kala asked, rushing to Beru's side to steady her. For a moment, Beru could not reply.

"Crush him! Crush him!" the crowd chanted around them.

"I'm fine," Beru said weakly, just as another sharp jab of pain radiated out from her side. She clutched at Kala, gasping, and looked back down at the pit.

The Bonecrusher had Hector raised above his head like a prized pelt. With a loud grunt, he heaved him into the air, tossing him into the side of the pit.

Hector turned in midair, hitting the side of the pit feetfirst, and then sprang off, sailing toward the Bonecrusher. His knees hooked over the Bonecrusher's broad shoulders. Twisting his body, Hector used his momentum to slam the Bonecrusher into the sand with a tremendous crash.

The crowd was dead silent for a moment as the hulking fighter lay still. And then a roaring cheer went up, blocking out all other sound.

Beru reached blindly for the bench behind her and sat down hard, the buzz of the crowd washing over her. Vaguely, she could hear Kala prepping the station behind her.

Hector Navarro. *Alive.* It wasn't possible. Was her mind playing tricks on her? Hector's face haunted her dreams each night—maybe the haunting had spread to her daylight hours.

She didn't know what to feel. She had been so horrified when she'd realized that Ephyra had killed him. That had been her breaking point, the moment she could no longer live with what she was. What they had become, together.

But now, as if it had never happened, Hector was alive. As if that awful day in the village of the dead had been erased.

And the way her body had reacted when Hector had been struck by the Bonecrusher—she hadn't imagined that sudden burst of pain.

"Beru, I need you over there," Kala said distractedly. Someone had already dragged the Bonecrusher into the medic station, and Kala was assessing his injuries. "Yandros, sit still."

Beru reached for another kit. It was only as she was making her way down the row of benches that Beru realized what Kala was asking her to do.

Hector Navarro sat on the bench at the very end of the medic station, his shirt shucked off as he pressed his fingers against a fresh scrape on his forehead. He hadn't seen her yet. She could still disappear into the crowd, make her excuses to Kala later.

Beru stayed rooted to the spot, just watching him. And it *was* him. The same mess of dark hair, the same tall, corded frame. She stared, forgetting herself until he suddenly looked up, spotting her, and went still. Feeling strangely detached from her body, Beru approached.

"Can I—can I see?" she said, indicating the cut on his face.

He didn't say anything, just slowly lowered his hand away from the wound without taking his eyes from hers.

Beru knelt, her mind swirling with panic, grief, and confusion. Hector was *dead*. How was he sitting here, looking perfectly unharmed save for the injuries he'd sustained in the fight?

She could not begin to ask him how he was alive, how any of this was possible, so instead she leaned toward him and gently touched his temple with her thumb. She felt a sudden stinging pain in her own temple, followed by a surge of dizziness. It felt as though the floor had dropped out from beneath her, like she had become unhooked from her body. Horror and anger and grief slithered through her like an invading poison.

He jerked away. The expression on his face was one she had seen before—the moment he'd realized she was a revenant. And she realized exactly whose anger she was feeling.

"What did you do to me?"

She couldn't speak. Her hand tingled where it had touched him.

"Sandstorm!" a voice boomed to Beru's right.

Beru let out a breath as Hector's attention turned to the Bonecrusher, who came stomping down the row of benches.

"I want a rematch!" the Bonecrusher demanded.

Hector's expression slipped into lazy insouciance. "You want to get beaten again? If you insist."

"No one beats the Bonecrusher. I'll prove it."

"Does it have to be right now?" Beru asked, rising from the ground.

"This doesn't concern you, little girl," the Bonecrusher growled, advancing on her. "Stay out of it unless you want a turn in the pit."

Hector stood so quickly Beru almost didn't see him move. "You want a rematch? Let me tie my arm behind my back so it'll be a fair fight."

The Bonecrusher roared in anger. "I'll break your arm, how's that?"

"Oh, for Keric's sake," Beru muttered, pushing herself between them. "You might as well take out your dicks and measure them."

The Bonecrusher and Hector stared at her with twin expressions of shock.

"Yandros, why are you so mad at him anyway? Your masters keep you like a dog, hungry and ready to attack when they need you," Beru said. "You should be angry at *them*."

"What did you just call him?" Hector asked, sounding perplexed.

"Yandros," Beru said, facing him. "That's your name, isn't it? You're not the Bonecrusher. You're not their attack dog. You're a human, and I bet that under all that . . . muscle, you've got a good heart. Maybe you've just forgotten how to use it because you've had to use your fists for so long."

Yandros blinked at her. So did Hector.

"We'll . . . we'll finish this later," Yandros said, but all the fight was gone from his voice. He backed away and lumbered off without another word.

Beru looked back at Hector, who was staring at her with an unreadable expression.

"I forgot how good you are at that," he said.

"At what?" she asked.

"Placating people who want to hurt you."

Beru knelt again, digging in her kit for a clean cloth, and then, taking care not to touch his bare skin, dabbed at his scrape. Their faces were inches away, and she could hear the sound of her own breath, ragged in her ears, as she worked. She fought to keep it even, to stop her hands from shaking.

"You're frightened," he observed after a moment.

"Did you come to this town looking for me?" she asked abruptly, holding his gaze.

He shook his head.

"I—How are you here?" she asked.

"I don't know," he answered. "I was hoping you would. There's a gap in my memory. I remember Medea. I remember your sister arriving. And the next thing I remember was waking up in the desert, alone. I was found by a prisoner's caravan. They brought me here, to the sandpits, to fight."

"You don't remember what happened in Medea?" Beru asked, her voice weak. She let her gaze drift over him and realized that the pale handprint that had marked his throat in death was no longer there.

What did it mean?

"No," Hector said. "What happened?"

He had no idea what Ephyra had done to him. What *Beru* had done.

She fastened a bandage over his scrape, pretending it took all her concentration. She didn't have to tell him. She could leave this place and let him find out on his own. Turn her back on him the way she and Ephyra had when they'd killed his family.

When she went to draw away, he caught her wrist, fingers curling around the black handprint that lay hidden under a cloth wrapping. His eyes were dark and intent, and she could feel her pulse racing under his thumb. And what was more, she could feel the desperate undertow of fear beneath his anger.

His grip tightened. "Tell me."

Beru closed her eyes as unshed tears gathered there. "She killed you," Beru said, her voice cracking. "Ephyra killed you to save my life."

"That's impossible," Hector said. He let her go, rising to his feet. A breath punched out of his chest. "She couldn't have. I'm still alive."

She shook her head, rising too. "I don't know how. It doesn't make any sense that you're here."

"Is she here?" Hector asked.

"I left her in Medea. I couldn't—*can't* stand knowing what she did to you."

His face shuttered, his expression unreadable. "You should go."

"Hector," she said, but he turned away from her.

Beru froze, breath catching in her throat. She stared at Hector's back, at the place beside his spine. There, just above his hip, was a black handprint.

It nearly matched the one on her wrist.

4

HASSAN

HASSAN'S COMPASS STILL POINTED TO THE LIGHTHOUSE. OR WHAT WAS LEFT of it, anyway.

His gaze faltered over the blackened ruins on the shore. It felt like his city was no longer truly his own without its lighthouse.

But here were more dire reasons why Nazirah was no longer the city he loved. Black and gold cloaked Witnesses marched their way down the street below. Hassan counted five of them, carrying chains and torches—not Godfire, just regular yellow flame— as they passed by the dark houses that lined the street. It was a quiet, residential neighborhood, far from the bustle of Ozmandith Road and the Artificers' and Alchemists' Quarters. There had been rumors that the Witnesses would be coming to this neighborhood, and the rumors had proven right. The Witnesses could only be here for one reason.

He nudged Khepri, who was perched beside him on the roof. Soundlessly, she shifted her position, her body tense, her hand going to the blade at her hip.

Hassan put a hand on her arm. *Wait*, he mouthed. With her Grace-enhanced sight, she could read his lips even in the dark.

They both leaned forward, watching as the five Witnesses approached the door of one of the darkened homes. They paused there. Waiting for something.

Three Herati soldiers emerged from the shadows at the other end of the street, wearing the distinctive uniforms of green and gold.

Hassan glanced at Khepri and saw his own fear and anger reflected in her eyes.

The Witness in the front of the group pulled out a hooked metal rod and the others stood back as he used it to break open the lock. The door swung in, and a light in the house turned on.

"Now," Khepri said, and prepared to jump.

But Hassan held fast to her arm. "No. We need to find out where they're taking them."

A woman appeared at the door, looking incensed.

"How *dare* you break into my home!" the woman yelled, facing down the Witnesses. "Who do you think you are?"

"We are the loyal servants of the Immaculate One," said the Witness with the metal rod. "We know you are harboring a heretic."

"Heretic?" the woman repeated. "Get out of my house! You have no right to be here."

"Hand over the heretic, by the order of the Hierophant," the Witness said.

The woman stared him down. "I would rather be paraded naked down Ozmandith Road than submit to you and your Hierophant."

"Restrain her," the Witness said to the soldiers. Two of them moved forward to grab the woman. She dodged, striking at one of them and backing farther into the house, out of Khepri's and Hassan's view. They could hear glass breaking and a loud thump against the wall. A few moments later, the soldiers dragged the woman out of the house.

"Let *go* of me!" she cried. Whipping her head around, she started to yell. "Help! Help!"

Hassan felt Khepri tense under his hand. His grip was tight with the effort of staying still, of not leaping down and putting the Witnesses in their place.

But they needed to know where the other Graced had been taken.

The Witnesses poured into the house. Hassan and Khepri could only wait, knuckles clenched tight and hearts pounding furiously, until the Witnesses came back out again. And when they did, they were dragging another person, bound by Godfire chains.

"Mom?" the girl asked, standing between the Witnesses and looking up at her mother, who stood helpless.

She was a child. A *child*. No older than twelve.

"Hassan," Khepri said. It was just his name, but she packed so much meaning into that single word. They weren't going to let a child get taken, no matter how much they needed to find out where the Witnesses would take her.

"Let's go," Hassan said, and Khepri leapt from the roof. Hassan scrambled down behind her, making considerably more noise.

"What is this?"

Hassan froze. Khepri, halfway toward the Witnesses, hand at her blade, froze too. The person who had spoken was one of the Herati soldiers.

"She's a child," the soldier said. "We're not going to lock up a child."

One of the Witnesses moved toward him swiftly. "We act under the authority of the Immaculate One himself. You think he's *wrong*?"

The Herati soldier visibly hesitated. Then straightened. "I don't care what the Hierophant says. We're not taking a child away from her mother."

"The Graced are abominations, no matter their age," the Witness snarled.

"She hasn't had time to hurt anyone! Look at her!"

The soldier's hesitance surprised Hassan. Evidently, the Herati soldiers hadn't all unilaterally started worshipping the Hierophant and condemning the Graced once Lethia took over.

"Are you saying you know better than the Hierophant?"

"Maybe I am," the soldier said, advancing on the Witness. "Maybe I'm saying that your creepy masked leader doesn't know what's best for this city."

Hassan held tight to Khepri's arm. If the disagreement between the Witnesses and the soldiers escalated into a full-blown fight, they could take advantage of it.

The Witness's face twisted in anger. "The only thing worse than an abomination is the one who protects them. Fall in line, or face the consequences of disobeying the Hierophant."

"You can't do this." He glanced at his two fellow soldiers, who were restraining the girl's mother. Even from Hassan's position he could tell the soldier would find no help from his comrades.

Hassan squeezed Khepri's arm and gave a short nod.

They sped over the road and toward the girl. Khepri leapt at the Witness who held her, laying him out with a single blow to the back of his head. Hassan suddenly had an opening to grab the girl.

But the four other Witnesses closed in on them, holding Godfire chains.

"It's our lucky day," one of them said. "Three heretics instead of just one. The Immaculate One will be *very* pleased."

"Hassan, *go*!" Khepri shouted, and Hassan hesitated only a half second before he tugged at the girl's arm, drawing her away from the fray as Khepri unsheathed her sword and struck at the Witnesses.

The Herati soldier who had tried to stand up to the Witnesses blocked Hassan's path. Hassan stopped short, heart in his throat as he eyed the soldier's hand, which rested on the hilt of his blade.

There was a moment's hesitation, and then the Herati soldier stepped to the side, leaving an opening to pass through.

Hassan cast a glance over his shoulder where Khepri was holding the other Witnesses at bay, and then steered the girl down the road. He ducked behind a house to unwrap the Godfire chains from her wrists.

"You need to run," he said.

The girl shook her head, sniffling and holding back tears. "I'm not leaving my mom."

Hassan sucked in a breath. He had once been in a situation just like this girl—the Witnesses and the Hierophant at his doorstep. His mother and father at their mercy. Then, he had run.

But he wasn't running now.

"All right," he decided. He squeezed her hand—he didn't know if it was for her comfort or his own. "Stay here. If you see anyone, yell as loud as you can. I'll be back with your mom."

He darted into the street. In front of the girl's house, Khepri knelt on the ground, her wrists bound by Godfire chains. Three of the Witnesses were incapacitated around her, but the other two stood over her.

White-hot rage filled Hassan's mind as he charged forward, tackling one of the Witnesses to the ground.

Khepri took advantage of the distraction to swing her bound wrists into the other Witness's face. He stumbled back, and Khepri kicked him between the legs. He crumpled. Khepri climbed to her feet and then reached down to yank Hassan up. He scrabbled furiously at the chains until they dropped from her wrists.

Together, they rushed toward the girl's mother, wrenching the two soldiers away from her. Hassan slid a protective arm around her shoulders. A glance behind him showed three of the Witnesses rising.

"Get her out of here," Khepri said fiercely, and Hassan obeyed.

Mother and daughter were reunited a few moments later. At the sight of her daughter unharmed, the woman let out a little sob and they embraced.

"I don't mean to be callous," Hassan said, "but you need to get out of here right now. There could be more Witnesses on the way. Do you have anywhere safe to go?"

The woman hesitated and then nodded. "My brother has a ship—"

"Good," Hassan said briskly. "Go. Get her out of this city."

The woman nodded, and Hassan could see how she steeled herself for her daughter.

"We're going to go on a little trip, all right?" she said, soothing. "We'll just get some of our things—"

Hassan shook his head. "No time."

The woman looked like she wanted to disagree, but she closed her mouth. "We never thought they would come for her," she said, her voice shaking. "Her Grace only manifested a few months ago. My husband wasn't Graced, and neither am I. How could they even—?"

"I don't know," Hassan lied. The likeliest explanation was that one of this woman's neighbors had reported them. "But it's no use wondering. The safest thing for you is to get your daughter out of the city. Don't look back."

The woman nodded. "Thank you."

"Thank me by getting to safety."

She took her daughter's hand, and they disappeared into the night.

Hassan raced back to the street and saw Khepri, scuffed up but barely injured. The Witnesses and the soldiers were gone.

Hassan paused for a moment just to take in the sight of her. The pale moonlight made her bronze skin glow. She had that fierce, unyielding look in her eyes, the one that had carried her across the sea to find Hassan and back again to save their home.

He couldn't help but reach for her, clasping her shoulder. "What happened to the Witnesses?"

"They took off. The soldiers, too," Khepri said, but she didn't sound relieved. "We should get out of here before—" She broke off suddenly. "Someone's here."

"Reinforcements?"

"Let's go," Khepri said, running down the road. Hassan followed at her heels.

"We can't go back to our hideout," Hassan shouted as he chased her. "Not until we're sure we've lost them."

"This way!" Khepri yelled back, banking a sharp right turn down an alleyway.

It was then that Hassan heard the footsteps pounding behind them. Buildings crowded on either side of the narrow alley, connected by low archways. And ahead, a dead end.

Khepri skidded to a stop and launched herself between Hassan and their assailants. She unsheathed her sword.

In the dark, all Hassan could make out were two quickly moving shapes.

Khepri soared toward one of the figures. Hassan advanced on the other, striking out with a fist aimed at his throat. He hit nothing but air.

The man had moved like a bolt of lightning.

Before he could recover, Hassan's attacker slammed into him. He hit the ground, knees first, pitching forward as his foe seized his arms and pinned them behind his back.

"Let go of him!" Khepri was yelling. "Don't touch him, you filthy—"

"Khepri?" the other attacker said.

Hassan jerked his head up and watched as Khepri went quiet. Her arms dropped hesitantly to her sides. Though he couldn't make out her features, he could see the confusion tightening the line of her shoulders.

Her voice whipped through the air, incredulous. "*Sefu?*"

She sheathed her sword and threw herself into the attacker's arms, sagging with relief. He responded in kind, embracing her tenderly.

Hassan's heart plummeted into his stomach as his mind whirred with awful scenarios of Khepri's lost love returning, ready to supplant Hassan in her affections.

Hassan's attacker let him go and quickly darted over to Khepri, wrapping his arms around her and lifting her into the air.

Khepri gasped and swatted at him, elbowing him sharply in the gut once he'd set her down. "Chike!"

Khepri turned to Hassan, her eyes sparkling with joy. "Hassan, these are my brothers."

Hassan blinked and looked at the two of them. They were both broad, nearly a head taller than Hassan, the sides of their hair shorn like Khepri's. Even in the dim moonlight, he could see the resemblance.

"Sefu, Chike, this is Prince Hassan," Khepri said.

Hassan could not see Sefu's expression, but he heard the shock in his voice as he replied, "You did it? You found him?"

The other one, Chike, turned to Hassan and fell to one knee.

"Your Grace." His brother followed suit. "We knew you would return to Nazirah. How long have you—"

"We can catch up later," Khepri said, cutting a glance at Hassan. "We should get out of here."

Her brothers exchanged a look as they rose to their feet. "We know a place. It's safe."

Sefu and Chike led Hassan and Khepri through the dark streets of Nazirah.

"What were you doing in that neighborhood anyway?" Chike asked.

"We heard a rumor that the Witnesses were planning to raid one of the homes there to capture someone with Grace," Khepri replied. "We wanted to find out where they've been taking the Graced. But the captive turned out to be a child, so we stepped in. What were *you* doing there?"

"Patrol," Chike replied. "A few of us make rounds every night to see if there are any Witnesses skulking around, causing trouble."

"The last time I saw you two, the Witnesses were dragging you off that ship," Khepri said, her voice tight. "What happened?"

"We escaped," Sefu said.

Chike shoved his brother. "More like we were rescued. After the Witnesses dragged us off your ship, they took us into the city and walked right into someone's trap. A bunch of smoke bombs went off, and in the confusion we took off. By then your ship was already long gone, and while we were searching for another way out of the city, our rescuers found us and recruited us."

"Recruited you?" Hassan repeated.

Sefu nodded. "There's a rebel faction operating inside the city. They—we—call ourselves the Scarab's Wing. We've been taking in the Graced before the Witnesses can capture them, hiding them at our safe house."

"The entrance is hidden," Chike cut in. "And the safe house itself is fortified by powerful artificery. You'll see when we get there."

"We're not the only ones who returned to Nazirah," Hassan said. "We came with a group—a whole battalion of soldiers. Others who fled from Nazirah. We returned about a week ago, and the rest of our soldiers have split up to hide. Is there room for them at the Scarab's Wing base?"

Chike smiled. "Oh, there's room. Anyone who's against the Witnesses is welcome there."

"I can't believe we found you," Khepri marveled. "I can't believe you're both still alive."

Hassan's throat tightened. He was happy that Khepri had gotten her brothers back, but there was a small part of him that couldn't help but envy her. His father was dead, his aunt had betrayed him, and his mother . . . he still didn't know where his mother was.

"Has there been any word of the queen?" Hassan asked. "The real queen, I mean. My mother."

"The Usurper"—Sefu spat the word out like a curse—"said she was killed. We don't believe it. The Hierophant wouldn't waste a chance to parade her death around. She's probably in hiding somewhere. Like you were."

The words were uttered casually enough, but Hassan felt a twinge of irritation. He had been in hiding in Pallas Athos, that was true. But hearing it spoken aloud so casually made him sound weak. Cowardly.

As the group approached a wine cellar, Hassan couldn't help but think of his mother, at the mercy of the Hierophant or worse. But he forced himself to look ahead—he had to believe his mother was safe.

Chike led them into the cellar, and they descended into the basement, where hundreds of barrels were stacked up along the walls. Sefu approached a barrel in the corner, gripped its sides, and twisted. The barrel descended into the ground, leaving a wide opening in its stead.

"After you," Sefu said, motioning them inside. Chike took the lead and Khepri followed, swinging her legs into the opening and dropping down into the darkness. Hassan went after her.

He landed in a pitch-dark tunnel. Hassan felt his way forward, until he bumped into someone.

"Sorry," Hassan muttered.

"Oh, right," Chike said. "You can't see in the dark. One moment."

There was a slight tapping noise, and then the soft orange glow of an incandescent light filled the space. A long row of lights winked on, one after the other, leading down a long tunnel.

"It only looks like a long walk," Sefu assured them. "We'll be there in no time."

When they reached the other end of the tunnel, Hassan saw that the door was barred with what looked like several interlocked wheels with seven sides, each with a different symbol on it.

"This," Chike said, "is the lock."

"And the key?" Khepri asked.

Sefu tapped the side of his head. "Right in here."

Methodically, he and his brother turned each of the wheels, working their way from the outside in. When the central wheel was in place, the door made a slight clank and Sefu pushed it open.

Hassan stepped out into a huge room, with shelves stacked floor to ceiling with books. Hanging from the ceiling were huge golden globes encircled by golden rings—armillary spheres.

"This . . . this is the Great Library," Hassan said, breathless with the realization. "How . . . *how?*"

"The Scarab's Wing has been operating out of here since the coup," Sefu answered. "The protections already put in place by the librarians have proved to be very helpful in warding off the Witnesses."

"Do they know you're here?" Hassan asked.

"They probably suspect," Chike replied. "But they haven't managed to get inside, so there's no way for them to be sure."

A short girl with dark, bluntly chopped hair strode briskly toward them. "Where in the Wanderer's name have you two been? Arash expected you back ages ago. He was this close to sending a search party."

"We ran into some friends," Chike replied. "Zareen, meet my sister, Khepri. Khepri, meet my pain in the ass, Zareen."

"You mean *alchemist*," Zareen replied. Her eyes lit upon Khepri. "I've heard so much about you. And frankly the fact that you've managed to put up with these two your whole life says everything."

"Khepri brought someone else," Sefu said. "This is Prince Hassan."

Zareen's eyebrows jumped up to her hairline. She bowed her head. "Your Grace. I—we didn't know you were in Herat. We thought you'd left during the coup."

"I did," Hassan said. He didn't like to admit it, that he'd run while all of them had stayed, but it had brought him here. "I came back, with Khepri and others who wanted to fight."

Zareen glanced at Sefu. "Does Arash know about this?"

"Does Arash know about what?"

Over Zareen's shoulder, Hassan spotted a tall young man approaching, his gaze focused intently on them.

"Arash," Chike said, sounding suddenly much more formal than he had with Zareen. He even stood up straighter. "Sefu and I found our sister. We brought her here, as well as—"

"Prince Hassan," Arash said smoothly, stepping toward Hassan. "I'd recognize you anywhere."

Hassan blinked at him. He stood nearly as tall as Chike, although he was much thinner, his brocade-clad shoulders perfectly straight. A rugged dusting of hair covered his narrow jaw and the skin beneath his pale eyes was dark, as if he hadn't slept in days. "Have we met?"

"Once," Arash replied, looking unfazed by Hassan's failure to remember him. "My father came to court a few years ago—you likely wouldn't remember. He was a minor nobleman."

"*Was?*" Hassan asked. "I'm sorry for your loss."

Arash's eyes darkened, his shoulders drawing even more taut. "We've all suffered losses since the Witnesses took over."

"Arash is the one who started the Scarab's Wing," Sefu said. "He recruited us. He's kept us all safe."

"Then maybe you can help us," Hassan said. "We have a force of soldiers—around two hundred of us. We're scattered around Nazirah now, hiding out wherever we can."

Arash nodded. "Faran's group."

"You know Faran?"

"We've seen a few of your people in the city," Zareen piped up. "Brought a few back here with us. I'd say we have a dozen or so who've joined us in the last week."

"We didn't know," Hassan said. "Thank you."

"Don't thank us," Arash said. "We need people who can fight. Do you think you'd be able to get all of your soldiers here? Do you know where they all are?"

He directed the question at Khepri, Hassan noted. She hesitated before answering. "I think so. Some may have moved since we were last in contact, but—we should be able to find them."

"Good," Arash replied. "The sooner you can get them here, the better."

Hassan noted Arash's curt tone, and the intensity of his gaze on Khepri. But Sefu, Chike, and Zareen didn't seem to register it.

"In the meantime, we welcome you," Arash said, his tone softening. "It's good to have more people here devoted to the cause."

Again, his words seemed directed more at Khepri than Hassan.

"Zareen," Arash said commandingly, "show them to their rooms. We'll break open some of the palm wine tonight in celebration."

With that, he swept off. Hassan watched him go, an unpleasant feeling churning in his stomach at the brief dismissal.

"Follow me, Your Grace," Zareen said.

She led them to one of the Library apprentices' dormitories and left them there to settle in.

"What do you think of all this?" Hassan asked.

"What do you mean?" Khepri asked. "This is exactly what we've been searching for. Somewhere safe to take the rest of the soldiers. Somewhere we can defend against the Witnesses. Regroup, and strike back. Just like you said, Hassan."

Hassan heard her words, the echo of his own. She was right. Of course she was right. But he couldn't shake the strange unease he felt.

"What do you think of Arash?" he asked.

"He seems smart. Capable. *Handsome*," she added with a smirk.

Hassan snaked a hand around her waist. "Oh, really?" he said, tugging her toward him. "More handsome than me?"

"Hmm," Khepri said, pretending to think. "I'm not sure."

They hadn't been alone and *safe* in so long. He remembered

with some longing the heat between them when they'd kissed on the *Cressida* the night before they'd returned to Nazirah. The night when everything had begun to unravel.

No. Hassan wouldn't let thoughts of his aunt's betrayal or the horror of the lighthouse ruin this moment. They were safe, in each other's arms. They finally had a path forward.

"Perhaps I should state my case, then," Hassan said, brushing his hand against the side of Khepri's face. Her eyes fluttered shut. He dipped his head toward hers, until their lips were only a breath away. "Who do you think is more handsome now?"

"Kiss me already," she breathed, not waiting for his reply before she clutched at his collar and pulled him down to her lips.

Hassan let himself go, losing himself in the feeling of their bodies pressed together, his fingers in her hair. All the exhaustion, all the fear and the worry that had built up in them since the lighthouse fell seemed to pour out of them.

A knock at the door had Khepri demurring, pulling away from Hassan. He chased her lips, not wanting to give up this moment together.

"One *second*," she called out, pressing his palm to his chest. She quickly smoothed down her hair, checked her clothes, and then went to the door.

"Khepri." It was Chike. Hassan could see Sefu just behind him. "We're supposed to come get you. There's food and drink up in the observatory. A celebration, of sorts, since we've found you."

"All right," Khepri said. "We'll be right along."

Chike hesitated in the doorway, his eyes darting past Khepri to where Hassan stood. Hassan was sure he looked much less put-together than she did and had no doubt as to what conclusions Chike had drawn.

Sefu leaned over his brother's shoulder. "Perhaps we better give you more time to *settle in?*"

Hassan flushed, but thankfully Chike dragged his brother away before he could say more.

Khepri spun back to Hassan. "Don't worry, they're just teasing." She let out a laugh. "Although, if we don't go join them in the observatory, I can't promise it will stay that way. Ready?"

She held out her hand.

Part of him wanted to beg Khepri to stay and continue where they'd left off. But they'd just arrived at the Scarab's Wing hideout, and Hassan was itching to know more about these rebels. And in particular to know more about their leader.

Hassan took her hand. "Lead the way."

5

ANTON

ANTON DREAMED, BUT NO LONGER DID THE LAKE, THE ICE, HAUNT HIS NIGHTS. The darkness that had swallowed him a thousand times on a thousand different nights did not open its maw to him anymore.

Now, Anton dreamed of light. The cold, white light of the Godfire flames licking out from the top of a tower by the sea. He dreamed of arms locked around him, wind rushing past, and that light shattering the sky as he and Jude plunged into the sea.

He dreamed of a face, covered by a gilded mask, wreathed in pale flames.

He dreamed of a red sky. Red like blood, red like flames, red like fury.

Anton opened his eyes with a gasp.

Warm water sloshed over him. The blue sky streaked with clouds greeted him, bracketed by vine-covered columns.

"What did you see?"

Anton startled at the sound of Penrose's low, melodious voice. He sat up, water sloughing off him, and let his gaze find the Paladin at the edge of the pool.

"The lighthouse again," he answered after a moment, wading toward her.

Penrose's mouth pressed into a thin line. "Nothing else?"

Just the nausea of falling, the searing flash of lightning behind his eyes, and the pounding of Jude's heart against his ear.

"No," he said.

It had been over a week since they'd arrived at Kerameikos, the secret mountain fortress of the Order of the Last Light. Every day, Anton came here, to the scrying pool that overlooked the river, trying to conjure the vision he'd seen twice before in his life—the first time as a child, a memory he'd repressed, and again just over a week ago, after his brother had nearly tortured him to death. Illya had tried to use Anton as a pawn to win the trust of the Hierophant and the Witnesses, almost drowning Anton so he would reveal what was in his vision. But Jude had rescued him before Illya could succeed and they'd escaped—diving off the lighthouse and into the sea.

Only under the water, on the brink of death, had Anton been able to remember.

Now, he drowned, again and again, searching for some clue that would tell him how to avoid the destruction his vision promised.

"We're getting nowhere with this," Penrose said, her voice edged with frustration. "We need to make sure you're ready for tomorrow's test."

"Why do I need to do this?" Anton asked, pulling himself out of the water and onto a nearby stone. "I fit all the signs. I told them what I saw. If they don't want to believe that I'm the Prophet, then that's their problem."

"The Order has grown cautious after what happened in Pallas Athos. When we—"

"Thought that the Prince of Herat was the Last Prophet and then let him drag everyone to Nazirah because of a fake vision, and then you all almost got killed, I know, I know," Anton said, grabbing the towel from her and drying himself off.

Penrose's lips thinned.

The thing was, Anton didn't necessarily care if the rest of the Order believed he was the Prophet. If they decided they'd been mistaken yet again, they might kick him out of Kerameikos—and, as far as he was concerned, that wasn't exactly a terrible option if it meant he'd no longer have to suffer the torture of reliving his vision. And if they really *were* wrong—well then that would mean Anton's vision would never come to pass.

"We're just being careful," Penrose said.

"Careful as in making me scry in the Circle of Stones to prove I'm the Prophet?"

"I explained it to you before," Penrose said, sounding less patient. "There are certain places in the world where the Prophets' powers of foresight were more in tune. The Circle of Stones at Kerameikos is one of them. The Stones will react to your Grace the same way they did to the other Prophets."

Anton rubbed the towel through his wet hair. He wasn't looking forward to this test—this trial—at all. He'd thought, now that he knew the vision that had haunted him nearly his whole life, he wouldn't panic every time he used his Grace. But if anything, the panic was getting worse. Just the thought of seeing his vision again, of reliving that nightmare, made his chest clench with terror. He dreaded these scrying sessions, dreaded the long stretch of daylight with nothing to do except think about the terrible possibilities in his head.

Jude may have rescued him from Illya's torture, but was this really so different?

A stab of resentment twinged in Anton's chest at the thought of the swordsman. He hadn't seen Jude since they'd arrived in Kerameikos. The moment they'd pulled into the harbor, the Order had convened a Tribunal to inquire about what had happened to the wayward member of the Paladin Guard, Hector Navarro. They'd whisked Jude away for questioning, barring anyone—and Anton in particular—from speaking to him.

It wasn't Jude's fault, but Anton couldn't help but blame him anyway, though his resentment tangled with worry. He'd felt Jude's Grace on the ship on the way back from Nazirah. Before, his Grace had been as loud and unrelenting as a storm. Now, it trembled like a faint breeze. He'd stopped himself from asking Penrose about it too many times to count. He didn't know what Jude had told the rest of the Paladin about how the Godfire had affected him. And if he wanted to keep that secret, Anton wouldn't expose him.

He refocused on Penrose. "You know what I saw in my vision. A shadow will cover the sun. The Six Cities will fall. A plague, a storm of fire, a river of blood, the cracking earth—"

"Yes, I know," Penrose said sharply.

"And nothing," Anton said after a beat, "that says how to stop any of those things from happening."

"There's a way," Penrose said. "There must be a way."

"Whatever I see will come to pass," Anton said. "If I'm really the Prophet, that's how this works, isn't it? Prophecies always come true. Something is coming, Penrose, and there's no dodging it, changing it, or stopping it."

"*To bring the age of dark to yield,*" Penrose said. "Those were the words of the Seven Prophets' last prophecy."

"*Or break the world entire,*" Anton returned. "That's the part you all always seem to forget."

Penrose's eyes darkened. "What do you know about the other prophecies, Anton? The other Prophets?"

Anton shrugged. Here he was, the first Prophet this world had seen in over a century, and he knew next to nothing about the ones who had come before him. It obviously bothered Penrose, and the rest of the Guard, but Anton couldn't bring himself to care.

"Come," Penrose said, turning on her heel to exit the courtyard.

Anton bit back a groan and followed.

They wound their way through the fort. Living at Kerameikos wasn't all bad—the grounds were lovely, tucked between the mountains and bathed in mist from the surrounding waterfalls.

And it was safe. That he was sure of. After nearly seven years of constant scrapping and scavenging whatever he could—food, clothes, affection—it certainly felt different to be somewhere where he didn't have to wonder where his next meal was coming from, or decide what he was willing to give up just to find a place to sleep that night.

The back of Anton's neck prickled as they neared the edge of the fort, tucked against the side of the mountain. A stone staircase wound up and around the mountain face. The twinge spread up his neck and into his head, throbbing. He stopped, clutching at his head with one hand.

"Are you all right?" Penrose asked, concern evident in her voice as she stopped beside him.

Anton sucked in a breath. "Just my head," he managed. He pointed to the stone stairs. "Where does that lead?"

"The Circle of Stones," she replied.

Anton's hand fell away from his head as he craned his neck to look up. He couldn't see the Circle from here, but the knowledge that it was up there sent a chill spiking down his spine.

Penrose frowned but continued past the stairs until they arrived at a building tucked against the mountainside. Thin, ornate columns welcomed them onto stone steps leading up to a tapered arch that opened into the atrium of the building. A glass-plated ceiling cast light onto the pale stone floor.

"Where are we?" Anton asked as Penrose walked up to a pair of stone doors and placed her hand on a square that jutted out.

The doors groaned, opening inward to reveal a cavernous room lined with shelves as tall as three men. Soft amber light suffused the room, although there were no windows. Instead, sunlight filtered through each marble brick in the walls.

"This is the Order's archives," Penrose replied. "Where we keep all the documents pertaining to every prophecy of the Seven Prophets— when they were made, their interpretations, their outcomes."

They stepped into the cavernous room, and Anton wondered just how many people had devoted their lives to writing down every detail of these prophecies. Enough to fill this entire room.

A slender woman wearing a dark gray cloak came toward them, writing something down in a journal as she walked.

"Good afternoon," Penrose said.

The woman slapped the journal shut and looked up at them.

By now, Anton was used to the stares he got from the people of Kerameikos—awe with a hint of fear. Like he wasn't a person, but a savior. It reminded him too much of the way his grandmother had treated him, not like a child but like something she could use to reclaim her family's legacy.

It made him lonelier than he'd ever been, lonelier than he'd felt growing up with a family who didn't love him, lonelier than when he'd survived on the streets by himself.

"We are honored by your presence at the archives," the archivist said, recovering herself. "What is it you hope to find here?"

"We want to learn more about who the Prophets were," Penrose said.

Anton glanced away. He did want to know more about the Prophets—who they *actually* were, which he didn't think he'd find in any records. To the Order, the Prophets were infallible. But he knew now that wasn't true—that the stories were just stories. Because he was a Prophet, and he was anything but infallible.

The archivist looked a little surprised by the request. "Where would you like to begin?"

Anton opened his mouth to reply before Penrose could. "I want to know about the prophecies that didn't come true. The ones that turned out to be wrong."

The archivist stared at him, a new expression on her face. Shock, and a hint of anger. "There's just one."

"You mean the prophecy about Emperor Vasili," Anton said.

"You know it." It wasn't a question.

It was the only prophecy, aside from the final one, he knew all the way through. His grandmother had made him learn it when he was six, certain that Anton would be the one to prove it wrong. To prove that the Prophets were wrong, that her grandfather's legacy would outlive them.

The archivist led them down one of the aisles and reached into the shelf to draw out a thick brown manuscript bound with leather. She handed it to Anton. "These are the writings of Emperor Vasili. We have the original copies—well, most of them."

Anton took the manuscript and leafed through the pages. The

beginning of the booklet was written in neat Novogardian script, each section dated. They seemed to describe various military plans and notes on who, if any, of Vasili's advisors were to be trusted.

Anton flipped toward the end. Here, the text was messier, as if written by a shaking hand, and broken up seemingly at random. Scanning a few pages, Anton couldn't make much sense of the writing. Gone was the careful, almost methodical notetaking, replaced by nonsensical raving.

The shadow creeps closer each day.

I know He wants to speak to me. He visits my dreams.

What the Seven did can never be undone. Their sin has stained the world and we all suffer for it. Myself most of all.

The Stone calls out to me. It knows that it was stolen, it wants to punish me for the sins of the Seven.

The light is beautiful and terrible. It wants to consume me. It wants to consume all of us. It is consuming me, burning out everything and leaving nothing but ash.

"This is the last page?" Anton asked, looking up.

The archivist nodded. "That one was written days before he took his own life. It may be the last thing he ever wrote."

"What does it mean?" Anton asked. "What is that light he talks about?"

The archivist shook her head. "Vasili was far gone by then. He was afflicted with terrible headaches that put him into fits for days. The light, they say, is an effect of those headaches."

Anton shivered. He didn't think it was just an effect of headaches. The way Vasili described the light sounded almost exactly like the light in Anton's vision.

"You said he took his own life," Anton said. "How did he do it?"

"You don't know?" the archivist asked.

Anton shook his head. His grandmother had loved talking about her grandfather Emperor Vasili, but she refused to ever mention what happened to him after he was defeated. As if she could erase that part of his legacy by never speaking of it.

The archivist looked at him sadly. "He drowned himself."

6

EPHYRA

SHARA WAS WAITING FOR HER OUTSIDE THE GAMBLING HALL THE NEXT morning.

"Are you ready to meet the rest of the crew?" she asked as Ephyra approached.

"Crew?" Ephyra repeated.

Shara raised her eyebrows. "You didn't think I became the world's greatest thief by myself, did you?"

It hadn't really occurred to Ephyra that there was a whole *team* to aid the Thief King. She couldn't hide the discomfort on her face. The Pale Hand was used to working alone.

"You'll like them, I promise." Shara paused. "Well. *Like* is a strong word. But we need them. Come on."

She pushed open the door, leading Ephyra inside. This early in the day, the gambling hall was devoid of patrons. There appeared to be only one other person inside, a server standing behind the bar, stacking clay cups. As they neared, Ephyra realized it was the same server she had spoken to the night before.

"Shar!" he cried, his cheeks dimpling as he spotted her. Catching sight of Ephyra behind her, his expression morphed to confusion. "Who've you brought?"

Shara jerked her head at Ephyra. "Ephyra, this is Hayu. He owns this shop. Hayu, this is Ephyra. She's, ah . . . looking for something."

Hayu's eyes lit with understanding. "Oh, the new job."

Shara leaned her elbow on the bar. "Hayu's like the mom of our household. We stay upstairs when we're in town to rest and regroup." She turned to him. "Where is everyone?"

He opened his mouth to reply when the sound of two loud, overlapping voices cut him off.

"I've *told* you ten thousand times not to touch my things!" a high, female voice shrilled from down the hallway that led out of the gambling hall.

"You have too many of them," a deeper woman's voice replied. "Why do you need all of it? A woman should only need her clothes, a knife, and a bowl. That's the way of the steppe."

"We're not in the stupid steppe," the first voice retorted. "Pallas forbid we have *anything* to make our lives a little easier."

Two women, who looked only a little older than Shara, emerged from the back room of the shop. One was pale and slender, with an aristocratic face, light hair, and eyes the color of the sky after a rainstorm. The other was tanned, with dark hair gathered into coils, and taller than any woman Ephyra had ever met.

"Hayu, please tell Numir that if she ever moves my books again she can sleep outside since she misses the steppe so much," the blue-eyed one said.

The tall woman snorted. "Hayu, tell Parthenia that her *books* are cluttering up the room, and that she doesn't even read them, she just keeps them so that we all think she's smart."

"Hayu, tell Numir that I *am* smart and that she'd know that if she'd ever even read a book—"

"Ladies," Shara said from her perch at the bar. She swept a hand back toward Ephyra. "We have a guest."

The two women, entirely focused on each other, suddenly stopped and turned toward Ephyra.

"How do you do?" the smaller, light-haired girl asked, her voice lilting and sweet. "I'm Parthenia."

She was one of the most beautiful women Ephyra had ever seen. It took her a moment to find her voice. "Ephyra."

"This is Numir," Hayu said, grinning at the tall woman beside him.

"My tracker," Shara explained. "Parthenia's the language expert. She knows just about every language in the world—even the extinct ones."

"Especially those," Parthenia said, her eyes gleaming. "I specialized in ancient Nehemian translation at the Great Library."

Shara craned her neck over the bar, as if searching for someone in the back room. "Where is Hadiza? I told everyone to meet here at midmorning."

"You know my sister," Hayu said with a sigh. "She considers 'on time' to be whatever time she shows up."

"What lies are you spreading about me now, little brother?" A voice sounded from the door of the shop. A woman stood there, hands on her hips. She had short, curly black hair and the same medium brown skin as Hayu and Shara.

She eyed Ephyra as she strode up to join them at the bar. "You must be our new client."

Ephyra was unnerved by the group's familiarity, not just with one another but with her. "Ephyra," she said. "Shara said you all could help."

"I'm Hadiza, Shara's lorist," the girl replied.

"She knows everything there is to know about legendary artefacts," Hayu said proudly. "Seriously. Everything. Just ask her."

"Do you know about Eleazar's Chalice?" Ephyra asked.

Hadiza's eyes widened, and Ephyra heard the others inhale sharply. The room was still for a moment.

Hadiza whirled on Shara. "You didn't tell us she was looking for *that*!"

"I didn't?" Shara asked. "That's so weird, I definitely remember telling you. Must've dreamed it."

"No, you did *not* tell us, and I'm betting it's because you knew we wouldn't show up if you did," Hadiza said. "Funny, that."

"Well, now you know."

Hadiza let out a heavy sigh. "Even if we *wanted* to find the Chalice, how exactly do you propose we do that?"

"You doubt me?" Shara asked. "As it so happens, this job comes with a head start." She nodded at Ephyra.

"My father was searching for Eleazar's Chalice," Ephyra said, pulling her father's journal out of her bag and flipping to the drawing of the Chalice. "I found his journal. The Thief King—the first Thief King, I mean, wrote to him about it. My father's notes say that the Thief King had something . . . a key."

"It's a start," Shara said encouragingly. "Badis left all of his possessions to me when he died, so we must have it somewhere."

"Shara, this is reckless, even for you," Hadiza said. She eyed Ephyra. "Let me see the journal."

Ephyra hesitated.

"If we're going to work together, you need to trust us," Hadiza said.

"I don't trust you," Ephyra said. She didn't trust anyone. "But I do need your help."

Reluctantly, she handed her the journal. Hadiza flipped through the pages, her eyes scanning.

"It looks like Badis had the good sense to turn this job down," she said at last.

"Badis isn't in charge anymore," Shara retorted. "But I'm not going to force anyone to do this. It's your choice. All of you. It won't be easy. Or safe. If word gets out that we're looking for the Chalice, we're going to start running into trouble."

"You mean the *mildly* inconvenient fact that we might get murdered just for looking for the Chalice," Hadiza said. "Seeing as it's happened to every other treasure thief who's tried. Someone doesn't want it found."

Ephyra set her jaw. Beru had always been the one who knew how to extract help from others, how to sweet-talk a captain into letting two penniless girls aboard their ship, or get a groundskeeper to overlook the two of them squatting in an abandoned house. She'd even persuaded Anton to help them find the Chalice—although that hadn't ended well.

Ephyra's skills began and ended with killing people, and protecting Beru. And she'd already failed at one of them. There was only one way she could think of to get them on her side: Tell the truth. But even the thought made her skin prickle.

"I don't expect you to agree to this," Ephyra said. "I know the risks. So do you. But this isn't about just treasure or power to me. I need to find the Chalice because . . ." She swallowed roughly, fighting against her urge to keep this secret at any cost. "I need it for my sister. She's been sick for a long time, and healers can't help her. I think the Chalice can save her."

She saw Parthenia's expression soften. Numir looked thoughtful.

"That's sad and all," Hadiza said. "But that only explains why you're willing to do this. Shara, why are you?"

"Because no one's ever found the Chalice before," Shara said. "If *we* do it, we'll be legends. The undisputed best thieves in the world. The others will bow before our glory, and we'll forever get the best jobs, the best pay, and no one will ever dare mess with us. No more getting our jobs scooped by other crews or having fences try to cheat us. Besides, aren't you just a *little* curious about this powerful artefact that so many have died trying to find?"

"No," Hadiza said.

"I am," Parthenia offered.

"You've both got a death wish," Hadiza said. "You really don't understand what the Chalice is, do you? It's not a treasure. It's a weapon."

Shara opened her mouth to reply, but Ephyra spoke first. "What if it was Hayu?"

Hadiza glanced toward the bar, where Hayu was putting away the cups.

"What if you had to watch your sick brother suffer? And what if you found a way to cure him? Wouldn't you do everything in your power to try? Or would you stand by and say it's too dangerous and let your brother die?"

Hadiza swallowed. "Of course I would try."

"Then you understand why I need to do this," Ephyra said. "You know why I need *you*. All of you. I promise, I don't want to hurt anyone. I just want to save my sister."

With all of their eyes on her, Ephyra felt uncomfortable, but she held herself still and didn't show it.

"Where's your sister now?" Numir asked.

Ephyra turned to her. This truth, she didn't need to give away. "She was too sick to come with me. I left her at home. If I don't go back to her with the Chalice, she'll die."

That part, at least, was true. Beru's time was running out. Ephyra had already spent a week tracking Shara down. She needed to find the Chalice, and once she did, she would hire a scryer to find Beru before it was too late.

"So," Shara said after a moment. "Are we in?"

"I am," Numir said without hesitation.

"Me too," Parthenia agreed.

Shara looked at Hadiza.

"Fine," Hadiza agreed. "I'll do it."

"Well, it's settled, then. Wrap up your affairs, do whatever you need to do." Shara grinned, quick and wolflike. "Next time we set foot in Tel Amot, we'll be legends."

Their first stop, according to Shara, was the original Thief King's hideout. Most of his possessions were still there, and if Ephyra's father was right, the key would be there, too. It was just outside the city, and Shara promised they would reach it before dark.

The morning was still cool as they set off, Numir warbling a traveling song from the steppe while Parthenia egged her on.

"Sing 'My Wife Is an Eagle' next!"

Numir glared at her. "That's not a real song and you know it."

Ephyra pulled ahead of their bickering, falling into step with Hadiza. "Your brother says you know everything there is to know about legendary artefacts."

"My brother is fond of exaggerating, especially about me," Hadiza replied.

"But you know something about the Chalice, don't you?"

Hadiza nodded, not meeting her gaze.

"Who made it?"

Hadiza was silent for a long moment. "The Chalice wasn't made," she said at last. "At least, not by an artificer. They say it was the original source of the Grace of Blood itself. Where did you think the Graces came from?"

Ephyra shrugged. "I hadn't actually thought about it, to be honest."

"Well, the legends state that there are four sources of Grace," Hadiza said. "The Prophets were the first to gain their powers, the Grace of Sight. And they then bestowed the sources of Grace upon those they believed were worthy."

"Who did they give the Chalice to?"

"The Chalice was given to a medicine woman. She was able to use its gift to heal the sick. At the time, there was a plague overtaking the city. The people went to their Prophet Behezda to ask if the plague would end. Behezda's prophecy said that the plague could be cured if the blood of an innocent queen was spilled at the Red Gate. The medicine woman told the people of the city that she would become their queen and sacrifice herself for them. They crowned her the next morning. By nightfall, she was dead."

Ephyra shivered despite the heat of the sun. She'd known only in vague outlines the story of the Sacrificed Queen. Now, it seemed to take on a new meaning, reminding her of Beru and the choice she'd made to leave Ephyra and let herself fade away.

"At first, the city thought the queen had sacrificed herself in vain," Hadiza went on. "The plague was still just as rampant as before. For *years* they asked Behezda what her prophecy had truly meant. But as they later found out, when their queen died, her *esha* was released back into the land and was remade. Children were born with the Grace of Blood, like the queen. Her death helped create new healers, and she became known as the Sacrificed Queen."

It was strange to think that Ephyra's own Grace was linked to this queen, the first person with the Grace of Blood. "What about the Necromancer King? How did he come to possess the Chalice?"

"Years after the queen's death," Hadiza said, "the Prophet Behezda had another vision. She saw a terrible war—the dead rising up against the living, an army of revenants that would sweep through the desert. And the Chalice would be at the center of the chaos to come."

"The Necromancer Wars," Ephyra said.

Hadiza nodded. "Yes. When the Prophet Behezda told this prophecy to the new healers, those who had been born with the *esha* of the Sacrificed Queen, they took the Chalice and hid it in their temple outside the city. They called themselves the Daughters of Mercy. Whenever a child showed signs of having the Grace of Blood, the Daughters of Mercy would take them back to their hidden temple to train them.

"A few hundred years passed in this manner. But for all the Daughters' efforts to track down those born with the gift, the Grace of Blood had spread beyond the desert. Still, the Daughters of Mercy kept the Chalice safe, and the Necromancer Wars seemed like they might never come to pass."

"But they did," Ephyra said. "How did they fail?"

"Four hundred years after Behezda's prophecy, a boy with the Grace of Blood came to the Daughters of Mercy to be trained. He was a curious child, with abilities that grew stronger every day. The Daughters of

Mercy became concerned about this child and banished him from their ranks, casting him out to the desert to die."

"But he hadn't done anything. They cast him out simply because he was powerful?" Anger came hot and swift and unexpected. She'd never known this part of the Necromancer King's story. Everything she knew about the man had taken place after he'd crowned himself the Necromancer King, when he was already powerful and terrifying.

Hadiza looked at her curiously. "He had only shown that his power was greater than what the Daughters of Mercy could control. They feared him, and that fear led them to turn him into an outcast."

Ephyra looked out at the dry land around them. She could imagine, a little, what that would have been like for the Necromancer King. Alone with his great power. Ephyra's own parents had been frightened of her, the way the Daughters had been frightened of the Necromancer King. But Ephyra—she'd had Beru, at least. She'd never been truly alone until now.

"The boy remained in the wilderness for years, living off the land," Hadiza continued. "Using the creatures and plants to keep himself alive. And he slowly started to push the boundaries of his power, the boundaries of nature. He learned how to raise the dead. Not humans, at first. Over the course of his travels, he glutted himself on the *esha* of people and creatures he found out there, taking their lives for his own. When he was strong enough, he returned to the Daughters of Mercy and demanded that they give him the Chalice. Having tasted the sweetness of power, he wanted even more of it. He used the strength he had stolen from others to take the Chalice. The Daughters, too fearful to use the Chalice themselves, were no match for him."

Ephyra curled her hands into fists at her sides. She could imagine the kind of power the boy had commanded. She could imagine him wielding it against those who sought to stop him. She almost understood it.

"The rest you probably know," Hadiza said. "He declared himself the king of Behezda, and with the power of the Chalice raised a revenant army to march on neighboring cities. Those who resisted were killed and then raised to become a part of his terrible army. He eventually marched on the Kingdom of Herat. His army had another effect, too—it sucked the land of life to keep the revenants alive, creating this desolate desert."

"How was he finally defeated?"

"He wasn't," Hadiza said. "In the end, he was stopped because the Chalice's power turned on him. Every revenant he made drew a little more of his power, until he was weak enough for the Daughters to seize the Chalice back. Without it, his revenant armies crumbled. The Prophets, who usually refused to meddle in mortal affairs, took it upon themselves to punish him for his crimes."

"Why didn't the Daughters just destroy the Chalice?" Ephyra asked. "Why hide it?"

"No one knows for sure what they did with it," Hadiza replied. "I've heard a lot of stories. All different. None with any proof. Some people believe they *did* destroy it. But I think they couldn't, that doing so would destroy their own power. So instead they hid it away where no one could find it."

"No one," Ephyra repeated. "Except us."

"It's my turn to ask a question," Hadiza said, narrowing her eyes. "I know you're hiding something from us."

"Everything I told you is true," Ephyra said. "My sister—"

"I believe that," Hadiza said. "But there's something else you're not telling us. And if what you're hiding means trouble for Shara and the rest of us . . . well, you better hope it doesn't."

She held Ephyra's gaze for a long moment. Ephyra didn't look away.

"Messing with that kind of power . . . it'll get you killed," Hadiza said at last. "So you better be sure it's worth it."

Ephyra swallowed. "It's worth it."

The hideout of the original Thief King turned out to be inside the ruins of what must have once been a colossally huge statue. All that was left now was a foot the size of a house and some rubble. It stood in the middle of nowhere, nothing but desert shrub surrounding them for miles.

"What is this place?" Ephyra asked.

"This was a monument to the very first rulers of this land," Hadiza said.

"You mean, before the Prophets?" Ephyra asked. "What's it doing out here?"

"No one really knows," Hadiza admitted. "Nehemian legend says that the Creator God was angry that the people of the desert city built such a grand monument to someone who was not divine—the stories say he struck down the statue and scattered it throughout the desert in his wrath. Most likely, it was destroyed by a windstorm or something."

"Some windstorm," Parthenia said.

Ephyra turned to Shara. "Your predecessor built a hideout here?"

"Not exactly," Shara replied. She had her ear pressed up against the large stone toenail, knocking at it carefully. "This hideout existed long before Badis found it. He was just the most recent occupant. Aha!"

She drew away from the toenail as it gave a low rumble and started to cleave open, revealing a stairwell that led into darkness. Shara flicked on an incandescent light that hung around her wrist, and led them down.

After a while, the stairs leveled out into a large stone chamber. The darkness faded into dimness as Shara darted around the room, turning on the lights.

With the room illuminated, they could now see what looked like a workshop. A large desk sat in the middle of the room, surrounded by tall bookshelves. The shelves were in disarray, books lying open on the ground, loose pages carpeting the floor as if a shamal had come through. Three wooden chests were splintered open, their contents scattered around them.

"Who else knows about this place besides you?" Numir asked.

"No one," Shara replied.

"Well, someone was definitely searching for something," Parthenia said, kneeling by one of the chests and righting it.

"The question is," Ephyra said, her heart thudding, "did they find it?"

"Maybe one of Badis's old crew returned to their former hideout?" Numir asked. Parthenia kicked her, not very subtly. "Ow. *What?*"

"They're all dead, too," Shara said, letting a telescope fall with a thunk.

A chill shivered down Ephyra's spine.

"What if . . ." Hadiza swallowed. "What if whoever broke into our hideout knew that Badis had the key to finding the Chalice?"

Before Shara could answer, a dull thump echoed through the room. It thumped again, louder. It was coming from the back wall of the hideout.

Shara's eyes widened and she strode briskly across the room. Ephyra stepped back, her hand going to the dagger at her belt.

Shara seized the handle sticking out of the stone wall.

"What are you doing?" Ephyra hissed. "Whoever's here could be dangerous!"

Shara rolled her eyes. "Relax." She tugged on the handle, and the wall began to move. "There's a reason Badis picked this place as his hideout. This secret room is where he kept all of his *really* valuable stuff. See, it's not that hard to find a secret room, if you know where to look. He made sure there were other precautions in place. Once you go into the room, it doesn't let you back out, unless you know the password."

The wall opened, revealing a steel cage behind it.

"I thought I heard voices," mused the man behind the bars. "I don't suppose you're here to jailbreak me, are you?"

It took a moment for Ephyra to realize she'd heard that voice before. Out of the shadows stepped a man she'd once tried to kill.

Illya Aliyev.

7

JUDE

JUDE WALKED BRISKLY THROUGH THE COVERED WALKWAY, KEEPING HIS GAZE level as he passed the Paladin practice yards and rounded the storeroom at the edge of the barracks.

Glancing around to make sure no one was watching, Jude slipped behind the main row of barracks to the outpost building. He didn't want to have to explain to anyone what he was doing visiting the Herati refugees.

At the request of Prince Hassan, over one hundred of the Herati refugees from Pallas Athos had returned to Kerameikos with the Order of the Last Light. And though the prince had turned out not to be the Prophet—had turned out, in fact, to be the Deceiver, the first of the harbingers spoken of in the final prophecy—the Order had nevertheless honored his wish to keep the refugees safe. A decision Jude was grateful for—for more than one reason.

He felt the refugees' eyes on him as soon as he entered. A young woman approached him.

"Keeper of the Word," she greeted him. "What brings you here?"

Jude's stomach dropped at the title. He was still Keeper, for now. Yesterday's questioning by the Tribunal proved that might not be true for long.

"I need to speak with your healer," he replied.

She glanced at him, and Jude fought the urge to touch the cloak that wound around his neck. "Of course. This way."

She led him toward a small patch of grass that the refugees had converted into a garden. Two women, both at least twice Jude's age, knelt in the dirt.

"Sekhet!" the woman beside Jude called.

One of the older women looked up.

"The Keeper of the Word would like to speak with you."

The healer hobbled toward him, her wrinkled face scrunched in bemusement. "What can I help you with?"

"There's a matter I wish to discuss with you," Jude answered. "A . . . delicate matter."

She seemed to understand at once. She signaled to her fellow gardener that she'd be back and then led Jude into a covered hut at the edge of the yard. As the door closed behind him, Jude undid his cloak, letting it fall from his throat and over his shoulders.

The healer's eyes widened as she took in the sight, but she said nothing.

"You've seen this before," Jude said, touching one finger to the pale scars that branched down his throat and clawed toward his heart. "Or something like it."

"I have," the healer agreed. "Once, after the Witnesses took Nazirah."

"Godfire," Jude said.

The healer reached toward him. "May I?"

Jude bowed his head in acquiescence. The healer's hands were cool and clinical as she pushed aside the cloth of Jude's tunic to see the span of the scars. She tilted him this way and that, examining him.

"The Godfire burns I saw were . . . much worse," she told him. "But the pattern of these scars are the same."

"I was burned in Nazirah," he said.

"I'm sorry to hear that," she replied, drawing her hands away. And she truly did sound sorry. "I've seen what it can do. I've witnessed the pain. Helped my patient through the worst of it."

"That's the thing," Jude said. "I don't feel any pain. When I first woke up I did, but now . . . nothing."

The healer blinked at him. "No pain is usually a good thing."

Jude swallowed, pressing his lips together tightly. "When the pain subsided, I thought that it might mean my Grace would return to me."

On one of their last days aboard the ship before they'd returned to Kerameikos, Jude had woken up and his first sensation had been hunger. Not nausea from the pain, not the hollow ache of the burns, not the waves of burning and freezing. He had simply lain in bed, his stomach rumbling, laughing with relief. He remembered closing his eyes and reaching for his Grace.

And feeling nothing.

"I haven't felt it. Not once since Nazirah." He looked up, meeting the healer's gaze. "It's gone, isn't it?"

The healer was silent for a long moment. "From what I saw of the soldier who suffered the Godfire burns, the pain of losing his Grace was . . . immense. By the end of it, he could no longer speak. He was all but catatonic."

"By the end of it," Jude repeated slowly.

"He died," the healer said gently. "It was as though without his Grace, his body slowly lost its will to function. It shut down."

A chill prickled over Jude as he touched his scar again. Is that what would happen to him? Was it happening already without his knowledge?

"There is hope," the healer said. "It's not as if we know everything there is to know about Godfire and its effects. Until a few months ago, we didn't even know it existed. And based on what you've told me, there may be a chance that your Grace was merely damaged and that there may be some way to repair it."

"How?"

"That, I don't know."

Jude closed his eyes. A chance. He needed more than that. Without his Grace, he could not fulfill his duties as Keeper of the Word. And in that case, the Tribunal might as well label him an oathbreaker. If he could not protect the Prophet, if he could not fulfill the promise he'd made to Anton aboard the ship, he had no place in the Order anyway.

"I wish there was more I could do," the healer said. "Perhaps the Order's scholars may know of something that could help you?"

"No," Jude said, too quickly. "I mean—there are far more important matters they need to be tending to."

The healer's eyes darkened with understanding. "Ah. How long do you intend to keep this a secret?"

Jude swallowed. "Until I know whether or not I can fix it."

The healer nodded. "I won't tell anyone. And I will keep looking for answers for you. I will ask the other refugees as well. Some of them knew others in Nazirah who were also marked by Godfire."

Jude didn't ask this time whether any of those people were still alive.

Jude entered the silent temple, consecrating himself with the chrism oil at the threshold. The last time he had stepped into this holy place, his father had told him that the Prophet had been found, and Jude's life had irrevocably changed.

Now, it was about to change again. His Grace was gone. The Pinnacle Blade, lost. And tomorrow, when the Tribunal delivered their verdict, he might lose everything else, too. His position as Keeper of the Word. His Guard. His place in Kerameikos. His destiny.

He wondered when the exact moment was that he'd broken his oath. Was it when he'd walked out of the villa in Pallas Athos, away from the person he believed was the Prophet? The moment he'd chosen Hector for his Guard?

Or even earlier, the night that Jude had turned to see Hector's body washed in moonlight and realized for the first time he wanted nothing so much as he wanted to touch him. Or perhaps it was much later, standing in a gambler's den, his golden torc clutched in his hand as a bartering chip. Throwing his lot in with sailors and scoundrels. Trusting his fate to a gambling thief he barely knew.

But then, that gambling thief had turned out to be the Prophet.

Maybe it was none of those moments. Maybe Jude hadn't broken his oaths at all. Maybe all that self-doubt and fear and yes, maybe even his faithless yearning, maybe it all had led him to Anton. To the Prophet.

But soon, if the Tribunal went the way Jude feared, Anton would no longer be his responsibility.

Someone drew up beside Jude.

"I've been looking all over for you," Penrose said.

Jude opened his eyes. "Should you be speaking with me? The Tribunal might consider this—"

"Jude," Penrose said. "Please. I came to explain myself."

"You don't have to explain anything, Penrose," Jude answered wearily.

"You deserved to hear it from me," Penrose said. "Alone. Not in front of everyone. I'm sorry it happened like that."

"You don't owe me anything," Jude said. "What you said yesterday was the truth, wasn't it? I abandoned my duty, and more than that, I—" He broke off. "I messed up in choosing my Guard. I chose Hector because I—well, you know why. And I left to chase after him instead of doing my duty. You all almost died in that lighthouse in Nazirah because of me."

"You found the Prophet," Penrose said, her voice low but steady. "You saved him. You brought him to us."

Jude turned, walking away from Penrose toward the threshold of the temple.

"He needs you, Jude," Penrose called after him. "He doesn't trust any of us, but he trusts you. He asks about you. Just talk to him, please."

Jude turned to her sharply. "Did you tell him?"

"That you asked not to see him?" she said. "No. He thinks the Tribunal won't let him."

"Good," he said, reaching up to touch his neck, where the scars webbed out. "I can't help him. I can't help anyone."

"So you're just giving up?"

Jude breathed in slowly, pretending he was doing a koah. Except he couldn't do koahs anymore because he had no Grace.

"After your testimony," Jude said tonelessly as he turned to face Penrose, "the Tribunal will have no choice but to strip me of my title, and at the very least exile me."

"You don't know that," Penrose said. "You don't—"

"I do," Jude replied. "And you do, too. It should have been you from the beginning. If you were born to the Weatherbourne line, none of this would be happening."

Penrose drew back as though he'd lunged at her. "You can't really believe that. That is . . . that is blasphemy against the Prophets. *They* chose you."

"Then they made a mistake." He looked away. He didn't want to tell her about his lack of Grace. It was too shameful, too horrible, and Jude was too afraid of seeing his own fear echoed in Penrose's eyes.

"How *dare* you," Penrose said, fire in her voice. "How dare you question the Seven. How dare you even think you know better than them. You were so desperate to fight for Hector, yet you've already given up on yourself."

Hector's name felt like a knife in an already bleeding wound. Jude had been willing to throw away everything—his duty, his oaths, the Order—just to keep Hector by his side.

And it hadn't been enough.

He turned his back on Penrose once more. "Take care of the Prophet."

He walked out of the temple before she could reply. He didn't know why he'd come. The Prophets were gone. They had no answers for him.

The last light of the sun was fading as Jude made his way over the bridge and toward the fort. He bypassed the pathway that would lead him back to his barracks. He didn't want to sleep. Usually, in such a state, Jude would go to his favorite place in all of Kerameikos—the foot of the highest waterfall, where he used to perform his morning koahs.

That place reminded him of Hector, the way they used to practice their koahs there together, the one place in the fort where they could be entirely themselves. It was in that place, too, that Jude had realized what he felt for Hector. And in the same moment, realized that he was never going to be the person he was supposed to be.

He didn't want to remember that person. He wanted to forget him entirely, forget his shame, forget his own name. He wanted to forget that Jude Weatherbourne had ever existed at all.

8

HASSAN

HASSAN AND KHEPRI SPENT THEIR FIRST MORNING AT THE GREAT LIBRARY
exploring the rebel base.

They had met most of the other rebels the night before in the
observatory over cups of palm wine and plates of spiced stew, although
Arash had not made an appearance. They'd reunited with some of
their own soldiers—Faran had found his way to the Scarab's Wing,
along with a dozen others. Their bellies full and their hearts warm,
Hassan and Khepri stumbled back to their room and into exhausted
sleep.

In the morning, after breakfast, Hassan had left Khepri to catch
up with her brothers, and explored the familiar rooms of the Library
alone, seeing how the rebels had transformed it into a functional
base. It was almost funny—as a child, he'd been wildly jealous of the
apprentices who got to live and work in the Library full-time. Nothing
would convince him that living in the palace was superior. And now
here he was.

"Your Grace!" One of the rebels Hassan had met the previous

night stood frozen in the doorway of a reading nook where Hassan sat, paging through a familiar volume of Sufyan's Histories. The boy was young, perhaps younger than Hassan, and clearly had not expected Hassan's sudden appearance.

"No need for that," Hassan said, waving him off. "Have you by any chance seen Khepri?"

They'd agreed to meet back up before dinner.

The boy nodded. "She was just in the workshops wing. Arash and the other leaders are having a meeting. They asked her to join them."

Hassan felt a prickle of irritation. Why would they have asked Khepri to join them but not him? It wouldn't have been hard to send someone to fetch Hassan.

His thoughts must have showed on his face, because the boy hastily added, "I'm sure you would have been invited, too."

Hassan nodded, shutting his book with more force than was strictly necessary. "I'm sure. Where is this meeting happening?"

The boy hesitated. He was not, it seemed, *sure* that Hassan would have been invited.

"The alchemy workshop," he said at last.

Hassan thanked him and then took off at a brisk clip. As he approached, he heard voices from within the alchemy workshop.

Steeling himself, Hassan strode to the door and pushed it open.

All conversation halted as he stepped inside. More than a dozen rebels, including Khepri, sat around a table in the middle of the workshop.

"Your Grace!"

Half the people seated rose to acknowledge Hassan. Arash, he noted, remained seated.

"I heard there was an important meeting called," Hassan said lightly. He kept his gaze on Arash and did not let himself glance at Khepri.

"Just our usual strategy meeting," Arash replied, matching Hassan's airy tone. "You're welcome to join us."

"As the Prince of Herat and sole heir to the throne, I think I should be here, don't you?"

Arash looked at him coolly. "Tirzet, please find the prince a cushion."

A willowy woman turned on her heel and carried a thick sitting cushion over to the table, placing it opposite from Arash.

Hassan kept his eyes on Arash as he sank onto it.

"We were just discussing our next mission," Arash said. "We'd love your help."

"What are you planning?" Hassan asked.

"As you may know," Arash said, "the coronation of the new Queen of Herat is to be held in a week's time."

Hassan's blood heated. Lethia's betrayal was still a fresh wound.

"We thought we'd make our own demonstration to the city," Arash went on. "During the procession."

"What kind of demonstration?" Hassan asked.

Arash glanced at Zareen, the girl Hassan had met the previous day.

"We want to create a disruption," Zareen said. "I've been working with the other alchemists on smoke bombs."

"Smoke bombs?" Hassan asked. "The coronation is going to be crowded with civilians. If we set off smoke bombs, it could cause a panic. And aside from that, Lethia's coronation is just a distraction. We should be learning more about what the Witnesses are planning."

Arash looked at him mildly. "We're not working defensively here. If we waited to find out what the Witnesses were doing in order to act, we'd be constantly at their mercy. We want *them* on the defensive."

"If we make plans without any knowledge of what the Witnesses are up to, we run the risk of causing even more mayhem," Hassan protested.

"We are rebels," Arash said dismissively. "Our job is not to keep peace in Nazirah. It is to overthrow this regime by any means necessary."

"Innocent people will be hurt."

"They are hardly innocent."

"What do you mean?" Hassan asked.

"Surely you must know," Arash replied. "There are almost no Graced left in the city. We've managed to rescue a few and bring them here, and others have fled. But the Witnesses have captured more than we thought possible. All thanks to their Graceless neighbors. Time and again we've heard stories of them giving up their Graced friends, even their family, in exchange for safety."

"You can't assume that all the Graceless are doing that based on the actions of a few cowards."

"It may only be a few for now, but if this regime continues, there will be more and more Graceless who turn. That is simply the way of things. I'm sure *you* understand. These people have nothing on the line, and even the most noble will eventually preserve their own selves over the lives of the Graced."

Hot anger flooded Hassan's chest. He was not imagining the way Arash directed the comment at him.

"How dare you," Hassan said, his voice shaking, his hands flat on the table.

Arash raised his eyebrows, as if taken aback by Hassan's anger.

"You think I have nothing on the line?" Hassan asked.

"Hassan," Khepri said placatingly. "I'm sure he didn't mean it like that."

"That's exactly what he meant," Hassan said, keeping his gaze on

Arash, who looked impassive. "That because I'm not Graced like the rest of you, I'm not to be trusted."

Arash didn't reply, which was as good as an agreement.

"The Witnesses took everything from me," Hassan said. "I was driven from my country. My father was executed. And my mother—I still don't know where she is. If she's even alive. I did everything in my power to stop their Day of Reckoning from happening. So don't you dare tell me I have nothing at stake here."

With that, Hassan stood from the table and stalked out of the room.

He got a third of the way down the hall when he heard footsteps behind him. He stopped, heaving a sigh.

"Khepri—"

"Not Khepri." It was Zareen.

"What do you want?" Hassan asked warily.

"Just to give you some friendly advice."

"Let me guess," Hassan said. "I shouldn't take things so personally. Arash wasn't trying to imply that I would turn on the Graced."

"Actually," Zareen said. "You were right. That's exactly what he was implying."

Hassan was so surprised he didn't know what to say.

"Look, Arash is a good leader," Zareen said. "I love him like a brother. But he grew up in a family where if you weren't Graced you were considered worthless. He's never really seen beyond that paradigm. Plus, the reason his parents were taken by the Witnesses was because their servants betrayed them."

"Who were his parents?"

"Lord and Lady Katari," Zareen replied.

"I do remember them," Hassan realized. "They stopped coming

to court when my father named me his heir. They said that having a Graceless king would be a disgrace on all of Herat."

His mother had tried to shield him from their words, but his father had told him when Hassan asked for the truth.

"When you are king, there are people out there who will disagree with almost everything you do," his father had said. "And there are people who will dislike you just because of who you are. You cannot hide from them. But you can choose not to let them rule you."

Hassan looked at Zareen, who returned his gaze without shame or apology.

"Is that what Arash believes, too?" Hassan asked. "If the Witnesses fall and we depose Lethia, he doesn't want me on the throne, does he?"

Zareen gave a thin-lipped smile. "He was glad when the lighthouse fell. He said it meant you no longer had a claim on the throne."

"And I suppose," Hassan said darkly, "he wants to claim it himself."

Zareen shrugged.

"Why are you telling me this?" Hassan asked.

"Just figured you should know who you're dealing with."

"Hassan."

Hassan and Zareen both turned toward the door of the workshop. Khepri stood there, one hand wrapped around her waist, looking contrite.

Zareen shot Hassan an indecipherable look and then flounced back inside.

"Things got heated in there," Khepri said.

"I lost my temper," Hassan said. "But the things he was saying . . . I had to do something."

"We need to work with them."

"They should be working with *us*," Hassan said, frustration bubbling in his chest. "I'm the Prince of Herat." He stopped, and realized

83

that what he had said was wrong. "I am the *King* of Herat, whether he likes it or not."

Khepri sighed, taking his arm and pulling him down the hall and into a little alcove. "We've been running scared since the lighthouse fell. This is a chance to actually *do* something."

"Yeah, ruin a parade," Hassan said, not bothering to conceal his derision. He stopped, glancing at Khepri. "You agree with me, right?"

Khepri closed her eyes. "Yes. I mean . . . I don't know. The situation here is worse than we thought. And I don't necessarily like everything Arash is planning, but he has a point. We don't have many other options."

"You're serious?" Hassan asked.

Khepri spread her arms. "What do you want me to say?"

"That you'll back me up."

"Did you think we'd just march in here and take over leading the Scarab's Wing?"

"*Yes*," Hassan replied.

"That's naive."

Hassan flinched, stung. "Herat is my country."

"And I know you care more about it than you do a crown," Khepri replied. "We *just* got here, Hassan. All I'm asking is that we try to cooperate with the only people who are actually on our side."

Hassan shook his head. "I'm happy to work with Arash. He would just rather not work with me."

Khepri let out a sound of aggravation. "You don't need to like each other. But I know you've been going crazy not being able to do anything since we got back to Nazirah. *This* is a chance to do something. Let your aunt know you're still here. That you're not giving up."

She was right of course. It *was* driving Hassan crazy not having anything to do.

"Go cool off," she said. "Do what you need to do. Then tonight, once you've cleared your head, talk to Arash."

"Fine," Hassan agreed.

Khepri looked mollified. "All right. Well. I'd better get back in there."

She turned on her heel and then was gone, leaving Hassan alone in the hall.

Hassan returned to the Library's reading rooms, doing what he always did when he was overwhelmed—turning to books. Late in the evening, someone joined him.

"Prince Hassan," Arash said, clearing his throat.

"Arash," Hassan said warily.

"I came to apologize." To his credit, Arash did look remorseful. "I think we got off on the wrong foot. I behaved . . . rudely during our meeting."

Hassan waited.

Arash sighed. "You had a right to be angry. I'm afraid I've grown less trusting since the coup. But I should not have doubted you."

Hassan tamped down the anger still swirling through him. *Try to cooperate*, Khepri's voice chided in his head.

"I think I can relate," he said at last. "As I'm sure you know, I trusted someone I shouldn't have. Her betrayal . . . well, perhaps it's affected me more than I thought."

"I would like to ask you to take part in this mission," Arash said. "That is, if you're willing."

"I'm not sure," Hassan replied. "I stand by what I said. It's dangerous, and I think there are better uses of our time and resources.

We need to find out more about what the Witnesses and my aunt are planning before we try to strike at them."

Arash pressed his lips together. "I understand your hesitance. I hope that, perhaps, you might come to the meeting tomorrow and present your case again. I'll hear you out."

"You'll hear me out?" Hassan said slowly.

"I am always willing to listen to the concerns of those I lead," Arash replied in a reasonable tone.

Hassan saw red. Arash really thought Hassan was going to defer to him, that his leadership was more legitimate than Hassan's. He met Arash's gaze evenly and rose from his chair.

"You know, Arash, I don't think that will be necessary. You see, I've read many, many of the books on these shelves, and do you know what I've learned? That the King of Herat does not defer to the sons of minor noblemen."

And with that, Hassan walked out of the room.

9

EPHYRA

"WHO IN THE WANDERER'S NAME ARE YOU, AND WHAT ARE YOU DOING IN Badis's hideout?" Shara demanded, stepping up to the bars of the cage, brandishing a knife.

Illya's gaze slid from her to Ephyra in the corner of the room. "Do you want to tell them, dear?"

Shara whirled around to Ephyra. "*Dear?*"

Ephyra tightened her grip on the hilt of her dagger as she watched the shadows flicker across the smooth planes of Illya's face.

"Are you working together?" Shara demanded. "What, you were going to get information from us while your boyfriend here robbed Badis's hideout?"

"He's not my boyfriend, and we are *not* working together," Ephyra said. "I have no idea what he's doing here."

"But you know each other," Shara said.

"Pardon me," Illya said, "I couldn't help but overhear you talking earlier, as I am literally trapped in here. You're all looking for Eleazar's Chalice, aren't you?"

Hadiza stalked up to the cage. "What do you know about the Chalice?"

Illya shrugged. "Well, that depends," he said, his voice going low and soft in a way that made Ephyra's hackles rise.

"Depends on what?" Shara asked, suspicious.

"On whether you're going to let me out of here."

Shara barked out a laugh. "You're bold, I'll give you that. But we need a little more to go on—and you're gonna tell me why you're even here."

"Same reason you are," Illya replied. "I'm looking for the Chalice, too."

"Then we're better off leaving you in here, aren't we? Usually I love a little competition, but in this case, I think I'll pass." Shara moved toward the handle on the wall that had revealed the little room.

"I thought you were supposed to be clever, Thief King," Illya said.

Shara paused.

Ephyra wished Illya would shut up. She knew exactly how manipulative he could be—after all, he'd tricked her into trusting him not too long ago. Then, Ephyra had been the one behind bars, and Illya had held all the power. Now the roles were reversed, but she couldn't help feeling like even behind bars, Illya was still the one pulling the strings.

"We're both here looking for clues to find the Chalice," Illya went on. "So maybe you'd like to know what I found."

"He's lying," Ephyra said, her eye trained on Illya. "He didn't find anything."

"Maybe you recognize this?" Illya said, holding up a mirror about the size of his head with an ornate frame and base.

Shara stilled.

"What is it?" Hadiza asked.

"That's Badis's," Shara said to Illya. "Give it to me."

To Ephyra's surprise, Illya handed it through the bars to Shara without protest. Shara took it in both hands, examining it. "One of the last treasures he ever found."

"What happened to him?" Ephyra asked.

"He was on a hunt with his crew, searching for some lost jewels in the Killing Caverns," Shara said. "They thought it would be their ticket to retirement. But they wound up getting trapped in a cave. A shepherd found their bodies a few weeks later."

She said it matter-of-factly. Like it didn't hurt anymore.

"When did it happen?" Ephyra asked.

"Six years ago, now."

Ephyra was silent. Six years ago. Right around the time the plague had come to her village. And, judging by the contents of her father's notebook, just a little while after Ephyra's father had asked for Badis's help finding the Chalice.

It *could* be a coincidence.

Shara held up the mirror. "He brought this back from a hunt just before he died. He didn't want to sell it, but I never knew why."

"I think I do," Illya said. "There's a clue in it. I believe it will help lead us to the Chalice."

"Badis didn't know where the Chalice was," Shara replied.

"Maybe he didn't know where it was," Illya said. "But he knew enough. Enough to get himself killed."

"What are you talking about?" Shara demanded, her fingers tightening over the mirror. "What do you know about Badis?"

"Enough to know his death wasn't an accident," Illya replied. "Look at the back of the mirror."

Shara turned it over. "'For those who seek the Sacred Relic, that which gives dominion over life and death . . . look no further, for I will show you the key to what you seek, if you have the power to wield it,'" she read slowly. She lowered the mirror. "You think Badis tracked down this mirror so he could find the Chalice?"

"Whether or not he knew the mirror was a clue, someone else certainly did," Illya went on. "Otherwise, I'm sure, he'd be here right now."

"Well if it *is* a clue, you just gave it to us and now you have no leverage," Shara said, smirking.

"That one was free," Illya said, smiling. "A gesture of my desire to cooperate with you. But I found something else that I think you'll need to locate the Chalice. A code. Which I destroyed. So I guess you'll need me if you want to use it."

"He's just trying to stall," Ephyra warned. "For all we know he has a dozen men waiting outside ready to ambush us. He's working with the Witnesses. I don't know what they want with the Chalice, but it can't be good."

"Is that true?" Parthenia asked sharply. She had studied at the Great Library of Nazirah—it made sense that she would be sensitive to rumors about the Witnesses.

"I *was* with the Witnesses," Illya admitted. "For a time. Until being among their ranks no longer served me."

"You are so full of shit," Ephyra said. She turned to Shara. "Don't believe anything he says, and for the love of Keric, do not let him out of that cell."

Shara's gaze shifted from Ephyra to Illya. "I thought all the Witnesses were fanatical zealots. What happened, did you hit your head and realize it was all horseshit?"

"Something like that," Illya replied. His eyes turned downcast. "The Witnesses, I have to admit, had me convinced for a while. The

Hierophant has a way of . . . understanding, completely, what it is that drives you. And twisting it to suit him."

Ephyra snorted. "Sounds like someone else I know, actually."

Illya ignored her. "For a while, I ate up everything the Hierophant told me. That the Graced did not belong in this world. That they needed to be cleansed."

Beside Ephyra, Numir tensed. "That is sacrilege. The Graced are divine."

Illya turned his gaze to her. "You're from the north, aren't you?"

"The Talin tribe," Numir said.

"The Novogardians believe in the Divine Graced, too," Illya said. "That is why I was so eager to be told they were nothing of the sort."

"We get it—your parents didn't love you," Ephyra said, rolling her eyes. "None of this is an excuse for being with the Witnesses in the first place. Or an explanation as to why you left, as you claim."

"You're right," Illya said. "I suppose nothing excuses it. It was youthful folly and a desperate need to feel like I was part of something greater than myself."

The words sounded similar to what Illya had told Ephyra when he was trying to convince her to trust him. *I found purpose. Somewhere I could feel useful, for once.*

"But then the Hierophant asked me to do something that chilled me to the bone," Illya said, swallowing roughly. "He asked me to torture my own . . . my own brother." He shut his eyes. "And I . . . I *did* it. I did what he asked because he told me it was necessary. That it was the only way to right the world. But when my brother tried to escape, I let him go. I was disgusted with myself. I realized that no cause could be good when it required me to do something so monstrous."

Ephyra narrowed her eyes at him. From what she knew of Illya, he struck her as an eternal pragmatist who acted out of self-interest, not out of deep-seated beliefs. If anyone would pretend to be a zealot for personal gain, it was him.

But even if he was telling the truth, even if his devotion to the Witnesses was out of self-interest, that was no reason to trust him.

"So why are you after the Chalice?" Shara asked.

"Because the Witnesses want it. And they're not too happy with me for leaving. I don't know what they're planning on doing with the Chalice, but I figure if I can find it before they do, then I can draw the Hierophant out and kill him before he kills me."

"What a convenient cover," Ephyra sneered. "So that when you find the Chalice, you can deliver it directly to the Hierophant and win back whatever favor you may have lost with him."

"There's a problem with your plan," Shara said. "You're much more likely to get killed looking for the Chalice than by the Witnesses. Someone doesn't want it found."

"It's a risk I'm willing to take," Illya replied. "Besides. The Witnesses are worse than whoever's protecting the Chalice. Trust me."

Ephyra scoffed. "Trust you? Are you serious?" She glanced around at the others. "The last time I saw him, he tricked me into helping him find his brother and then tried to *kidnap* me."

"Yes, and you tried to kill me," Illya replied. "Which I think we'd all agree is worse than kidnapping."

"I didn't try to gain your trust first!"

But by the expressions of Shara and the others, Ephyra could tell Illya had already done his damage.

"All right," Ephyra said, taking a step back. "That's it. I'm not listening to this anymore. You can all do whatever you want, but there's no way I'm working with this guy."

She threw up her hands and stomped back up the stairs, out of the hideout.

The desert heat had cooled into evening. Ephyra plunked herself down beside two sand skiffs tied up by one of the statue's toes.

She knew exactly what was happening below. She'd seen how easily Illya had sunk his poisonous claws into Shara and the others.

Shara, who thought herself invincible, believed that even if Illya was lying to them, she could still get what she wanted without putting the rest of them in danger.

Only Ephyra knew how wrong she was.

A few minutes passed, and then Shara emerged out of the statue. She was alone.

"You're going to let him out," Ephyra said. It wasn't a question.

"We'll keep him on a leash," Shara replied, moving past Ephyra, toward the sand skiff tied up beside her.

"You're making a huge mistake," Ephyra said, getting to her feet. "He may seem charming and sympathetic now, but the next thing you know he's got six paid swords behind him and he's holding a knife to your throat."

"Kinky," Shara said, eyebrows raised.

Ephyra drew the dagger from her belt and held the point at Shara's throat. "Don't ignore me. I've dealt with this guy before. If you don't get rid of him, we're all going to pay the consequences."

Without missing a beat, Shara reached up and plucked the dagger from Ephyra's grip, using it to cut through the skiff's ties.

"Your concern has been noted," she said. "But let me remind you who's in charge here, as it seems you've forgotten. Let me also remind you that I didn't become the youngest, most successful treasure thief in the Pelagos by making stupid decisions. You can either trust that I know what I'm doing, or you can go find someone else to track down Eleazar's Chalice for you."

Ephyra glared at her. Shara didn't blink.

"What will it be?"

Frustration bubbled in Ephyra's gut. She pressed her lips together.

"Great," Shara said brightly. "Now help me set up camp."

They left Illya in the cell while they camped in the first room of the hideout. Once Ephyra was certain the others were asleep, she lit a lamp and crept over their sleeping forms and pushed open the wall to the hidden chamber.

Illya was sitting behind the bars, his elbow slung over one knee. He looked up as she approached. "Something told me you'd come in here sooner rather than later."

"You are absolutely shameless, do you know that?" Ephyra asked, coming closer. "I've met a lot of liars in my life, but you're something else."

He smiled, his face half-shadowed by Ephyra's light. "Everything I've ever told you has been true. To some extent. But if you want me to be honest with your little crew, maybe I can start with the fact that you're a legendary killer known as the Pale Hand."

Ephyra stopped. Panic rose in her throat. She swallowed it down. "You've no proof of that."

He shrugged.

In an instant Ephyra was up against the bars. "Say anything and I'll kill you. We both know I don't need a knife to do it."

Illya's smile grew. "You know, you never said why *you're* searching for the Chalice."

"That doesn't concern you."

"Does it have something to do with your sister?"

She glanced at him, startled.

"Just a guess. You were so desperate to find her the last time we saw each other, and yet she's not with you now, is she?"

Ephyra regretted ever telling him anything about Beru. "Why don't you tell *me* something?" she asked. "Back in Pallas Athos, you tried to capture me along with Anton. Why did the Witnesses want me?"

"You're Graced," Illya said. "And powerful."

"Is that really it?" Ephyra asked. In the back of her mind, she heard Beru's low warning the last time they'd spoken. *An Age of Darkness is coming. And we're the ones who will cause it.*

"Why, what else would it be?" Illya asked.

Ephyra narrowed her eyes. Did he know about the prophecy, too? As always with him, she couldn't tell truth from lies. Easier just to assume it was all lies. But that meant she would get nowhere.

"You may have convinced Shara you can be trusted, but you will never, ever, be able to convince me," she said. "Do us both a favor and stay away from me."

One corner of Illya's mouth tugged up into a twisted smile. "You're the one who came to me."

Ephyra turned on her heel. "Not a mistake I'll be making again," she called over her shoulder as she strode from the room.

"We'll see," Illya's voice, quieter than hers, floated after her, echoing in her head until sleep finally found her again.

10

ANTON

THE HIEROPHANT SWEPT DOWN THE CORRIDOR, TORCHLIGHT GLINTING OFF the gold mask that obscured his face. Two robed figures flanked him.

He drew to a stop in front of a circular room. Another robed figure guarded the door.

"Take me to the prisoner," the Hierophant said.

"Yes, Immaculate One," the robed man said, heaving open the heavy door.

The room was dim, reeking with the scent of burned flesh. It was unfurnished save for the table in the center. A man lay on top of it, his skin raw and scorched in places, scarred over in others. Tattered robes hung around his thin frame, and his ankles and wrists were chained down to the table. Another man stood at the perimeter, holding a torch of white flame.

The Hierophant drew closer to the prisoner.

"No more," the prisoner moaned, his voice trembling. "Please, no more."

"I'm not going to hurt you," the Hierophant said, in a voice that was almost gentle. "I'm here to listen."

"L-listen?"

"Yes. You are going to tell me where the covenant is."

"I don't know," the man on the table whimpered.

"I'm afraid I don't believe you."

The Witness holding the Godfire torch lowered the flame to the prisoner's chest. Screams echoed through the room, desperate, almost animal noises. The Witness withdrew the torch and the screams cut off.

"I see you will not make this easy for either of us," the Hierophant said, sounding tired. "You are not the first follower of the Lost Rose I have tracked down. Some of them gave up their secrets quite easily, but others took more . . . convincing."

The Hierophant laid a slender hand on the man's shoulder lightly, and the Witness lowered the torch again, its flame dancing above the prisoner's skin. The prisoner whimpered, his body jerking against his chains.

"I don't know where the covenant is," the prisoner gasped. "I don't even know what that is. The secrets of the Lost Rose are kept hidden even from its members."

"You are stalling," the Hierophant said. "You truly expect me to believe that you've never heard of the *only* written record of the Lost Rose? Of the Relics they protect, and what they can do?"

The prisoner glanced at the Godfire flame, drawing closer to his skin. "I—I've never laid eyes on it."

"So you *do* know of it," the Hierophant said, satisfied. "I thought so. And I think you know exactly where it is. I think that you believe you will protect this secret from me, until your dying breath, because you fear what will happen if I find it. But I assure you, whether or not you die screaming on this table, what happens next has already been set in motion. The ancient power you have tried to protect will be unleashed, to propel us into a new and glorious era."

The prisoner did not answer, his face warped with anguish.

"But if you die here without giving me what I want," the Hierophant went on, almost tender, "your daughter will be next. We will rip this secret from her, and your death will be for nothing."

"No," the prisoner rasped. "No, please. I'll tell you. I'll tell you anything you want to know." He flinched as the masked man stroked a long finger over his forehead.

"I'm listening."

Anton startled awake, light bursting behind his eyes.

"What is it, boy?" His grandmother stood over him. Her face was cracked and wizened, her mouth set cruelly, her eyes like two black marbles.

"I was dreaming, Babiya," he said, blinking in the dark.

"Anton," she croaked. "My child. Come home. You belong with us. This is your destiny, just like it was Vasili's. You will finish what he began."

"No," Anton tried to say, but no sound came out of his mouth. "No, no, I'm not. I won't be like him."

He was sinking. Hands reached down to grip him. Anton thrashed and fought against the hold, but it did not let up. He breached the surface of the water and found himself floating in a crumbling fountain. He pushed himself up and climbed over the rim, toppling into a courtyard filled with amber light and bustling voices.

He knew this place.

"There you are."

He knew that voice, too. He turned. Surrounded by the shadowy, indistinct figures of the rest of the crowd stood the Nameless

Woman. She looked exactly like she had the last time Anton had seen her. Her dark painted lips formed the hint of a smile.

"I've been looking for you," the Nameless Woman went on. She was suddenly right in front of him. She held out her hand. In it were four playing cards, one in each suit—cups, crowns, stones, swords. Anton's fingers closed around the cards.

"How did you find me?" Anton asked.

"You think my powers only work when we're awake?" she asked, sounding amused. She waved her hand, and she was suddenly holding a glass of dark wine.

He shook his head. "You've never done this before."

"You were never ready," she replied.

"I'm not ready now." Anton swallowed. He tasted ice in his throat. "I'm going to be just like him. They're going to make me. It's happening already. There's a light in my vision and the light, it wants—" He stopped. The *light* wants? That wasn't what he intended to say. "It drove him mad. It's going to do the same thing to me."

The cards in his hands were gone. Instead, he held a sword. It felt heavy, but Anton knew he could not drop it.

"Endarrion," the Nameless Woman said. "You'll find it there."

"What?"

Something passed over the Nameless Woman's face, like a shadow. "Anton," she said, the glass in her hand cracking, wine spilling from it like blood. "Wake up."

Anton sat up, gasping in the darkness. His sheets had been pushed off the bed, his neck and forehead damp with cold sweat. He raised a shaking hand to his face to wipe at a stray tear.

The images from his dream swam behind his eyes. The Nameless Woman, his grandmother . . . and the Hierophant. It had felt so *real*, like he'd really been in that room, watching the Witnesses torture that prisoner, his screams ringing around them.

He'd never seen the Hierophant before, but he knew that was who the masked man was. He'd dreamed of him, but not in such visceral detail.

Could it be real? Or had it been conjured from Anton's own terror?

But it was impossible. It was a dream, nothing more. Just his mind churning through its worst fears.

He gazed out through his window at the black sky, cold dread pitting his stomach as he thought of what awaited him in the morning. More nightmares. More of the same. The thought of facing it again made him suddenly, impossibly weary, a kind of exhaustion that sleep could not soothe.

What was he even doing in Kerameikos? Subjecting himself to some test devised by people who didn't care about him, only the visions in his head, the way his grandmother had, the way his brother had, the way the Hierophant had. It didn't matter to them what Anton wanted, and it never would. And if their digging and prodding turned him mad, they wouldn't care, either.

The thought came to him, sudden and inevitable—he could leave.

It would mean at least a week's hike in either direction—Anton wasn't sure exactly where in the Gallian Mountains they were, but he knew if he followed the river long enough, he'd hit a coast eventually. From there, he would figure the rest out. He always did. He would be alone, but he'd been alone his whole life. Why should now be any different?

It was supposed to be, a voice in the back of his mind whispered. *This time, you were supposed to have someone to protect you.*

He shoved the thought away viciously, climbing out of bed and throwing a few changes of clothes into one of the sheets, tying it up like a sack. He slipped outside, closing the door behind him as quietly as he could, and crept across the darkened courtyard toward the barracks' storeroom. In the absence of the fort's usual noise, the rush of the river sounded twice as loud.

The storeroom was unlocked, the door slightly ajar. Anton supposed that as isolated as they were here, they didn't need to worry about petty thieves.

He crept inside, tapping on the incandescent light until it illuminated the cavernous storeroom. Starting down the first row of shelves, he began gathering his provisions, fingers skimming the shelves and plucking out whatever looked serviceable—a few root vegetables, a skin of water, a sack of grain. He turned the corner to the next row of shelves and peered at a row of unlabeled jars. He grabbed one at random, opening the lid to sniff at it carefully.

"Why is it," a voice spoke from the darkness, "that whenever I can't sleep, there *you* are."

Anton jumped, fumbling and knocking a stack of crates into the nearby shelf. The jar broke open at his feet, spilling salt grains all over the floor.

Anton didn't move to pick it up. Instead, he stared ahead, eyes adjusting to the dimness until he could see Jude half leaning against the shelf that ran along the storeroom's back wall. His posture was crooked and slumped, like he was hurt.

"You dreaming about me, Jude?" Anton asked. This was, he realized, the first time they had been face-to-face since arriving at

Kerameikos. Since the Tribunal had barred them from seeing each other.

Jude's head lolled to the side, his gaze focused on Anton. "First the Hidden Spring," he went on, as if he hadn't heard him. "Then on the ship. Now here."

An uncharacteristic bitterness suffused Jude's words, and there was something else about his voice that sounded *wrong*. As Jude lifted a jug to his lips and took a long gulp, the whole image of him came together. The heavy slump of his shoulders. The unfocused gaze. The slur of his words.

Jude wasn't hurt. He was drunk.

The impossibility of this simple fact rendered Anton speechless for a long moment. He recalled the disdain with which Jude had refused even the smallest cup of wine by the crew of the *Black Cormorant* in Pallas Athos. Before arriving in Kerameikos, Anton had assumed all the Paladin abstained—but it was just Jude. Until now, anyway.

In the silence that stretched between them, Jude raised the jug of wine, taking a long drink from it.

"All right," Anton said, kneeling at Jude's side and gently tugging the jug away from him. "I think that's enough."

Dealing with overindulgent patrons was something Anton had gotten a lot of practice at when he'd worked as a server at Thalassa Gardens. This wasn't any different, really.

Jude let Anton drag the jug away from him, his eyes unfocused and bleary.

Anton set the jug down behind him. "Why don't we get off the floor?"

Jude wiped at the corner of his mouth with his palm. "I am exactly where I belong."

Anton swallowed and pushed himself to his feet. He stood there, considering Jude for a moment.

"What are you doing in here?" Jude asked, as if the question had just occurred to him.

"Nothing, Jude," Anton said, hitching the sack up on his shoulder. "Go back to your room and go to sleep. You look terrible."

Jude's gaze caught on Anton's sack of stolen goods, and he lurched to his feet abruptly. He stood over Anton, his cheeks flushed from the wine and his eyes burning in the dim light. "You're leaving! You—You can't do that. You're the Prophet."

Anton set his jaw. "So?"

"This is where you belong," Jude said sharply. He wasn't slurring anymore.

"Says who?" Anton retorted, turning to leave.

Jude spun and took a wavering step toward him. His brows drew into a taut line. "Says . . . me. I say. I won't let you do this."

A sudden stroke of anger flared inside Anton, a spark of the resentment that had been kindling inside him since they reached Kerameikos. "Really? The drunk swordsman who can barely stand up straight is going to stop me?"

Jude flinched and then went rigid, steeling himself.

"You are the Prophet," he said, raising his voice. "You are destined to fulfill the final prophecy and stop the Age of Darkness. I have spent my whole life praying for you, waiting for the day when the world would find its savior. Yet you turned out to be nothing but a coward."

"At least I'm not hiding down here and drowning my problems in a bottle of wine," Anton replied evenly. "You're the one who's so obsessed with your duty, Jude. You know none of that means anything to me, so why should I pretend that it does?"

Jude's mouth twisted. "If the Prophets were still here, they would be laughing at us for ever pinning our hope on you."

Anger grew bright in Anton's chest and behind his teeth as he met Jude's blazing eyes.

"Then find someone else," he bit out. "Let me go, and find someone else to be a savior or whatever it is you think I am, because I never wanted any of this."

"There is no one else!" Jude roared, backing Anton into the shelf. The scent of sweet wine hit his nose as Jude loomed over him. "You were the one who was meant to do this! From the moment you were born, from the moment the skies lit up for you, it was always going to be you. Don't you *get* that?"

Jude gripped the front of Anton's tunic, pinning him in place. Silence crackled between them.

"It's hard, isn't it?" Anton said, working to keep his voice from trembling, willing himself not to look away from the tempest in Jude's eyes.

Jude swallowed thickly. "What is?"

"To believe in something so much, only to have it disappoint you."

Jude made a low noise like he'd been struck. His hand fell away from Anton and he stepped back, stricken.

A wave of guilt swelled inside Anton. He forced it down, turning toward the door.

Jude's voice sounded behind him, quiet and small. "They're going to exile me."

Anton froze. He felt suddenly cold, as if a draft had whisked into the storeroom. *Exile?*

In the hold of the ship Illya had imprisoned them on, Jude had been utterly defeated and without hope. That was how he looked now. Crushed. Back then, it was because Jude had thought he failed the Prophet. Failed *Anton*.

"How can they do that?" he asked. "After everything you did? After everything you sacrificed?"

Without meaning to, he glanced at the pale Godfire scars on Jude's throat.

"The oath of the Paladin is sacred," Jude replied. "And I tarnished it."

"But you found the Prophet," Anton argued. "They can't just deny—" He stopped. They *could* deny it. Because Anton hadn't proven himself. And without that proof, Jude's sacrifice meant nothing. Without that proof, he had failed in their eyes.

"The Tribunal will deliberate tomorrow, but my heart already knows what the outcome will be," Jude said, bowing his head. "I will accept the punishment for my mistakes."

Mistakes. Those mistakes had put Jude in Anton's path. Those mistakes had led to Nazirah. To the top of the tower, to the bottom of the sea. To Anton finally facing the vision that had haunted him almost his entire life.

And now they meant Jude would lose the one thing that meant anything to him.

"Come with me," Anton said suddenly, the words tumbling from his mouth before he could consider them. He took a step toward him, suddenly overcome with this foolish, reckless possibility. "Jude— come with me. Leave before they can make you."

But when Jude raised his eyes, Anton saw the hollow resignation in them.

Keeper or not, Jude would stay. He would accept whatever the Order decided because nothing was more important to him than his duty.

Not even the Last Prophet.

11

BERU

SULFUROUS MIST CLUNG TO BERU'S NOSE AS SHE PRESSED HERSELF AGAINST the wall of the springs. The cacophony of the camp was beginning to quiet as the fighters settled in for the night, oblivious to the girl who stood vigil in their midst.

The day before, Beru had been face-to-face with Hector, staring in horror at the black handprint that marked him as something not quite alive, but no longer dead.

"Hector," she'd said, her voice faltering. "You're a revenant."

She'd feared meeting his eyes, but she'd made herself face the pain she saw in them.

"No," he'd choked out. "No, that's impossible. I can't be . . . an abomination."

When she'd reached for him, he'd caught her wrist, and again she'd felt a flood of horror and grief. *His* horror and grief. His eyes had widened in confusion, and then he'd dropped her wrist like it had burned him. Before she had a chance to speak, he'd fled back into the crowd.

Beru had watched him go, turning her hand over, as if she could find some sign of what their strange connection was. But her hand remained just a hand.

Ephyra had used Hector's *esha* to restore Beru from the brink of death. But now Hector was alive again. It must have created some connection between their *esha*, the energy given to Beru still bound in some way to Hector.

That explained why she had felt Hector's pain in the fighting pits. And his reaction when she'd touched him made her suspect that it wasn't just her—that whatever seepage existed between their *esha* went both ways.

And what if . . . what if the *esha* in Beru was given back to Hector? If the energy was restored to Hector, then maybe . . . maybe it would make him whole again. Maybe Hector wouldn't have to live a cursed half-life as a revenant. The half-life Beru had been living for six years.

He could have his life back.

This was how Beru could finally atone for the lives she'd taken as a revenant. A thread of *esha* connected her to Hector, and it was that thread that she would follow. Ephyra had taken his life. As her last act, Beru would give it back.

But first, she had to free him.

Which is exactly what had brought her here, waiting in the dark, dressed in a cloak and a cloth mask that covered the bottom of her face. The faint sound of someone whistling drifted toward her, growing louder. She peered around the wall to confirm it was the owner of the fighting pits, and then shrank back, listening to his footsteps and the creak of the wooden door as it swung open. A few moments later, she heard a splash and peeled away from the wall.

It was a low wall, just a few feet taller than she was, and the shoddy masonry made it simple to climb. She paused at the top, peering down into the bath area. Steam rose up from the spring pool, partially obscuring the man within. The steam would make it easy to get in without him realizing.

Carefully, she climbed down the other side of the wall. The stones were slippery from the steam, and Beru had to go slowly to avoid losing her footing. When she was safely on the ground, she crept behind him.

She gripped his hair, pulling his head back with one hand, and held a knife to his throat with the other. "Scream and your throat gets cut."

The man whimpered.

"Do you know who I am?" she said, pitching her voice lower. "You can answer."

"N-no," he stammered.

"You should," she said. "They call me the Pale Hand."

The man whimpered again.

"So you do know who I am," she said. She hadn't been certain he would—the Pale Hand had never been sighted on this side of the Pelagos, but it seemed the rumors had spread far. "I'm here because of your so-called fighting pits. What you're doing to these people is wrong."

"They're prisoners," he spat. "They're lucky to even get the chance—"

Beru tried to imagine what Ephyra would say. She pressed the knife, which she had stolen from the caravanserai kitchens, closer to his skin. "You're the lucky one. I'm letting you speak instead of killing you right now."

"Please," he said. "Please, I—"

"I'll give you a chance to live," she said. "I don't often do that. But I can sense that you have a conscience somewhere in there."

"I'll do anything," he said at once.

Beru smiled beneath her mask. "Good. I want you to finish your bath. Go back to your room, gather your things, and leave this place. Alone. Tell no one. If I come back here tomorrow and see that you haven't left, well—I don't give second chances. Tell me that you understand."

"I understand," he said pitifully.

Beru let go of his hair. "I'm going to go," she said. "And if you try to have me followed, or send anyone after me, I'll kill you. If you turn around, I'll kill you. Understand?"

"I understand," he said again.

She withdrew her hand and backed away from the bath. He didn't turn around. She climbed back over the wall and ran back to the caravanserai, her heart hammering the whole way. Pretending to be the Pale Hand filled her with awe and horror at what Ephyra had done to all those people. Beru had never threatened anyone's life before, and Ephyra had done worse—she'd actually killed. It made Beru sick with guilt, and in some twisted way it also made her miss her sister desperately.

But she was more sure than ever that leaving had been the right choice.

Beru woke before the sun the next morning. Dressing quickly and creeping out to the stairs overlooking the stalls and courtyard, Beru watched the caravan that had arrived the night before rush around to ready themselves for departure.

A deep voice floated up from below. "I'm telling you, we need to hire some protection. After that close call in Tazlib—"

"We can't afford it," another voice, this one much higher, argued. "You know that."

"Well, we can't afford to have our wares stolen by bandits, either."

"Look," the higher voice said. "If we make it through the rest of the summer, maybe we can do something during the harvest."

"Through the summer? We might not even make it to Behezda!"

Beru knew all about the bandits who plagued the Seti desert. Her father had been a merchant, and each time he'd left on a journey Beru would cry herself to sleep, worried that he'd be taken by bandits. Ephyra had always been the one to calm her, reading to her and telling her all kinds of ridiculous stories just to distract her.

Her chest twinged at the memory, and she shoved it away as she padded down to the kitchens to grab a piece of bread and strolled into town as the sun rose.

When she arrived at the fighters' camp, the dawn twilight had just lifted into morning. The fighters were already awake, and seemed to be engaged in some sort of altercation involving breakfast. Beru stood back to watch.

A short man was cowering behind an overturned table.

"If Sal's gone, that means we're not your slaves anymore!" yelled one of the fighters.

"What are you doing here?"

Beru startled, whirling around to find Hector standing several paces away, glaring at her in the morning sun.

"You're freed, right?" she said.

He stared at her for a moment, disbelief and understanding crashing together. "It was *you*, wasn't it?"

Beru bit her lip. Horror curled in her gut, rising through her like nausea.

"What did you do to him?"

She looked at him, shocked. "I didn't *kill* him! I'm not—" She stopped herself.

"You're not your sister?" Hector said.

Beru set her jaw. "I just *maybe* sort of scared him. A little."

Hector's eyes narrowed, and Beru felt a storm of emotion she could not quite parse, but it sent her heart kicking against her ribs and her fists clenching. Almost like she was angry.

It wasn't *her* anger, she realized, as Hector turned and abruptly started walking away.

"Hey!" Beru called, trotting after him. "Hector, wait, just—*wait*." She caught him by the arm as they passed the side of the barracks. "I saw the handprint. Someone brought you back to life."

"*Who?*" he said. "Your sister? Where is she?"

Beru shook her head. Ephyra was the only person she knew who was capable of bringing someone back from the dead. And she had been left with Hector's body.

But Beru could not believe that Ephyra had done it. The last time Ephyra had brought someone back from the dead, she'd killed an entire village in the process. She wouldn't risk that again. Not for Hector.

"I think someone else brought you back," she said.

"That's impossible. That would mean that there's—"

"Another necromancer," Beru finished. They stared at each other, the enormity of her words permeating the air. "Another necromancer who wants you alive."

A shout cut through the air, startling both of them. More

shouting followed. When Beru glanced behind her, she realized that the fight she'd encountered in the camp had escalated into a full-blown riot.

Hector grabbed her arm, pulling her out of the camp, and past the fighting pits. Beru's breath shortened as she struggled to match Hector's brisk pace.

"What exactly do you want from me?"

She glared up at him. "To help you."

Hector let out a mirthless laugh. "*Help* me?"

"Yes," she replied, defensively. "There's a . . . connection between us. Between our *esha*."

"So what?" he spat.

Again, that *anger*, roiling through her chest and buzzing beneath her skin. It almost made her want to turn around and forget this whole thing. But his appearance here, in this middle-of-nowhere town, was the sign she'd been searching for. She wasn't going to let him slip away.

"We're both revenants," she said. He flinched at the word. "What's happening to me right now, that's going to happen to you, too. You'll start to fade. But . . . what would happen if the *esha* in me was given back to you? You could have your life back."

There was nothing, Beru knew, that Hector loathed more than what he was now. What she was. He had called her a corruption, an abomination. He had taken her halfway across the world to kill her because he couldn't stand to let such an unnatural creature live. She, and what she was, was the reason his family was dead.

"It's not possible," he said. "I *died*."

She shook her head. "Not like I did. You died because your *esha* was stolen from you. If we could give it *back*—"

"I'm not supposed to be alive!" His words bit off in a furious growl and he stopped short. "What is this? Why would you want to do this?"

Beru looked away. "I left Ephyra behind in Medea. I won't be able to survive much longer without her anyway. But . . . if I can do any bit of good in this world before I go, it will be worth it."

She felt a small spark of surprise, and something akin to astonishment. He didn't say anything for a long moment, and for all that Beru could apparently feel his emotions, she had no idea what was going through his head.

"You wish to atone," he said at last.

Beru's gaze cut back to him. "Yes. I know I can never make up for the things I've done. For your family . . . for all the people whose lives were lost because of me. But I want to leave this world knowing I caused more than just pain."

His jaw tensed. She felt his anger rise again, but now it was tinged with bitterness.

"You think that's selfish," she guessed.

He shook his head. "How would you even begin to do such a thing?"

"I don't know," Beru said. "But I know one place where we might start. The Daughters of Mercy in Behezda. They're said to have a better understanding of the Grace of Blood than anyone. If there's someone who knows what this connection between us is, it will be them. And maybe they'll know how to set it right."

She and Ephyra used to argue about the Daughters. Beru had wanted to go to them, to see if their long history and knowledge of the Grace of Blood could help them. Ephyra had always refused, too afraid of what the Daughters would do to a necromancer and a revenant.

"You want to go to Behezda," he said slowly. "And just . . . walk up to the Temple of Mercy?"

"What are you going to do?" she shot back. "Stay here?"

She waved a hand at the dusty sandpits, empty at the early hour but littered with trash and soaked in blood and sweat and piss.

He narrowed his eyes. "How are you even going to get there?"

"There's a caravan heading out right now," Beru said. "If we hurry we can catch them. And it sounded like they need protection. I figured you'd be pretty good at that, right?"

She offered a tentative smile.

"This is foolish," he said. "You can't change what happened. You can't save me."

"Please," she said, desperation cracking her voice. "Let me try."

He shook his head, turning away.

Beru's breath gusted from her lungs as he started to walk away from her. Sorrow ached through her bones. She was going to fail. She was going to die, and she would have done nothing, *nothing* to fix any of it because Hector didn't want her to save him.

And then he stopped.

"You . . ." he said softly, his voice wracked with grief. "I can feel it. This . . . pain."

Her pain.

"You made me a promise, once," she said, her voice shaking. "Do you remember?" Her grief was huge, and heavy, but within it she could feel the echo of Hector's.

"I remember."

She stepped toward him, wielding her grief like a blade. "So will you come with me?"

He turned back to her, and something had changed in him, the words he'd said to her back then haunting them both like a shadow. She felt his resolve, hardening in her chest as he spoke them again.

"Until the end."

12

JUDE

JUDE HAD BEEN DRUNK ONLY ONCE BEFORE IN HIS LIFE, AN EXPERIENCE THAT had ended with him waking up slumped over the horses' trough. Hector hadn't let him live it down for *months*.

This time, he'd at least managed to make it back to his barracks, but everything before that was a blur. His mouth tasted like something had died inside it, and the pounding in his head protested vehemently against even the thought of sitting up.

The Tribunal was deliberating today. They were probably deciding his fate right now. Maybe if he just stayed inside this room he would never have to find out their decision and everything would remain precisely the same as it had been yesterday.

Jude sat up quickly, his head screaming in protest. He was struck suddenly with the sensation that there was something *very* important he needed to do. Memories from last night flashed back to him. Dark eyes, staring up at his. Lips curled in anger.

Anton. He'd come into the storeroom. What had he been doing

there? Jude couldn't remember, but he did remember the gambler's anger. What was he so angry about?

It hit Jude at once. Anton had been in the storeroom gathering supplies. He had been trying to *leave*.

Jude scrambled out of bed, panic overriding everything else. Penrose. He had to find Penrose.

He was dressed in the clothes he'd been wearing last night. Even his boots were still on his feet. He flung open the door of the barracks, groaning when a bright beam of sunlight lanced through him.

"Captain Weatherbourne!"

Jude blinked against the bright sunlight to find one of the stewards approaching with an alarmed expression. The Guard already knew, then. Perhaps they'd already gone after Anton.

"You're expected in the Tribunal Chambers at once," the steward said.

"Where's Penrose?" Jude asked hurriedly.

"The Guard is in the Tribunal Chambers," the steward said patiently. "The Tribunal is about to announce their decision."

Jude paused. The steward wasn't talking about Anton. It seemed the Guard still had no idea he was missing.

He tore past the steward, sprinting across the courtyard toward the Tribunal Chambers. He may not be Keeper of the Word for much longer, but he wasn't going to let losing the Prophet be his last act. He reached the Tribunal and slammed through the stone doors, gasping for breath.

Immediately his gaze landed on the Guard, who were gathered around the central dais. They turned as he entered, and Jude felt himself flush. He hadn't spoken to any of them except Penrose in over six days, but he knew what they were all probably thinking—that he'd failed them.

"Captain Weatherbourne!" a terse voice cried. The magistrate stepped out from behind the Guard. "Have a seat, please. The Tribunal has reached their—"

"I need a word with Paladin Penrose," Jude said quickly. "It will take a moment only. I—"

"After the Tribunal declares its decision, you will be free to—"

He caught Penrose's eye and gave her a pleading look. Penrose cleared her throat. "I, uh, I do need to speak with Captain Weatherbourne about some . . . lingering Guard business. It will only take a moment. We beg your apology, magistrate."

Jude could almost hear the magistrate grinding his teeth as Penrose took Jude's arm and led him back toward the doors. He must look like quite a mess for Penrose to breach protocol that readily.

"What's going on?" she asked under her breath as they pushed back through the doors and ducked around the side of the Chambers.

"Do you know where the Prophet is?" he asked.

She looked at him quizzically. "What?"

"Last night," Jude said, "Anton said he was going to leave Kerameikos Fort."

"You spoke to the Prophet last night?" she said sharply.

"*That's* the part you're upset about? He could be anywhere. We need to find him."

"Right, yes," Penrose said, a grim set to her mouth. "I'll send Annuka and Yarik to his room, and Osei to the temple. I have a few other ideas about where he might be. But, Jude—you need to go back inside and pretend nothing's wrong."

"What?" Jude said. "I need to find the Prophet."

"No," Penrose said firmly. "If he's truly gone, we *will* find him. But the Tribunal can't know that you're involved in this."

"I'm not involved, I just—"

The doors opened behind them, and the magistrate stalked out, looking incensed. Planting himself in the open threshold, he demanded, "What makes either of you think it's acceptable to have an unsanctioned chat while the Tribunal is trying to declare their decision?"

"Our apologies," Penrose said swiftly, stepping out in front of Jude. "The Guard can't be here for the Tribunal's decision. We have important matters to attend to with the Prophet."

The magistrate nodded, still looking at her coldly. "Well then, attend to them."

Penrose signaled to the rest of the Guard, who filed out without question. A strange sense of loss filled Jude as he turned and walked inside the Tribunal Chambers. He knew what the Tribunal was about to decide, and despite what she'd said the last time they'd spoken, Penrose seemed to know, too.

Jude wasn't captain of the Paladin Guard anymore.

"Have a seat if you please, Captain Weatherbourne," the magistrate said as they reached the center dais.

Jude stiffly took his seat on the stone bench in the center of the room, feeling as though he might jump out of his skin. Despair clawed at him as the seven veiled members of the Tribunal filed in from the back of the room.

"The eighty-first session of the Tribunal of Kerameikos is called back to order," the magistrate said. "The Tribunal has reached a decision in the matters of the oathbreaking of both Hector Navarro and Jude Weatherbourne."

The Magistrate droned on about the specifics of the Tribunal's deliberation, the precedence of their decision-making, and all sorts of esoteric rules Jude could not begin to pay attention to. Jude shifted in his seat, trying to stop himself from leaping to his feet and tearing the fort to shreds in search of Anton. He couldn't have left. He *couldn't* have. The Guard would find him.

"Never before has a Keeper of the Word been accused of oath-breaking," the magistrate went on, continuing some line of thought that Jude had already lost. "It is therefore this Tribunal's decision that should the Keeper step down, his predecessor will reassume the role."

He could not bear to think of what his father's face would look like if Jude was forced to return the mantle of Keeper to him. He'd already lost the Pinnacle Blade. But he fought down the shame, firm in the knowledge that his father would protect Anton, and Jude would . . . he would just . . .

He would be alone. More alone than he'd been in his Year of Reflection. More alone than he'd been when Hector had turned his back on him. More alone than he'd been in front of the Hierophant, waiting to have his Grace burned out of him. He had no Guard, no duty, no Prophet. He was a name to be skipped over and struck from the record. He was a shadow.

The ivory doors burst open, and Annuka rushed in, an out-of-breath Yarik trailing behind her, their footsteps echoing on the tiles.

"What is the matter with you?" the magistrate demanded, wheeling on them. "First the delay and now you interrupt—"

"You need to stop the Tribunal," Annuka said. "The Prophet is gone."

Penrose appeared at the doorway, and when Jude met her eyes, she just shook her head minutely. "They're right. And if the Prophet is truly missing, Jude can help us find him."

Jude was already on his feet.

"Absolutely not," the magistrate replied. "Jude Weatherbourne stays here. The others can search for the Prophet."

"Jude knows him best," Penrose argued. "If there's anyone here who can find him—"

"*I said no!*" the magistrate cried. "If you will not respect my authority as Magistrate of the Tribunal of Kerameikos, then perhaps I should convene a new session to look into your own wrongdoing, Paladin Penrose."

Penrose looked indignant but fell silent.

"Now, if there are no further objections, can we—"

The doors opened again, and the magistrate spun toward them furiously. "We will not tolerate any more interruptions!"

"I hope I'm not too late."

Jude froze. So did everyone around him.

In the doorway, against a backdrop of bright light, stood Anton. Jude could only stare as he swept down the main aisle of the Tribunal Chambers, looking as casual as if he'd arrived late to breakfast.

Penrose reacted first, striding briskly toward him. "Where *were* you?"

"I was on my way here," Anton said mildly. "I thought perhaps the Tribunal would like to hear what I have to say."

Penrose looked speechlessly from Anton to Jude. Anton didn't even glance at Jude. His gaze was fixed on the magistrate and the veiled members of the Tribunal behind him.

A sudden memory of the night before flashed in Jude's mind. It was nothing more than an impression—just the cold fury on Anton's face and the word Jude had hurled at him—*coward*. His face now was almost blank, impassive, but Jude could see the nuances in his expression, the same icy anger underneath.

"I—we have not called you to speak, there is a *procedure* for—" the magistrate began.

Anton smiled brightly, and still the anger crackled. "I call myself to speak."

What was Anton *doing*? Jude wondered frantically, his breath coming in short bursts. He could not decipher anything beyond Anton's anger.

"You have no authority over this Tribunal. We are deciding whether Jude Weatherbourne broke the oaths of the Paladin Guard. It has nothing to do with you."

"Why does the Paladin Guard take oaths?" Anton asked.

"Why?" the magistrate scoffed. "Because they must cast aside their worldly desires and devote themselves completely to—"

"To the Prophet," Anton finished. "To me. So I think my opinion here is very relevant, don't you?"

The magistrate gaped at him, practically vibrating with outrage.

Anton apparently took this as an invitation to keep talking. "The Keeper of the Word is supposed to protect the Prophet, and from the moment I first met Jude, that's what he has done. He found me. He saved me."

His gaze at last met Jude's across the Chambers, and Jude felt all the blood rush into his face as it held there. "He's the only person who ever has."

Jude swallowed heavily, wanting to look away but unable to. He had spent nineteen years perfecting his koahs and learning the history of the Seven Prophets, readying himself to find and protect the Last Prophet. But none of it had prepared him for Anton.

Anger, gratitude, and breathless hope spurred his heart to an unsteady gallop. He felt like he was back at the Hidden Spring, watching the game of Trove and River, waiting for Anton to turn over his last card.

"If you want to punish Jude for finding me, then go ahead," Anton said, finally looking away from Jude and back at the magistrate. "But just because he didn't do it exactly the way you wanted him to, doesn't mean it was *wrong*."

"That is not for you to decide," the magistrate said.

"It *is* for me to decide," Anton said, eyes darkening. "I'm the one who has to live with the consequences. I'm the Prophet—and you want to take away my Keeper, right when I need him the most. I saw something last night. Not a vision—I think it was something happening here and now. The Hierophant is searching for something. Something that could start the Age of Darkness."

Penrose looked at him sharply. "You saw the Hierophant?"

"Even if that were true," the magistrate said testily, "you have not proven you're the Prophet."

"Fine," Anton said. "Then I will. Right now."

The magistrate looked taken aback. Penrose even more so.

"We'll go to the Circle of Stones," Anton said. "If I prove I'm the Prophet, Jude stays as Keeper of the Word. If I don't, then we'll both leave."

Jude could hear his own heartbeat ringing in his ears. There was one part about their argument the night before that he hadn't remembered until now. Anton had asked Jude to go with him when he left Kerameikos. Jude hadn't even answered. He hadn't needed to.

Even so, Anton hadn't left.

One of the cloaked members of the Tribunal raised a hand and beckoned to the magistrate.

"One moment," he said to the rest of the room, and then he retreated toward the rest of the Tribunal to confer with them.

Jude slid his gaze back to Anton, his stomach lurching. The morning sun streaming in from the high windows caught Anton's hair in a halo of light. He looked perfectly at ease, standing there in the center of the seven-pointed star. Jude desperately wished his drunken self had not called Anton a coward. Anger and gratitude and shame wrestled in his chest as he marched over to where Anton stood. He did not know what he would say.

But a crash of bells shattered the air before he could even try. Jude startled, pushing Anton behind him before he even registered what was happening. Those were not the bells that tolled the hour or the bells that called the Paladin to meditation.

These were another set of bells, ones that Jude had never heard rung in his nineteen years living at the fort, ones he had never hoped to hear in his life.

Kerameikos was under attack.

13

EPHYRA

WHEN SHARA HAD SAID THEY'D KEEP ILLYA ON A LEASH, EPHYRA HADN'T
thought she meant it *literally*.

She eyed the cuffs in Shara's hands. They were a pale, brushed silver, a green gem set in the center of each, gleaming like two eyes. Shara had gotten them during a previous heist, taken from a vault belonging to a retired general of the Behezdan army. They'd been hired to steal a helmet, but Shara had taken the cuffs, too, thinking they looked pretty. It was only later that she'd discovered their true purpose.

Ephyra watched with distaste as Illya held his left wrist out to Shara.

Shara placed one of the cuffs on it, and it tightened, fitting him perfectly. She started to put the other cuff on herself. Ephyra grabbed her arm.

"Give it to me," she said. "I'm the only one I trust not to get tricked by him."

Shara didn't argue. She simply slipped the cuff over Ephyra's wrist.

Ephyra didn't take her eyes off Illya. He flexed his hand and held up his wrist, as though admiring the cuff. The cuffs were connected through artificery, as if an invisible rope tethered them to each other.

"They're not a fashion item," Ephyra snapped. "You're our prisoner. *My* prisoner. You can't get more than thirty paces away from me. Step one toe out of line and I'll have you on the ground before you can blink. Got it?"

"I have so missed your warmth and sweetness," Illya replied, shaking his sleeve over the cuff. "I'm looking forward to all this quality time we get to spend together."

"*One* toe."

Shara glanced at them and grinned, throwing her arms around their shoulders. "Come on, you two, we're a team! Let's see some camaraderie."

"That's not really a concept Illya is familiar with," Ephyra muttered, moving out from under Shara's arm.

"She's just a little irritable," Shara whispered conspiratorially to Illya. "Usually she's a lot nicer."

Ephyra rolled her eyes and started to retreat over to one of the sand skiffs.

"No, she's not," she heard Illya mutter behind her.

Ephyra paused, glancing down at the cuff on her wrist and then threw her arm sharply out in front of her. The soft sound of a body hitting the sand followed, then a hissed curse. Ephyra suppressed a grin and then made her way over to where Numir was restringing the sand skiff sail with Hadiza's help, while Parthenia pored over one of Badis's books in the shade.

"You three are all right with this?" Ephyra asked.

"It's not like we've been able to stop Shara from working with unsavory characters before," Hadiza said, giving Ephyra a pointed look.

"Illya's different," Ephyra insisted. "He's manipulative."

"Shara can handle herself," Hadiza said. "We all can. And besides. There's five of us, and only one of him."

Ephyra gritted her teeth. She was not getting through to any of them. They seemed utterly unconcerned about the snake in their ranks.

Ephyra would just have to be vigilant enough for all of them.

"All right," Shara said, striding over to them with Badis's stolen mirror in hand. "Who wants to admire their pretty face in the mirror? Parthenia?"

Numir laughed, covering it badly with a cough.

"Is anyone else a little creeped out by this whole thing?" Parthenia asked. "I mean, who exactly would leave a clue to find the Chalice? Who is it even for?"

"The Daughters of Mercy?" Hadiza suggested. "Maybe they needed a trail back to the Chalice, just in case they ever needed to find it again."

"It must have been the Daughters," Illya said from behind her. "Because only someone with the Grace of Blood can use that clue."

Shara turned to him. "And you know that . . . how?"

"'I will show you the key to what you seek,'" Illya recited, "'*if you have the power to wield it.*' Only someone with the Grace of Blood can wield Eleazar's Chalice. Therefore, only someone with the Grace of Blood can *find* it." His gaze slid to Ephyra.

She grimaced. If the mirror really did exactly as it said, she was the only one who could use it. But she hadn't yet told Shara and the others what she really was.

"I know a few healers in Tel Amot," Shara said thoughtfully. "But I'm not sure if—"

"We don't need to go to Tel Amot," Illya said.

It seemed Illya was going to force her hand. Ephyra glared at him and then turned to Shara. "Give that to me."

Shara swung toward her in surprise. "What? You have the Grace of Blood? But you don't have—" Her eyes flickered to Ephyra's arms.

Ephyra resisted the urge to hide her arms behind her. They were bare, the brown skin unmarked by the usual tattoos that healers wore to aid them in their trade. She did not dare look at Illya, but she knew he was delighted by what was transpiring. The less Ephyra and Shara trusted each other, the more easily he could slither his way into getting what he wanted.

"Shara, no," Hadiza said firmly, grabbing her arm as she held the mirror out to Ephyra. "You can't give that to her."

"We don't really have another option," Shara said.

"You don't understand," Hadiza said, casting a distrustful glance at Ephyra. "She's dangerous. She's Unsworn."

Ephyra had heard that term before. It was used for people with the Grace of Blood who had never been trained how to use it. People who hadn't taken the oath that said they would use their power only to heal, never to hurt. The stigma against people like her existed everywhere, but it was more acute in certain places. Places like Tel Amot, which had been touched by the destruction of the Necromancer Wars.

"We can't trust her," Hadiza said. She whirled on Ephyra. "I *knew* you were hiding something."

Ephyra dug her nails into her palms. "I'm not going to hurt anyone."

"Even if we believed you, that doesn't mean you aren't dangerous," Hadiza said. "The Unsworn . . . those without the knowledge of binding and unbinding *esha* are prone to misuse their power. The laws are strict for a reason. Without training, their Grace is unpredictable. Even if they don't mean to hurt people, they do."

Ephyra kept her gaze on Hadiza, anger building in her gut. Hadiza didn't know anything about Ephyra, what she had managed to learn about her own Grace. What she could do. But a part of what Hadiza said rang true, and that made Ephyra angry, too.

"I didn't lie to you," Ephyra said, her voice shaking. "I want to save my sister. That's the only reason I'm here."

"She's telling the truth."

All of them turned to stare at Illya.

"Are you . . . vouching for her?" Shara asked after a long pause.

"Yes," he replied without hesitation.

"You *do* realize we have no reason to trust you, either," Hadiza pointed out.

Illya shrugged. "You need me because I'm the only one who knows the code that was on that mirror. You need her to use the mirror. Seems like you're going to have to put your notions of trust aside if you want to find this Chalice."

"*She's* the one who said we can't trust *him*," Parthenia said thoughtfully. "And if we can't trust her, then maybe *he's* trustworthy. But if *he's* trustworthy and he says we can trust *her*, then—"

"This is making my head hurt," Shara declared. She thrust the mirror toward Ephyra. "Just take it."

"Shara!" Hadiza protested.

"Don't make me regret this," Shara warned as Ephyra took the mirror.

Ephyra took a deep breath and held it up. At first, all she saw was her own face staring back at her—thick black hair framing a fairly average face, with a long, thin scar running from her forehead down to her jaw. The mark Hector Navarro had left on her when she'd killed him.

Then the image rippled like water, and in its place, a structure appeared, but not like any Ephyra had ever seen. It looked almost like a mountain, triangular, with steps leading all the way up to its peak.

Ephyra lowered the mirror and then raised it back to her face. It showed the same thing. "I'm not really sure what this is."

She crouched down into the sand to draw it.

"It doesn't look like anything I've ever seen," Shara said. "Hadiza?"

Hadiza was still staring at Ephyra. "I told you this was a bad idea from the start."

"So, what? You're out?" Shara asked. "Come on, Hadiza. If you can't trust her, then trust me."

Hadiza bit out an irritated sigh. "Fine. For you, Shara. I'm only doing this for you. To make sure you don't get yourself killed."

She crouched down in the sand beside Ephyra's drawing. "This looks like one of the four main temples that was built by the Nehemians in worship of the old god. What did the top of it look like?"

Ephyra looked back into the mirror, and this time focused on the top of the temple. "There's some sort of . . . sculpture. Or statue."

Ephyra drew it in the sand. A circle with a line through the right side of it and curving lines above it.

"The Temple of the West," Hadiza said, nodding. "It's in a city called Susa."

"Susa?" Ephyra repeated, frowning. "I've never heard of it."

"That's because it doesn't exist anymore," Hadiza replied. "It was one of the cities that was destroyed in the Necromancer Wars."

Ephyra felt a prickle of unease.

"You know the way there?" Shara asked.

Hadiza nodded. "It's over a week's journey."

"All right, then, I guess we're heading out."

The others mobilized around Ephyra, finishing up their preparations and climbing into the skiffs. Her gaze found Illya as he approached her, smiling. It was a nice smile, handsome, warm.

Ephyra hated it.

"Well, guess we're in the same boat," he said, gesturing to the skiff.

"You're awfully lucky we don't just drag you behind us in the sand," she replied, pushing past him.

He grabbed her wrist, halting her. Still smiling, he said, "I bet if these people knew who you *really* were, and what you've done, it wouldn't just be Hadiza who wants out. Don't forget, I know your secrets."

Ephyra felt her pulse skip against his thumb. "Yes. And I know yours."

14

JUDE

JUDE'S HEART THUDDED OUT ITS OWN WARNING AS THE BELLS OF KERAMEIKOS clanged.

A messenger burst inside the Tribunal Chambers.

"What's happening?" Jude demanded.

"There are ships approaching from downriver," the messenger said. "They—they have Godfire."

"The Witnesses," Jude said, understanding at once. He spun back to Anton. "We need to get you out of here."

"Annuka, take the rest of the Guard and go to the gates," Penrose ordered. She turned to Jude, and he did not have time to feel chagrined at her easy command of the Guard. "We should head to the passage in the mountains. If the Witnesses breach the fort . . ."

"How did they even find him?" Jude asked.

Penrose only shook her head. "We'll need to figure that out later, but right now we need to move."

Jude turned to Anton, whose eyes were wide and frightened. "Let's go."

They made for the exit.

"Where are you going?" the magistrate demanded.

They didn't slow. "We're under attack," Jude said. "We're getting the Prophet out of here. I suggest you and the rest of the Tribunal get to the Keep."

Panic pumped through Jude's blood as they wound through the fort, passing other Paladin running in the opposite direction.

"This way!" Penrose led them into the armory, where she grabbed a sword and tossed it to Jude. Jude balanced the sword in his hand, biting his lip. He wanted to tell Penrose about his Grace, that he would be next to useless in a fight, but now wasn't the time. Once they got Anton to safety, he would tell her everything.

They dodged more Paladin racing to the outer fortifications. The cadence of the bells had changed, growing more urgent.

"What's happening?" Penrose asked, stopping one of the passing Paladin. "Have the Witnesses breached the fort?"

The Paladin nodded, looking very pale and very young. "They're within the outer walls. We were forced to draw the footbridges."

That would slow the Witnesses' progress into the fort, but not stop them completely.

"What about the Herati refugees?" Jude asked, knuckles tightening on the hilt of his sword.

"They're in the Keep," the young Paladin replied. "A force of two dozen are already there to defend it."

Jude sucked in a breath. He didn't know if that would be enough to protect the Herati refugees, but there was no way to gather them all and escape. Keeping Anton safe was the priority. "If the Witnesses breach the inner wall, pull everyone back to the Keep. Protecting the refugees is now your mission."

The Paladin nodded and took off.

Jude, Anton, and Penrose made for the rocky outcropping that led them on a steep hike up to the surrounding mountainside. Jude paused for a moment as the path flattened off, looking out at the river. Here he could see the ships surrounding the fort, and the cloaked figures pouring off them, brandishing Godfire torches and crossbows with bolts aflame. There must have been over two hundred of them.

Penrose took Anton's arm. "Did you really see something last night?"

Anton hesitated, and then nodded. "I had a dream, or—I don't know, parts of it seemed real. Felt real. I saw the Hierophant."

"You never saw him in Nazirah, did you?" Penrose asked. "How can you be sure it was him?"

Anton shook his head. "I just . . . knew. He was wearing white robes, and this gold mask so I didn't see his face but—"

"That's him," Jude confirmed. His heart thudded in his ears.

"He was torturing someone with Godfire," Anton said. His gaze skittered over Jude. "He wanted information about something that he said would awaken some kind of . . . I don't know. An ancient power. Something old enough and powerful enough to remake the world."

"I've never heard of such a thing," Penrose said.

Jude shook his head. An ancient power? The only ancient power was the Graces, bestowed upon a few by the Prophets centuries ago. "We'll figure this out, Anton. Once we get out of here."

Penrose led them through the trees, Jude at Anton's heels as the forest thickened. They staggered up a hill of dense vegetation toward a clearing.

"Jude," Penrose said, her voice tense. She had reached the clearing first, her gaze trained on the trees beyond.

Jude turned as three cloaked Witnesses emerged from the trees, crossbows and Godfire torches held aloft. The Witnesses had already penetrated the fort.

Automatically, Jude shifted into a defensive position, putting himself between the advancing Witnesses and Anton. Beside him, Penrose did the same.

One Witness stepped out in front of the others. He was covered head to toe in black, the bottom half of his face hidden by a mask, so all Jude could see were two bright gray eyes. His hand rested on a sword sheathed at his hip.

"Give us the Prophet," the masked Witness said calmly, "and we will leave your little fort intact."

Jude heard the metallic sound of Penrose unsheathing her sword. His hand went to the hilt of the sword she had procured for him.

"Take the Prophet and go," Penrose said, before he could draw it. "I'll hold them off."

The command was so startling Jude whipped his gaze to her.

"No," he said. "I can't—" He cut himself off. He couldn't let the Witnesses know that he was Graceless and vulnerable. "You take the Prophet."

"The Prophet," the masked Witness said, placing his hand on his sword, "will be coming with us."

"Jude," Penrose said. "Go."

With a cry, she ran at the Witnesses, her sword gleaming in the sunlight. The sharp clap of firing crossbows filled the air, and Jude reacted on instinct, pulling Anton to him and shielding him with his body.

The crossbows flew wide, and Jude tightened his grip on Anton's arm, spinning around to search for Penrose in the chaos. Another bolt sailed toward them, and then she was there, leaping in front of it, her sword a silver arc slicing through the air. The bolt dropped and Penrose landed at Jude's side.

"Jude, *go*," she urged. "Keep him safe."

Another protest died on his tongue. He knew it was futile. He should have told Penrose that his Grace was gone, but it was too late now. He would do whatever he could to get Anton out of danger, and then pray that the rest of the Guard found them.

"This way," Jude said, steering Anton toward the trees. He cast a glance back at Penrose, who was fending off two Witnesses as they rushed toward them. She would be all right. She had to be.

They wove through the copse, toward the head of a waterfall that cascaded about fifty feet to the river below. They would have to cross over the stream that fed it, and then climb down twenty feet of a precarious slope studded with loose rocks to reach the passage that lay behind the waterfall. It would lead them out of the river valley and into the mountains, where they could hide.

Jude stepped into the ankle-deep water, reaching back to help Anton over the slick rocks. He waded in farther, keeping his hand on Anton to help him balance. When they were over halfway to the other side of the stream, he glanced back at Anton again and saw another figure appear at the edge of the stream. The masked Witness.

Panic jolted through Jude as he thought of Penrose. If the masked Witness had gotten past her—he couldn't even think it. He shouldn't have left her. If she was hurt, it was his fault.

Jude's eyes found Anton's. "Keep going. Climb down the path. The passage is through the falls. I'll be right behind you."

Anton opened his mouth, as if to protest, but before he could say anything, Jude whirled around. The Witness stepped into the water, drawing toward him.

"Jude Weatherbourne," he said. "The Hierophant has told me much about you."

"Then you must already know that your Godfire chains won't work on me," Jude bluffed.

The masked Witness unsheathed his sword.

For a moment, Jude was blinded. The sword blazed in the light of the sun. And then Jude realized it was not the sun's glare that lit the sword. The blade itself was engulfed with pale white flame.

Godfire.

Jude flinched back on instinct. The scars on his throat tingled with heat, as if remembering the scorch of those pale flames.

"You fear it," the masked Witness said. The sword blazed between them. "You shouldn't. This is not your destruction, Paladin. This is your salvation. You are too blind to see it now, but in time you will know the truth. Now, step aside."

Jude closed his eyes and breathed in, stepping into the position for the koah of speed, willing his Grace to respond.

Nothing.

The masked Witness lunged forward, his sword cutting through the air toward Jude's chest.

Jude unsheathed his sword, parrying the blow. The masked Witness struck again, and Jude ducked beneath the blazing sword, water splashing around him. The Godfire sword thrust forward and Jude maneuvered away, realizing too late that the Witness was slowly working them both toward the other side of the stream, where Anton stood despite Jude's command.

"Go!" Jude hollered back at Anton, keeping enough of his attention on the Witness to parry his next strike.

The attacks kept coming. There was something familiar about

the way the masked Witness moved, something that reached back into the foundations of Jude's training. Jude was barely able to keep ahead of the attacks, too accustomed to his Grace-enhanced speed. The Witness would soon have Jude hemmed in against the sharp drop of the waterfall, and Jude was powerless to stop him.

The Godfire sword blazed toward Jude, and Jude had only a split second to make a decision. He dropped his own sword, diving to avoid the Witness's strike. He landed on his hands and knees, turning to watch the Witness as his momentum launched him toward the edge of the waterfall.

The Witness wheeled back from the edge, catching himself on one knee. Jude lurched to his feet, but the Witness was already up, racing away from Jude and toward the edge of the stream.

Jude followed. Anton had finally obeyed Jude, climbing carefully down the steep slope that ran alongside the waterfall. He glanced up, saw the Witness barreling toward him, and Jude watched in horror as his eyes widened and his foot slipped off a loose rock. Suddenly Anton was tumbling down the slope, hands and knees scrabbling for purchase as he rolled off the edge of the path.

"*No!*" With a burst of speed, Jude flung himself down the slope after him.

The Witness reached Anton first, catching him by the shirt and dragging him back over the edge.

Jude froze.

"So," the Witness mused, his hand still gripping Anton's shirt. "You are the Prophet."

"And you are?" Anton asked, his sarcasm betrayed by the tremble in his voice.

The Witness pulled Anton closer. "I am the most loyal of the Hierophant's servants. I am the one who will deliver you to him."

Anton drew back and spat directly in the Witness's face. The masked man reared, his hand going slack, dropping Anton over the cliff's edge. Jude leapt forward, barely managing to catch his arm and haul him back to safety.

The Witness stumbled back, raising the Godfire sword. "Step aside, Paladin."

"You cannot have him," Jude said, blocking Anton with his body.

The Witness lunged for another strike. Jude dropped to the ground, sweeping the Witness's feet from under him. The masked Witness rolled to the side, springing to his feet against the rock face. Jude charged. The Witness swung his sword, the Godfire blade wheeling inches from Jude's face. Jude leaned back, using the rock face for support as he kicked forward. He struck the Witness square in the chest and he stumbled back, arms flying out to his sides to try to steady himself. But there was nothing to catch him.

He slipped off the edge of the rock, falling backward into the waterfall and disappearing into the river below.

Jude turned back to Anton who was staring, wide-eyed.

"Look out!" Jude cried, his gaze catching on movement above them, where several crossbow-wielding Witnesses fired from the top of the waterfall. He leapt at Anton, pinning him against the rock face and shielding him from the bolts raining down.

Anton's breathing was quick and labored. Jude recalled with sudden clarity the night before, pinning Anton against the shelf, their breath mingling in the dark storeroom.

"On the count of three," Jude said, his eyes locked on Anton's. "One, two—"

He cried out as a crossbow bolt struck his right side. Pain seared through him as Jude fell against the rock, sliding to the ground.

"Jude!" Anton twisted beneath him, clasping Jude's forearm, and pulling him to his feet.

"Go," Jude said, breathless with agony, clutching at the bolt and tearing it from his side with a roar.

"No," Anton said. "I'm not leaving you."

Before Jude could argue, Anton tucked himself under Jude's good side and half dragged him to the edge of the cliff, where the waterfall rushed past them in a deluge.

Anton glanced up at Jude uncertainly, and Jude had a sudden image of Anton, half-drowned in the cistern in Nazirah. He took a breath, and together they ducked into the falls. There were a few seconds of silence and submersion, and then they emerged onto the other side. The water rushed past them, echoing in the passage and enclosing them inside.

Jude turned to Anton, who was smiling.

"What?" Jude asked.

"This is just like old times," Anton said. "Running away from Witnesses. Wandering through dark caves."

Jude looked away and didn't say anything. Back then, he could rely on his Grace. Back then, he was able to protect Anton. "We need to move quickly. The Witnesses won't be far behind, but we can . . . we can lose them in the mountains." Jude gulped in air, the pain on his right side blotting out all thought. "There's an outpost," he went on, "a few miles away. It should have plenty of supplies."

"What about the others?" Anton asked.

Jude shook his head, guilt clawing at his chest. It felt like he was abandoning his Guard all over again. "They'll be all right."

Anton didn't press the issue, and let Jude lead them slowly through the dark passage. Jude's wound throbbed steadily with the beat of his heart, and with each step he grew more faint, until he was barely conscious, but still moving, one step after another. After a few silent, struggling minutes, Jude saw the light ahead.

"The exit," he breathed. They reached the mouth of the passage. On the other side, tall grass and trees rose around them. Jude stumbled, his hand going out to catch his fall, and found himself on his knees, his head swimming, his chest heaving.

"Jude!" Anton's voice cried, but he sounded far away. "Jude, stay with me."

Jude couldn't keep his eyes open any longer. He laid his head down in the dirt and let the darkness take him.

II

BLOOD AND MERCY

15

HASSAN

HASSAN CAME TO THE NEXT SCARAB'S WING STRATEGY MEETING PREPARED. He arrived early to the alchemy workshop, claiming the seat at the head of the long table—the seat Arash usually took. Adopting a look of placid welcome, he waited for the others to arrive.

Khepri smiled and sat beside him, while Zareen shot him a look of mild amusement as she plopped down onto one of the cushions. Arash was one of the last to arrive, and he paused in the doorway for a brief moment before taking a seat beside Zareen. He didn't look at Hassan, and Hassan schooled his look of satisfaction. He'd already thrown him off balance.

As the rest of them took their seats, Arash cleared his throat. "Prince Hassan," he said, his tone pleasantly cheerful. "I'm so glad you've put aside our differences to join us. I know that you're against what we're trying to do, and I know many of us are interested to discuss your thoughts."

Hassan smiled. "Actually, Arash, I've changed my mind. I think we should go forward with the coronation plans."

He watched Arash's eye twitch slightly. "Oh. Well that's wonderful news. We're pleased to have your support."

"Good," Hassan said. "And as we're now working together, I thought I would share some ideas as to how we can best take advantage of this opportunity."

"There will be time for that—"

"Disrupting the parade is a great way to get the attention of not only the queen and the dark forces that prop up her rule, but also the Herati public," Hassan said, as if he hadn't heard Arash. "We have an opportunity here to appeal to those who are feeling helpless over the coup, to show them that they have something to fight for." He paused, looking around at the others to ensure he had their full attention. "I think it would be the perfect time to tell the people of Nazirah that their king has returned."

He watched the panic flash across Arash's face. "I don't think that's a good idea." Arash cleared his throat. "It's a mistake to show our hand already. If we reveal to the public that you're still alive, those loyal to the Usurper will only target the Scarab's Wing harder."

Hassan turned to him. "I know the people of Herat. If we tell them what Lethia has truly done, they will rise up against her and join us."

His gaze flickered over to Khepri. She was the one who'd given him the idea. *Let your aunt know you're still here*, she had said. Rather than creating a haphazard disruption, as a fringe group of radicals might, Hassan would issue a direct challenge to Lethia's claim to the crown.

"Prince Hassan is the true heir to the throne," Sefu said. "The public knows that. If they know he's alive, I think there's a good chance they'll throw their support behind him."

"I love this idea," Zareen said. "I'm shaking just thinking about the Usurper's face when she sees you. How is she going to argue against your right to rule? She'll be trapped."

The rest of the table broke into conversation. Hassan's plan seemed to be catching like fire, and Hassan watched with satisfaction as Arash's face grew drawn and grim. But he didn't offer any counterarguments.

For Hassan's part, he could oversee the plans and make sure it minimized the risk of hurting innocents. And by the end of it, everyone would know who led the rebellion. Everyone would know who their king was.

Over the course of the next few days, more and more of Khepri and Hassan's refugee soldiers found their way to the Library, led by a search party sent out each evening. Hassan and Khepri established a routine at the Scarab's Wing base. Mornings were for strategy sessions. In the afternoons, Khepri trained with the other soldiers. Sometimes Hassan joined them, other times he disappeared into the Library's endless collections of books or perused the workshops where the alchemists and artificers were developing new weapons to use against the Witnesses, and new protections for the Library.

Today, that was where Hassan found himself, helping Zareen in her corner of the workshop, which was cluttered with beakers of every size and strewn with various brass instruments. Somehow, Zareen seemed to instinctively know where everything was when she needed it, despite the lack of organization.

"You titrated that?" she asked, pointing to a beaker in Hassan's hands.

"Yup," he answered, setting the beaker down. "What's it for?"

"Paralytic powder," she answered. "It's not very useful in combat—you have to ingest it for it to work. And it takes *forever* to make."

"What about these ones?" Hassan asked, pointing to a collection of glass cylinders filled with various tinctures.

"Uh, they're mood modifiers," she replied distractedly, squinting as she poured some of Hassan's mixture into her own. "They calm people down, wake them up, make them feel happy, stuff like that."

"So if I drink this I'll suddenly feel deliriously happy?" Hassan asked, peering at a bright amber glass.

"If you drink it you'll probably die, or at least puke," she answered. "They work through exposure. They store as liquid and release as gas at high temperatures."

"Ah, Prince Hassan. Just the man I wanted to see," Arash's cheerful voice called from the threshold of the alchemy workshop.

Hassan looked up at the Scarab's Wing's leader. They'd hardly spoken a direct word to each other since the morning Hassan had taken over the strategy meeting, and if they interacted at all, it was usually with Khepri as a buffer.

"We're busy, Arash, what do you want?" Zareen inquired, sounding irritated.

"Just a word or two with the prince here. It won't take long."

Zareen shot a questioning look at Hassan.

"It's fine," Hassan assured her, pleased that she looked to him for permission and not Arash. "Just—maybe try a different catalyst for the paralytic powder. Could help speed it up."

He followed Arash into the hallway.

"Who would have thought the Prince of Herat knew so much about alchemy?" Arash asked.

"It's thanks to my father," Hassan replied.

"I thought he trained in artificery? My masters at the Library talked about him a lot. They said he was one of the greatest artificers of the Seif line. We all thought his heir would succeed him in that, as well as the crown."

Hassan felt a stab of irritation. Arash never missed an opportunity to remind Hassan that he was Graced and Hassan was not.

"He was a great artificer," Hassan agreed, ignoring the rest. "But he dabbled with alchemy as well, and I always found it interesting."

"You are full of surprises," Arash said, managing to sound both impressed and condescending.

"What can I do for you, Arash?" Hassan asked, unable to keep the weary note out of his voice.

Arash gave a tight smile. "I'd like your help with something."

"That's what we're here for, isn't it?" Hassan asked. "To help the rebel effort. So just tell me what it is."

"It would be easier to show you."

Arash took him down to the Library's basement vaults. This was where they kept the most ancient texts, the ones that would be damaged without careful regulation of the air's temperature and moisture levels. Hassan had been down here only a few times in his life, and every visit had left him feeling claustrophobic and cold. Yet he couldn't deny that there was something awe-inspiring about seeing such ancient texts in person.

The original mosaic depicting the founding of Nazirah stretched across the back wall of the vault. Parts of it had crumbled away with age before it had been properly preserved and moved to the vaults, but the main elements of the story were still clear, if faded. Hassan recognized the visage of the first King of Nazirah, as well as the Prophet Nazirah herself. She was placing something on his head—the Crown of Herat.

"The stories say that the Crown Nazirah gave the first king

imbued him with Grace," Arash said. "They say it allowed him to create great machines, the likes of which haven't been seen in all the centuries since. But the Crown went missing centuries ago. I want to know what happened to it."

"What for?" Hassan asked.

"We have some of the most brilliant minds right here in this Library," Arash said, his fingers hovering just over the mosaic. "What if we could make them even more powerful? We could build weapons that would take out the Witnesses in an instant. We could save so many lives."

"We?" Hassan asked. "Or you?"

"All of us," Arash replied, dropping his arm and turning to Hassan. "All of us with the Grace of Mind, in any case. But, you're right. I've been working on something I think could help us reclaim the city. But my Grace . . . it's not enough for what I want to do. But if you told us where the Crown is—"

"You're assuming I know where it is," Hassan said. "I don't."

Arash pursed his lips. "You're the heir to the throne. I thought that your family had been keeping it safe all these years. You really have no idea?"

"None."

Arash's expression tightened. "This could really help, Hassan." It was the most sincere Hassan had ever seen him. "We need *something*."

They had something. A king.

Hassan hesitated. "Arash, you do know the stories about the Crown, don't you?"

Arash didn't reply.

"They say the Crown turned on the last person who wielded it," Hassan said. "The first king's grandson. That he used it to build a machine that ended up killing him."

"That's just a story, told to dissuade people from searching for the Crown."

Hassan sighed. He wasn't so sure. "Even if that's true, I still don't know where the Crown is. No one does."

Arash looked at him with a careful gaze for a long moment. "Well, then. I suppose I should return you to Zareen now. She won't be happy with me taking her assistant away."

That evening, Hassan sat up in bed, Khepri curled against his side, recounting the success of her training session.

"That armor they've started experimenting with is already *really* impressive," Khepri said. "The artificers here must be geniuses or something."

"Yeah," Hassan said absently.

Khepri turned in his arms to face him head-on. "Are you actually listening to me?"

"I'm sorry," Hassan said, shaking his head. "It's just—I had this strange conversation with Arash today."

Khepri sighed, and Hassan sensed her fatigue at the subject. She'd already been on the receiving end of a fair number of irritated tirades from Hassan.

"It's not what you think," Hassan said. He quickly recounted his conversation with Arash.

"What do you think?" he asked when he was done.

Khepri took a moment, rubbing her thumb absently over the muscle of his forearm. "I think we should try whatever we can to fight the Witnesses."

"I thought you'd say that."

"Well, don't you agree?"

"Of course." He paused. "But don't you wonder if . . ."

"If what?"

"If putting that kind of power into someone's hands is dangerous?"

"Not if they use it to save lives," Khepri replied. "A tool is only good or evil depending on how it's used—and by whom. Do you think I'm dangerous?"

Hassan leaned into her, smiling. "Very," he said against her lips.

She laughed, pushing him away. "You know what I mean. Is what Arash wants so wrong?"

"I don't know," Hassan said, sobering. "It's . . . there are stories about the people who wielded the Crown that don't end well. I'm afraid if Arash has it . . ."

"Arash wants to save this city as much as we do."

"I know," Hassan said. "But what if the Crown's power proved to be too much for him and he accidentally hurt people, or destroyed the city? I'm not saying he would do it on purpose. But the Crown . . . there's a reason my family hasn't gone looking for it."

"We need to focus on the things we *can* do," Khepri said. "Which is more than it was a week ago."

"Do you worry . . ." Hassan trailed off for a moment. Even with Khepri, it was difficult for him to admit his uncertainty. His fear. "Do you worry about what's going to happen after all this? If we defeat Lethia and drive the Witnesses out?"

She pressed her lips together, plucking at a stray thread in Hassan's sleeve. "Do you?"

Hassan nodded. "I just hope that winning doesn't mean losing sight of who we are and what we believe in. I hope it doesn't end in a choice like the one we made with the lighthouse. Letting it fall into Lethia's hands or letting it fall, period."

Khepri's face crumpled in sadness. "Oh, Hassan. You don't regret the choice we made, do you? Even if the lighthouse isn't there anymore—"

"I know," he said. "We did what we had to."

She took his hand, kissing his knuckles. "Whatever happens from here, we'll rebuild. You, and me, and everyone who loves this city, this kingdom."

He closed his eyes and Khepri pressed in closer, kissing his shoulder.

"But first, we have to take back the country," Khepri said. "Right now that means using every tactic at our disposal. And taking allies wherever we can find them."

He knew she was right. But he couldn't shake the fear that Arash and his rebels were proving everything the Witnesses said about the Graced to be true.

16

ANTON

ANTON MADE THE HIKE TO THE OUTPOST IN LESS THAN AN HOUR, HIS HEART pounding the entire way. He couldn't stop picturing the Witnesses stumbling upon Jude's unconscious body.

Once he'd packed a bag full of anything useful he could find—food, bandages, a fire starter, a tarp, and anything else they might need—he started making his way back down the hill. He wanted nothing more than to sprint back to Jude but had to force himself to tread quietly and listen for signs of the Witnesses.

Only the sound of wind and the flow of the river greeted him as he reached the edge of the clearing. He stopped between two trees, focused on the other side of the clearing, where Jude lay hidden in the soft brush.

A branch snapped loudly.

Anton froze, hardly breathing for almost a full minute. Maybe it was just an animal, or a branch that had fallen on its own.

Then a voice hissed through the clearing.

"Keep searching!"

Rustling grass and snapping twigs followed.

Anton ducked behind a tree, setting his pack down silently. The footsteps neared. He pressed himself farther back.

"They can't have gone far," another voice said, higher, much closer. Too close.

Anton fought to keep his breath silent. He gazed up at the tree branches above him, calculating how long it would take to climb up and considering whether the Witnesses would see.

"Wait," the first voice said.

The footsteps stopped.

"There," the voice said. "Look over there."

The footsteps sounded like they were getting farther from Anton again. He let out a relieved breath.

"They could be hiding in the brush."

Jude. Anton's heart kicked in his chest. He peered around the side of the tree and the sight in front of him made his blood go cold. Four Witnesses were striding across the clearing, heading straight for Jude's hiding spot.

Anton held his breath as they surrounded the brush, poking into it. One of them was mere feet from where Jude's head lay. He reached into the brush, and Anton tensed, ready to act, though he didn't know what to do exactly—rush at the Witnesses, call out to them and distract them, just *something*. The Witness was right on top of Jude. Anton stepped out from behind the tree.

But then the Witness turned away. "There's nothing here. Let's go."

Anton's stomach dropped. There was no way the Witness would have missed Jude from his position, which meant the swordsman was simply *gone*.

Anton barely had the presence of mind to slip back into the shadows as the Witnesses crossed the clearing and disappeared through the trees. Heart hammering, Anton stayed perfectly still, breathing hard, for another few long minutes until he was sure the Witnesses weren't coming back.

Then he grabbed his pack off the ground and sprinted across the clearing to kneel down by the brush, searching desperately for Jude. But the Witness had been right. He wasn't there. Had he been taken by an earlier patrol? Had he wandered off to bleed out in the woods alone?

Anton pushed himself to his feet, wanting to call out to Jude, but terrified the Witnesses would hear him.

A low groan drifted through the air.

"Jude?" Anton said, pitching his voice a shade lower than usual.

He heard another groan and hurried toward the sound. A moment later, he caught sight of Jude's crumpled form leaning against a tree. Relief gusted through him. Jude groaned again, pained, and Anton dropped to his knees at his side.

"Hey," he said gently, his chest still tight with worry. "It's all right."

Jude's eyes closed. "Thought you were gone," he panted. "I thought—"

"I'm here," Anton said at once. "You were passed out, and I went to get supplies at the outpost. The Witnesses—"

"I saw them," Jude said. "Hid."

"Good," Anton said firmly. "I don't think we can go back to the outpost, though. It's not safe."

"It's not safe to go back to Kerameikos, either," Jude said, wincing as Anton helped him sit up.

Anton let that statement wash over him, along with the guilt it inspired. "Are they going to be all right? The Guard, and the rest of the Order?"

Jude's face clouded over. "They will," he said, more like an incantation than a true answer. "They're the strongest fighters in the world."

Anton bit his lip. "The Witnesses know you and I escaped. Maybe they don't care about the fort, maybe they just want to find us. We can outrun them."

Jude nodded. "We need a plan. A place to go, somewhere safe, so we can contact the Order and—" His face crumpled as he sucked in a sharp breath and doubled over.

Anton reached out to steady him. "First order of business is taking care of that."

Jude lifted his hand from his side, and Anton saw that his shirt was wet with blood. "I'll be fine."

"You're completely delusional," Anton replied, turning to rifle through his bag of supplies. "Take that off."

Jude averted his eyes, staring studiously at the tree next to him as he shrugged out of his tunic. At first Anton thought Jude was embarrassed out of prudishness, but a moment later he realized the true source of Jude's discomfort.

Over a week ago, Anton had sat beside an unconscious Jude on the ship back to Kerameikos, horror filling him as he saw the full extent of the damage Jude had suffered from the Godfire. Now, Anton's eyes traced the white scars webbing down Jude's throat to his chest. That same sick feeling rose in his throat like bile. Back on the ship, he had run, unable to face what his own fear had cost Jude. Now, Anton stepped toward him.

"Here," he said quietly, moving into Jude's space as if to embrace him. Jude watched, jaw tense, as Anton wrapped the cloth bandages around his rib cage, over the wound and around his back. He reached for Jude's discarded shirt. "You need to put pressure on the wound," he advised, balling up the shirt and pressing it against Jude's side.

Jude grunted in pain and then reached over to take the shirt from Anton.

Anton dropped his hands, but something stopped him from moving away. His gaze drifted back down to the scars on Jude's chest, and without thinking, he reached up and brushed his fingers against them.

Jude flinched beneath his touch, and Anton went still.

"Why didn't you leave?" Jude asked after a moment. His eyes were on Anton's hands. "Last night, in the storeroom."

"I changed my mind."

"Why?"

The question appeared to be entirely earnest. Jude, evidently, had not figured it out on his own. Anton dropped his hand. "You said they were going to exile you. And I wasn't going to let that happen."

Jude pressed his lips into a thin line. "You shouldn't have gotten involved."

"What does it even matter anymore?" Anton asked. "You just said we're not going back there."

Jude's brow wrinkled in confusion. "You're . . . angry at me," he said at last. "You just defended me to the Tribunal, you went against the entire Order of the Last Light, but—you're angry."

Anton sat back on his heels. The awful thing was that he *was* angry, even after Jude had just risked his life to protect him.

"Whatever I said to you last night, I apologize," Jude said solemnly. "I was not myself."

Anton stood. "I don't care about last night." He snatched up his bag and began stalking across the grass. "Let's get going before the Witnesses find us."

Jude trailed after him. "If it's not about last night, then what is it about?"

"Nothing," Anton said. "I'm not mad."

"I don't believe you," Jude said. "And right now we need to depend on each other to get to safety. Tell me why you're angry so we can—"

"Because!" Anton burst, whirling on him. "Because you broke your promise!"

"Promise?" Jude repeated. "What—"

His confusion resolved into understanding.

Anton met his gaze, his jaw clenching against the words. He couldn't say them aloud.

Jude said them instead. "Whatever happens, I'll protect you."

A tremor ran through Anton. He hated how much he'd believed those words when Jude said them. Hated how much he'd wanted them to be true. He'd learned long ago not to rely on anyone else—not to trust a helping hand that didn't come with strings attached.

But then he'd met Jude, and for some stupid reason, Anton had believed that he would protect him. That he was *meant* to protect him. Maybe it had to do with the way Jude's *esha* had called out to him before they'd even met. Or the way Jude had thrown in his lot with Anton over a game of cards in Pallas Athos.

Or the way he'd come for him when Anton had been trapped in the dark pit of his own nightmares, and pulled him out.

"All I've ever done, my whole life, is run," Anton said, looking away from Jude's bare, vulnerable face. "And you told me to stop, and that night on the ship after Nazirah I thought—well, I thought maybe I could. Because you would be there, just like you were in Nazirah."

"Anton," Jude said softly.

"But you haven't been," Anton went on, squeezing his hands into tight fists. "In Kerameikos, I was forced to relive that awful vision over and over and over. Alone."

Silence followed this confession, filled only by the sound of Jude's soft breath.

"There was nothing I could do," Jude said at last, sounding miserable. "I can't . . . I can't be the Keeper of the Word anymore. I can't protect you." He looked away. "My Grace. I haven't been able to use it. Not since . . ."

"Nazirah," Anton said. He'd suspected as much, but to hear Jude confirm it made guilt burrow in his chest. "That's why you could touch the Godfire chains."

Jude bowed his head.

"But I can feel it," Anton said. Even now, he sensed it, fluttering hesitantly, a faint buzz in the air. Not the storm he used to feel, but not gone completely. "It's faint, but I can feel it, Jude."

Jude looked pained. "Well, I can't," he said, choking out the words. "When I try to summon it, I . . . it doesn't come. I think it's not just the Godfire. I think it's *me*. Something happened on that lighthouse and now . . ."

Anton wilted. Something had happened on the lighthouse. *Anton* had happened. If he hadn't been so scared, Jude never would have been near the Godfire flame. It was his fault that Jude was . . . broken.

"We'll find a way to fix it," Anton said. "Maybe a healer—"

Jude shook his head. "I went to a healer. There was nothing she could do. And it doesn't matter, anyway, now that I've lost the Pinnacle Blade—"

"The Pinnacle Blade," Anton interrupted. His dream from the night before came back to him, the heavy weight of the sword in his hands. "Jude, that's it."

Jude stared at him.

"That's what you need to—you know, to get in touch with your Grace again." He remembered the sheer power that Jude had channeled when he'd unsheathed the sword. Power like that—maybe it could make Jude's Grace whole again.

"I don't . . ." Jude trailed off. "We have bigger problems than my Grace."

"No, listen," Anton said, heading off what he knew would be another round of objections. "I saw your sword in my dream. The same dream where I saw the Hierophant. Why would I have seen it if it wasn't important?"

"That's exactly what I meant when I said we have bigger problems," Jude replied. "The Hierophant. The Age of Darkness. *That's* what we need to focus on."

"Jude, just—please," Anton said. "All I have is my vision and now this dream to guide me. I can barely make sense of them but I'm *trying*."

Jude shook his head. "We don't even know where the Pinnacle Blade is. One of your brother's mercenaries stole it from me when we were captured."

Anton's dream tugged at him again. Someone's voice—the Nameless Woman?—called to him.

"I know where it is," Anton said. "You have to trust me, Jude. We need to do this."

Jude opened his mouth and looked like he was struggling for words. "I—where?"

"Endarrion," Anton said. "It's in Endarrion."

Anton had taken only enough salted meat and nuts from the outpost to last them five days. Eight, if they really stretched it. Jude had estimated that Endarrion was about a ten days' journey from Kerameikos, but their pace was slowed by Jude's injuries and the winding terrain itself. They kept close to the river, but not so close that the Witnesses would easily find them, and they changed into a spare set of clothes from the outpost to disguise themselves.

They slept side by side each night, sheltered by the tarp Anton had taken from the outpost. He hadn't slept beside someone since he was young—before his brother had turned on him, they'd used to curl up on the rug beside the hearth to keep warm in the winter. He'd never allowed himself to be that vulnerable in front of someone since.

But now, it wasn't his own vulnerability that troubled him—it was Jude's. They were both light sleepers, and Anton would sometimes wake in the dark and watch Jude's profile, lit by the moon, and the soft rise and fall of his chest. He looked so young when he slept, and Anton wasn't sure exactly how that made him feel, except sometimes it drove him to get up and pace around their campsite to loosen the weight in his chest.

On the sixth night, they camped in a copse of trees, and when Anton awoke the next morning, it was drizzling lightly. The soft tap of rainfall was so relaxing, Anton almost forgot about all the dangers stalking them. Almost.

Jude was no longer beside him, and Anton carefully picked himself up, crawling out from under the tarp and shielding his eyes against the bright gray sky.

He found Jude by the river, moving stiffly through familiar forms that Anton identified as koahs. Anton leaned against a tree to watch, unsettled by how easy it would be to sneak up on Jude now that he couldn't use his Grace. But even without it, Jude's movements were elegant, almost mesmerizing.

It was several minutes before Jude spotted him, and he quickly fell out of his form, looking as though Anton had caught him doing something shameful. They stood there for a moment, rain misting around them.

"It's habit," Jude said.

Anton tilted his head. "You think you can summon it."

Jude shook his head, but his next question betrayed him. "Can you feel it?"

Anton closed his eyes and searched for the familiar whisper of Jude's Grace. He felt it now, as light as the rain that fell around them. He opened his eyes and met Jude's gaze. "I can always feel it." He touched the bark of the tree. "Even before I knew you, I felt it."

"What do you mean?"

Anton bit the edge of his lip. "The moment you arrived in Pallas Athos, I felt your Grace. I can feel everyone's *esha*, but yours was . . . different." That was a mild way to put it. When Anton had first felt Jude's Grace in the harbor of Pallas Athos, he'd been nearly struck down by the force of it, how it had swept over him like a crackling storm. "It scared me."

Jude's thick brows drew together in concern. "Why?"

He wasn't quite sure how to explain what he'd felt. Even now, he didn't understand it fully. "It overwhelmed me. Made me want to find you, but made me terrified of what would happen if I did. It felt like if I faced you, you'd know everything about me, even the things I didn't understand myself."

Jude's lips parted in surprise. His eyes flashed with something like recognition, and then he let out a huff of breath that sounded almost like a laugh.

"What?" Anton asked.

Jude shook his head, almost smiling. "Nothing."

Anton dug his thumbnail into the tree bark, feeling somewhat foolish, as if he was missing some part of a joke. He pushed himself off the tree and cleared his throat. "We need to find something to eat."

He had taken some fishing line from the outpost, which Jude

cut between two rocks and tied to a tree branch while Anton rooted around in the mud for worms. When he came back, he was so muddy that Jude let out a startled laugh at the sight of him. Anton retaliated by hurling a glob of mud at Jude, which he dodged. Anton pounced on him, scooping up mud and letting it ooze down the back of Jude's tunic, smooshing it against the side of his neck for good measure.

"Mercy, mercy!" Jude said, laughing and shoving Anton away.

Anton grinned, triumphant, and thus was not expecting it when Jude dropped a handful of mud onto his head. Anton wiped at it furiously and then charged at Jude. Three quarters of an hour later found them both breathless with laughter, washing off as best they could in the river. By then, the sun had peeked out from the clouds and they left their clothes on a rock by the side of the river to dry, changing back into their old clothes.

It was almost midday by the time they caught any fish.

That evening, several miles downriver, they cooked the fish over a fire, stripping the outer layers off damp wood.

Anton had spent most of the past six years in cities, so it was strange to be out in the wilderness where the only sounds were the river and the rustle of leaves. He watched the firelight flicker over Jude's face. He seemed more at peace here than anywhere Anton had ever seen him. This was also, Anton reflected, the most at peace he himself had ever been—despite the Witnesses, despite his nightmares, despite what lay ahead.

"How does your wound feel?" Anton asked that night as they lay side by side on their bedrolls, embers from the fire casting warmth over their toes.

"Better," Jude replied.

"We might want to let it breathe after we get to Endarrion. It'll heal faster that way." Or maybe they'd find a healer to patch him up properly.

Jude shifted onto his uninjured side. "How did you learn how to do this?"

"Do what?"

Jude's gaze dropped to his bandaged ribs.

"I was on my own for a while as a kid. When I got hurt there usually wasn't a healer around."

"When you got hurt?" Jude asked slowly. "Hurt how?"

Anton shrugged one shoulder. "Things happen. The world is a dangerous place."

"And there was no one to protect you," Jude said quietly, as if to himself.

Anton's eyes flickered up to meet Jude's. For the most part, Anton tried not to think too much about the years he'd spent between leaving Novogardia and coming to Pallas Athos. Nights on the street, nights searching for refuge any place he could find it, nights weighing a bad option against a worse one. He hadn't had anyone back then, but that had been . . . well, not fine, but it was what he knew. He'd seen kids his age in worse states than him. He'd gotten by.

But now, looking at the horror in Jude's eyes, Anton considered his past through a different lens for the first time. Jude had grown up in the safety of Kerameikos Fort. He'd never had to wonder where his next meal would come from, nor what he would do the next time an older, stronger person demanded something he didn't want to give.

"Jude," Anton said. "It's fine. Really. I'm fine."

"It's not fine," Jude said sharply. "It's—they should have found you earlier. I should have found you. And because I didn't, you—you had to—"

Anton stared at him, not knowing what to say. "It is what it is, Jude. Whatever happened back then . . . whatever *I* did, it got me here. Maybe it would have been better if the Order had found me sooner. But maybe not."

Jude didn't answer for a long moment. Then, looking up at the sky, he said, "There's just . . . a lot about your life that I don't know. Sometimes when I look at you, it's like I'm seeing two people. The Prophet, and the boy who bet my sword on a game of cards."

"I'm not two people, Jude," Anton said.

"I know," Jude replied. He closed his eyes and turned on his side, silent for a moment that stretched long enough that Anton started to doze. But then Jude's voice drifted back over him, quieter than before. "Sometimes I feel like it would be easier if you were."

Anton opened his eyes and looked over at him. "What would be easier?"

But the only answer was Jude's gentle breathing.

17

BERU

PERSUADING THE CARAVAN TO TAKE THEM TO BEHEZDA HAD BEEN EASIER THAN anticipated. The leader of the caravan, Orit, had been quick to accept Beru's offer to have Hector guard them against the bandits who plagued the caravan route.

He kept his distance from Beru throughout their first day of travel. She busied herself by asking the caravan merchants about their wares and letting them teach her how to guide the camels.

Dust choked the air as they marched through the desert. The sun was already beating down on them by midmorning. Beru ceased trying to wipe the sweat from her face. Orit's daughter, Ayla, lent her a scarf to wrap around her head to protect her from the elements.

When they stopped at midday to rest and water the camels, Beru found that despite the heat, she couldn't sit still. When one of the other merchants asked if she could bring some straw reeds up to the top of the wagon to dry, she readily agreed.

"We used to make baskets in my village with these," Beru said, watching Vira the cat bat at the reeds like they were particularly slow-moving prey.

"We use them for flooring," the merchant replied. "Surprisingly sturdy stuff. Keeps things dry."

It was as Beru was climbing down from the wagon that she noticed Hector standing beside the cart, looking up at her.

"Oh," she squeaked, and dropped to the ground beside him.

"You were always like that," Hector said. "Even when we were young."

"Like what?"

"Curious," Hector said after a beat. "You wanted to know how everything worked. Didn't matter if it was the fish tackle or mother's woodworking, you were always getting into everything."

Beru opened her mouth to reply and then stopped. It was the first time Hector had spoken of their past before his family had died. It was the first indication that he remembered the girl she'd been back then.

"I guess I just like to be useful," Beru said.

"You were probably a bigger help to them than I ever was," Hector said. He was almost smiling, but then the expression faded and Beru felt a heavy wave of sadness from him. Perhaps he was remembering that she was the reason he no longer had parents.

The sun suddenly felt too hot on her back. Her head felt light. She stumbled.

"Whoa!" Hector's arms went around her, holding her up.

She let herself sag for a moment, face tucked into his shoulder, his heartbeat a steady drum against her chest. It was only when she realized what she was doing—being *comforted* by him—that she pulled away.

"Sorry," she said, her head swimming.

He was still holding on to her arm. "How much longer . . . ?"

She understood the unasked question. How much longer until she faded again.

"I'm not sure," she answered. "Enough." She hoped.

By the time they stopped to rest that evening, Beru was dead on her feet. Hector had probably had a point about resting.

"You'll get used to it," said Orit, steering her into a tent.

Beru was so exhausted, it took her several moments to realize she was not the only person inside. Hector lay in an untidy sprawl across his bedroll, his face angled away from her.

"Sorry," Beru said hastily. "I think they assumed we—" She cut herself off. It didn't matter what the caravan had assumed. "I'll just go."

She started to roll up the bedroll.

"It's fine," Hector said after a moment. "You don't have to go."

Beru hesitated. "I think I probably should. You don't want me here. I'll find somewhere else to sleep."

"It's not that." He sat up, the thin sheet falling to his waist, leaving his chest bare. He wiped his hand over his face, and Beru felt a twinge of something that curdled her stomach like guilt.

"Really. You should stay. I mean, unless you don't want to."

Beru looked off toward the corner of the tent. "You don't need to be nice to me. Not after everything I've done."

"Just sleep here," he said, with finality. "It's late."

He was right. And Beru was too tired to go bother Orit and find another place to sleep. She unrolled her bedding at the very edge of the tent, as far from Hector as she could get, and curled up to sleep. Even with her eyes closed, she was too aware of Hector and every sound he made as he turned over in the dark. It was like she was twelve again, watching the steady rise and fall of Hector's chest from across the room, Ephyra snoring softly next to her. She cringed, remembering her unbearable crush on him back then. The countless fantasies of marrying him and becoming a part of his family for real.

Now, miles and miles away from that home by the sea, she listened as Hector drifted to sleep, and slipped into her own uneasy slumber.

Faces swam before her. Marinos's face, with that tiny scar above his right eyebrow. His eyes were closed, still. Beside him, she saw his parents. They were resting on their backs, on the floor of a home that was both familiar and not. A pale handprint appeared on Marinos's shoulder, spreading like a bruise. The handprint appeared on his mother and father, too, and then they began to bleed. Blood dripped from their eyes, their ears, overflowing their mouths.

Help us. Help us.

Their eyes flashed open. *Help us, Hector.*

A low, choked-off moan woke her. Beru sat up, blood hammering through her veins. The echoes of the nightmare swam at the edges of her mind.

The tent was dark, Hector just an indistinct shape on the other side of it. But he was moving, thrashing back and forth like a bird caught in a trap.

Beru scrubbed a hand over her face and went to wake him. It was a risky endeavor. His Graced strength could crush her before he'd even woken.

She knelt over him. "Hector." She shook him gently, and then again, a bit harder. "*Hector.*"

He sputtered awake, his chest heaving with the force of his breath.

"Are you all right?" Beru asked after a moment.

"I was dreaming," Hector said. His sheets were bunched up in his hands. He was staring straight ahead, not at Beru, as if still caught in the claws of his nightmare.

"It's all right," Beru soothed, not sure what else to do. "You're fine now."

"I saw my family," he said. "They were calling out to me."

Beru's own dream snapped its teeth in her mind.

"Oh," she said faintly. His gaze shifted to her. She wasn't sure if she should utter the words that were on the tip of her tongue. She couldn't quite make out his expression in the dark. That made it easier. "I think . . . I saw your dream, too."

He was staring at her. "What do you mean, you saw my dream?"

"The connection between us," Beru said. "It's stronger . . . or just, *more*, than we realized."

Hector was silent for a long moment. Then he rolled over. "Stay out of my dreams."

A bolt of irritation flashed through Beru as she retreated to her own bedroll. "I wasn't *trying* to see them."

There was no answer from the other side of the tent.

Beru had thought she was making progress with Hector, but the next morning she knew that the night's events had eclipsed whatever good will he'd felt toward her. She let him avoid her most of the day, occupying herself with tossing bits of dried meat to Vira and trying to make herself useful.

In the evening, when they stopped to make camp, she found him sitting beside one of the wagons, idly stroking Vira's fur as he looked out at a dark shape in the distance.

"It's a shamal," Beru said after a moment. "Sandstorm. It won't hit us here, though. It's headed south."

He looked up at her, unsurprised by her sudden presence.

She sat down beside him, holding her hand out for Vira to rub her head against. "My father used to say that long before the Prophets, people used to think the shamal were omens."

"What do you think this one means?" he asked.

"You're on the right path?" she suggested. "That's what I hope it means, anyway."

He didn't answer, but he didn't make a move to leave, either. Beru scratched under Vira's chin.

"It's strange," Hector said, looking down at the cat. "I thought she would instinctively know what we are."

"Maybe she does," Beru countered. "But she just doesn't discriminate when it comes to chin scratches."

Vira purred in agreement.

They shared a tent again that night, and this time it was Beru who dreamed. She knew it was her own dream, because in it she saw Hector's lifeless body staring up at the acacia trees in the yard of her childhood home. A pale handprint wrapped around his throat, and Ephyra stood above him, her own hands dripping with blood.

She woke to Hector's face, alive, above her, and by his expression she knew he had seen the dream, too.

Beru sat up, wanting to say something to him but not knowing what.

He spoke first. "You want absolution. You think I can give it to you."

She closed her eyes. "I want . . . I want to know my life hasn't been for nothing. That I haven't brought only suffering to the world."

"And why do you think saving me is going to change that? I'm . . . I'm not exactly a good person."

She stared at him. "What do you mean?"

"I abandoned my duty," he said, looking down. "I abandoned my only friend. I . . . I threw away the only thing that had ever been given to me."

"You mean the Order of the Last Light."

Something seemed to close in his expression.

"They took me in," he said at last. "When I had nothing. And they offered me a life. The friend I abandoned—he was like a brother to me. No one could replace what I lost, but . . . he was good. I wanted to be that, too. I think I would have tried, for him, until the day I died, if I hadn't . . ."

"Found me," Beru finished softly.

Hector's fists tightened and Beru felt a wave of anger that dissipated—his anger, she realized belatedly. Twice, Hector had lost his family. Twice, Beru had been the cause of his suffering.

"What would happen if you went back?"

Hector shook his head. "When I left, I broke an oath. The punishment for that . . . well, I suppose I've already experienced it."

"That's . . ." Beru didn't know how to finish the thought. She felt furious and sad. "That's not fair."

"Not fair?" he asked, scornful.

Beru swallowed. What wasn't fair was Ephyra murdering him to keep Beru alive. But that's why she was trying to fix it. "Hector, I'm sorry. I never wanted—"

"What is done cannot be undone," Hector said. "Not by you, not by the Daughters of Mercy—not by anyone. I am a revenant now. And that means that the prophecy could refer to either one of us. *That which sleeps in the dust shall rise.* I thought it meant you, but now . . . either way, I know what I have to do."

"What are you talking about?" Beru said. "We're going to Behezda, and we're going to make this right."

Hector shook his head. "I didn't agree to come to Behezda so you could save me. I'm going there to end my life for good."

18

EPHYRA

THE JOURNEY TO SUSA TOOK THEM DEEPER INTO THE DESERT. EPHYRA HAD never been this far into the Seti, and the absolute nothingness was as breathtaking as it was terrifying. The desert around her village, Medea, teemed with life—shrubs and grasses and lizards and even trees. This desert was nothing like that. It was sand, as far as the eye could see, and sloping dunes that had been built by the wind.

They slept through the hottest part of the day, shaded by their tents and the sails of their skiffs. Numir and Hadiza guided them by the stars and the early-morning sun, but Ephyra couldn't help but feel like they were going in circles.

She spent most of her days thinking about Beru, and keeping an eye on Illya, who had quickly made himself useful aboard the skiff, helping to tack and jibe with the wind. Ephyra was deeply suspicious of his helpfulness, and irritable whenever he asked Hadiza to tell them stories about the desert, or commiserated with Numir about the heat, or got Parthenia jabbering on about her favorite languages, and how much their grammar reflected their cultural precepts.

It didn't help that there was sand in every crevice of Ephyra's body, trapped between the curls of her hair, crusted behind her ear, in between her toes. About two days in, she'd stopped bothering to scrub it off.

On the tenth day, Ephyra was dozing in the skiff as the sun rose over the golden dunes. The pitch-dark desert landscape brightened and Ephyra realized that for the first time, the land didn't look exactly the same as it had the day before. The sand here had hardened into loose dirt, and they seemed to be in a valley between two slopes. Wide grooves fanned out through the valley, long and waving like estuaries.

"What is this?" Ephyra asked.

Hadiza glanced over at her. "This used to be a river. There was a whole system of villages and travel networks that connected this area to Tel Amot and Behezda."

"What happened?" Ephyra asked, her eyes scanning the landscape, trying to imagine what it must have looked like when the river was flowing and lined with bustling villages.

"The Necromancer King happened," Hadiza answered. "All this loss of life, of civilization"—she gestured at the desolate land surrounding them—"was the cost of his greed."

Ephyra shivered, despite the heat.

Hadiza wasn't finished. "This is what the Chalice can do. This is the power of the thing you seek. Knowing that, you still want to find it?"

Ephyra closed her eyes. Someone else had asked her that question before. *Knowing what it costs, do you still want to save her?* She had been sure of her answer then.

With the nothingness of the desert surrounding her, she was less sure.

They reached Susa the next day. Fractured domes and broken towers rose abruptly from the sand, shimmering in the midday sun like a mirage.

They tied their skiffs up at the city gates and entered on foot, Numir leading them carefully over the decayed road. Ephyra's eyes scanned the buildings that rose up on either side of them. The architecture was like nothing she'd seen in the Six Prophetic Cities. The tops of the city walls and gates were jagged with uneven crenellations and decorated with three-dimensional figures—people and winged creatures that Ephyra had never seen before. The buildings were all crumbling and eroded. Some of them gleamed in the sun with the remains of some kind of copper plating.

"This place was built before the Prophets, wasn't it?" Illya asked.

Hadiza looked surprised. "Yes. This city is ancient—one of the oldest we know of."

Despite the heat of the sun, Ephyra felt a chill slide down her spine. The silence and desolation of this place reminded her of somewhere else—Medea, the village she and Beru had come from. The village that Ephyra had destroyed. She could almost see the bodies splayed across the cracked ground.

"The temple should be at the center of the city," Hadiza said.

"Stay alert," Shara said sharply. "We don't know who—or what—else could be here."

Unease crept over Ephyra as they made their way into the heart of the city. She felt eyes on her, like they were being followed, watched. But when she turned to look, there was nothing there.

The temple rose into view, looking exactly as it had in the mirror. A triangular base tapered up to a peak. Wide stairs ran down one side of it. As they got closer, she could see the sculpture at the top.

They stopped at the temple's colossal stone door, intricately carved with winged serpents and lion-headed birds, along with geometric symbols.

Parthenia made a face. "What if there's . . . dead people in there?"

"What if there's *living* people in there?" Numir added. "The kind that want to kill us?"

"I'll go in first," Shara said. They shuffled toward the entrance. Shara ran her hands over the right edge of the door, while Hadiza did the same on the other side.

"Maybe we can bust through it?" Numir suggested.

"This is probably four to six feet of solid stone," Hadiza said, shaking her head.

Parthenia rolled her eyes at Numir. "That *would* be your suggestion."

"What's *your* suggestion then?"

Ephyra turned to face the door as they continued to bicker. There was a border of raised stone along the bottom, in some sort of pattern. Ephyra knelt to get a better look. The pattern wasn't consistent, although there was clearly repeating lines of some kind. Almost like . . . letters.

"Wait," Ephyra said. She glanced up and saw that no one was paying attention to her except Illya.

"Parthenia," she said, louder. "I think there's writing on the door down here. But not in any language I know."

Parthenia stopped her argument midsentence and trotted toward Ephyra.

Parthenia squinted at the writing. "It looks quite a lot like

Nehemian . . . but I'm guessing since we're at a temple it's High Nehemian, which would have only been used by priests for religious ceremonies."

"So you can't read it?" Ephyra asked impatiently.

Parthenia gave her a saccharine look. "I can read it. It'll just take me a second."

She drew a slate out of her bag and a little piece of chalk along with a book. She kept glancing from the book to the writing on the door, and then scribbling something down on the slate.

The sun scorched above as Parthenia worked at her translation. Sweat slid down the side of Ephyra's face.

"All right," Parthenia said at last, looking down at her slate. "It says to get inside, we need to give a sacrifice."

"Like a *human* sacrifice?" Shara asked, alarmed.

Ephyra glanced at Illya. Maybe he would be useful after all.

"It could be," Hadiza replied. "They used to sacrifice people to the old god."

A heavy silence fell over the group.

Then Parthenia spoke again. "Oh, wait," she said with a little laugh. "I mistranslated this. It doesn't say sacrifice—it says *secret*."

"Like a secret password?" Shara asked.

Parthenia shook her head. "No, a secret of *yours*. The words *sacrifice* and *secret* are related in Nehemian—offering up a secret is a kind of sacrifice." She stepped up to the door and cleared her throat. "My real eye color isn't blue. I just convinced an alchemist at the Great Library to change them for me."

Numir barked out a laugh. The door didn't move.

"What's wrong?" Shara asked. "Did you get the translation wrong? Maybe it *is* 'sacrifice.'"

Parthenia pursed her lips and shook her head. "There are about

179

twelve different words for *secret* in High Nehemian, all associated with different body parts. There's *fumaya*, which roughly translates to a 'mouth-secret,' and *zamaya* which is 'bone-secret.' They used *coraya* here, which I think translates to 'heart-secret'?"

"What's the difference?" Shara asked impatiently. "Secrets are secrets."

"Not to the Nehemians," Hadiza said. "They believed secrets have power and that the secrets you keep could present themselves as a sickness or ailment. As though secrets take up physical space in our bodies—in our mouths, bones—"

"And hearts," Ephyra finished. "And so a heart-secret is . . . what?"

"Something to do with the heart," Parthenia said simply. "A secret about who you are, truly."

"So not just a secret about changing eye colors," Shara said.

Parthenia gave her a sarcastic look and then stepped up to the door again and took a breath. "I haven't seen my parents in five years because I think if they saw me now they would be ashamed of me."

The door began to rumble, and then it ascended, exposing darkness within the temple. Parthenia didn't hesitate, stepping over the threshold and into the darkness. The door slid shut behind her.

Ephyra caught sight of Numir's face, which looked stricken, as she stepped up to the door. She told the door that during the traditional First Hunt that women in her tribe had to perform, she had tracked a hawk to its nest, but when she saw its baby chicks, she'd let it go. Shara went next.

"So . . . I guess we're all going to share secrets," she said. "Great. Um. I never told Badis how much he meant to me, and I regret it every single day." She paused, and when the door didn't open, she said, "All I ever wanted was for him to be proud of me."

The door slid open again, and Ephyra watched Shara disappear inside. She looked at Hadiza.

"After you," Hadiza said.

Ephyra eyed her. She didn't want anyone to hear her *heart-secret*, but Hadiza certainly didn't look like she'd let her get out of it. But that didn't mean that Illya had to hear it, too.

"You go first," she said to him.

He swallowed. "Fine." He approached the door and touched it lightly with one hand. "My brother hates me."

The door didn't move. Illya bowed his head and went on, even quieter, "I think he's right to."

Ephyra's eyes widened, and her pulse jumped as the door slid open. Somewhere, deep down, Illya really *did* regret what he'd done to Anton. He swung his gaze back to Ephyra for a moment before disappearing through the door.

Ephyra approached it slowly, reaching her fingers out to brush the face of the door. A real secret. Something she'd never told anyone before. She took a deep breath, and said, "I'm afraid I'm going to fail."

The door didn't move.

Ephyra tensed and continued, quieter, "I'm afraid of what's going to become of me if I do."

The door rumbled open, and Ephyra crept inside. The room was illuminated by the incandescent lights Shara and Numir held. The others all seemed to be avoiding each other's eyes. A moment later, the door slid open and Hadiza entered.

"All right, that's all of us," Shara said.

There was a doorway directly in front of them. Through it, they emerged into another nearly pitch-black chamber—completely dark, except for a single beam of light that cut down from the ceiling into the center of the sanctum. Judging by its height, they were in the main chamber of the temple, which filled out the entire building.

They fanned out across the interior of the temple, searching with the help of their incandescent lights. They seemed weak and dim against the sheer size of the temple's interior.

Ephyra found herself walking straight toward the column of light that beamed down from the ceiling, stopping to look up at the perfect circle of fading blue sky above.

"There's something over here hanging on the wall," Parthenia called out.

"I found something, too," Hadiza said. "It looks like the same mirror we found in Badis's hideout."

"There's one over here, too!" Shara cried. "Not sure what good a mirror is going to do in the dark, though."

Ephyra's hand flew to her bag, where the first mirror was stowed. She flipped it so the mirror side faced up, and immediately the glass became so bright she had to shield her eyes. She tilted the mirror away from her gaze. Suddenly, an oval of light was projected onto the far wall.

She continued to experiment, moving the mirror this way and that, watching the light dance on the sloping walls, until she finally aimed it at the mirror Hadiza had found.

The light bounced off the mirror and illuminated Illya, who was standing a few feet away.

"Move," Ephyra demanded.

He stumbled out of the way, revealing another mirror behind him, and the light zigzagged around the sanctum, hitting each mirror and bouncing off to the next. Ephyra followed the beam of light to its end point, a circle impressed into a stone wall, which began to move, revealing a secret chamber on the other side.

Ephyra put the mirror back in her bag. The light vanished, but the door stayed open. She approached it, the others at her heels. Plucking the incandescent light from Shara's hand, Ephyra entered the secret chamber. It was much smaller than the colossal main sanctum, and crammed full of ceramic vessels.

"What are we looking for, exactly?" Parthenia asked.

"Hopefully we'll know it when we see it," Shara replied.

"That's your plan?" Ephyra asked. "Just hope the next clue falls into your lap?"

Shara shrugged, and Ephyra bit back a frustrated sigh. Despite Shara's bravado, Ephyra was beginning to think that she wasn't actually a very good treasure thief. She seemed capable only of barking commands and making hasty decisions. What did she bring to the group, like Parthenia's languages or Hadiza's histories? Sure, Shara had gotten them this far, but none of that mattered if they didn't find the Chalice.

"Over here," Illya said from one corner of the room. Shara and Parthenia, who were nearest to him, hurried over. "Look at this. It has the same symbol as the code I found behind the mirror."

Ephyra pushed her way over to them. "You mean the code you purposely destroyed so that we'd be forced to drag you along with us?"

Illya glanced up at her. He held one of the ceramic vessels in his hands, and she could see clearly from the light that there was an impression of a circle with lines through it. It looked like a compass rose.

Shara plucked the urn from his hands, weighing it in her palm. Then she hurled it at the wall.

"What are you doing?" Ephyra demanded as the ceramic shattered against the wall.

Shara just smirked and stooped down in the debris. When she stood again, she was holding up a long ribbon of leather.

"What is that?" Ephyra asked, leaning toward her. There seemed to be writing on the leather. "What does it say?"

Shara looked down at the leather. "Just a bunch of letters."

Ephyra whirled toward Illya. "What was the code? The one you found on the mirror?"

"If I tell you," Illya replied, "then you won't need me anymore."

"If you don't tell us, no one is getting the Chalice," Shara said.

A loud rumbling sound cut through the air.

"What was that?" Shara asked, alarmed.

Another rumble, this one louder. The chamber shook, small chunks of rock breaking off and raining down on them.

"We need to get out of here," Numir said. "Now."

She strode over to the entrance to the chamber. Ephyra moved to follow her—and then the floor started to shake. Gently at first, and then quicker still until it felt like an earthquake was erupting beneath their feet. Ephyra had the distinct sensation of falling.

"The temple is sinking!" Parthenia cried, bracing herself against the wall.

That, it seemed, was all it took for the rest of them to leap into action. They scrambled through the doorway and back into the main sanctum, rocks falling from the sloped ceiling. Ephyra ran hard for the entrance, Illya keeping pace beside her.

A large chunk of stone crashed down in front of them, nearly crushing Parthenia. Numir leapt toward her, pushing her to the ground and shielding her from more falling debris. The rest of them scattered around the fallen rock as Numir hauled Parthenia to her feet by the elbow and sprinted for the threshold.

They reached it first, disappearing outside. Hadiza followed. As Shara approached the threshold, rocks cascaded down, blocking her way. Shara leapt back, and suddenly the door was no more. Ephyra and Illya looked on in horror.

They were trapped.

19

JUDE

JUDE DEMANDED THAT THEY STOP AT THE TEMPLE OF ENDARRA BEFORE TRYING to find the Pinnacle Blade. They arrived in the late morning, tired, hungry, but most importantly, alive. If any members of the Order had made it out of Kerameikos safely, they would have contacted the acolytes here.

The temple lay just outside Endarrion, surrounded on all sides by the river. The entrance was accessible by riverboat or via a narrow, serpentine bridge that wound up to the temple steps.

Jude reached for Anton's arm to hold him back as they approached the bridge. "We don't know who's in there. Could be friends."

"Could be Witnesses," Anton said, completing the thought.

Jude nodded. "Stay close."

The sun peeked out of the clouds, casting pockets of bright light on the river as they made their way to the temple's entrance. They stopped at the threshold to anoint themselves with chrism oil. Jude caught Anton sneaking glances at him, as if he was copying the movements, and Jude had the startling thought that this might be the first time Anton had ever set foot inside a temple of his forebears. He opened his mouth to ask as much when an acolyte appeared before them.

"Keeper of the Word," the acolyte breathed. "We've been expecting you."

Jude moved toward Anton, shielding him, but there was no malice in the acolyte's voice. "We seek the shelter of Endarra the Fair."

The acolyte bowed his head. "Endarra grants you shelter most readily."

The acolyte was not dressed like the ones Jude had met in Pallas Athos. These acolytes wore silk robes of lilac, trimmed in pale gold and patterned with small bursts of white flowers. Delicate gold bracelets hung from their wrists, and thin circlets lay over intricately braided hair.

An auburn-haired acolyte approached them as they entered.

"This is our head acolyte," the first acolyte said. "They will see that you are taken care of."

The auburn-haired acolyte peered at Jude and Anton with undisguised astonishment. "You. You must be him. The Prophet."

Anton's eyes went wide. "What? Jude, you never told me!"

The acolyte paled.

"He's kidding," Jude said belatedly.

The acolyte looked unnerved.

Jude also felt unnerved. Not by Anton's joke, but by the way the acolytes were looking at Anton, like he was the sun rising in the east. He remembered what he'd told Anton after escaping from Kerameikos—that he often felt like Anton was two different people. Over the past ten days, traveling with Anton in solitude, depending on each other, it had been easy to lose sight of what Anton meant to the rest of the world.

He couldn't afford to forget that. Especially now.

"Kerameikos is under attack," Jude told the auburn-haired acolyte. "The Witnesses assaulted the fort almost two weeks ago, in search of the Prophet. We don't know how they found us."

"We heard all this from your Guard," the acolyte said.

Jude let out a breath he felt like he'd been holding since they'd escaped from Kerameikos. "They're all right? They survived the attack?"

"A small number of Paladin managed to escape downriver," the acolyte said. "The Guard contacted us a day ago, saying they'd reached Delos. They also told us that you and the Prophet escaped alone, and advised that you should stay here under our protection until they arrive to retrieve you."

"Is the city safe?" Jude asked. "Are there Witnesses here?"

The acolyte looked grim. "There were reports of a group of Witnesses arriving here several days ago, but none have approached the temple."

Jude's stomach plummeted. "They've been waiting us out. If they saw us arrive here, then we've put you all in danger."

"The Witnesses don't have a large presence in this city. I don't think they would risk attacking the Temple of Endarra in broad daylight, and we have certain precautions in place to deter unwanted visitors."

Anton glanced at Jude again, concern etched onto his face. "Do you have somewhere we can relax, maybe?" he said to the acolyte. "Something to eat? It's been a long journey."

"Of course," the acolyte said, pressing a palm to their chest. "I should have offered to begin with. Come with me."

"What about a healer?" Anton asked. "Jude was injured in the attack."

"Of course," the acolyte replied, sweeping through the main sanctum. They led them through a door that opened out into a lush garden shaded by canopies, overlooking the river.

Jude hadn't realized how exhausted he was until the acolyte sat him down on a plush circular cushion and disappeared to bring him a tray of food much more sumptuous than anything they'd eaten in Kerameikos. He and Anton picked at the plate of candied fruit and sliced meat, and then the acolyte returned with the temple's healer in tow.

The healer sat down beside Jude and got to work.

"Wait," Anton called out as the acolyte turned to leave. "I have a question I hope you can answer. We think that Jude's sword—the Pinnacle Blade—might be here in Endarrion. Do you know anything about that?"

The acolyte's gaze swung to Jude, and Jude wanted to recoil from the horror on their face.

"It's true, then?" the acolyte asked. "The Pinnacle Blade was lost?"

Jude looked away and didn't answer.

"What do you know?" Anton asked.

"A rumor, only," the acolyte replied. "There's a famous collector here in Endarrion who trades in rare items. There's been talk that she's acquired a new sword for her collection, said to be as old as the Prophets themselves. We didn't believe it was truly the Pinnacle Blade, but . . ."

Jude realized he was shaking with rage. The Pinnacle Blade was forged for the first Keeper of the Word, made to serve the Prophet. It wasn't some pretty trophy to be paraded about by a *collector*.

"A collector," Anton repeated. "Can you tell us anything else about her?"

The acolyte shook their head. "I'm sorry."

They left the room, and the healer finished her work on Jude's wound.

"Should be good as new," she said gently, smoothing her fingers down Jude's side where the wound had been. The pain was entirely gone, and when Jude moved there was no twinge or stiffness.

"Thank you."

Anton got to his feet as soon as she disappeared out the door.

"Where are you going?" Jude asked with a frown.

"We need to go into the city," Anton said. "We need to find this collector and get your sword back."

"It's too dangerous. You heard what the acolyte said. The Witnesses are searching for us here. If one of them finds us—"

"Are you kidding?" Anton said. "This is the whole reason we came to Endarrion!"

"We should wait for the Guard."

"And who knows where your sword will be by then," Anton said. "We know where it is right now. We know—sort of—who has it."

Jude hesitated. He knew he should keep Anton here at the temple, where they were safe. But he couldn't shake the possibility of it—of returning to the Order with both the Prophet and the Pinnacle Blade safe.

It could mean absolution.

And more than that, it might mean his Grace being restored. He hadn't been able to stop thinking about the possibility since Anton had brought it up. If anything could fix his Grace, it was the Pinnacle Blade. Maybe that was why Anton had seen it in his dream. If Jude's Grace was fully restored, he could once again serve the Prophet and help him stop the Age of Darkness.

He glanced back at Anton, who was watching him intently.

"Even if we wanted to reclaim the Pinnacle Blade," Jude said slowly, "how would we get to it? It doesn't seem like we can just walk into this collector's house."

Anton grinned. "That, I *have* figured out. All we need is to find someone who knows her, and then get an invite to see the collection. Rich people love showing off their wealth. And as it so happens, I know just the person."

"I thought you've never been to Endarrion before."

"I haven't," Anton replied. "But I used to be a server at a taverna in Pallas Athos, and there was a merchant who used to stay there a lot with his son. We were . . . friendly."

Friendly. Jude wondered what details, exactly, that word glossed over. Again he was struck with the uncomfortable knowledge that there was a lot about Anton's past that Jude knew nothing about—and might never understand.

"Anyway, his father specialized in selling valuables, so if anyone knows the collector it'll be him."

"And you think this merchant's son will help us?"

"I know how to be persuasive," Anton replied, and Jude's frown deepened. "We'll just go over there and say hello. The worst that can happen is he says no."

There were plenty of worse things that might happen, especially with Witnesses in the city. It was selfish to put Anton at risk for the Pinnacle Blade—selfish like he'd been in Pallas Athos, chasing after what he wanted and denying the oath he'd sworn. *To serve the Prophets above all else. Above our lives. Above our hearts.*

But selfish choices had led him to Anton. And now they were here together in a city of hidden enemies, with no way to defend themselves.

If there was a chance that Jude could regain his ability to protect Anton, the risk was worth it.

"Fine," Jude said at last. "We'll go."

Anton beamed at him all the way into the city.

Jude rowed them down the river in one of the acolyte's small boats. He'd rolled up his sleeves, the sun warming his arms. Without his Grace, rowing was more of an effort, but he didn't mind the strain on his muscles. In fact, the exertion was almost comforting.

He glanced over at Anton, who sat across from him, trailing one hand lazily through the water. He'd gotten a little too much sun during their journey, and the pinked skin of his face and neck was now freckling.

"You could help, you know," Jude suggested, leaning back as he dragged the paddles through the water in one smooth stroke.

Anton propped his chin on one hand. "I prefer to watch."

Jude's face heated under Anton's considering gaze. His paddle slapped against the surface of the water as he missed the rhythm of the next stroke.

"Oh!" Anton said, swiveling to look at the side of the canal. "There it is. The one with pink trees in front."

Jude angled the boat toward the dock that jutted out from the bank of the canal. This appeared to be where the richest citizens of Endarrion lived, just outside the Floating Gardens that occupied the city's center. The only way to access this merchant's estate was by boat, and only approved visitors could dock in front of the estate.

Anton and Jude were not approved visitors, a fact that the guard manning the dock seemed eager to inform them.

"I know we're not expected," Anton repeated. "But I promise you, if Lord Cassian knew we were here, he'd want you to let us in."

"Lord Cassian is out of town on business," the guard replied gruffly.

"I meant his son," Anton said. "Evander Cassian. Look, just go ask him."

The guard seemed affronted. "I'm not going to bother my lord's son over some ruffians in his backyard."

"Sir—what's your name?" Anton asked sweetly.

"Favian," the guard replied, looking at Anton with suspicion.

"Favian," Anton repeated, pronouncing each syllable laconically. "You look like a very smart man."

Jude snorted, and then quickly covered it with a cough. The guard glared at him.

"And I can tell you're good at your job," Anton went on. "I know Evander well, he's a friend of mine, and I know he and his father would only hire the most capable guards—"

"If you want to see him," the guard cut in, "you can leave a card like everyone else. If you're as good a friend as you say, I'm sure he'll get back to you."

Anton glanced at Jude. Jude knew what he was thinking—if they left and waited for Evander to get in touch, it might be too late. If the guard even passed along the card at all. But it didn't seem like they had another choice.

"Come on, Anton," Jude said, dipping his paddle back into the water. "Let's just do what he says."

Anton seemed ready to give up as the guard returned to his station.

Then he paused, his gaze lighting on something behind the guard. He slinked over to the guard's table, picking up a jar of what looked like silver beads and shaking it.

"You play canbarra?" Anton asked the guard.

The guard snatched the jar back, returning it to the table. "I've only won the Endarrion canbarra tournament five times and counting."

Anton lit up. "All right, then how about this? Play one hand with me. If I win, you go tell Evander we're here. If you win, we'll leave you alone with no further argument. What do you say?"

The guard eyed him. Jude resisted the urge to bury his face in his hands.

"One hand," Anton said again. "If you're as good a player as you say, then it'll be a breeze, right?"

Twenty minutes later, Jude and Anton waited on the dock while the guard summoned a servant to inform Evander of their presence.

"I can't believe that worked," Jude said, shaking his head. "*Again.*"

"Gambling always pays off, Jude," Anton said sagely.

"Should I be grateful you didn't wager anything of mine this time?"

Anton smiled. "Progress."

The guard shuffled back to them, looking embarrassed. A servant followed at his heels.

"Well?" Anton said, clearly already gloating.

"Lord Evander requests you be brought up immediately," the servant said. "Come with me."

Anton shot Jude a triumphant look as he all but skipped past the guard. Biting back a laugh, Jude followed.

The servant led them through the grounds of the estate, winding up a tiled path that led into the grand entrance of the main house. A sparkling glass chandelier lit with incandescent light cast rainbows on the walls and floor. Two sweeping ivory staircases wound up to the next floor. Jude stared dumbly at the beauty and opulence. Anton appeared similarly entranced.

"Right this way," the servant said, leading them out into a sunlit garden.

At first Jude was too distracted by the lush beauty of the garden to register the presence of the dark-haired boy, no older than he, lying redolently on a cushioned lounge beneath a tree that wept pale lavender blossoms. A chilled pitcher of honey-colored liquid sat on the filigreed table beside him, a crystal glass held delicately in the boy's hand.

"Anton!" the boy cried, leaping to his feet and throwing his arms around Anton, honey liquid sloshing out of his glass. Jude stiffened to see such an effusive display of affection—they were not something the Paladin engaged in, even between the closest of friends.

"It's good to see you, Evander," Anton replied as the boy dragged him over to the lounge, leaving Jude standing by himself.

"What a lovely and utterly unexpected surprise," Evander gushed. "Come, we have so much to catch up on."

"First," Anton said, "I'd like to introduce you to my friend Jude."

Evander's gaze slid over to Jude, and his hand flew to his mouth. "Oh dear, how rude of me! I thought you were his servant or something."

Technically, that was true—in that the Order of the Last Light were the holy servants of the Prophets. But he sensed that Evander didn't mean it that way.

"Not exactly," Anton said.

"Back when I knew you at Thalassa, you wouldn't have been able to afford a servant," Evander went on with a laugh. "But I thought perhaps you'd run off with someone rich and gotten married. You know, my father and I were in Pallas Athos not two weeks ago— by the way, did you hear about those ghastly attacks last month? Apparently the Temple of Pallas almost burned down!"

Jude looked up sharply, but Evander was already prattling on.

"Of course it was perfectly safe at Thalassa, where we always stay, only the owner told us you'd up and disappeared! I was devastated, and hoped that maybe you would write one day. What a shock it is to see you here! You *must* tell me everything that's happened since we last met, spare no detail, my dear, I want to hear every last thing."

Jude had never heard someone say so many words in such a short amount of time.

"It's a long story," Anton replied.

Evander smiled, familiar and fond. "Not getting into *too* much trouble there, were you?"

"Just the right amount," Anton returned with a flash of teeth.

His tone caught Jude off guard. It was one he hadn't heard since he and Anton had first met that night at the Hidden Spring. It bothered Jude to hear that tone again now. And directed at this . . . Evander.

Evander clapped his hands suddenly, and a servant appeared beside him. "Bring us two more glasses, and another pitcher." He turned back to Anton. "You must tell me *all* about it, and what it is that brings you to Endarrion."

Anton glanced at Jude. They hadn't actually discussed what they would be telling Evander, although it seemed obvious to Jude that it wouldn't be the truth.

"Well," Anton said, "after hearing so much about it from you, I couldn't help but want to see it for myself."

Evander looked pleased by the answer. "Isn't it everything? The most beautiful city in the world. Endarra would be thrilled with such a lovely namesake."

"Endarra didn't believe in the beauty of artifice and material things," Jude said. "Her belief was that all things held beauty in them, from the humblest worker bee to the most majestic mountain."

The moment the words left his lips, he immediately wished for them back.

Anton and Evander both stared at him. Then Evander clapped his hands gleefully. "Well, isn't that a lovely sentiment. The humblest worker bee. How utterly brilliant! I love it."

The servant arrived with their drinks, pouring the honey-colored liquid into tall, crystal glasses.

"Magnolia wine," Evander told them. "A delicacy here."

Anton tipped the liquid into his mouth. Knowing it would be impolite to refuse, Jude took a single sip. The wine melted on his tongue like morning dew on a flower petal.

"Divine, isn't it?" Evander asked. "I swear my mother weaned me on it. It's too bad she's not here to see you, Anton. She did always adore you so. Although it's probably for the best that Father isn't here." Evander glanced at Jude conspiratorially. "He thought it beneath me to dally with the serving staff, but I just couldn't help myself, I mean—could you?"

Jude did not have the slightest idea how to answer that. He felt his left eye twitch.

Evander draped his chin over Anton's shoulder. "I was heart-broken when I learned you'd left Thalassa. I thought I'd never see you again, and yet here you've gone and shown up on my doorstep like a Moon Festival cake! You *must* stay here with me. I insist. The house is so terribly empty while Mother and Father are away."

Anton raised his eyebrows at Jude, and Evander followed his gaze, now turning his large blue eyes upon Jude, as well. Any attempt to protest, it seemed, would be futile. And Jude could not deny that staying here with Evander was probably safer than at the temple. The Witnesses weren't likely to come looking for them here. And if they did, Evander seemed to have a whole staff of guards.

"We can stay," Jude said, flicking a purple blossom off his shoulder.

Evander leapt to his feet, throwing his arms around Jude. Jude's body went into a panic, and he only barely stopped himself from throwing Evander off him and pinning him to the ground.

Over Evander's shoulder, he saw Anton stifle a laugh.

"Let's go get you settled, and then I'll have the cooks start dinner," Evander said, pulling away. He chattered on as he led them inside, through more opulent hallways with marble floors and gilded ceilings.

"This is going to be easy," Anton said, his breath warm on Jude's ear. "We'll have dinner, butter Evander up, and get more information about this collector."

Jude pulled away. "Just don't get distracted."

Anton narrowed his eyes. "You agreed to come here, remember?"

"Yes, to get the Pinnacle Blade," Jude hissed. "Not to—"

"Anton?" Evander called from the bottom steps of a grand staircase. He had evidently noticed that neither of them were paying attention to him.

"Coming," Anton called. He shot Jude a glare and then hurried ahead, smiling brightly at Evander.

Jude watched their backs as they climbed, unsure if he was mad at Anton or himself. They had gotten along so well during their journey from Kerameikos, but here in Endarrion, Jude remembered how different he and Anton were, and how Anton knew exactly how to get under Jude's skin without even trying.

Dinner at a house like Evander's was an elaborate affair, with cooks bringing out decadent dish after decadent dish—game hens roasted in honey and pomegranate, candied squash, chilled cucumber soup drizzled with mint. Evander carried the majority of the conversation, which surprised Jude not at all, but made it difficult to find opportunities to find out more about the collector.

But between dinner and dessert, an opportunity presented itself.

"That's a nice vase," Anton said idly, gesturing at a glass-blown vase in the corner of the room.

"Oh, that was a gift," Evander replied, sipping his magnolia wine. "One of my father's clients gave it to us. Lady Bellrose."

"A client?" Anton asked. "What does she do?"

Evander looked thoughtful. "You know, I'm not entirely sure. She collects all sorts of curios."

Jude went still, and Anton crushed a wide grin into a look of mild curiosity.

"I've never even met her," Evander went on. "She's quite evasive. But she always throws the most extravagant celebrations. They're the talk of the city for *weeks*. I heard she just arrived back in town a few days ago after chasing down some new item for her collection."

This was it. The Pinnacle Blade. Jude cleared his throat. "What kind of item?"

"I think a sword . . . ?" Evander trailed off. "I can't really remember to be honest, but her parties are such fun!"

Jude opened his mouth to speak again but a sharp stab of pain in his foot silenced him. Anton had stomped on his foot, and it could not have been an accident. He bit off a hiss of pain and glared, gripping Anton's knee underneath the table in a fruitless demand to know what he was up to.

Anton betrayed nothing, gently plucking Jude's hand off and smiling up at Evander.

"I miss the parties we used to have at Thalassa," he said. "We met at their midwinter ball, do you remember?"

Evander sighed, dreamy, which launched them into a detailed remembrance of the first time Evander had set eyes on Anton. It took them all the way to the dessert course, a cloud of whipped egg whites and sugar drowning in a bowl of rich cream, topped with a delicate sugar-lace dome.

"And you know, it wasn't like I'd never had a beautiful boy, or girl for that matter, make eyes at me across the room but there was just *something* about him!" Evander cooed to Jude. "Even serving drinks in that ridiculous uniform, he was the most luminous thing in the room."

Jude very dearly wanted to pour the dessert over Evander's head, if it would stop him talking.

"It's been so long since I was at a party like that," Anton said after Evander was done recounting the precise way the light had struck Anton's hair. "The last time Thalassa had a party you weren't there, and I had to suffer through the company of the other guests."

Evander clapped his hands together. "I've just had a wonderful idea. Lady Bellrose is throwing one of her parties tomorrow night. Why don't you two come along with me as my guests?"

Jude stabbed the top of the sugar dome with the dainty little dessert spoon and very pointedly did not look at Anton, certain that seeing his barely concealed smirk would shred what was left of his self-control.

"Oh, I don't know," Anton said. "The parties at Thalassa are one thing, but I don't think I belong at a party that elegant."

"Nonsense!" Evander cried. "You belong anywhere I belong, Anton. You two absolutely must accompany me. I won't take no for an answer!"

"I suppose," Anton said with a sigh. "If you insist."

When Jude looked down, his dessert spoon was bent in half.

20

EPHYRA

AS THE TEMPLE KEPT SINKING, EPHYRA FEARED THEY MIGHT FALL STRAIGHT through the earth.

"What do we do?" Illya shouted at Shara, clinging to one of the temple walls.

Shara looked terrified.

Ephyra almost wanted to laugh. She had trusted in Shara to help her, not realizing that the famed thief was just a girl who'd bitten off more than she could chew. A stolen identity who failed to live up to her namesake. She was no one, not really, and she wasn't going to save them.

The temple lurched, throwing Ephyra to the floor as the walls started to buckle and cave.

They were going to die. Ephyra was going to die, and that meant Beru would die, too. And that would be it. There would be no one else to remember her.

"Get up," Illya's voice barked. His face appeared above hers. "Get *up*."

He sounded pissed. She didn't get up.

"If you stay here, then I have to stay here, too, and I am *not* dying like this."

"Feel free to die however you want," Ephyra replied, but she dragged herself to her feet, stumbling into him.

"Shara!" Hadiza's voice cried from above.

All three of them jerked their heads up. A rope dangled from the top of the temple ceiling, where the roof opened to the sky. Shara was the first to register what was happening, sprinting toward the rope. She grabbed hold of it, and the others, above, pulled her up.

"We have to go together," Illya said as they reached the rope. He was right. The cuffs meant that he would get dragged along with her, his weight pulling her down.

They each grabbed hold of the rope, facing each other.

"Pull us up!" Ephyra cried as rocks pelted toward them and the floor began to crumble beneath them. She let out a scream as the floor collapsed and they were left dangling. She felt her hands drag and slip down the length by a few inches.

She hissed, tightening her grip.

"Wrap your legs around me," Illya instructed. He had his arm wrapped around the rope, looping it through the crook of his elbow to maintain his grip as they were slowly pulled upward.

She gave him an indignant look.

He rolled his eyes. "Do you want to fall? I can help support your weight."

Feeling like she was about to do something incredibly stupid, Ephyra tentatively circled her legs around his waist, glaring at him as they were pulled higher and higher. This close, she could see the dark sweep of his eyelashes against his pale skin, and smell some spiced scent under the layers of dust and sand.

The temple ceiling groaned as more debris plummeted toward them. The rope swayed, and Ephyra squeezed her eyes shut.

"It's all right," Illya murmured soothingly, which was so unexpected it made hysterical laughter bubble in her chest.

"Don't comfort me."

"I can threaten you, if you prefer," Illya replied, and this time she couldn't help but let her laugh spill out.

She opened her eyes to find him smiling with genuine mirth.

They dangled, entangled and breathless with terrified laughter, for a few more moments before Numir and Hadiza dragged them over the edge. They grabbed Ephyra first, hauling her up. She collapsed beside them, panting, as they yanked Illya up. Parthenia pulled Ephyra to her feet.

"We have to move!"

The six of them skidded over the rapidly sinking roof of the temple. As they reached the edge, the ground rose to meet them.

Numir went first, sliding down the sloped wall of the temple on her feet until she was close enough to the ground to jump. Hadiza and Parthenia followed, sitting with their knees pulled toward them. Then Shara, her hand braced against the wall to control her descent.

"Come on!" Illya yelled, grabbing Ephyra's hand and leaping down the wall. Ephyra glided after him, using him as a counterweight to stay balanced. When they reached the bottom, Illya landed on the ground, planted his feet, and turned to catch Ephyra's fall.

The others were already running away from the sinking temple, the ground rippling beneath their feet. At last they reached stable ground and stopped, gasping for breath.

"I think someone *really* did not want us to retrieve that object," Shara said. She glanced at Ephyra. "You do *have* it, right?"

Ephyra reached into her bag and withdrew the inscrutable leather ribbon. "For all the good it'll do."

They walked back to the skiffs under the setting sun. Ephyra's feet dragged with exhaustion and defeat.

Shara made her best attempt to rally them. "I know we're all tired after almost getting buried alive, so why don't we just get some sleep and figure out what to do tomorrow."

"We need to get out of the immediate area, at least," Hadiza said. "We can't stay here. Someone might have heard the commotion and could come poking around."

Shara rubbed her forehead. "Fine. We'll travel two hours in any direction and *then* sleep. Everyone get in."

They all boarded the skiffs, Numir and Shara taking the helm of each. Ephyra turned the leather over in her hand, examining it. Out of the corner of her eye, she saw Illya staring at it, too.

She shoved the leather back into her bag and turned her gaze to the horizon.

Later that night, Ephyra sat awake while the others slept, staring at the ribbon of leather they'd found in the temple. She needed something, *any* kind of hint that would tell her what it meant. But no matter how she looked at it, all she saw was the same string of letters, too random to form words in any language.

Maybe it was just a stupid trick. Maybe whoever was leaving these clues was leading them nowhere. She felt like she was no closer to finding the Chalice. And each day, Beru slipped further and further away. What if she couldn't get to her in time?

What if she was already gone?

A rustling noise disturbed her thoughts. A figure rose, walking toward her. Illya. Of course.

Ephyra scrunched up the leather in her hand and watched him approach with narrowed eyes. "What do you want?"

He held up his hands, as though to pacify her. It was a gesture she'd seen his brother make a number of times. Based on what Anton had told her, he had learned it to placate Illya. She wondered who Illya had needed to placate.

"I just want to say thank you," he said.

From anyone else, it would've sounded like kindness. From Illya, Ephyra suspected a different angle.

"What are you thanking me for?"

"Helping me get out of the temple," he said. "Especially since you didn't have to."

She held up her wrist. "Did you forget that we're bound by these?"

"You could have taken it off. Left me there."

Ephyra stared. It hadn't even occurred to her. "You claim to have information I need."

Her skin prickled under his golden gaze. In the moonlight, his face seemed to glow. It made her wish she *had* left him to get crushed inside the temple. Maybe then his face wouldn't be so infuriatingly pretty.

"All right," he said, plopping down beside her. "I'll show you what I found."

Ephyra watched as he bent his head, drawing in the sand with quick precision. He drew a circle with a horizontal line through it. Next to the circle he wrote the number seven. He sat back, looking at his handiwork.

"That's it?" Ephyra asked.

He nodded. "I had no idea what it meant, at first."

Ephyra pressed her lips together. She did not want to admit that she also had no idea what it meant.

"But now that we have a clue from the temple, I understand." He glanced at her and seemed to read that she had absolutely no idea what he was saying. "They're measurements. This one is the diameter of a circle. It's instructions on how to build a cylinder."

"Why would we . . ." Ephyra paused. She looked back at the leather ribbon in her hand, and the seemingly random line of letters. Slowly, she wrapped the leather around her wrist three times. The first letter on the ribbon now lined up with the fourth and the eighth. They were still a random jumble, but she suddenly understood how, if they were wrapped around the right size cylinder, they could line up to form words.

"Are you two awake?" a grumbling voice asked.

Ephyra turned toward Shara, who was rubbing at her eyes and standing. "Shara, look."

She came over to them and stared at their markings in the sand, bemused. Illya explained what he'd figured out and she paused for a moment and then said, "We need Parthenia."

"The sun's not even up yet," Parthenia complained when Shara poked her awake with her foot.

Numir let out a yawn, having woken when Parthenia did. "What, you need your beauty sleep?"

Parthenia batted her eyes. "Aw, you think I'm beautiful."

"No, that's not—I meant you *need* beauty sleep because you're *not*—"

"Focus, please," Shara cut in.

After Parthenia had inspected both the measurements and leather ribbon, she said, "We actually don't need to build anything. If we know the diameter of the circle, we can calculate its circumference and then just measure out the space between the letters. Then we'll know how many letters fit around it once, and we can simply count them off and line them up accordingly."

Ephyra just stared at her. "I thought you studied languages."

Parthenia tossed her hair. "We were taught the basics of all fields. This is very simple mathematics."

Ephyra sat back as Parthenia did her calculations. The letters were spaced about three inches apart, and according to Parthenia's calculations, the circumference they needed was twenty-four inches. She wrote out:

$$24 / 3 = 8$$

"Mark off every eighth letter," she instructed.

Illya wrote the letters in the sand as Parthenia called them off. Ephyra peered over his shoulder.

When he was done, he had six lines of eleven letters each:

THETOMBOFTH
EQUEENHIDES
THECHALICEO
FFERASACRIF
ICENOTOFBLO
ODBUTOFLIFE

"'The tomb of the queen hides the Chalice,'" Ephyra read. "'Offer a sacrifice, not of blood but of life.'"

She raised her eyes to Illya's and saw her own exhilaration and incredulity reflected in them. Hastily, she broke his gaze, an angry flush rising to her cheeks to remind her that she did not want to share anything with Illya, and especially not this.

"The Sacrificed Queen," Shara said. "It must be."

Ephyra stood. "We should leave now and get as far as we can until the sun hits its peak."

Shara hesitated for a moment but, to Ephyra's relief, nodded. They woke Hadiza and prepared to leave, the others clearly as practiced at rushed departures as Ephyra was.

Illya started to climb into one of the skiffs. Ephyra took him by the elbow and tugged him back. "You aren't coming."

He watched her with careful eyes. "I'm the only reason you even know where to go."

"Yes," Ephyra replied. "And that means that your services are no longer needed."

He grimaced. The others paused in their tasks, alerted to the brewing argument. Ephyra pressed down the part of herself that worried they had grown to like Illya more than her, that they would take his side.

"You can't just leave me here," he said.

"You knew this was coming the moment you convinced us to take you along," Ephyra replied. "Unless you thought you'd be able to manipulate us into trusting you by now. I guess you're not as talented as you thought." She gave him a sympathetic smile drenched in condescension.

Illya met her smile with his own. "All right. You caught me. I thought I could get in your good graces, but alas. Perhaps you *have* no good graces."

Ephyra's smile tightened with irritation.

"But," Illya went on. "If you leave me here, you're certainly trusting that I won't tell the Daughters of Mercy that you're planning on stealing the Chalice. Or that I won't send my own people to get it first."

"Your people?" Ephyra scoffed. "Thought you said you turned on them."

"Did I?" Illya replied. "Thought you didn't believe anything I said."

Shara cleared her throat behind them. "He's right, Ephyra."

Ephyra whirled on her. "Don't tell me you actually *believe* him."

"I don't," Shara replied, eyeing Illya. "But he can do more harm away from us than with us."

"Horseshit," Ephyra spat.

"He's a liability one way or the other," Shara said steadily. "So might as well be one we can keep our eye on."

Ephyra turned back to Illya, burning with rage. He had *played her*, yet again. He'd thought about this, about every single move she would make. Every move he could make to counter it. And after everything, he *still* won. She couldn't stand it. "Then we kill him."

Dead silence met her suggestion. She watched Illya's jaw twitch. Maybe that was the one possibility he hadn't considered.

Shara barked out a laugh. When no one joined in, she paused. "You're kidding, right? She's . . . kidding . . ." She seemed to become less certain with each syllable.

"You said it yourself," Ephyra said. "He's a liability. Easiest way to deal with a liability? Get rid of it."

"Behezda's Mercy," Shara groaned. "You're *serious*."

"Of course I'm serious," Ephyra answered. It was starting to bother her, how ridiculous Shara seemed to find the idea. She looked around at the others and saw their expressions were also disbelieving.

"That's . . . not really how we deal with our problems," Shara said slowly.

"You mean by solving them?"

"By *killing* people."

"He's not a good person," Ephyra said. "Trust me."

"I don't really care what kind of person he is," Shara replied. "Except that he stays an alive one."

"But—"

"I'm in charge here," Shara said. "It's my decision."

"Oh, *you're* in charge?" Ephyra said, whirling on her. "And why exactly is that? Hadiza's the one who found Susa. Numir's the one who got us there. Parthenia's the one who got us into the temple. Face it, Shara, you're no master thief. You're just a girl who's in over her head."

Shara's face went rigid for a split second. Then she relaxed. "Are you done?"

Ephyra gritted her teeth. She felt like rather than insulting Shara, she'd just spilled her own darkest secrets to everyone. Because everything she'd said was true about herself, too, wasn't it? Ephyra was known as a vicious killer, as a specter of retribution, the Pale Hand. But she was just a girl facing an impossible task, and no matter how much control she thought she had, moments like this made her realize she'd never had any at all.

21

HASSAN

THE MORNING OF LETHIA'S CORONATION ARRIVED WARM AND CLEAR. HASSAN and Khepri woke early, dressing in the dawn light. He reached for her hand when they were done, tangling their fingers together.

"Whatever happens today, I just want you to know—I couldn't do any of this without you," he said.

She pressed a kiss to his knuckles instead of answering.

By sunrise, they were all gathered in the alchemy workshop to go over the plan one last time with the six team leaders, who would each disseminate the information to their squads of nine. They all wore regular civilian clothes, stashing away dark green scarves that they would use to cover their faces during the blockade.

"We think there will be up to four hundred guards stationed along Ozmandith Road," Sefu said. He had led most of the intelligence gathering for the mission. "Khepri, Chike, and Arash will lead the blockade here, about halfway through their parade route. Meanwhile, Zareen and the alchemists will create distraction points at the statue of Queen Berenice and the Golden Square. They'll set off the first smoke bombs once the dancers pass the blockade point. Hassan will arrive last, and we've scoped out a spot along the arcade where he will deliver his speech. We'll have six more people to cover him."

"The prince will stay back here until the blockade is in place," Arash said, pointing to a side street.

Hassan's gaze snapped up. "That's not what we decided."

Arash looked at him calmly. "Change in plan. We don't want to risk you before our position is secure."

"I can hold my own in a fight," Hassan replied, forcing himself to remain calm. He should have guessed that Arash had something up his sleeve to throw off Hassan.

Arash made a sweeping gesture with his hand. "Nevertheless. We don't want anyone getting in the way while—"

"Getting in the *way*?"

"Arash, Hassan is just as capable as any of us," Khepri said. "If it weren't for him, we all would have died in the lighthouse."

"I don't doubt the prince's ability," Arash replied. "But this mission will be pointless if he gets hurt and fails to confront the Usurper. I think we can all agree on that."

"Fine," Hassan replied. "I'll stay out of the way, on the arcade."

"Now that that's settled, I think the time has come," Arash said.

They left the Library and dispersed into the streets in teams. Crowds were already beginning to gather along Ozmandith Road. The coronation procession would begin when the sun was at its peak, which gave them roughly thirty minutes. Khepri's squad maintained their position at the midway point of the procession. Once the bombs went off, they would move in to block the parade. And then Khepri would light a black smoke bomb, signaling Hassan to take his position on top of the arcade that ran alongside Ozmandith Road, where his guard would be waiting.

From his perch on a rooftop that lined the arcade, Hassan ran through his planned speech in his head. He tried to imagine confronting Lethia. The last time he'd seen her was in the atrium of the burning lighthouse. She'd turned her back on him. Left him to suffocate on poisonous smoke. He wasn't sure what he would feel, coming face-to-face with her again.

It wasn't long before the pounding of drums announced the beginning of the procession. Hassan chanced a peek over the edge of the arcade and found Khepri's team hidden in the crowd. Khepri and Arash stood together, eyes focused on the street.

In the distance, Herati soldiers dressed in gold and green marched forward. There were at least a dozen different groups in the parade— soldiers, dancers, musicians, fire twirlers, even elephants—that would precede Lethia's arrival on her palanquin.

Hassan watched the fire twirlers go past, then the soldiers. It should have been the Legionnaires next. If it were Hassan's coronation, it would have been. But by tradition, the Legionnaires were all Graced. And they had all fled or been captured.

Instead, a line of Witnesses marched down the processional. Hassan felt his chest go hot with anger when he saw them—welcomed members of the Usurper Queen's court. How *dare* she.

Behind them, he could just make out Lethia's palanquin, gilded gold and covered in rich emerald silk. The sight of it made his anger flare hotter.

A crack, audible even over the volume of the crowd, struck through the air. The first of the smoke bombs.

The crowd seemed to think the smoke was part of the parade,

applauding as the next ones went off, enveloping them in a cloud of red smoke. It covered the street, so Hassan could no longer see where Khepri and the others were. He would just have to trust that the blockade had been formed.

Another crack split the air, and Hassan saw a plume of black smoke—Khepri's signal—rise from the center of the street. The crowd had begun to panic, realizing the smoke bombs were not part of the parade. Hassan scrambled to his feet, climbing over the lip of the arcade's roof, to where his six guards were waiting for him.

Below, the crowd was a frenzy of movement. It was a moment before Hassan realized they weren't panicking—they seemed to be rioting. Hassan stood frozen, looking down at the turmoil. People were hitting one another, ripping clothes, their faces distorted in anger and aggression. He saw an old woman baring her teeth, locking her bony hands around a man's throat. A little girl clawing at her brother's arms until she drew blood.

Hassan looked on, panic rising in his throat, trying to make sense of what was happening. Another smoke bomb went off and suddenly the horrifying scene came into focus. Dread turned his blood to ice.

Zareen. He closed his eyes, not wanting to believe it, but her words from days before came back to him. She had *told* him what she was doing. Inventing mood modifiers that could be dispersed quickly and indiscriminately. An alchemical gas that could calm people down, or wake people up . . . or cause them to unleash aggression.

More screams and shouts curdled the air. This wasn't the plan. The smoke was meant to be harmless, a way to get people's attention, to halt the procession, not—not this. They weren't supposed to hurt anyone.

He wheeled around, facing the guards. "Did you know about

this?" When none of them replied, he advanced. "Are there more smoke bombs?"

Their faces were hidden by green scarves, which Hassan quickly realized were not just to obscure their faces. The scarves protected the Scarab's Wing from breathing in the smoke. Only the unsuspecting crowd would be affected.

He tugged his own scarf over his face and looked back down at the roiling crowd below. A woman was shrieking, hitting an already unconscious man over and over. Two other men were grappling on the ground, blood running from gouges where they'd torn into each other's skin with their bare hands.

He had to find Zareen, Arash. He had to stop this.

He fumbled with the device in his pocket that one of the Library artificers had given him for his speech, a sphere of copper and gold wires. When Hassan spoke into it, it amplified his voice.

"Hey!" he yelled, his voice booming out over the crowd.

None of them paid any mind to him. They were too lost in their violence, to the senseless riot carrying on below.

"People of Nazirah!" He tried again, to no avail. These people were beyond reaching.

His city had become a war zone.

22

ANTON

ANTON SMOOTHED THE LAPELS OF HIS JACKET AND CHECKED HIMSELF ONE last time in the gold wreathed mirror in Evander's palatial guest room.

Evander loved nothing as much as he loved clothes, and Endarrion fashions were ever-changing. He would probably rather suffocate himself with magnolia wine than be seen bringing two unfashionable guests to the party of the season. He'd provisioned Anton with dark, narrow trousers tucked neatly into soft boots, a trim cream jacket over a pale blue floral blouse, and finished it off with a flourish that was wholly Evander: a silk scarf, patterned with pink flowers, around Anton's neck.

He went out into the hall and spotted Jude peering down over the banister. He turned as Anton approached, looking overwhelmed and somewhat embattled.

"Tell me you're not about to throw yourself over the banister," Anton said. "Is everything all right? Is your Grace—?"

"I'm fine," Jude said quickly. He looked down, clearing his throat, cheeks glowing. "You look—different."

"Evander really likes clothes," Anton said with a sigh. "Every time he came to Thalassa, he'd try to give me a jacket or a scarf. I see you didn't escape his wrath." He nodded at Jude's attire, which was similar to Anton's, but in toned-down dove gray, with a bottle-green jacket that brought out the color of his eyes. One of the jacket's laces was undone, trailing off his sleeve.

"Why did we agree to this again?" he asked.

"Because we're about two hours from finding the Pinnacle Blade," Anton answered, taking hold of Jude's sleeve and doing up the laces of his jacket. "And besides, this will be your first party, Jude. An exciting day."

"I've been to a celebration before," Jude said. "The Order had feasts to commemorate the Prophets' Days."

Anton bit his lip to stifle a laugh. "Now that I've seen Kerameikos for myself, I can confidently say that place has never seen anything remotely close to a party. I'm guessing these feasts were just a bunch of abstinent swordsmen quietly eating plain vegetables, wearing the exact same expression you have on right now."

"Sometimes we would salt the vegetables," Jude said, and Anton glanced up to see he was trying to suppress a smile.

Anton laughed and Jude's smile broke free, surprised and pleased. It was like glimpsing the sun through the trees.

Anton realized he was still holding on to Jude's sleeve, but suddenly he didn't want to release him. He wanted to reel him closer, to say something quiet and teasing to make him blush. The desire surprised him. He'd flirted with Jude before, a lifetime ago at the Hidden Spring, but that had been something different, a way to keep Jude at arm's length. Now, he just wanted to see the swordsman's smile again. He curled his fingers around Jude's wrist.

Evander emerged from the other hallway. He was a riot of bright pinks and lavender, his jacket decorated with gold buttons and jeweled epaulettes. A glittering crystal earring dripped from each ear, and Anton realized that he and Jude had been spared from Evander's more boisterous inclinations.

"Well, don't you both look handsome? See what a little sartorial upgrade can do?" Evander frowned. "Jude, *what* is going on with those shoes? Didn't you like the ones I set out for you?"

"Well—"

"This simply won't do," Evander said. "Go take those dirty boots off at once."

Jude shot Anton a pleading look.

"Come now, we're already running late," Evander said. He looped an arm through Anton's, marching him toward the stairs. "We'll meet you at the dock."

Evander shook his head at Jude's retreating form, and led Anton down the stairs and out into the yard. Now that the sun had set, the grand front lawn was lit with soft yellow lamplight, stretching out to the little dock that cut into the river. The water glinted silver in the moonlight.

"This is going to be so much fun," Evander said. "I'll have the most interesting guests at this party—*everyone* will want to know where I found you."

"Actually," Anton said. "It would be best if we . . . went unnoticed."

Evander's eyes lit up. "Oooh, keep things *mysterious*. I like it!"

"Sure."

"You always were very mysterious." Evander sighed. "I missed you terribly on our last trip and I'm afraid I can't help myself from asking if you ever missed me, too."

Back then, Anton had collected friends like Evander collected clothes. It was easy enough to make them, and just as easy to forget them. Evander had adored him the way a child adores a favorite toy, and when he'd wanted something other than just friendship, Anton hadn't had any objections.

But the truth was, as much as Anton enjoyed Evander's attention and company, he hadn't missed him at all. He'd barely thought of him.

Now Evander was looking at Anton with wide eyes, a faint blush tinging his cheeks, expecting Anton to answer with pretty words to match Evander's pretty face.

"I loved the time we spent together at Thalassa," Anton told him, which was close enough to the truth. As selfish and self-centered as Evander was, he was also *kind*, and that wasn't something Anton ever got used to. "And I'm glad we have this time together now."

"I feel the same way," Evander said, satisfied. He tugged coyly on the scarf looped around Anton's neck. "You know, I was worried when you showed up with another boy that perhaps you'd forgotten me completely."

He closed his eyes and pressed his lips against Anton's. Anton let himself be kissed, responding to the familiar softness and warmth.

Then, quite suddenly, Evander pulled back.

"Ah, Jude!" he exclaimed. "See, aren't those shoes so much better? You look like a proper Endarrion gentleman now."

Anton stared past Evander at Jude's stony face in front of them. He had seen Jude angry before—had, in fact, *made* Jude angry. On those occasions, he'd had the same stiff posture, the same furrowed brow. But Anton wasn't sure what Jude was feeling now. There was something raw about his expression, a vulnerability that Anton had last seen in the storeroom at Kerameikos.

"Oh, look, our boat's arrived," Evander said, looping his arms through both Anton's and Jude's and leading them aboard.

What followed was potentially the most awkward half hour of Anton's life.

He and Jude sat on either side of Evander, who prattled away, oblivious, while the boatman rowed them through the canals. Jude was silent, staring out at the banks of the canal as they drifted past. Anton thought back to Jude's shy smile at the beginning of the evening, hating himself for wanting to see it again.

Then their boat turned, and all thoughts fled Anton's mind at the sight before them. Tiny glowing lights lit the Floating Gardens gold. Platforms laden with flowering trees and lush green plants surrounded a circular pavilion of slender columns, draped in vibrant blossoms and crawling vines.

The boatman rowed them toward a barge lit up from the inside and bursting with colorful flowers. Music and mingling voices drifted toward them, and Anton realized the barge was their destination.

They steered onto a floating platform with a fountain and a man dressed in white who greeted them by handing them each a glass of magnolia wine. Evander swept up the ramp that led them aboard the barge, and when two guards stopped them at the top, Evander merely told them his name, and they waved all three of them through.

They entered a huge, bright ballroom. Glass cases were displayed throughout the room, where guests could peruse the collection. Anton's heart sped up and he glanced at Jude. The Pinnacle Blade could be in any one of those cases.

Jude caught his eye, looking more nervous than the situation warranted. Anton opened his mouth to say something and then Jude turned swiftly on his heel. "I'm going to take a look around the room."

Anton watched him go, wishing he could take back the last hour. But they had a mission, and no matter how annoyed Jude was at him, Anton wouldn't lose focus.

Evander was at his elbow, steering him through the crowd. "Oh, Anton, let me introduce you to the contessa and her daughter."

They approached two elegant women dressed in fine gowns who were conversing with another woman and her husband. Anton was drawn into the conversation easily, laughing at the right moments and interjecting his own comments with a small dose of wide-eyed wonder that immediately charmed the group.

"Evander, wherever did you find him?" the contessa asked, already giddy on magnolia wine.

"As you all know, a collector doesn't like to share their secrets," Evander said with a wink.

The others laughed, and just like that, Anton had the perfect opening. "I've heard so much about this mysterious collector. Have you heard about the private collection? Apparently she keeps the good stuff hidden away."

It was a gamble, assuming that there was a private collection. The others paused, and for a moment Anton worried he had overstepped and showed his hand, but then the contessa's daughter leaned in. "She keeps everything worth seeing upstairs. But only a select few get an invitation."

"You've been angling for one for years, haven't you, Lord Hallian," the contessa said, nudging the man beside her. "Trying to cozy up to whomever you can."

They chatted for a few more minutes before Anton excused himself to get food, knowing he'd squeezed all the information out of them he was going to get. He waylaid one of the servers and struck up a conversation, flirting more and more outrageously until the server coyly asked him to meet later in one of the service corridors that led to the upper deck.

Anton grinned suggestively. "Looking forward to it."

He let the server go and was engulfed back into conversation by a new set of guests, laughing and conversing with ease, while simultaneously sweeping the room in search of Jude, whom he had not seen since they'd arrived. Anton's group erupted into laughter as the archduke's son concluded some story about the swans at his brother's manor. Anton laughed, too, and looked up to see Jude heading toward him, his eyes focused.

The woman at Anton's elbow put a hand on his shoulder, trying to get his attention, but Anton didn't look away from Jude. The green jacket Evander had chosen for him made his eyes look dark and mossy.

As Jude reached their circle, he seemed to realize at the same time as Anton that everyone was staring at him.

"Anton," he said, his voice coming out a little strangled. "I need . . . a word."

"Quite popular this evening, aren't you?" the archduke's son said, eyes twinkling.

Flashing an apologetic smile at his new friends, Anton placed his empty drink on a server's tray.

"Enjoying yourself?" Jude asked as they retreated to the edge of the room.

"What?"

"Did you forget why we came here?" Jude asked. "We're here to find the Pinnacle Blade, not so you can—can flirt and—"

Anton narrowed his eyes. "Have you decided to be mad at me again? Is this about what happened with Evander at the dock?"

"No," Jude bit out. "It's about you wasting time hanging off the arm of some Endarrion lord while we still don't know where the Pinnacle Blade is or how to—"

"It's on the upper deck," Anton said.

"What?"

222

"The Pinnacle Blade," Anton replied easily. "It's on the upper deck. And I can get us there. See, while I was *wasting time* and *flirting*, I happened to talk to one of the servers. He told me there's a service corridor that goes up there."

Jude just stared at him for a moment. "Oh. Well. That might work."

Anton hooked his finger through the laces on Jude's jacket sleeve, tugging him toward the door. When he was sure no one was looking, they slipped out and around to the service corridor. The corridor wasn't empty, but their attire and a confidently brisk gait carried Anton and Jude through the corridor unbothered, and they were let out into an outdoor deck that surrounded the perimeter of the barge's upper deck. From up here, they could see all the glittering lights of the party, but they were removed from it, the sound muted by the walls of the ballroom. It felt intimate and secluded, with the legendary Floating Gardens spread out around them.

It made Anton remember standing on the ship as they sailed to Kerameikos, how Jude had touched his hand in comfort.

Jude glanced around. "How do we find it?"

"What, you've never snuck onto a boat with the intent to steal a priceless artefact?" Anton asked, leading the way. "Wouldn't have guessed."

"We can't all be master sword thieves," Jude replied seriously, but he was smiling.

Anton felt warm despite the cool evening air, and a thrill of pride went through him.

"We should just search all the rooms we can," he said, refocusing. "If we run into anyone, we'll just say we were invited up and got lost."

"And if there are guards stationed with the Pinnacle Blade?"

"Fight them?" Anton suggested.

"We could tell the collector that it belongs to me," Jude replied. "Which is true. I don't like the idea of taking it like a common thief. I shouldn't have to steal it, when it was stolen first from me."

"Sometimes, Jude, not everything is as it should be," Anton replied, pushing open a door that led into another corridor.

It was dimly lit and gleaming with gilded frames and wall sconces. They crept down, and Anton tried the first door in the corridor. It pushed open, revealing a wide bed elevated on a platform and a balcony that opened out to the gardens.

"I don't think it's in here," Jude said. "Let's try a different room."

The next room was a study with shelves of books and a brass astrolabe on the desk. They searched in silence, pausing every few moments to listen for voices or footsteps. There was no sword in that room, or the one after it.

As Jude and Anton emerged again into the corridor, the sound of voices carrying from the outer deck hit them.

"This is a rare treat," a man's voice was saying. "Few people get invited to see the lady's private collection."

Anton and Jude exchanged wide-eyed glances. Whoever was up here was going directly to where the Pinnacle Blade was, but there was the more pressing issue of what would happen if they were caught sneaking around.

As the voices drew closer, Anton made a decision and threw open the door across the corridor, dragging Jude by the front of his shirt. The door closed with a soft click behind them, which Anton hoped would go unheard by the approaching party.

But when he whirled around, he realized his error. They were surrounded by three walls of glass, which encased gleaming vases, bowls, and ceremonial weapons. Other trinkets, like hair combs and jewelry, were displayed on pedestals of various heights. What little furniture there was in the room was more ornate than anything Anton had seen in Evander's house.

It appeared they had, at last, found the collector's private collection. Which meant the people outside were about to come in and discover them.

Anton glanced at Jude's panicked face. Thinking quickly, Anton shoved him against the wall and started mussing his hair and tugging at the laces of his jacket.

In a tone bordering on hysterical, Jude hissed, "What are you doing?"

"Shut up." Anton slapped a hand over Jude's mouth. "Do not say a word." He persisted in his tussle with the Endarrion clothing.

Jude's eyes met Anton's, green swallowed by wide, dark pupils.

Without breaking his gaze, Anton removed his hand, curling it instead around the back of Jude's neck, thumb resting just under Jude's jaw, where his pulse fluttered. He heard Jude's sharp intake of breath, felt him exhale warm air against his cheek, as the door of the room swung open.

"Oh—oh dear," a voice said.

Anton spun around, smiling sheepishly.

"This is so embarrassing," he said with a small laugh. "We were just looking for a bit of privacy! We thought this was a guest room."

The man in the doorway glanced from Anton to Jude. Anton followed his gaze.

Jude looked as thoroughly disheveled as Anton had intended. The addition of a bright flush on his cheeks only sold the act further.

"This is not a guest room," the man said. "How did you even get up here?"

"We'll go," Anton said, seizing Jude's wrist and towing him from the room. The man stopped him with an arm on the doorframe.

"No," he said. "You'll be escorted back downstairs."

With his other hand, he signaled two guards who stood behind him. Anton and Jude followed wordlessly as the guards led them outside.

Then one of the guards stopped abruptly, turning back to Jude. "You might want to . . ." He trailed off, flicking his gaze over Jude's disheveled form. Jude's hands shook as he hastily did up the laces of his jacket, pointedly avoiding Anton's gaze.

As the guards escorted them down a stairwell that led back to the ballroom, Anton stole a glance at Jude, trying to catch his eye, but Jude was gazing determinedly, steadfastly, ahead. They descended the staircase back into the glittering ballroom, where the guards left them.

"I didn't see the Pinnacle Blade in there, did you?" Anton asked.

"No," Jude replied curtly. He wasn't looking at Anton but rather staring at the ground, face still flushed, his breath uneven.

"Look, I'm sorry about that back there," Anton said, rubbing a hand over the back of his neck. "I know that's not something you—I know you're not—"

"It's fine," Jude said abruptly. "It's—it was smart."

"It's just," Anton ventured, stepping toward him. "You seem mad."

"Anton." Jude's eyes, at last, slid to his, and Anton almost recoiled from the intensity of his gaze. "Please. Leave it alone."

The request cost him something, Anton realized. He went still, understanding, all at once, what Jude could not say. The way Jude had treated him after witnessing his kiss with Evander, how he'd reacted to the ruse, and now, the tension and restraint that Anton could only interpret one way.

Jude wanted him.

It wasn't a wholly new thought. He'd sensed it before, even going as far back as at the Hidden Spring in Pallas Athos, repressed beneath layers and layers of control and denial. But now, Jude's desire stood between them in a way it never had before, and Anton could see how deeply it strained the swordsman. He suddenly wanted nothing more than to make Jude *relax*, to smooth his hands across the taut line of his shoulders and watch the tension bleed away.

He moved toward him, not certain, exactly, what he was about to do.

A sudden and familiar voice aborted the movement.

"And just *where* have you two been off to all night?" Evander demanded, sweeping through the crowd toward them. Two men dressed in the servants' uniform flanked him.

"We—"

"There was—"

They both broke off into awkward silence. Evander looked back and forth between the two of them, but neither offered up anything else.

"Well, I'm sure you can return to whatever it was later," Evander said. "We've something far more important to attend to."

"What?" Anton asked.

"The collector summoned us to her private chamber," Evander said. "She wants to speak to you."

23

BERU

BEHEZDA. THE CITY OF MERCY.

Nestled in a canyon cut by an ancient river and riddled with narrow passages and hidden gorges, Behezda was just as Beru had pictured it. Most of its buildings were carved from the red rock itself, crowded along the river and climbing up the canyon walls. In the east, the great Red Gate of Mercy stood sentinel, the ruins of what was once ancient Behezda spread at its feet.

Beru and Hector picked their way down to the canyon. They parted ways with the caravan at the city gates.

"You'll find the Daughters' temple up there," Orit said, pointing off beyond the edge of the city. "May Behezda's Mercy find you."

The caravan pulled away from them, and Beru looked over at Hector, whose gaze rested on the canyon walls, where the Temple of Mercy perched above the city.

"You don't need to do this," she said in a low voice. It was the first time she'd spoken of Hector's plan to end his life since he'd revealed it to her. She'd tried to talk him out of it then, had stayed up until nearly dawn arguing with him. "There's another way."

"Neither of us should be alive," he said, shaking his head.

"But we *are*."

"You were ready to die in Medea," he said. "What changed?"

"Haven't you ever had anything you wanted to atone for? Something you wanted to make right?" she asked. "You told me about the Order, about your friend who you left behind. Wouldn't you at least want to tell him you're sorry?"

Hector's lips pressed into a thin line, and Beru felt a pang of guilt coming off him. "I am making things right."

"You're not," she said. "You're giving up. You're running away."

He turned and started to stalk away from her. "You don't know anything about me."

But the anger that jolted through her—unmistakably Hector's—told her she'd hit home. She hurried after him.

"You betrayed the only person who loved you, and now you're afraid to face the world alone," she said. Another bolt of anger, bright and hot. "You don't want to confront the people you've hurt. Trust me, I get it. But this isn't the answer."

He stopped. "You think you can just solve everything by saving me. It doesn't work like that. Sometimes things are just broken and there's nothing you can do."

"I don't believe that," Beru said. She reached for him, her fingers brushing his shoulder.

He flinched away. "Don't."

A spike of fear. She wondered what he felt from her—frustration, sorrow, hesitance.

"You didn't come all the way here just to end your life. Some part of you knows I'm right. We have to at least try, Hector. Both of us. I can't do it without you."

He shivered, but this time he didn't shy from her as she laid her hand on his shoulder. Touching him always seemed to strengthen the connection between them. She felt everything pour from him—a potent mixture of fear, grief, and awe. And in turn, she let everything that she felt pour into him, willing him to understand what it all meant.

He broke away, gasping. "What if the Daughters of Mercy can't help us?" he asked after a long moment. "What if they won't?"

"Then we'll find another way."

He turned his head to the side, hiding his expression. "You know, when I told you what I was planning, I assumed you'd find a way to talk me out of it."

"And?" she asked.

He shook his head ruefully. "And I was right. Come on, let's go."

Beru's stomach grew tight with anticipation as they wound their way up the face of the narrow canyon to the Temple of Mercy. Her head was light and she felt like she might faint, so she stopped and leaned against the canyon wall.

Hector stood in front of her, his face grim. "It's getting close to the end, isn't it?"

Beru closed her eyes, panting. "Yes. But I'll make it."

A moment later she felt him at her side, supporting her. She opened her eyes in surprise and let him take some of her weight until they reached the mouth of a cave. Carved into the red sandstone was the facade of a temple. In front of them, two great doors stood, etched with intricate swirling lines and ancient symbols.

"We wish to speak to the Daughters of Mercy," Beru said in a loud, clear voice.

Nothing happened.

Beru cleared her throat and chose her next words carefully. "I am Beru of Medea. Please."

With the sound of crunching earth, the rock began to move. A gust of wind swirled through the sand toward them. Beru and Hector threw up their arms, shielding their faces from the wind.

At last the wind died down. It seemed that her name, or that of her village, had granted her access. That alone was enough to make her apprehensive.

The Daughters already knew who she was. But did they know *what* she was?

Swallowing her last bit of fear, Beru stepped into the temple. Several tiered platforms were sculpted out of the rock face. It looked like a stadium fit for over a thousand people, but only twelve faced Beru and Hector at the entrance.

The Daughters of Mercy. They dressed in white, and wore crimson scarves over their heads. Each of them bore tattoos more intricate than anything Beru had ever seen on the healers in Charis and Tel Amot—tight, swirling lines that looked like the symbols they'd seen on the door outside.

Their eyes followed Beru and Hector as they made their way from the threshold to the platform that stood at the end of the canyon, upon which three Daughters of Mercy stood.

"Merciful Daughters," Beru said, kneeling before the platform. "We most humbly request an audience."

"*Medea*," intoned the one closest to Beru. She looked slightly younger than the others. "I know of this place."

Beru swallowed.

"The Daughters of Mercy saw what happened there. The corruption we found was . . . foul. We have searched for its origin for many years."

"Then you need search no longer," Hector said. "I have come to tell you what happened in Medea."

The Daughter's gaze flickered to Hector. "And who are you?"

"Hector Navarro," he said. "Of Charis. I am—I was, a Paladin of the Order of the Last Light."

"The Order of the Last Light," the Daughter spat. "Those devoted servants who hide themselves away from the world. If you are part of this Order, what is it that brings you here?"

"I left."

"Oathbreaker," several Daughters hissed.

"We do not look kindly on those who forsake their vows," the younger Daughter warned.

Hector ignored them and forged on. "I came here to tell you that the world is in danger. A necromancer walks this world. Not just *a* necromancer—two of them."

"That's impossible," the Daughter said.

"He's telling the truth," Beru said, her voice shaking. "I can prove it."

Beru fumbled with her wrapping, feeling strangely exposed as she lifted her bare wrist to show them the handprint.

A hush filled the canyon.

"I died in Medea. But I was brought back. Only it—it wasn't permanent," Beru said, stumbling onward. "And so this necromancer took more lives to keep me alive. Including . . . his."

Hector glanced at Beru and she nodded. He pulled the scarf from around his neck and then shucked off his shirt, revealing the dark handprint on his back.

232

The Daughter reached out, her bony fingers just passing over the handprint.

"We need your help," Beru said. "His *esha* is connected to mine, somehow, because it was used to heal me. But if it can be given back to him, then maybe—it can save him, can't it? You can restore his *esha* to him. You can put this right."

"The Daughters are glad you have found your way here," said the Daughter.

"So you can help us?"

"We can help you reach the place you were meant to be."

Hector and Beru exchanged a glance. "What . . . what does that mean?"

"The powers of the Grace of Blood were granted to us through sacrifice," she said. "Sacrifice and mercy. That is our legacy. And that, in turn, is *our* gift to the world. Mercy."

A wave of relief broke over Beru. At last, she could atone.

The Daughter inclined her head. "Come with us."

They led them through the canyon and into a narrow crevice that branched out from the main chasm. Archways hewn out of the rock and curtained off with sheer fabric lined the passage. The Daughter leading them stopped at one of the archways and pulled the curtain aside.

"Please," she said. "We ask that you partake of our hospitality."

Hector and Beru ducked inside hesitantly. The room was warm, glowing with soft light filtering through a small opening in the rock above. Violet and cream cushions were spread out around a low table.

Hector and Beru just stood there, looking around, until another Daughter arrived, carrying a tray laden with bread and figs and olives, and little bowls of chutney. Another Daughter appeared with a second tray of delicacies, and a third with a pitcher and glasses.

They all settled onto the cushions, and as Beru took the first bite of a fig, she realized she was ravenously hungry. A Daughter poured her a glass of whatever was in the pitcher, and Beru gulped it down readily.

This might be my last meal, she thought, and suddenly the sweet fig turned to ash in her mouth. She had known for a long time that death was coming to her, but somehow it had never felt closer than it did now. Part of her wished she could remember what it had felt like, the first time. She felt half a shadow, waiting for darkness to swallow her.

She looked up and saw that Hector was watching her. He set down his glass and reached toward her, touching her shoulder.

"We can leave," he said softly, his eyes intense. "You don't need to do this."

It was what she had said to him at the city gates. Why was he hesitating now?

Beru looked down at her lap. After all this time, even now, she wanted to live.

His hand was still on her shoulder, and Beru felt her stomach flutter at the warmth and the way his gaze stayed pinned to hers. For the space of a breath, all she wanted was to say yes. To leave here with him. To find another way—another way to live, another way to atone.

But there was no other way.

The Daughter who had led them into the room reappeared inside the curtain. "Do you need more time?"

"No," Beru said, rising to avoid Hector's gaze. "We're ready."

The Daughter nodded, satisfied, and took them back into the main chamber of the temple. There were hundreds more Daughters now, crowded on the tiered platforms along the canyon walls. Beru felt a twinge of fear as the Daughter ushered them to the center dais. She couldn't tell if it was coming from her or Hector—maybe both of them.

"We hope that you have partaken of our hospitality," the Daughter in the back of the room said. "And that both of you have enjoyed your final moments here."

Hector tensed beside Beru. The Daughters of Mercy nearest to them seemed to move closer. Advancing.

"What do you mean, final moments?" Hector asked, at the same time that Beru was thinking, *What do you mean both of us?*

The Daughter went on. "You are revenants, dead things that were never meant to cross back into the land of the living."

The approaching Daughters formed a tight circle around Beru and Hector, effectively sealing them in. As if they expected the two of them to flee.

"What are you doing?" Beru demanded, looking around at the flat expressions of the Daughters. "You said you would help us."

"I said we would help you return to the place you were meant to be. And you do not belong here," the Daughter said. "You belong to the desert."

24

JUDE

JUDE'S STOMACH SANK. THE COLLECTOR WANTED TO SPEAK WITH THEM. Personally. Jude could think of only one reason—somehow the collector had figured out that they intended to steal the Pinnacle Blade.

His gaze zeroed in on Evander. "You," Jude said. "What did you tell her?"

"Nothing!" Evander's brow furrowed. "*Is* there something to tell her?"

Of course. Evander didn't know who they truly were, or why they had come here. But there was no other explanation.

"Jude, let's just go see what she wants," Anton said.

Jude avoided his gaze. They didn't have much of a choice, unless they wanted to leave now and lose any hope of getting the Pinnacle Blade back.

Evander summoned one of the servants to his side. "Take us to see Lady Bellrose."

The servant nodded, leading them to a door across the ballroom. He pushed it open, shepherding them inside.

Evander looped his arm through Jude's and held him back.

"Excuse us one moment," Evander said, and let the door swing shut, with Anton on the other side.

"I don't know what just happened with you two," Evander said, eyes searching Jude's face. "But can I give you some advice?"

Jude didn't know what sort of advice a self-absorbed lordling could have for a member of the Paladin Guard, but he was sure he wouldn't like it.

"Don't pin any hopes on him."

Jude startled, wondering for a brief moment if Evander somehow knew what Anton was, knew about the prophecy and their roles in it.

But then Evander continued. "He's got a tendency to collect admirers and lead them on. He'll make you feel like you're his favorite person in the world, and then the next day he'll have moved on."

"I am *not*," Jude bit out, even as he felt himself flush, "an admirer."

But the memory of Anton's body pushed up against his, every angle lined up, cut through his denial. He could still feel the phantom weight of Anton's hand, firm against the nape of his neck. And he was still reeling from his own sudden realization of how easily he could have leaned forward and captured Anton's lips with his, and of how terribly he'd wanted to.

"Not what it looked like to me," Evander said. "I know you saw us out by the dock. You didn't like that I kissed him."

Because Anton was the Prophet. Because dallying with lordlings was beneath him. But despite himself, the scene Jude had witnessed flashed in his mind. Evander drawing Anton close beside the moon-lit river. His thumb brushing over the hinge of Anton's jaw, inching down to his throat where his pulse beat.

Jude curled his hand into a fist. "He can do whatever he wants. It doesn't make a difference to me."

Evander laughed. "Don't be mistaken—it's not that I'm jealous. I'm just giving you a friendly warning." He pushed the door open again. "Come on. Lady Bellrose is waiting."

Jude followed, averting his eyes from Anton's questioning glance as they followed the servant down a corridor. He was as big a fool as Evander thought him to be. No, a bigger fool. Because even if he recognized this ache for what it was, even if he admitted it to himself, it was not something he could ever allow himself to act on.

It wasn't as if Anton was the first person Jude had ever wanted in this way. But with Hector, it had been different—as much as Jude loved him and wanted him, he had known that his yearning would lead nowhere. So he'd been willing to take what he could get—Hector by his side, but never more than that.

But Anton did not operate by the same rules. Anton pushed closer, Anton was careless with his touch, with his teasing, in a way that felt utterly dangerous to Jude.

He had accused Anton of forgetting what they had come here for, but Jude was the one distracted now. He struggled to focus as the servant led them down a set of stairs into a hallway that ended at a single doorway.

At the foot of the stairs, Anton stopped suddenly, swaying against the wall.

"What is it?" Jude asked. Anton was staring at the doorway with an unrecognizable expression on his face. It wasn't quite fear, but something close to it, and beneath that was a sort of weary resignation.

The servant pushed the door open and smiled placidly. "Welcome. The lady is expecting you."

The room was surprisingly plain, decorated as a very simplistic sitting room, with a couch along one side and plush chairs around it. A table sat in the middle, laden with sweets and wine.

The most elegant thing in the room was the woman who lounged in one of the chairs. She wore an Endarrion-style dress of deep purple stitched with an intricate pattern of silver stars. The red jewels that adorned her throat were so dark they looked black, except when the light caught them, as it did when she rose to greet them.

"Lady Bellrose," Evander said, sweeping into a bow as soon as he crossed the threshold.

Jude was not sure if he was meant to bow, but he copied Evander's movement anyway. Anton, however, didn't move.

"We are honored that you called us here," Evander said.

She waved the servant off with a flick of her fingers and he departed, shutting the door behind him.

Evander sat on the couch, closest to Lady Bellrose. Jude sat beside him, leaving room between them for Anton, who did not join them. He remained at the door, staring at Lady Bellrose with a hard, calculating gaze.

"Your friend is rather shy," she remarked, pouring four glasses of wine as dark as her jewels.

Jude had never heard anyone describe Anton as *shy*, and the very notion of it was absurd.

"He's never been in the presence of someone as high-ranked as you, my lady. Come sit down, Anton," Evander said, as if Anton were a pet he could command.

Jude bristled, but he stayed silent as Anton sat between them, his gaze trained on Lady Bellrose.

"That's better," she said. "Now. I'm sure you can guess why I've summoned you here."

Her piercing gaze shifted from Anton to Jude, and Jude felt like he was back in the Tribunal Chambers, his every secret flayed open to her.

"Jude Weatherbourne," she said. "I've been expecting you. Both of you."

Jude's skin prickled. He had not told Evander his full name. And if she knew who he was, she more than likely could guess who Anton was.

"Who are you?" he asked.

It was Anton who answered. "She's a bounty hunter."

Both Evander and Jude turned to him in shock.

"You know her?" Jude asked.

"She's a collector," Evander said. "Anton, what are you—"

"I am many things," Lady Bellrose replied, smiling. "All of them a little bit true. But none of them the whole truth."

Jude narrowed his eyes. If she was a bounty hunter, she could be working for anyone. She could be working for the Witnesses.

"What do you want?" Anton asked.

She smiled briefly, as if this was an old joke between friends. "The better question, I think, is what do you want?"

Anton fell into restless silence.

"We want the Pinnacle Blade," Jude said. At this point, it made more sense to speak plainly.

"Ah," she said knowingly. "I might have guessed as much."

"It belongs to me."

"That sword was given to the Keeper of the Word by the Prophet Pallas," she replied.

"Keeper of the—" The rest of Evander's words were cut off in indignation. "What is she talking about?"

"Did you know?" Anton asked abruptly. "When you came to warn me about my brother in Pallas Athos, did you know why he was looking for me? Did you know what I—who I am?"

"Yes," she replied evenly. "Does that surprise you?"

Jude looked at Anton sharply. Was she saying she knew he was the Prophet?

"You could have told me."

"You weren't ready to hear it."

"I wasn't ready anyway," Anton replied, and then snapped his mouth shut, as if his own words had surprised him.

"Perhaps not."

"Where is the Pinnacle Blade?" Jude asked, swallowing his alarm. The longer they spent in here with Lady Bellrose, the more uneasy he felt.

"Your Grace," she said. "It's abandoned you, hasn't it?"

Jude reeled back, stunned. How could she possibly know that?

"The Pinnacle Blade won't restore it," she said. "The problem is within you, Jude. Your heart is in conflict."

Before he could stop it, Jude's gaze flickered to Anton.

Lady Bellrose rose from her couch, crossing the room to the armoire in a few fluid steps. She unlatched it, opened the doors, and lifted something from within with both hands.

When she turned back around, Jude leapt to his feet.

The Pinnacle Blade lay in her hands. The sheath gleamed in the low light, obsidian struck through with silver.

Lady Bellrose traced the seven-pointed star etched into its ornate hilt. "As soon as I laid eyes on it, I knew exactly what I was looking at."

"How?" Jude asked.

"I know everything there is to know about the Order of the Last Light," she said. "More than anyone alive."

"That's not possible."

"Do you want your weapon back, Jude Weatherbourne?"

Jude clenched his hand, remembering the weight and balance of the sword, the power that had saturated his Grace.

"What do you want?" Anton asked, cutting his gaze to the woman. "Whatever it is, it's yours. In exchange for the Pinnacle Blade."

"So mercenary," the woman said reproachfully. "What if I told you the sword is a gift?"

Anton and Jude exchanged wary glances. On Anton's other side, Evander looked entirely lost.

Lady Bellrose sighed. "Anton, when have I ever done anything that didn't help you?"

"You told the Pale Hand about me," Anton replied. "That wasn't very helpful."

"Wasn't it?" she asked. "As I said. The sword is a gift."

She held it out to Jude. He reached for it.

"There is, of course, one thing you must do," she said, and Anton made a noise of distaste. "The Pinnacle Blade is yours if you can wield it."

"What do you mean?" Jude asked.

"The Blade will know," she said, "whether you are truly the Keeper of the Word."

Jude's heart leapt into his throat. Again, he felt as though he were back in the Tribunal Chambers. "I am the heir to the Weatherbourne line."

"A birthright is not a destiny," she said. "What must you surrender to meet yours?"

Jude curled his hands around the sword's hilt and closed his eyes, searching for the strength to rid his heart of its treacherous desires.

The silence of the room was abruptly broken by a loud knock at the door.

"Lady Bellrose!" someone cried. "We have to get off the ship right now."

Jude, Anton, and Evander all startled. Yet when Jude looked at Lady Bellrose, she did not seem alarmed.

"Ah. I think your friends are here."

"Our friends?" Jude repeated.

"The ones who attacked your fort," she replied, as if this were obvious.

The Witnesses.

Jude advanced on Lady Bellrose. "Did you tell them where to find us?"

"Of course not."

"Then—" His gaze swung to Evander.

The boy's eyes widened and he held up his hands. "I don't understand *anything* that's happening right now."

"We need to go." Jude fastened the Pinnacle Blade to his belt and moved to the door. "Stay here. I'll see if it's safe."

He opened the door and stepped into the corridor. He could hear frantic chaos below, partygoers screaming and stomping on the lower decks, but the corridor was empty. He waved the others forward and they followed him into the corridor.

"There are lifeboats on the starboard side," Lady Bellrose said.

Jude nodded. "Then we make a run for them."

He led them down the corridor and out onto the deck to a row of lifeboats. Jude flew to the first one and knelt to begin hastily untying it. The metal shriek of a sword being unsheathed froze him cold.

He turned. Across the deck, the bright white flame of Godfire flared, illuminating the form of the masked Witness from Kerameikos.

He should be dead. Jude had seen him fall.

"Get on the boat," Jude said to the others, and slowly stood.

Anton grabbed Jude's sleeve, yanking Jude toward him. "I'm not leaving you."

Lady Bellrose had the lifeboat rigged up, she and Evander inside it. They started to lower themselves down as Jude looked from the boat to Anton's face.

Without pausing to think it through, Jude planted his hand on Anton's chest and pushed him over the side of the ship. It was only a short drop into the lifeboat, where Evander helped brace his fall. Anton scrambled to his feet, staring up at Jude thunderously.

Jude turned to face the advancing Witness. He gripped the Pinnacle Blade and pulled on the hilt. It didn't move. He tried again, now frantic, but the sword would not be unsheathed.

The masked Witness drew closer. "Step aside, Paladin."

"You know I'm not going to do that," Jude replied. He could still hear the sound of the lifeboat being lowered.

The Witness attacked, his flaming sword striking toward Jude's shoulder. Jude gripped the Pinnacle Blade's sheath just below the hilt and raised it to block the Witness's attack. He moved with his parry, sidestepping the Witness as he surged forward.

They separated, and Jude skidded backward. He risked a look down at the lifeboat and saw that it was now in the water. The Witness shot toward the prow of the ship and leapt up onto the long wooden beam that ran perpendicular to the mast. Jude tore after him. The Witness spun, his sword swinging toward Jude's head.

Jude ducked, and the Witness struck again. This time, Jude moved toward him, grabbing the hilt of the Godfire sword with one hand and sending his elbow into the Witness's throat. The Witness fell back, throwing a hand out to grab on to the nearby rope net to catch himself, his mask slipping down and off his face.

In the light of the sword's flame, Jude saw the Witness's face for the first time. Pale scars crept up his throat like vines, curling over his cheeks and branching around his eyes.

Scars that looked like the ones on Jude's body.

"You've been burned by Godfire," Jude said. He suddenly understood why this man's fighting felt familiar. He stepped back in astonishment. "You have the Grace of Heart."

"Had," the Witness replied, pulling himself up. "I burned that vile affliction out of my body."

Shock and horror rippled through Jude. "You burned your Grace out *deliberately?*" His eyes roved over the Witness, taking in the scars. "Why?"

"To purify myself of its corruption," he answered. "And to prove that I am the most loyal of the Hierophant's followers. The others can threaten the Graced and burn down temples, but only I have endured the searing pain of the Godfire flame. The flames destroyed me and they remade me. I emerged from them brand-new, pure and whole at last."

Jude suppressed a shudder. As he had been desperately trying to find a way to restore his Grace, here was someone who had willingly sought out the Godfire's devastation. He could not fathom it, and the mere idea of it filled him with such disgust he almost wanted to retch.

The Witness hurled himself back onto the beam and attacked Jude, forcing him to retreat until Jude was at the edge, staring down at the dark waters below. Ropes stretched down alongside the mast. Jude grabbed one as the Witness advanced.

"One day, Paladin, I hope that you come to see the truth," the Witness said. "To realize that the Grace that you cherish is an evil aberration, a symbol of all your sins and the sins of those you worship."

He raised his sword, and Jude jumped off the beam, rope still in hand. The rope caught fire as Jude swung above the water, Lady Bellrose's lifeboat below. The rope pulled taut at the height of Jude's arc and then snapped, sending Jude plummeting into the river.

The water enveloped him and Jude kicked hard, slicing through it until he emerged, gasping.

A hand gripped his collar and then another joined it, pulling him up out of the river. He flopped over the edge of the lifeboat, panting. Above him, Anton's face appeared, his eyes furious.

"He could have killed you," Anton said.

Jude closed his eyes. "You know what I am. You know what I have to do."

Anton didn't answer.

On the ship, they'd been playing pretend. Pretending they were not the Prophet and the Keeper of the Word, pretending their destinies didn't matter. And it had been easy—too easy—to mistake the game for something else.

But Jude realized that he'd been pretending a lot longer. Since that first night in Pallas Athos, Anton's face shadowed by candlelight in that tiny room in the taverna, pretending Anton hadn't seen everything Jude had been trying to hide. Since the night in Kerameikos before the attack, pinning Anton against the shelves and pretending he was the cause of Jude's fury.

But Anton had pushed and pushed until the facade cracked and Jude could no longer tell himself he didn't know why his Grace wouldn't work, why the Pinnacle Blade would not allow him to wield it. Jude's heart was in conflict, and he could no longer pretend it wasn't.

25

EPHYRA

AT SUNRISE, THEY REACHED THE PART OF THE DESERT THAT NUMIR CALLED THE salt pan. The skiffs could not travel over the salt the way they did over sand, so they left them behind. But Ephyra was almost grateful when they were forced to continue on foot—she had not been looking forward to being cooped up with Illya the rest of the way to the tomb of the Sacrificed Queen. She would rather bury herself in the sand. At least if they were walking, Ephyra could get up to thirty feet away from him.

Instead of the golden sand Ephyra had grown accustomed to, white crystal covered the ground as far as the eye could see. It shone brilliantly in the sun, broken by pockets of sand that made it look almost like seafoam. Long ago, this whole area had been covered in water. This was what it had left behind.

Frustration built inside Ephyra as the sun set behind them. They were as close to Eleazar's Chalice—to a cure for Beru—as they'd ever been. Yet she'd never felt farther away. The others kept up a steady stream of chatter. Just ahead, Shara and Illya were talking about something evidently very funny judging by how often they broke into laughter.

Ephyra gritted her teeth and marched faster toward them.

"*Then* he told me that the real treasure was the friends—" Shara paused to glance at Ephyra. A shadow of panic passed over her face and Ephyra froze. Obviously Shara still wasn't over the argument they'd had yesterday.

Illya raised his eyebrows. "Can we help you?"

"I need to talk to you," Ephyra said to Shara.

Illya fell back, allowing the two of them a few feet of privacy.

"You can save the apology," Shara began.

"What apology?"

Shara huffed in irritation, but there was something else in her eyes, and the way they would not quite meet Ephyra's. It was a moment before Ephyra realized what it was—Shara was afraid of her.

Usually that was not something that would have concerned her. In fact, much of the time, fear was useful. Here, it complicated matters. Would Shara let Ephyra have the Chalice if she feared what she would do with it?

Ephyra steeled herself. "When it comes to it, when we get to the Chalice . . . I just want to know that you're not going to renege."

"Why would I do that?" Shara asked.

Frustration twisted in Ephyra's chest. "I don't know. Maybe because you've been listening to what that snake has to say."

"Illya has been nothing but helpful to us since we found him," Shara argued. "I'm not worried about him."

"But you are worried about me," Ephyra finished for her. Shara's expression confirmed it.

"Ephyra, you were perfectly fine with killing someone!" Shara said. "That's—that's not a normal response to this situation."

"You don't get it," Ephyra said. "This is *life and death* to me. My sister is dying."

Shara narrowed her eyes. "I just want you to know—I have been honest with you from the start. I've never lied to you, and in return, you've consistently hidden things from me. So I'm sorry if I can't exactly trust you."

"Then why are you even here?" Ephyra asked. "I know where the Chalice is. I don't need your help anymore."

"You think *finding* the Chalice is the hard part?" Shara laughed. "Sure, you don't need me."

"Then tell me that when we find it, you'll hand it over to me like we said."

"And if I don't?" Shara asked. "Will you solve that problem by killing me, too?" Her jaw was set, challenging, but Ephyra saw that same shadow of fear. She was never going to win her over.

You don't want to find out, she thought viciously.

The lake was filled with blood.

Ephyra blinked, wearily rubbing at her eyes. Maybe the desert was starting to mess with her head. The landscape on the other side of the salt pan was different from the rolling hills of sand they'd crossed to get there. Huge boulders and rock formations impeded their route. There were even a few plants dotting the ground—small, shrubby little things with spiky branches and rigid leaves. In the moonlight, they looked like hungry little monsters.

She was still staring at the blood lake when she realized everyone else had slowed.

"What *is* that?" Shara asked, her gaze on the lake ahead. "Is that a mirage?"

"No, it's real," Hadiza replied. "The people of Behezda call it the Lake of the Slain."

"Because it's literally filled with them?"

"It's not *actually* blood," Parthenia said. "I'm guessing it's a chemical reaction of some kind, likely the water interacting with sulfur in the lake bed."

"It's a good sign," Hadiza continued. "We're close to the tomb. Behezda's about five miles that way"—she pointed across the lake to where a large formation of rock rose from the ground—"and the tomb should be right ahead."

Even with the rational explanation, the lake was unsettling, and as they drew closer, Ephyra felt some strange pull toward it.

"Are you sure it's not cursed?" she asked uneasily. She edged closer as they looped around it, and found herself standing with her toes at the edge of the water, looking down at her reflection in the moonlight. She looked more dirty and miserable than she'd imagined. Her hair was matted and grimy. The thin scar that Hector Navarro had left on her cheek seemed to cut her face in two.

"I see the tomb," Shara said.

Ephyra startled, turning away from the lake and trailing after Shara, squinting into the distance. She could see a dark shape ahead, rising from the rock. A wide, tiered rectangular stone base supported a colonnaded top. It looked like a blend between the architecture of the temple in Susa, and the more familiar architecture of the Six Prophetic Cities.

Ephyra felt that pull again and she realized it was not the lake she'd been drawn to. It was the tomb. The Chalice.

"Someone should stay behind with him," Ephyra said, gesturing to Illya.

"We can't afford to go in shorthanded," Shara said tersely. "We don't know what's waiting for us in the tomb. I'm not risking it. So either *you* can stay behind with him, we leave him here by himself, or we take him in with us."

Ephyra took a deep breath. Soon, she would have the Chalice in her grasp. She would be rid of Illya. She would find a scryer in Behezda who would find Beru for her. And then Beru would finally be healed. "Fine. Let's just go."

They crossed a long, paved courtyard lined with crumbling columns and gnarled, leafless trees. The closer they got to the tomb, the larger it loomed.

"Everyone, stay sharp," Shara said as they reached the stairs that led up to the entrance doors. "I'm willing to bet we're about to encounter some nasty surprises. Stick together and stay on guard."

They climbed the stairs to the tomb's entrance.

"How do we get in?" Numir asked, staring at the solid stone door. "Another hidden message in an ancient language?"

Parthenia inspected the door. "I don't see any clues."

"What was it the message said?" Illya asked, looking at Ephyra. "Offer a sacrifice . . ."

"Not of blood but of life," Ephyra said.

"What does that mean?" Shara asked. "Of *life*?"

"The mirror that led us to Susa was designed so that only someone with the Grace of Blood could use it," Hadiza said slowly. "So it would make sense if this one was the same. What if by 'life' they mean *esha*?"

They all looked at Ephyra.

Her mouth went dry. "I . . . no, I can't do this."

She didn't want to explain that she didn't know how to take part of someone's *esha* without taking all of it. That the only thing she'd ever done with her Grace was kill.

"Use mine," Illya said.

Shara looked at him like he was speaking in tongues, but Illya ignored her, rolling back his sleeve.

"She just threatened to murder you," Shara said. "Barely a day ago."

Ephyra narrowed her eyes at Illya in suspicion. He must be up to something, to offer himself up so easily.

"Doesn't seem like anyone else is eager to volunteer," he said.

He was right, of course. He was her shot at getting into the tomb, and even if he was planning something horrible, she'd take it.

The others watched as Ephyra moved toward him and laid her hand on his arm, just above his elbow. She could feel his pulse jumping beneath his skin.

Ephyra closed her eyes. *You can do this*, she told herself. It sounded like Beru's voice in her head. She raised her other hand and put her palm against the mausoleum door. She took a breath, concentrating on Illya's pulse, and then felt for the flow of his *esha*.

How did healers do this? As a child she'd pulled and pushed *esha* purely on instinct. Later, when she'd brought Beru back to life, she was so possessed by grief and pain that she couldn't control herself. And as the Pale Hand, she took *esha* only to kill, seizing it by any means necessary.

She was powerful. She wasn't gentle.

She thought of Beru, of her life getting cut short if Ephyra failed. She felt Illya's pulse and tried to tug on his *esha*. Nothing. She was concentrating too hard, overthinking what she'd done dozens of times without thought.

A moment later, she felt his hand on her wrist, picking it up off his arm and setting it at his throat. Ephyra sucked in a sharp breath, eyes flying open to stare at him. His face was drawn and serious as he pressed her thumb against his pulse, his skin warm beneath her hand. A shiver ran down her spine.

Breathe, she told herself, blocking out everything else around her until all she could hear was his breath and his blood rushing through his body. She followed the sound to the thread of his *esha*. She coaxed it gently, like a baby chick fluttering onto her hand. His face twisted in discomfort and she released his *esha*, as if it had burned her. But she could still feel it, like warm water lapping at her fingertips. She breathed in and took it in hand, not pulling, just holding it there, working by instinct, and then slowly drew it toward her hand that was touching the door.

It began to move. Ephyra jerked her hand away from Illya, gaping at the door as it opened fully.

"I . . ." She'd done it. She hadn't killed him. She hadn't even hurt him. He was staring at her, one hand raised to his throat where she had touched him.

"Shall we?" Shara said, gesturing them forward.

Ephyra broke Illya's gaze and went in first. As they crossed the threshold, the entrance sealed shut behind them. No going back.

Shara tapped her incandescent light until it glowed, illuminating the antechamber of the tomb. The others followed suit, and with their combined light Ephyra could see they were standing in a huge, cavernous space. She took a step forward.

"Wait—" Hadiza warned.

A cacophony of clicking sounds drowned out the rest of Hadiza's words and Ephyra dropped to the ground before she could process what was happening.

A hundred arrows streamed across the mouth of the chamber.

She heard a sharp cry of pain from somewhere behind her and a beat later, the arrows ceased. She remained on the ground for a long moment, just to be sure.

"You *idiot*!" Numir's voice cut through the silence, edged with anger.

"You're welcome," Parthenia gritted out, her voice wracked with pain.

Ephyra pushed herself off the ground, catching sight of Shara helping Hadiza up. Behind them, Numir was crouched beside Parthenia, who lay on the floor, clutching her arm against her chest.

"Why did you do that?" Numir asked, a hint of desperation creeping into her voice.

"It was a reflex," Parthenia replied.

Ephyra suddenly understood the source of Numir's anger. Parthenia had pushed Numir out of the path of the arrows, and as a result had gotten struck instead.

"It doesn't look too deep," Numir said, inspecting Parthenia's wounded arm. Parthenia hissed in pain. "Don't be a baby."

"Looks bad enough that you should stay here," Shara said. "Too dangerous."

"I'll stay with her," Numir said at once, helping Parthenia to her feet.

"I don't need a nursemaid," Parthenia said irritably.

"Numir's right," Shara said. "Stay safe."

Parthenia looked like she was about to protest again but a sharp look from Numir silenced her.

"The rest of us should keep going," Ephyra said. Her gaze slid to Illya, who was looking around the tomb with curiosity. "He can go first, to test out the other traps for us."

Illya grimaced.

"That's . . . actually not a bad plan," Shara said. She glanced at Illya and shrugged. "Sorry, but if it has to be one of us and all. Knew you'd end up being helpful."

"Fine," Illya said. "Then give me one of those." He held out his hand and Hadiza handed over her light. Shining it directly in front of him, Illya crept farther into the chamber and then paused, as if waiting for more arrows to fly. Nothing happened.

He led them down a narrow passageway branching off from the first chamber. At the end of the passage, he stopped.

"Dead end?" Shara asked.

"No, there are stairs going down," Illya replied.

He was clearly apprehensive. Being inside this dark tomb was bad enough, but going underground? Even Ephyra shivered a little bit.

He hesitantly went down one step, and then another. Ephyra could see his light disappearing downward. "Seems fine!" he called back.

Ephyra followed, the others at her heels. The stairs were so narrow they only allowed one person through at a time. She inched along behind Illya, pausing to wait for something to spring out of the walls at her, but nothing did. Shara and Hadiza followed her.

"Guess it's safe," Shara said in relief. "Which is either a good sign or a sign that there's nothing—"

She cut off with a yelp. Ephyra lurched backward, her feet scrabbling for purchase, but the stairs had transformed—they now formed a smooth ramp. A scream tore at her throat as she fell onto her back and plummeted down into darkness.

She slid down and down, unable to stop herself, until finally she was spat out onto stone floor. She lay there for a moment, her head spinning, and then shifted over. Something cracked beneath her.

A moment later, there was a hollow tapping noise and an incandescent light illuminated their surroundings.

"Is everyone all right?" Hadiza asked.

Ephyra heard a groan and then Shara's voice. "I think I broke a rib."

"Illya?" Hadiza asked.

"Here." He tapped on his light, too. Ephyra realized that hers had broken beneath her.

"If we can't find a way out, we'll starve to death," Hadiza said matter-of-factly. "No way we're getting back up there."

Ephyra looked back toward the passage and what had once been stairs. They were at least fifty feet below the top level, with no means to climb up in sight.

"Come on," Illya said. He was several paces away from them, his light illuminating another passage. "I think this is the only way forward."

This time, Ephyra gave Illya a wide berth before following. As wide as the cuffs would allow. He stopped about thirty paces ahead. When Ephyra reached him, she saw why. The passage abruptly ended, plunging down into a deep cavern below. A thin rope bridge led across it.

"One at a time?" Ephyra suggested.

"I'm pretty sure this bridge is longer than thirty feet," Illya replied. "Unless you're planning to free me, we need to go together."

The bridge swayed with every one of Illya's steps. Ephyra waited a moment and then stepped onto it after him, holding tightly to each side.

"I think it can hold our weight—" He cut himself off as his foot went through one of the planks of the bridge.

Ephyra's heart slammed against her ribs. Illya's eyes were wide with panic as he stared down at the boundless abyss.

A second later he seemed to compose himself and pulled his foot free. He toppled onto the next plank in the bridge.

"Are you all right?" Shara yelled after them, clutching her injured rib.

"Fine," Illya gasped back. He waited as Ephyra took her turn approaching the gaping hole in the bridge.

"Here," he said, holding out his arms.

"I really don't need your help," she replied shortly, and with her hands braced on the ropes, she launched herself across the gap, landing neatly in front of him. They were far too close for Ephyra's comfort, but she wasn't going to be the one to move.

Illya didn't move for a moment, either, breathing heavily, his eyes flicking down.

"Move," she said, and he stepped back, shaking his head a little, and spun on his heel. Ephyra's eyes stayed pinned to his back as they crossed the remainder of the bridge.

Shara followed behind them once they were safely on the other side, tucking her light into her belt to hold on to the ropes with both of her hands. She moved slowly, gritting her teeth in pain.

Hadiza came last, moving tentatively across the bridge. When she reached the piece that Illya had broken off, she leapt over. The bridge swayed as she landed hard on the next wooden plank, and Ephyra sensed what was about to happen before it did.

The rope snapped.

The bridge collapsed, and a high-pitched scream tore through the air as Hadiza was sent plummeting down into the chasm.

"Hadiza!" Shara cried, moving as if to lunge over the edge of the cliff, but Ephyra grabbed her arm to hold her back as Hadiza disappeared into the blackness.

"Hadiza!" Shara cried again, swinging her light over the dark chasm.

There was no answer. Shara called her name over and over again, her voice shaking.

"Stop it," Ephyra snapped. "She's gone."

"She can't be," Shara said, biting down a sob. "She—"

"We can't stay here." Ephyra turned away from the cliff.

Shara looked at Ephyra as though she were seeing her clearly for the first time. Frigid silence stretched between them, absent the echoes of Hadiza's screams.

"Oh, so you're ready to just keep going?" Shara snarled at her. "You don't care about Hadiza and the others and what happens to them, do you?"

"You all knew what you were getting yourselves into," Ephyra replied. "If you don't think it's worth it, you should have left a long time ago."

"You're right, I should have. This was a terrible decision, and I did it anyway because I have a habit of making terrible decisions, and yet somehow it's always fine in the end. No one dies. But this time, *you're* here."

"This isn't my fault," Ephyra said.

"It *is*!" Shara yelled. "None of this would have happened if you hadn't gone looking for that *stupid* Chalice! Hadiza would still be here. And if your father hadn't gone looking for it, Badis would still be here, too. You dragged us here, and you cursed us."

Ephyra sucked in a breath. "If that's what you really think, you can stay here."

Shara's eyes burned with anger in the dim light. "Fine. Go on without me."

They stared at each other for a long moment, blinking in the darkness, and then Ephyra turned her back and started to walk. It was a moment before she heard Illya's footsteps catch up to her.

They climbed the path that wound around the cavern. Ephyra could hear faint sounds from below, like skittering animals. She shivered, keeping her eyes focused on Illya and the light in his hand just ahead of her.

The rumble of stone sliding over stone sounded, faint at first but growing louder. Ephyra instinctively looked up, and saw a column plunging down onto the path.

She leapt forward, rolling away from the impact as it crashed to the ground, dust spraying up at them.

Illya grabbed her hand, pulling her to her feet. "We need to go, *now*."

"What?" Ephyra said, trying to jerk her arm away from him. He dragged her forcefully down the path. "Let *go* of me—"

The rumbling sounded again and Ephyra abruptly stopped trying to pull away from Illya and instead shoved him forward, running after him.

Another stone column slammed down behind them and they sprinted as hard as they could. Ahead, Illya's light illuminated a juncture in the path. She ran harder, feet flying, mere steps behind Illya. They were nearly at the juncture when Ephyra's foot caught the edge of a rock and she went flying to the ground. The rumbling was so loud, ringing between her ears, there was nothing in her mind besides *get up, get up, get up!*

She pushed herself up and suddenly there were arms around her waist, lifting her to her feet and slamming her against the wall. Ephyra shut her eyes as the sound of the rock column crashing into the path boomed in her ears. After a moment there was silence, punctuated only by sharp pants of breath.

The breathing, she realized, was not her own. And after a moment she understood what had just happened. Illya had pulled her to safety.

The same Illya who was now pinning her between the rock wall and his body, his head tucked against her shoulder.

He pulled back and in the darkness she could not make out his expression. She didn't move, didn't push him away, just waited. He shifted his weight, bowing his head and ghosting breath across her lips, and Ephyra went very still.

A sudden realization sliced through her—she was waiting for him to kiss her. On the heels of that realization came another—despite his timely rescue, she still hated him, every bit as much as she had in Pallas Athos.

"Should be safe, now," he said, leaning away from her.

In the span of a breath, Ephyra gathered herself. She was here for one reason—to get the Chalice. Either Illya was going to help her get it, or he was going to try to take it himself and that was the extent to which she needed to think about him.

"So," Illya said, gesturing at the junction. "Which way?"

Ephyra stood in front of a fork in the path, which led to two possible routes. The silence seemed to crowd with whispers, words she couldn't make out. She felt a tug. The Chalice.

"Left," Ephyra said, following the direction of the pull. "After you."

Illya led the way, casting glances back at her every few minutes. It irritated her, made her feel jumpy and anxious.

"I know why you saved me," she said.

"Oh?" A smile played at his lips.

"You're not fooling me. You've been cozying up to Shara and the others this whole time, trying to win them over, and maybe it's working." She faced him head-on, putting steel into her voice. "But it will *never* work on me. You saved me so I would think, oh well, he did those terrible things, but maybe deep down he's a good person. After all, he helped me, didn't he? And maybe I'd be a little less on guard, a little less cautious. And maybe, over time, you'd start to win me over. You'd keep being helpful, charming, and I'd have to wonder, maybe he really did change. Maybe I can trust him."

An unreadable expression flashed over his face. Was he annoyed to be caught out? Was he calculating what his next move should be, now that Ephyra had thwarted this one?

"But I want you to know that no matter what you do, no matter how much you seem like you've changed, I will never let my guard down. Not an *inch*. Because I know who you really are."

He swallowed, shadows and light dancing on his face. "Fine," he said, a smile slowly curling his lips. "You're right. You have me figured out. I thought saving you would win you over, but I should have realized that will never work on someone like you."

"Someone like me?" Ephyra said, and immediately regretted asking. He was trying to manipulate her again.

"You really don't trust anyone, do you?"

One person. Ephyra trusted one person, and had only trusted one person her entire life.

"Do you?" she asked.

He looked off into the blackness. "I trust that people will act how I expect them to act. I trust that they will do whatever they need in order to continue believing the story they've told themselves about who they are."

"What story do you tell about yourself?" Ephyra asked.

He grinned. The expression looked lethal in the dark. "One you don't want to hear."

Ephyra bit down on the inside of her cheek. Despite herself, she *did* want to hear it. Every single time he spoke to her he wove another thread in a twisted web and dared her to untangle it. And Tarseis take her, *it was working*. She wanted to get to the bottom of all his lies, to peel back the layers of his deceit and see what slithered out.

Illya's light suddenly dimmed and then went out.

"What just happened?" Ephyra asked. "Why did you turn it off?"

"I didn't," Illya said. She could hear him smacking the light, but could see nothing.

She reached out and brushed her fingers against the rock wall. She was trapped here. Trapped in the dark with only a snake for company.

26

BERU

THREE OF THE DAUGHTERS TOOK BERU AND HECTOR INTO THE DESERT. THEY
walked, their hands bound, beneath the light of a crescent moon, the
lonely desert spreading out around them.

Fury howled in Beru's chest. "You could save him," she pleaded.
The Daughters ignored her, marching on. Beru's anger curdled and
festered, and she knew that Hector must feel it, too.

He was silent at her side. They walked for hours, the passing time
marked only by the moon that slowly rose in the sky. The dry desert
air, so hot in the afternoon, now chilled her to her bones. She felt
the weight of every life she'd cost, like their spirits were following her
steps, waiting for the justice they'd been denied. Beru's strength faltered with every step. Death reached for her.

She closed her eyes.

"Move," one of the Daughters said, and Beru realized she had
stopped walking and was listing to the side like she might collapse.

They continued on. The desert landscape shifted—gone were the rocky crags and low brush that surrounded Behezda. Here it was just sand—empty and desolate. There was nothing living in this land.

The moon was high in the sky when they finally came to a stop. Two of the Daughters pushed them down into the sand to bind their ankles.

When they were done, the Daughters stood facing Beru and Hector.

"The desert will take you," they crooned in unison. "And the desert will release you."

Without another word, they turned and walked away. Beru could almost imagine that the desert stretched on endlessly. That she and Hector were the last two people left in the world.

The wind whipped at their cheeks, tossing sand around them. Beru ducked to shield her face. A storm was coming. She could see its shadow looming on the horizon like a great beast.

When she looked back at Hector, he was tugging himself free of his bonds. "What are you doing?" she said, the words heavy in her mouth.

His ankles free, Hector crawled over to start undoing Beru's. "We can get out of here."

Beru shook her head. "Hector, I—I can't. I'm too weak. I don't even know if I can stand. Just leave me here. You can still find a way to cure yourself."

The wind howled around them, so loud that Beru couldn't hear what Hector said next. He looked at her, breathing hard. Before she knew what was happening, he leaned forward, his arms going around her.

"I told you in Medea," he said softly. His breath was warm on her ear, and as close as they were, she could hear him clearly over the wind. "I'm staying with you. Until the end."

Beru squeezed her eyes shut. The sand whipped fiercely around them, swirling like a vortex, tearing mercilessly at their skin. The whole world was in pieces. She felt Hector's breaths and the beat of his heart as her mind ebbed in and out of consciousness.

"I wanted to save you," she whispered. "I'm sorry. I'm sorry."

He held her and said nothing as the storm swallowed them.

27

ANTON

JUDE HAD NOT SAID A WORD SINCE JOINING THEM IN THE BOAT. SOMETHING
had shaken him thoroughly during his fight with the masked Witness,
though Anton knew that he hadn't been injured.

They were miles from the center of the city when the boat pulled
over to one of the canal docks.

"Out you go," the Nameless Woman said. Jude rose, but she shook
her head and pointed at Evander. "Just him."

Evander got to his feet unsurely.

"Take that boat," the Nameless Woman said, gesturing to an empty
canal boat tied up at the dock. "It will take you back to your estate."

"I'm not leaving Anton," he said, with a ferocity that surprised
Anton.

"This doesn't involve you," the Nameless Woman told him. "Best
you stay safe."

Without warning, Evander pulled Anton into a fierce hug. "I don't
want you to get hurt."

Anton didn't know what to say.

"I'll be all right," he assured Evander, patting him awkwardly on the back. Then suddenly Evander was untangling himself from Anton and lunging toward Jude. Anton watched Jude's eyes go wide and shocked as Evander embraced him.

When he pulled back, Evander said, "Keep him safe, all right? Whatever it takes."

Jude hesitated, and then gave him a short nod. Evander climbed out of the boat.

"Anton," Jude said, his gaze on the Nameless Woman. "Maybe we should get out, too."

"You can," she said. "But then you won't hear what I have to say."

Jude glanced at Anton, and he understood that Jude was letting him take the lead. If Anton trusted the Nameless Woman, then so would Jude. It was a surprising amount of faith to place in him, much more than Anton was willing to place in the Nameless Woman.

But this was a rare offer from her, to give him answers. Even if they were filtered through her usual combination of ambiguity and equivocation.

"We'll hear you out," Anton said, and Jude sat back down beside him. "But you're going to tell us *everything*. You know who I am. You know who Jude is. If you're really trying to help us, you need to tell us who you are."

"All right, then."

They pulled away from the dock, continuing along the canal.

"Where are you taking us?" Jude asked.

"Somewhere safe."

Anton crossed his arms in front of him. "Start talking."

"Why don't we play for it?" the Nameless Woman asked. "A rematch, of sorts, from the night we met."

She withdrew a deck of cards from a pocket in her sleeve. The backs of the cards were decorated with gold foil and shone in the moonlight.

"I'm serious," Anton warned.

"So am I." The Nameless Woman began to deal out the cards.

Jude watched them both warily.

"You get first play," the Nameless Woman said.

Anton gritted his teeth and snatched up his hand. For once, he didn't want to play canbarra. He drew a card anyway. A five. He pulled out the five already in his hand and played them both to the center.

"Very good," she commended. "Now you may ask me your question."

"Who are you? Really."

"Have you ever heard of the Protectors of the Lost Rose?" she asked, drawing a card and tucking it into her hand.

"They're a myth," Jude said.

But Anton realized he *had* heard of them. The night before the attack on Kerameikos, when he'd dreamed about the Hierophant. He'd been . . . torturing someone. Someone with ties to the Lost Rose. It had been meaningless to Anton at the time but now—it couldn't be a coincidence.

"The Lost Rose is very real. And I am its leader," she replied. "Anton, what do you know about where the Four Bodily Graces came from?"

Anton laid down a six, seven, and eight of cups. "The Prophets gave them to their faithful subjects. Right?"

The Nameless Woman smiled. "Yes. But how did they do that? Where did they get these great powers?"

"I . . . I don't know," Anton admitted.

The woman looked at Jude. "The four sources of Grace," Jude said slowly. "The Four Sacred Relics."

"Yes. And the Lost Rose was formed to keep the Relics safe." She laid down four aces, naming each suit as she played them. "The crown. The sword. The chalice. The stone."

"The chalice," Anton repeated, with another startling bolt of recognition. "Eleazar's Chalice?"

"Yes," she said, sweeping the aces to the side. "There were times when the Protectorate could not do what we had been formed to do. Times when one of the Relics fell into the wrong hands. The Necromancer Wars being the worst example."

"So where are they now?" Jude asked.

The Nameless Woman set her piercing gaze on him. "You're holding one in your hands."

Anton and Jude both stared at the Pinnacle Blade. The reason they had come to Endarrion. Jude's hands tightened around the hilt.

"That explains why you wanted the Pinnacle Blade," Anton said. "But why are you telling us this?"

She nodded down at the cards. With an irritated huff, Anton snatched up the eight of cups, added it back to his hand, and discarded a ten at random. She picked up his ten, discarding a six.

"You are the Last Prophet," she said. "You have received visions of destruction and ruin. The fall of the Prophetic Cities."

"I thought only the Order knew about the prophecy. About me."

Maybe the Nameless Woman had once been a member of the Order—an acolyte who'd broken her oaths. But that seemed unlikely. She was far too self-interested to join the Order.

"The Order believes that the Prophets entrusted them alone with their secret. But that isn't quite true. There were others . . . a trusted few, who were given the secret, too. As a matter of insurance."

"In case something happened to the Order?" Anton asked, drawing a card without prompting.

"In case the Order failed at finding you. In case they got the prophecy wrong."

Jude bristled, but even he couldn't deny that they *had* gotten the prophecy wrong—at first, anyway.

"So it's you and who else?" Anton asked, playing his three eights to the center. He now had only three cards remaining. She still had six. Yet he didn't feel at all like he was winning.

"It's me and whomever I deem important enough to know," she replied.

"And the Relics . . . what do they have to do with the prophecy?"

"Everything." She drew her next card and immediately discarded it. "The Age of Darkness is here because of the Relics. Because of what the Prophets did to create them."

Anton reached for a card and then froze, peering at her. "You're saying the Prophets *caused* the Age of Darkness."

"Something like that."

"No," Jude spoke. "No, that's not possible. The Prophets were *good*. They were blessed with Sight because each of them demonstrated their pure virtue. Wisdom, faith, justice, beauty, charity, and mercy. The *esha* of the world filled them with divine power because they were worthy of it."

"You're right, of course," the Nameless Woman said. "They *were* chosen by the world's *esha*. But once, that *esha* had a name. A form. A will. Once, it was a god—a god who created all other beings. But he could not speak to his creations. His voice was too great and his words too powerful for mortal ears. And so he chose the Seven to be his Prophets. He gave them their ability to peer into the future so that they could communicate his bidding to the people. They were his servants. His voice. And later, his betrayers."

Anton heard Jude's sharp intake of breath and looked over to see his hand clenched on the edge of the boat.

"There was no god," Jude said, his voice hard. "That's just a myth the people of the Prophets' time believed, until the Prophets showed them the truth."

The Nameless Woman smiled over her cards. "The Prophets spent two millennia convincing their followers that the god of old was nothing but a lie. They did it well."

"What happened to the god?" Anton asked, watching Jude's expression harden with betrayal. He finished up his turn, playing a four to his existing run of cups.

"They killed him," the Nameless Woman said, playing two poets. "And they did not stop there. They took pieces of their Creator, divided up his divine body and from it created the Four Sacred Relics. His heart was forged into the Pinnacle Blade, which bestowed the Grace of Heart. His blood became Eleazar's Chalice, bestowing the Grace of Blood. His skull they crafted into the Crown of Herat, granting the Grace of Mind. And his eye became the Oracle Stone, imparting the Grace of Sight. With these Relics they proclaimed they would rule in the god's stead, bestowing these Graces on those they judged worthy."

"None of this is true," Jude said, heated. "The Order of the Last Light—"

"Do you really think," the Nameless Woman said, "that the Prophets would have told *them* the truth?"

Anton could see the fury and conflict on Jude's face, the stiff line of tension that ran through his shoulders. He looked like he was a moment from pulling Anton out of the boat and swimming away.

"You can't just tell us these lies and expect us to believe them," he said. "Pull the boat over and let us out."

Anton's gaze drifted over the Nameless Woman, searching for signs of deception. He didn't trust her to tell the truth, but at the same time he couldn't see a reason why she would lie. He knew enough about her to know she wasn't working with the Witnesses. And unlike Jude, Anton did not have any allegiance to the Order's version of events.

When the Nameless Woman did not reply, Jude pushed himself to his feet and stalked to the other end of the boat.

Anton turned back to the Nameless Woman. "You still haven't explained what the Relics have to do with the Age of Darkness. With my vision."

"I'm getting there," she replied, drawing a card. "The Relics spread some of the god's *esha* in the form of Graces. A little bit of the god's power spreading was acceptable. But to let it flow freely into the world was too dangerous. Too unpredictable. So, in secret, the Lost Rose locked the god's esha away, using the only things powerful enough to do it—the only things imbued with the god's power itself."

She set down her remaining cards—one herald of each suit, and placed them around the rest of the deck.

"The Relics?" Anton asked.

"Yes," the Nameless Woman replied. "They used the Relics and some of their own Graces—Heart, Mind, Blood, and Sight—to create a seal that kept the god's *esha* contained. But at some point, the Four-Petal Seal began to break. Some of the god's *esha* has been slowly seeping out. Spreading fear, disease, corruption. If the seal breaks completely . . ."

"The Age of Darkness," Anton finished grimly, his nightmare about the Hierophant flashing back to him. He knew what it must mean now. "That's what the Hierophant wants. That's what he's trying to do. He wants to break the Four-Petal Seal." He glanced back at the Nameless Woman. "You knew all this and yet you waited until *now* to tell me any of it?"

"You said yourself, you weren't ready," she replied. Anton's own words echoed back in his head—not the ones he had said on the barge, but rather what he had said to her in his dream in Kerameikos. "When I met you, you were still running away from everything that could cause you harm, telling yourself that what you feared was your past—not your destiny. I tried to help you along, to guide you, and you refused me."

"Because I don't trust you," Anton said. "I still don't. You could be lying to us, like Jude said."

"I could be," she agreed. "But you think I'm telling the truth, don't you?"

Anton could not deny it. What she was saying sounded too close to what he had heard in his dream for it to be a lie. "What am I supposed to do with this information? How do we stop this?"

"You must return the Four Relics to the place where the god was slain and use your Grace to repair the Four-Petal Seal. Only the Last Prophet can do it. *The final piece of our prophecy revealed. In vision of Grace and fire. To bring the age of dark to yield.*"

"*Or break the world entire,*" Anton finished.

"Well, we must endeavor to avoid that outcome. It won't be easy. And you asked for none of it." She almost sounded sad. "Yet, here you sit."

"I'm the Prophet," Anton answered, remembering the words Jude had hurled at him. "I don't have a choice."

28

HASSAN

HASSAN STORMED INSIDE THE GREAT LIBRARY, HEART THUNDERING WITH rage.

"Where is Arash?" he demanded.

Khepri met his gaze from across the room and started toward him. "Hassan—"

"Where is he?"

Khepri lowered her eyes. "He's . . . in the mess. With the others. Are you—"

"I'm fine," he said curtly. "But those people at the parade aren't."

He stalked across the room, the other rebels openly staring at him, and marched down the hall. He could hear voices from the mess, and then the sound of soft laughter. His blood seared with anger as he quickened his step.

He slammed open the door to the mess, scanning the rebels gathered. Arash stood just a few paces in front of him, glancing coolly at Hassan.

"Prince Hassan," he said. "I'm so glad you're all right."

He didn't sound glad at all.

"What in the Six Cities was that out there?" Hassan demanded, not even trying to make his tone calm. "That wasn't the plan."

"It was, actually," Arash said mildly. "Little speeches are nice and all, but the Scarab's Wing is more interested in action than talk."

"Innocent people got hurt," Hassan said, blazing with anger. "That is unacceptable."

"They aren't innocent," Arash replied. "They were there celebrating the coronation of a usurper. A false queen. Your *aunt*."

"That doesn't mean they deserve to be used like this!"

"They *should* have been rioting," Arash hissed. "They should be storming the gates of the palace and demanding the death of the Usurper but they're not. And they never will—you know why? Because they don't care about us. They don't care about the Graced."

"And why should they, after that?" Hassan demanded. "You just showed them exactly how dangerous you are."

"Good," Arash said. "I told you, we aren't playing nice or fair. Some of us can't afford civility."

"You'll turn this whole city against us," Hassan said. "You're doing the Witnesses' job for them."

"You're naive. I am doing what needs to be done. What you refuse to do."

"This isn't what I signed up for when we joined you," Hassan bit out.

"Then by all means, leave. The door is that way," Arash said, lifting his chin imperiously.

Hassan's nails dug into his palm. "I'm not going to let you tear this city apart."

"The Witnesses tore apart this city, not us," Arash replied. "If you can't see that then I question whose side you're really on."

Hassan felt like he'd been struck. "The Witnesses took *everything* from me. My father is dead because of them!"

"And if he were here right now, I bet he'd be ashamed of his coward son—"

Hassan didn't think before he raised his fist and struck him. Arash stumbled back, hands flying to his face.

Hassan swallowed, instantly regretting his actions. He reached for Arash, his lips formed around an apology. And then Arash's gaze hardened and he lunged at Hassan. A blow to his stomach had Hassan crumpling to the ground unable to do anything to stop the fist headed toward his face.

Before it struck, Khepri appeared in front of him, her arm up to block Arash's fist.

"Khepri," Hassan breathed, relief coursing through him.

She turned to face him. "Hassan," she said. "I think . . . I think it might be a good idea for you to go."

"What?" Hassan asked, dumbstruck.

"You clearly can't work with Arash, and I don't think that continuing to be here is—"

"You're siding with *him?*" Hassan asked. He couldn't believe the words that were coming out of her mouth, couldn't look at the pained expression on her face. "After what he did?"

She looked away. "I'm sorry. I just . . ."

He narrowed his eyes. "Did you *know?* Did you know what he was really planning to do?"

She didn't meet his gaze.

"Did you know, Khepri?"

"I'm sorry," she said, her voice feeble.

Hassan couldn't speak. He'd thought that Khepri would always be at his side. That she would always choose him.

He'd thought wrong.

"Fine," he said, straightening. "I'll leave. I want no part of this *rebellion*. I'm *done*."

He spun on his heel and limped from the room, Khepri's silence deafening in his ears. She didn't follow him.

When Hassan arrived back at their room, someone else was waiting for him. Zareen.

"That was your work," he said hollowly.

She leaned beside his door, arms crossed over her chest. "Yes, it was."

"Did you know what they were going to do?" he asked.

She gave him a look, as if to say that neither of them were stupid enough to believe otherwise.

Hassan unlocked the door and went inside. Zareen followed him.

"For the record," she said, "the riot wasn't supposed to start until after you spoke."

"You're fine with that?" he asked. "You're fine with the way Arash does things?"

"More than fine with it," Zareen replied, her eyes blazing. "You don't get it, do you? It's not just about the Witnesses. This whole city has stood aside while they impose their ridiculous beliefs on us. Our so-called countrymen did *nothing*. The girl I—" She took a breath. "The girl I loved was caught by the Witnesses, just after the coup. They tied her up in the middle of a square and beat her. They said it was punishment for her use of Grace, that she *deserved* it for . . . for doing nothing but *healing* people. And the people in that square, they just watched it happen. The people she had risked her life to heal, the people who would have been *dead* without her, they just . . . *watched*."

"I'm sorry," Hassan said, feeling sick. "I didn't know."

Tears had formed in Zareen's eyes. She wiped them furiously.

"So, yeah. I don't care about the people at that parade. I don't care if they got hurt because of me. I *want* them to hurt. I want to burn this whole city down."

Hassan didn't know what to say, so he focused on packing his things. When he was finished, he went to the door where Zareen stood watching him, and paused.

"What happened to her?" he asked. "The girl you loved?"

Zareen looked away. "After they beat her, the Witnesses took her. They experimented on her. She came back to me covered in white scars, like her skin had shattered and been put back together. She wasn't the same. Her Grace was gone and so was her will to live. She just . . . wasted away. I couldn't do anything. One day I came home and found her lying on her bed. Not breathing. Her lips were stained silver. She'd gone into my workshop and drunk a bottle of mercury."

Hassan closed his eyes, gripping the doorframe so tight he thought it would splinter. "I can't imagine what that was like. And I understand why you can't forgive the people who stood by and let it happen. I can't, either. But hurting them won't bring her back. This is my city, and every single person in it is my responsibility. Including them. Including you. I want to bring them to justice, but I can't do it like this."

"Justice?" Zareen asked. "Does such a thing exist? I've never seen it."

"I don't know," Hassan said. "But if we're not trying for that, then what's the point of all this? What comes after rage, Zareen?"

She looked up at him, her lips twisting. "I don't know. I guess I'll let you know when I find out."

He nodded at her and then left the room, following the corridor to the passage that led out of the Library. Half of him wanted to find Khepri waiting there for him, to take back her words and beg him to stay. But the other part of him knew she was right—he couldn't be part of this anymore.

It gutted him that Khepri would stay, with or without him. It tore him up that she had trusted Arash, *lied* to Hassan, and been part of something so unforgivable. But then, she'd never shied away from lying, from doing the unconscionable in order to achieve her goals. Maybe he was a fool for being so surprised.

He arrived at the passage and turned to take one last look at everything—the gleaming armillary spheres, people going about their business oblivious to his departure—and then climbed into the dark passage alone.

29

EPHYRA

EPHYRA AND ILLYA JOURNEYED DEEPER INTO THE TOMB. THE DARKNESS WAS so complete, Ephyra felt like she was floating in a void. A whisper hissed past her ear and she whirled around to find its source. But there was only Illya beside her.

Another whisper curled like smoke around her. She shivered. Neither of them had spoken in what felt like hours—she didn't even know how long they'd been in this tomb. Maybe it was already morning outside. Maybe they'd been trapped down here for eternity.

The whispers grew louder, resolving into words.

"Pale Hand," they whispered. "Ephyra. *Murderer.*"

Ephyra tightened her jaw as they forged onward. The whispers followed them, wending their way through Ephyra's ears, beckoning her.

"I'm sorry," someone murmured, but it was not the same whispers coming from the tomb. It was *Illya*. Startled and somewhat disturbed, Ephyra stumbled into him. "I'm sorry, I don't know why I'm like this. There's something . . . something wrong with me. There always has been. I can't . . . It never goes away. I'm sorry—" His voice broke off, high and frightened.

Ephyra grabbed his elbow and spun him toward her. "Illya, it's not real. Whatever you're hearing, it isn't real."

"Please," he said. He was shaking. "Please, I didn't want to hurt you. I don't know why I did. I don't—"

"*Murderer*," someone wailed behind her. Ephyra spun, her hand on her dagger. In the blanket of darkness, she could see a face right in front of her. It was familiar, like someone she'd known as a child.

"You *killed* us," another whisper said. Ephyra turned and there was a different face staring at her accusingly.

The whispers grew louder, and then a trembling scream cut through the darkness.

Ephyra knew that scream. It was Beru. She stumbled forward in the dark.

"Beru!" she cried.

"Ephyra!" Beru's frightened voice called back.

"Beru, I'm coming!" Ephyra yelled, charging forward into the abyss. Her foot caught on something and she was thrown to her knees, and in the darkness she almost thought she would keep falling, until her hands hit the ground. "Beru!"

"This is your fault, Ephyra," Beru's voice said. "This is all your fault."

"No, Beru—"

"Why did you do it?" Beru asked. "Why did you kill them? You killed them all, Ephyra. You're a monster."

"Beru, please," Ephyra said. "I'm sorry. Please."

"You're not sorry, Ephyra," Beru said in disgust. "You don't know how to be sorry."

Ephyra choked on a sob, head hanging down between her shoulders. Beru was right. She felt no remorse. She was a monster.

"You killed me," another voice said. And Ephyra looked up to see Hector standing above her. "You murdered my family and then you murdered me and you *still. Don't. Care.*"

Ephyra squeezed her eyes shut and stumbled to her feet. She reached out, searching for anything to anchor her. Her fingers brushed against rock.

"You're a monster," Hector said. And Beru's voice joined him. "Who could love a monster?"

Ephyra gasped and lunged toward Hector. He disappeared like smoke and suddenly Ephyra was falling, and this time, there was nothing to catch her. A scream tore from her throat as she plummeted into blackness.

When Ephyra woke, she wasn't alone.

She stared up at a gilded ceiling. Rich amber light suffused the room, and the scent of incense curled around her nose. A face swam above her, wrinkled and wizened.

Ephyra shot up, scrambling back. Hands caught her shoulders and she tried to jerk away. A dozen figures stood around Ephyra like mourners at a pyre. But mourners would not be armed with scythes.

"Who are you?" Ephyra demanded, her voice echoing in the chamber.

"We are the Daughters of Mercy," the woman in front of her said. "And we know who you are, Ephyra of Medea. We know what you seek."

Ephyra sucked in a sharp breath. "What do you mean?"

"Your father came to us," she said. "Many years ago. He, too, sought the Chalice. But we made sure he never found it."

It was *them*. They were the reason that no one survived the search for the Chalice. They had killed Badis.

"Where is it?" Ephyra asked.

"It is here," another Daughter said. Ephyra turned. In the woman's hand was a silver chalice, studded with jewels. "You will not have it. We will not let you."

The other Daughters moved in front of her, holding their scythes aloft.

Ephyra drew herself up. "I need it to save my sister."

"Your sister," the Daughter with the Chalice repeated. "Beru of Medea. She came to us."

"Beru?" Ephyra asked, her stomach dropping.

"She asked for our help."

Ephyra's heart hammered, her chest tightening. "What did you do to her?"

"We did what you should have done," she replied. "We gave her back to the earth."

Terror gripped Ephyra's heart. It couldn't be true. This was another trick, like hearing her sister's voice call out to her in the dark.

"You turned her into something vile. Something profane. She came to us, and we put right the evil that you let inside her. We allowed your sister to complete her journey through this world."

"No."

"We took her into the desert and left her there," the Daughter said. "Her *esha* belongs to the sands now."

"*No!*"

Blind with rage, Ephyra charged at the Daughter and grabbed for the Chalice. But another one lunged toward her, swinging the scythe to meet her throat. Ephyra ducked beneath it, skidding to the ground. A hand reached out and grabbed her arm. Ephyra was face-to-face with the wrinkled Daughter, struggling against her hold.

"We do not wish to kill," the Daughter said. "That is not our way. But we will do what we must to protect the boundaries of life and death, which you have trespassed."

The other Daughters advanced, their scythes gleaming in the low light. Ephyra closed her eyes and focused on the *esha* of her captor. She sucked in a breath and pulled. A gasp echoed through the chamber and the grip on her arm slackened. The Daughter hit the ground.

Ephyra rose to her feet, the Daughters' cries of anger and anguish drowned out by the blood pumping in her ears and the thrum of the Chalice's power around her.

"You have perverted the sacred power of the Grace of Blood, the power bestowed on us by the Sacrificed Queen!" one of the Daughters snarled.

"You killed her," Ephyra growled. "You took her from me!"

She lunged at the Daughter holding the Chalice. The others surrounded her, tearing at her clothes and hair, but Ephyra ignored them like white noise and grasped the Daughter's ankle with both hands. She pulled her *esha* from her, like stripping the skin off an orange. The Daughter collapsed and the Chalice clattered to the ground. Ephyra dove for it. The Daughters pounced a heartbeat later.

Her fingers locked around the stem of the Chalice, knuckles burning white with the intensity of her grip as the Daughters tried to push her away.

Ephyra closed her eyes and clutched the Chalice. They had taken Beru from her. They had taken every glimmer of hope. And Ephyra wanted them to *pay*.

She heard the first hollow gasp behind her. Her eyes flew open.

The Daughters of Mercy were on their knees.

The Chalice was warm in her hands. Ephyra realized what was happening, what she was doing.

She was taking the Daughters' *esha*. The power of the Chalice let her do it without touching them. Let her take from them, all of them, at the same time.

The Daughters of Mercy had taken Beru's life. And now Ephyra would take theirs.

Their *esha* flowed into her, like a river surging against a broken dam. Ephyra closed her eyes and let it in. The *esha* swallowed her, cocooning her in bright white light. She felt it fill her, screaming through her body until it *hurt*. Gasping, she let her grip on the *esha* slacken and dissipate.

The light vanished and Ephyra was left inside the darkened tomb, the bodies of the Daughters of Mercy spread out around her.

The Chalice glowed softly, its power almost palpable in Ephyra's hands. It was hers now.

But it had come too late. Beru had returned to the earth.

Ephyra fell to her knees and let out a terrible cry.

30

JUDE

THE LIFEBOAT PULLED SMOOTHLY INTO A CAVERNOUS CHAMBER. THEY WERE outside the city now, having navigated the canals and turned down an estuary of the Endarrion River. Columns bordered the chamber and moonlight shafted through the ceiling, casting shadows across the water. It seemed like some sort of indoor harbor, though Jude had never heard of such a thing in Endarrion.

"What is this place?" Jude asked as they pulled up to a dock.

There were steps on either side of the bank, leading to long colonnaded walkways.

"A hideout, of sorts," Lady Bellrose replied, sliding out of the boat. "This is where I reside, when I'm in Endarrion. Being on the water allows me to move through the city sight unseen. And allows others to come to me."

Jude climbed out of the boat after her and held his hands out to Anton for support.

"Others like who?" Anton asked, hands curling around Jude's arms.

"Other members of the Lost Rose. We typically try to communicate through coded correspondence, but some matters require a visit."

Jude pinched his mouth in distaste. He still thought this woman was lying about the Lost Rose. He *knew* she wasn't telling the truth about the Prophets. Part of him wanted to grab Anton and the boat and row them back to Evander's place, or the Temple of Endarra, but that would bring danger to them. That wasn't tolerable. And it seemed that even though Anton didn't trust the woman, he trusted that she wouldn't hurt them, or allow anyone else to.

Still, it was with unease that Jude followed her down the walkway and up another set of stairs that led them inside an echoing hallway, with a glass ceiling that peeked out to the night sky. She took them through double doors that landed them in a sitting room that overlooked the river.

"I'll make up rooms for you," she said, and swept away.

"*She'll* make up a room?" Anton asked. "No servants?"

"How do you know her?" Jude asked.

Anton ran his fingers across the edge of a bookshelf. "We met a few years ago. She tried to teach me to use my Grace. It didn't work, I ran off, and she found me again in Pallas Athos."

"You don't trust her." It wasn't a question.

"I don't trust anyone, Jude," Anton said, weary.

"You trust me." That wasn't a question, either.

"Yeah," Anton said. "I guess I do."

Jude felt unsteady under his dark gaze, and looked away. There was a new tension in the air between them, and Jude wasn't sure if it was because of what had happened on the barge, or if it was just in his own head.

He felt the weight of the Pinnacle Blade at his hip and brushed his fingers over the cold metal hilt. This was why he couldn't draw it. This was why his Grace would no longer answer to him.

The door clicked open, and Lady Bellrose reappeared. "Let me show you to your rooms. You both look like you could use some rest."

She led them into another hallway lined with a series of maps that seemed to depict the Six Prophetic Cities over the past two thousand years, as well as a few of the Novogardian Territories and the Inshuu Steppe. The woman opened a door near the end of the hallway.

"This is you," she said to Anton. Anton glanced at Jude. "Don't worry," Lady Bellrose said, amused. "He'll be right next door."

Anton slipped into the room, but instead of leading him to the next door, Lady Bellrose drew Jude back up the hallway. "Let's talk for a moment, Keeper."

Her hand on his arm felt strangely cold. "I don't have anything to say to you."

"You couldn't draw the Pinnacle Blade, could you?"

Jude froze. "You know why."

"It's as I said."

"You said the sword would know whether I am Keeper of the Word. So that means I'm not."

She stepped through an archway and into a small study. Leaning back against the writing desk, she said, "Keeper of the Word is just a title. It holds no power. The power is in you."

"My Grace doesn't work." It was too late to wonder if he should keep that to himself. At this point, he was desperate.

"Not your Grace," she said. "Your actions. Your intentions. Your purpose, I suppose."

"I know my purpose," Jude said, more harshly than he'd intended. He'd known his purpose since he was three years old, and still, after all this time, he let himself be distracted. He let himself think thoughts and feel feelings that a Keeper of the Word shouldn't.

"And what if you're wrong about what your purpose is?"

Jude jerked his head up to meet her gaze, startled.

"I must ask you," she continued. "Have you ever been honest with yourself? Even just once?"

"Have you ever been honest with him?" Jude shot back, heart thudding.

"I was tonight," she said. "Whether or not you believe me."

"What do you want from me?" Jude demanded. "Do you want the Pinnacle Blade back? Fine, take it back. I can't use it anyway." He unclipped it from his belt and held it out to her.

She curled her hand around the hilt. "This sword can only be drawn by the Keeper of the Word. The man who sold it to me was desperate to get rid of such a useless weapon. So is that what it is to you, Jude? Is that what you are to it? To him? Useless?"

Shame welled up in his chest, suffocating. Anton had been right before. Jude had made him a promise he couldn't keep. And breaking it would break them both.

"You don't know me. You don't know anything about this." But his heart thundered out the truth. "I'll fight for him. No matter what, I'll fight for him. Even if I lose."

She looked at him almost pityingly. "If that's what you want, Jude, then that's what you'll have. But maybe one day, you'll learn to *stop fighting.*"

Before she could say another word, Jude fled.

Jude sat on a balcony overlooking the river. The sky was pitch-black, the only sound the rush of water below. He wasn't sure how much time had passed since his conversation with Lady Bellrose, he only knew he couldn't get her words out of his head. Sleep was a far-off thing.

"Still awake?" Anton's voice sounded behind him and Jude turned toward it.

How many times had they met like this before? In the middle of the night, their defenses lowered, truth struggling toward the surface like the sprouts of new spring.

Anton approached, half-shadowed by moonlight, and Jude felt—

He didn't know how he felt. He didn't move, just watched as Anton sat beside him.

"You're upset," Anton observed.

"I thought," Jude began. "I thought it would be simple. My whole life, I knew what my destiny was. All I wanted was to be worthy of it. And I thought when I found you that I would know what to do. And when I didn't, I—"

"Gave up," Anton said quietly.

Jude looked down. "I called you a coward that night at Kerameikos. But I'm the one who's been running away."

Every cruel word he'd said to Anton that night he had really meant for himself. All the shameful things he hadn't been able to admit. He couldn't stand knowing that he'd taken it out on Anton.

"You're scared, Jude," Anton said. "That doesn't make you a coward."

"Aren't you?" Jude asked, before he could stop himself.

"Always."

"And you just . . . live with that?"

"I wasn't aware there was another option," Anton replied drily.

"I just mean . . ." Jude rubbed at his forehead. "The Prophets were the one thing I always believed in. My faith is all I have. The one certainty in my life, when I was uncertain of everything else. And I . . . I don't know how to go on, if I don't have that. I don't know how to get it back."

"Maybe you're not supposed to," Anton said.

"But I need to," Jude said. "My Grace . . . it's gone because I no longer know how to be who I'm supposed to be. I can no longer follow the path of the Paladin. I couldn't even draw the Pinnacle Blade. It knows I am not worthy of it."

"If you're not worthy of it, Jude, then no one is," Anton said.

Jude shook his head. "You don't know. You don't know what selfish thoughts I—" He couldn't look at Anton. He couldn't say more. He closed his eyes and tipped his head back toward the sky. "All I've ever wanted was to serve the Order."

"We both know that isn't true."

Everyone wants something, Jude. Even you. Anton had said that to him, the night they met. He'd known, even then.

Jude wanted to hide his face. He didn't.

"You see too much," he said, his voice trembling. It was the most terrifying thing about Anton. More terrifying than the teasing jokes or the way, even without his Grace, Jude always seemed to know exactly where he stood in a room.

More terrifying, even, than the way Anton was looking at him now, swathed in moonlight, his dark eyes clear.

"I see you, Jude."

Anton's hand came to rest on Jude's, his thumb brushing the knob of Jude's wrist. The weight and the warmth of it felt more intimate than the way their bodies had been pressed together in the private collection room on the barge. Jude knew he should put distance between them, but he could not keep stepping away from this boy who invited him closer, close enough to smell his skin, to hear the gentle thump of his heart in his chest. He could not.

He must.

Jude's own heart stuttered against his ribs. He felt dizzy as Anton leaned toward him, touching his back. He closed his eyes and they stayed there a moment, a breath away, until Anton pressed their lips together and everything went still.

The kiss lasted only the length of a breath before Anton drew back. Jude's chest ached with the absence and before he knew what he was doing he surged after him, pulling him close, seeking his lips and his warmth. Kissing him felt like waving a hand through fire, wanting and wanting not to be burned. Like diving off the top of a lighthouse, without hope or sight of safe landing.

Like sinking to the bottom of the sea, knowing he would surely drown.

31

ANTON

"PLEASE," JUDE WHISPERED AGAINST ANTON'S LIPS. ANTON CURLED HIS fingers around a handful of Jude's shirt and leaned in to kiss him again.

Jude pulled back. "Don't—don't offer me this. Please."

Anton opened his eyes. Jude was trembling under his hand, his eyes dark.

"Are you so afraid of having what you want?" Anton asked, searching Jude's face.

"You're the Prophet." On his lips it was a refrain, a mantra, a *warning*, and only now did Anton realize what a chasm those three words created between them. "And I'm the Keeper of the Word. I shouldn't want anything from you."

Anton reached for him. "But you do. Is that so bad?"

Jude caught his wrist. Anton felt his pulse beat against Jude's thumb as his grip tightened, like he was fighting himself. "It would mean breaking my oath." His eyes flickered up to meet Anton's. "It would mean never restoring my Grace. Please."

Neither of them moved for a moment. Then slowly, Anton drew his hand back.

"All right," Anton said, lowering his gaze. "I won't do it again. We'll go back to how things were."

He looked up with a smile that he was certain looked as false as it felt. He didn't recognize this tender feeling inside him, wasn't sure if he wanted to squash it or cradle it close against his heart.

He watched as Jude stood up in one swift motion, hands clenched at his sides, putting distance between them that Anton knew they would not cross again. He thought he'd been giving Jude something he wanted, but he saw now how dire the conflict was in him. And it was Anton now who couldn't shake off the taste of Jude's lips, the warmth of his hands, the soft press of his body. He wasn't used to wanting these things, and it seemed only now that Jude had taken them away that he realized how much he did.

"Anton," Jude said, shifting his weight and looking like a storm. But it seemed he did not know what to say, and neither did Anton.

So he just sat there, staring out at the river and listening to Jude's footsteps as he walked back inside and closed the door.

Anton dreamed of the lake for the first time since Nazirah. Everything in the dream was the same—the snow, the gray sky, the razor cold water—except instead of Illya above him, it was Jude. He was reaching for Anton, calling his name, but no sound came out.

The world turned on itself, and it was suddenly Jude falling, drowning, while Anton reached for him, screaming his throat raw.

He woke gasping, hand searching for Jude beside him instinctively. Only Jude was not there. He was behind a wall. Anton resisted the urge to duck out to the balcony that adjoined their rooms and slip into Jude's room to tell him about the dream. Instead, he crept down the hall, toward the Nameless Woman's study. The door was cracked open, and golden light spilled from within. Anton pushed it open further.

"You're up awfully early," the Nameless Woman said as Anton entered the room.

"I had a dream."

"A bad one, it looks like."

"They're always bad," Anton replied. "But I'm not talking about just now. I had a dream a few weeks ago. You were in it."

She raised her eyebrows. "That's flattering."

He stepped farther into the study as she poured a glass of dark bronze alcohol.

"You knew that, though, didn't you?" Anton said slowly. "I wasn't dreaming about you. You were really *in* my dream." He shook his head. "How is that possible?"

She slid the glass across the desk to him. "With a great amount of practice. Not all scryers can do it."

"But you can," Anton said, sitting across the desk from her. "Did you see what was in my dream?"

"Bits and pieces."

He wondered if she'd seen the piece of his vision that had been in the dream. He wondered if he lay down right now and went to sleep dreaming of it, if she could step into his mind and see it all. The destruction of the Prophetic Cities, that cold, consuming light, Beru's body in the broken tower. At least that way, he wouldn't have to bear knowing it alone.

"You were trying to tell me something," he said. "Was it about the Relics?"

She nodded, pouring herself another glass.

"The Hierophant was in that dream," Anton said. "He was searching for the Relics. And my grandmother—she was in it, too. It's been years since I dreamed about her. But that day I'd been reading Vasili's last writings . . ." He paused, recalling a specific entry. *The Stone calls out to me. It knows that it was stolen, it wants to punish me for the sins of the Seven.*

"The Relic of Sight," he said. "The Stone. Vasili had it, didn't he?"

The Nameless Woman nodded. "The Relic of Sight is what led to his madness. It consumed him. He knew its origin and he believed it would allow him to communicate with the slain god. To overthrow the Prophets. In a way, it worked."

"What do you mean?" Anton asked.

"Isn't it obvious?" the woman asked. "Vasili's was the last prophecy that the Prophets saw fulfilled. Vasili failed to defy their prophecy, but they disappeared shortly after that. And left behind their final prophecy."

"The Age of Darkness," Anton said.

The Nameless Woman bowed her head. "What Vasili did with the Relic of Sight—whether he was truly able to communicate with the god or not—I believe it set all of this in motion. The last prophecy. The disappearance of the Prophets. The Age of Darkness."

"Tonight, in my dream, I was in the lake again, at my grandmother's house," Anton said, the words tumbling out of him. "And there was . . . something pulling me down. Something at the bottom of the lake. Not a person. More like . . . a power. Stronger than anything I've ever felt." Stronger, even, than Jude. "It felt like every thread of my power was being pulled to it."

He met the Nameless Woman's gaze. It was steady and alight with realization.

"The Relic of Sight is there, isn't it?" he said. "When Vasili died, he must have passed it on to his son. And he must have passed it on, too. My grandmother has it."

"I'd long suspected that," the Nameless Woman said. "Anton, how do you feel about going home?"

Dawn was just peeking over the mountains when Jude, Anton, and the Nameless Woman gathered in her study. Anton explained his dream to Jude, and how they'd figured out the Relic of Sight was back at Anton's old home.

"We need to go find it," Anton finished.

Jude's lips pursed. "We need to discuss this with the Order before we decide anything. They'll be here soon."

"We don't need the Order," Anton said stubbornly.

"Anton, I can't—"

"Protect me, I know," Anton replied. "I don't need you to. I need you to *trust* me."

"I do," Jude replied softly. "But that doesn't mean we don't still need the Order."

Anton let out a frustrated sigh. "I'm not going to change your mind about this, am I?"

Jude shook his head, and then turned to the Nameless Woman. "Can you send a messenger to the Temple of Endarra?"

"I *can*," she hedged, shooting a glance at Anton that told him she would only do so if he agreed. Anton chewed on his lip. What would meeting the Order mean for Jude? Would they separate them, stick Anton with the rest of the Guard and keep Jude from him?

Anton thought miserably of how Jude had rebuffed him the night before. Did Jude *want* them to?

He wouldn't care, Anton decided. He'd grown too attached to Jude as it was and it was better this way. But even as the thought formed, he couldn't bring himself to believe it.

"Send the message," Anton said, and the Nameless Woman rose to do so, leaving Anton and Jude alone in the study.

Anton looked over at Jude, acutely aware of the fact that this was the first time they'd been alone together since he'd kissed him. Jude looked as though he'd slept even less than Anton had. His dark hair was rumpled, his eyes bloodshot, and there was a pallid tint to his face. It made Anton's chest ache.

Jude's gaze slid over to Anton and it seemed to take him several attempts to speak. "Why do you want to go after the Relic?"

"The dream that I had about the Hierophant," Anton began. This wasn't exactly safe ground, but it felt safer than any other topic of conversation. "He was searching for the Relics. Even if the Nameless Woman is wrong about the god, we still need to stop the Hierophant from finding them. And I . . . I saw the lake in my dream. I think that means we need to go there."

Anton didn't know what waited for him, but when he'd left he'd intended never to return. His home was the place of his nightmares. But going back was the brave thing to do. And Anton was trying to be brave.

"You saw it in your dream?" Jude asked.

Anton nodded.

"You're trusting your Grace."

He was right. Anton's dreams had led them to the Pinnacle Blade. And now they were leading him home. This was what the Order had wanted him to do all along, but he'd been too afraid.

Anton knew what the difference was, why he was able to trust the visions in his head now when he hadn't before. It was the same reason he could even consider returning to the nightmare of his childhood.

"If you think we need to go, then we'll go," Jude said. "I'll convince the Guard."

The Nameless Woman appeared back at the door.

"The message is on its way," she said. "We should hear back soon."

The day seemed to drag by. Anton haunted every room of the Nameless Woman's hideout, while Jude sequestered himself in his own room, to the point where Anton had no choice but to believe he was avoiding him.

Finally, the Nameless Woman summoned them both back into the study.

"It appears," she said, "that the Paladin Guard is already waiting for you at the Temple of Endarra."

Jude nodded, looking grim, and rose. "We should go meet them."

He turned to leave the room, and Anton rose after him.

"Wait," the Nameless Woman called as he reached the door. "You're forgetting something."

Anton watched with surprise as she held out the Pinnacle Blade. Jude turned back, approached her, and then hesitated. His mouth pinched into an expression Anton couldn't quite read. He looked almost annoyed, with a hint of confusion.

"Take it," she said. "It's yours."

With a slow nod, Jude took the sword and secured it back at his side. Anton looked at the two of them, unsure what had just passed between them. But Jude turned and left the room without another word.

"You're not coming," Anton said to the Nameless Woman. "Are you?"

He didn't just mean to meet the Paladin Guard.

She smiled, a little sadly. "No. But I'll make sure you get to your destination safely."

Anton wasn't sure why he felt disappointed. He didn't trust the Nameless Woman, and he knew the Guard wouldn't, either. Accompanying them to Novogardia would only complicate things.

Maybe it was just the fact that she seemed to understand his power, and everything that came with it, better than anyone—even himself. That was what had made him run when they'd first met, but now it seemed like a reason to keep her near.

"Will I see you again?" he asked.

"Getting sentimental, are we?" She sighed. "If all goes well, then I suspect not."

"And if it doesn't?"

She gave a thin-lipped smiled. "Then we'll have much bigger problems to worry about."

32

BERU

BERU AWOKE TO THE SOFT SOUND OF HUMMING. FOR ONE DELIRIOUS MOMENT she thought it was Ephyra's voice in her ear, humming a song from their childhood. The first thing she saw when she opened her eyes was the wide fronds of a date palm spread against a bright blue sky. Slowly, she pushed herself up.

"You're awake!" a bright and unfamiliar voice greeted.

Beru turned and pushed herself off the ground to stand. A wave of dizziness hit her, and she nearly collapsed before a pair of strong hands caught her by the forearms.

"Don't strain yourself," the voice said. "Let me help you."

Beru leaned heavily on the stranger, allowing them to help her upright. Panting softly, she raised her gaze.

Before she had a chance to speak, there was a flurry of sprinting footsteps and she was suddenly shoved backward. Beru wavered, catching herself as the sharp sound of metal scraping against metal rang out around her.

"Get away from her!" another voice roared.

This voice, Beru recognized. Hector stood in front of her, his sword unsheathed in one hand while the other was flung out behind him, as if to keep Beru back.

She was not his target.

With her breath coming in short spurts of exertion, Beru looked across the few feet of distance between Hector's taut form and the stranger who'd woken her. The stranger was tall and thin, almost delicate, with long black hair and tattoos running up and down his arms. He held his hands out to them, palms first, his shoulders hunching as if he was trying to make himself smaller.

"Don't come any closer," Hector warned.

Beru wasn't sure what surprised her more—the presence of the stranger out here in the middle of the desert, or the ferocity with which Hector had charged to her side, sword in hand.

"I'm sorry," the stranger said, sounding almost tearful. "I didn't mean to frighten you. I was just trying to help her."

A moment of tense silence passed, and Beru realized Hector was waiting for the stranger to make another move.

Beru reached out, touching the curve of Hector's bicep with the tips of her fingers. Instead of flinching away, his shoulders softened at her touch. She could feel his fear, mingling with her own unease.

Emboldened, Beru pressed her palm against his arm. "It's all right," she said in a shaking voice. "He's telling the truth."

"Who are you?" Hector demanded, staring across the distance at the stranger. "How did you find us?"

The stranger lowered his hands. "I—I found you both collapsed in the sand not far from here. I brought you here to heal."

"Where is *here*?" Beru spoke up, looking around at the clear blue pools scattered between craggy rock formations. Lush green trees and reeds spilled out of the land, and she even thought she could hear the faint chirping of birds. "What is this place?"

The stranger spread his arms in welcome. "This is my home."

"Who are you?" Beru asked.

"My name is Azar," he replied. "I am a healer."

"Did you heal me?"

Azar raised his eyes to hers. "I did."

"How?" Hector asked.

"The oasis provides all I require," Azar replied. "Come, come."

He spun on his heel, loping away from them.

Hector lowered his sword and turned his head slightly to catch Beru's gaze, as if checking to see what she wanted to do.

"Are you all right?" he asked. The tender concern in his voice rendered Beru speechless with confusion for a moment.

"I'm fine," she replied at last. "Are *you*?"

Aside from his baffling behavior, he looked sort of shaky and drawn. Like he was beginning to fade.

She shoved the thought away.

"I'm fine," he replied. "But there's . . . something familiar about this place." He ran his hand over the leaf of a palm tree.

"Familiar?" Beru repeated. "What do you mean?"

"I'm not sure," Hector replied. "I just feel like . . . I've dreamed of this place."

Ahead, Azar turned back to them expectantly.

She tilted her head toward the healer. "Let's see what this is all about."

He led them into a squat hut at the edge of one of the springs. There was a table surrounded by cushions in the center, already set up for tea. Hesitantly, Beru took a seat as Azar poured them tea, humming.

Beru reached for the cup, and with a jolt realized her wrist was uncovered. She instinctively grabbed it with her other hand to hide the handprint.

"I know what you both are," Azar said, his tone even. "And I know who brought you to the middle of the desert and left you for dead. They were my teachers, once."

"The Daughters of Mercy?" Beru asked.

He nodded. Hector was still staring at him, suspicious.

"What happened?" Beru asked.

"They cast me out," Azar replied. "Gave me to the desert, much like they did to you. But I found this place. An oasis. A refuge. And I've remained here ever since."

"By yourself?" Beru asked.

Azar inclined his head. "Occasionally, a wayward traveler will stumble into my path, needing aid. As you did. But they never remain long. And no one in quite some time. No, it's just me and Prickly."

"Prickly?"

Azar pointed to a sharp-looking plant in the corner. "Don't worry, he loves visitors. Don't you, Prickly?"

Beru glanced at Hector, not sure if she should be horrified or amused that their savior, or whoever he was, apparently talked to his plants.

She cleared her throat. "You helped us, even knowing what we are?"

"Yes, yes," Azar replied. "I'm not one to discriminate between those who are living and those who are . . . living again. Who was it who brought you back?"

The question was so casual he might have been asking their favorite kind of tea.

Beru glanced at Hector. She wasn't sure yet if they could trust the healer, despite what he'd done to help them. He said he didn't believe in the doctrine of the Daughters of Mercy, but how far did that extend? A revenant was one thing. The necromancer who'd made her was another.

"You don't want to tell me. Oh dear. Well I won't pry, then. It's not polite," he said, almost like he was chastising himself. "You are welcome to stay here and recover your strength. The oasis will happily provide for you, too."

"How did you really heal her?" Hector asked. "And don't give us some line about the oasis."

Azar tilted his head. "An odd way to treat someone who just saved your life. But I suppose you've had quite a busy day, so I'll forgive you."

Hector's expression darkened and Beru suddenly had the urge to laugh.

"The two of you," Azar said after a moment. "There's a connection between you. Your *esha* feeds off each other."

Beru's laughter suddenly vanished and she felt like she might be sick. "Do you mean . . . you used Hector's *esha* to heal me?"

It explained why Hector had seemed so much weaker than before. She couldn't look at him. Didn't want to see his expression when he realized that, once again, Beru had done nothing but take from him.

"You're upset," Azar said softly. "I—I only meant to help you." He seemed lost suddenly, hurt in a way that surprised her, his eyebrows crinkling and his mouth pulling down at the corners.

She had the sudden urge to comfort him. "It's . . . it's complicated. You couldn't have known, but Hector's death was because of me. Because my . . . because someone wanted to use his *esha* to heal me."

"I see," Azar said.

"I wanted to try to undo it," Beru went on. "That's why we went to the Daughters of Mercy."

"What is done cannot be undone," Azar said.

It was exactly what Hector had said the night he'd confessed he wanted to end his own life.

"But I think you know how to make it right," Beru said. "You can help us, can't you?"

Azar didn't answer at first. He was looking down at his hands. Then, quietly, "Alone, I'm afraid I—I cannot do what you ask. It will require another. The one who did this to you."

Beru's eyes widened. Ephyra. She would never, ever agree to it. She would never give up Beru's life, least of all for Hector.

"Please," Beru said. "There has to be another way."

"I can think of no other way," Azar said. "Unless—"

"Unless what?" Beru asked, leaning toward him.

"There is something," Azar went on. "An object. An ancient Relic that belonged to the first queen of Behezda. A chalice."

"Eleazar's Chalice," Beru said.

Azar's eyes glittered in the candlelight. "You know it."

Beru nodded. "We . . . I was searching for it. But I never even came close to finding it."

"Many have tried." Azar bowed his head. "Yet without it, I know of no other way. I'm sorry I can't be of more help."

She felt anger coming from Hector, but she could not make sense of it.

"Please," she said. "You've done more than we could ask for. Thank you."

"I'll show you your rooms," Azar said. "And the baths, if

you'd like. There's a particularly nice pumice stone that—well, you'll see."

He rose from the table and ushered them both back outside and into a honeycomb-like structure with doors that faced out to a small garden. Azar opened one of the rooms and let Beru inside.

"Here you are."

Once shut inside, Beru felt suddenly *alone*. She'd gotten used to Hector's presence beside her in the tent during their journey to Behezda. She also felt completely exhausted. It couldn't be past midday and yet she felt like she wanted to lie in the musty bed and sleep for hours.

A knock came at her door.

"It's me," Hector's voice filtered in.

Beru went to the door and pulled it open. Hector stood on the other side, looking uncertain.

"Come in," she said. He did, and she shut the door behind him.

"Does this seem strange to you?" Hector asked as soon as Beru had turned to face him.

What was strange was that Beru's heart wouldn't sit still in her chest when she looked at Hector. What was strange was that he was coming to her. She waited for him to continue.

"This healer just happens to find us out in the desert?" Hector asked. "And he just happens to be able to heal you? It seems too good to be true."

"I guess that depends on your definition of *good*," Beru replied.

She felt his jolt of surprise.

"Hector," she said, "you wanted to kill me not that long ago."

He grimaced, and she felt a pang of something like regret. "When the storm came, I thought you were going to die and I—" He looked at her beseechingly, like she might be able to tell him what he was trying to say.

Beru wanted nothing more than for him to finish his thought.

But when he spoke, he said, "We can't stay here."

"Then don't," she said. "Find your way back to civilization."

"And leave you with this creep?" Hector said, incredulous. "Not a chance."

Beru pulled up short, feeling protectiveness and frustration radiating off of him. It was a moment before she found her voice. "Sure, he's a little weird, but he's harmless. And besides, you don't owe me anything."

"I didn't say I did," he returned, his voice heated. He paused. "You don't—Do you want me to leave?"

"No," Beru answered at once. She felt even more like she needed to lie down.

A smile flickered tentatively on his face. It was the first time she could remember seeing him smile since they were children, and her heart fluttered at the sight of it, warmth rushing into her face. She wasn't a little girl with a crush anymore. So why did she still feel like one?

"Let's just be careful, all right?" Hector said. "We thought we could trust the Daughters and look how that turned out. I don't want to make the same mistake again."

"All right," she answered faintly.

He remained standing by the door for a long moment, as if waiting to say something else. "I'll let you get some rest," he said at last, and left the room, closing the door behind him.

Once she heard the sound of his footsteps leading away she let out a sigh and leaned her head back against the door. She felt a bone-deep exhaustion, but when she lay down on the bed, sleep did not claim her.

She should be dead. She should have died in the desert, like the Daughters of Mercy had intended. But once again, against all odds, she had been saved. Hector was right—it was too good to be true. Something was wrong here, but she didn't think it was Azar.

She was beginning to think it was her.

33

EPHYRA

EPHYRA DIDN'T KNOW HOW LONG SHE STOOD IN THE TOMB, HOLDING THE Chalice, looking down at the bodies of the Daughters of Mercy spread out around her.

A sharp inhale wrestled her from her trance. She swung her gaze to the edge of the room where Illya stood, his mouth covered by one hand.

"What did you do?" His voice was clipped, bloodless.

"They killed her," Ephyra said. "They *killed her*." She looked down at her hand and the Chalice clutched in her fingers.

"I don't need it," she said. "It's yours if you want it."

He eyed her, as if he thought this was some kind of trick. But there was something else in his eyes. Hunger.

She held the Chalice out to him, watched his gaze follow it and then drag back to hers. His breath hitched.

"Or maybe," Ephyra went on, "there's something else you want."

She felt rage—powerful, unyielding—a ring of fire around an abyss. Anger would fill it, but even that would burn out, leaving nothing but this chasm of nothingness.

If she let herself fall into it, it would hollow her out and tear her apart.

She stared into Illya's golden eyes and stepped smoothly into his space, her hand curling around his neck. The Chalice dropped to the ground between them. Her thumb pressed gently against the hollow of his throat, and she felt his pulse jump the way it had outside the tomb when she'd taken his *esha*.

"I could kill you, you know," she said. "Easily. I should have done it the night we met."

His eyes darted to her lips. "So do it."

Her hand tightened on his throat. She pressed on it as the emptiness pressed in on her. Killing him would fill the void. It would feed her hunger, but when it was over, when he was dead at her feet, it would be back, gnawing and endless.

Beru was gone, and she was alone in the world.

Her hand slid up, cupping his face, drawing it to hers. The kiss crackled like a wildfire between them, uncontrollable. Ephyra's rage was gone. Need burned in its place. Ephyra pressed herself closer as Illya's hands tangled in her hair, his lips searing against hers.

And then, just as quickly as she'd begun it, she ended it, shoving him away from her. They stood there for a moment, breathing heavily, sizing each other up as if for a fight. Then Ephyra leaned down and picked up the Chalice.

"We need to get out of here," she said.

He nodded, still staring at her. "We can't go back the way we came."

They both turned away at once, searching the walls of the vault.

"Here," Illya called. "I think there's an exit."

Ephyra followed the sound of his voice and saw he was standing before an opening in the wall. Ephyra let herself be led, her feet moving but her mind blank. The rest of the journey out of the tomb was a blur, until finally they were stumbling out to the light.

Dawn had broken in the time they'd been inside the tomb, the sun's glare turning the sandstone blood red.

Ephyra stumbled away from Illya and collapsed in the sand. She closed her eyes and breathed, not knowing how long she sat there.

"You're alive," a voice said.

Ephyra didn't turn to look at Shara standing behind her.

"You got the Chalice," she went on.

Ephyra dug her fingers into the sand.

"What happened to her?" She heard Shara ask Illya.

Ephyra got to her feet. Gripping the Chalice, she faced Shara. The others were standing with her, Parthenia propped against Numir. Hadiza was not with them.

"I killed them," Ephyra said, enunciating each syllable clearly. "The Daughters of Mercy killed my sister, so I killed them."

Shara's face was a swirl of confusion and fear.

"Now the Chalice is mine," Ephyra said. "And if you try to take it from me, I'll kill you, too."

Shara's expression resolved into anger. "No, you won't."

"I won't have to kill you," Ephyra said. "If you stay around me, you'll die anyway. You were right, Shara. I'm cursed."

That was what Hector had said, too, in his own way. A harbinger of darkness. A pale hand in the night, bringing death and destruction wherever she went.

"What are you going to do with it?" Shara asked, her eyes flicking to the Chalice.

There's something dark inside of us. It was one of the last things Beru had ever said to Ephyra.

Ephyra could feel the darkness inside her now, clawing at her insides like a frantic, trapped beast. It would tear her heart to shreds, and Ephyra would tear the world to shreds just to make it feel one ounce of her pain. This was her destiny.

"Just stay out of my way," Ephyra said, "and you won't have to find out."

She turned and started walking east, toward the sun and Behezda. A few seconds later, she heard Illya's footsteps behind her. He had no choice but to follow.

Ephyra held the Chalice close and kept walking. She could feel its power coursing through her still. The dark thing inside her grinned wickedly.

III

FAITH AND LIES

34

JUDE

TWO TORCHES BURNED AT THE ENTRANCE OF THE TEMPLE OF ENDARRA. ANTON and Jude stood side by side at its steps, the river flowing gently beneath the walkway. Jude's gaze rested on the darkened threshold of the temple.

"We don't have to go in," Anton said, his eyes soft. "We can just leave, right now, you and me."

"We need them." Jude dug his nails into his palms. "I let my feelings get in the way of my duty before, with Hector. It could easily happen again." It already had. "They're waiting for us."

Without waiting for Anton's reply, he began to climb the stairs, apprehension threading through his bones. At the top he paused, dipping his forefinger and his thumb into the chrism oil in one of the wide ceramic dishes that sat before the entrance.

Anton walked past him to go inside, and without thinking, Jude caught his wrist, reeling him back. Anton looked up at him, inches away, as Jude drew the pad of his thumb across Anton's forehead, leaving behind a glistening streak of oil. Anton blinked in surprise and Jude stepped back, releasing him.

Jude shook himself, dipping his fingers in the oil again to consecrate himself. He wasn't sure what had come over him. It was an incredibly intimate act, to consecrate someone before entering a temple of the Prophets. Only parents did it for young children, or married couples for each other. Jude had no business consecrating the Last Prophet, even if Anton had no idea how to do it for himself.

When he turned back, Anton was exactly where he'd left him, staring at Jude, his cheeks coloring. He touched the line of oil on his brow and Jude looked away as they entered the temple, balling his treacherous hands at his sides. He had to pull himself together.

The same acolytes who had greeted them before stood in the circular antechamber, the Guard fanned out behind them. Upon seeing them, Penrose broke away from the others and strode toward the temple entrance.

"Jude." There was affection in her eyes as she came toward them. "You're safe. Both of you."

Relief coursed through him. The acolytes had told them that Penrose and the rest of the Guard were safe, but he hadn't truly let go of his worry until now.

Petrossian pulled up beside her. "Is that—the Pinnacle Blade? How?"

Jude rested his hand on the hilt. "It's a long story. There's much we need to discuss. Is Father with you?" His gaze swept briefly over the gathered Paladin.

Penrose's face crumpled. "The acolytes didn't tell you?"

Jude stilled. "Tell me what?"

"The . . . the Witnesses," Penrose said, shaking her head slowly. Her eyes were wide and haunted. "They killed him."

The words howled in his ears like a merciless wind. A storm of grief crashed over him.

No.

"I'm so sorry," Penrose said, and she sounded it. "You are the last of the Weatherbourne line."

Jude crumbled. He covered his face with his hands, a wretched sob rising in his throat, and he trembled with the effort of keeping it down. He and his father had never been close. If the elder Weatherbourne felt affection for his heir, it had been wrapped up in his hope for Jude's devotion to their shared duty. And sometimes, it had been enough. His belief in Jude had made him feel like he belonged.

He felt as if his world had already shattered but this—this was the final piece to break. How could the Order of the Last Light exist without Theron Weatherbourne?

"Do you know what that means, Jude?" Penrose asked. "You need to be Keeper of the Word."

"No," Jude said, desperate. "No, I—the Tribunal—"

Penrose shook her head. "It doesn't matter. The Prophets were very clear that the Keeper of the Word must be from the Weatherbourne line. No other can stand in your place."

"So you put him through all that," Anton said, "for nothing?"

The vehemence in his voice was enough to shock Jude out of his grief for a moment.

"Anton," he said sharply.

"No," Anton said, his dark eyes flashing with challenge. "Either they think you're fit to be Keeper of the Word or they don't. It doesn't change what I already know. I need you."

Jude watched Penrose's gaze flicker to Jude, and Jude dropped his eyes. Anton's declaration made his chest feel light. But he also knew how Penrose would read into it.

"I see," she said.

"There's something else you should know," Anton said. "We aren't planning to stay in Endarrion. Or go back to Kerameikos. We're going north."

Penrose looked taken aback by Anton's commanding tone for a moment. There was a new certainty in him, a decisiveness that Jude had only seen glimpses of before.

"Why north?" Osei asked.

"I need to go back to where I was born," Anton replied. "I think that's where the Relic of Sight is."

"The Relic?" Penrose asked. "What does that have to do with—"

"You remember the dream I had about the Hierophant?" Anton said. "He's after the Relics—all of them. We need to find them before he does, to stop the Age of Darkness."

Penrose watched him with careful eyes. Jude knew that if Anton tried to tell them the rest of what the Nameless Woman had said, the Guard would react as Jude had. It was a ridiculous story, but Anton seemed sure about needing the Relic of Sight.

"We need to go somewhere safe," Penrose said. "The Witnesses found us at Kerameikos. We'll need to find a place where we can protect you."

"They already attacked us in Kerameikos," Anton said. "Where else can we go that will be safe from them? Where will we find safety if the Age of Darkness begins?"

"He's right," Osei said. "Our best chance is to keep moving."

"We should do as he says," Jude said, startling the others. "Anton is the Prophet. He says finding the Relic of Sight will help him. So we should go."

Penrose watched him for a moment, and Jude got the distinct

sense that she was seeing something brand-new in him. He wasn't sure if it was something she liked. But then, he realized, it didn't matter. His father was gone. She was Jude's to command. They all were.

They boarded Lady Bellrose's barge, which was docked outside the temple. The barge, which Jude noted was actually named *The Bellrose*, was outfitted with a skeleton crew. Jude was wary of allowing anyone else to know what they were doing and where they were going, but he swallowed his objections.

"Who is this Lady Bellrose exactly?" Osei asked.

"An old friend of mine," Anton answered. "She helped us get away from the Witnesses."

"And she's just giving you a riverboat?" Penrose asked.

"Loaning," Anton replied. Along with more money than they could possibly need for the journey, but Anton didn't elaborate. "She wants to help. She won't do anything to hurt us."

It was clearly not the answer Penrose was looking for, and when her gaze rested on Jude he could not bear to return it. He looked instead out at the water, thinking of the last time he had spoken to his father. His faith in Jude had not wavered, not once. He trusted Jude, trusted his devotion to the Prophet even in turmoil. Jude looked over at Anton, and realized that he was the only other person who believed in him like that.

They settled in a room on the upper deck with glass walls that overlooked the rest of the ship as they set sail along the river, the sun sinking below the horizon. The Guard peppered Jude and Anton with questions, wanting to know what had happened to them since escaping

Kerameikos. Anton took over answering most of them, which Jude was grateful for, and when it was dark Jude slipped out onto the outdoor deck.

The cool night air was a balm as he sat down, letting his legs dangle off the edge. He didn't know what waited for them in the Novogardian Territories, but he knew the Nameless Woman was at least right about one thing. If he didn't get himself together, he would remain utterly useless to everyone.

"Jude?" Penrose stood behind him. "Are you all right?"

He wanted to lie to her. More than that, he wanted to believe the lie. He shook his head. "There's something I need to tell you. Something I should have told you a while ago."

She waited, holding on to the rail, knuckles turning white.

"My Grace is gone," he said.

Her mouth fell open in surprise. In horror. "Oh, Jude."

"I didn't tell you because I didn't want to face it," he said, coming to rest his hands on the rail beside hers. "I thought there was some way to regain it, because the Godfire didn't seem to affect me the way it affected the others."

"And is there?" Her voice was wracked with hope.

"Anton thinks so," Jude said. "Lady Bellrose . . . it's hard to get a straight answer about anything from her, but she says that it's not gone. That there's some weakness in . . . me."

"If there's a way to get your Grace back, you will," Penrose said, her eyes intent. "I know you. And there's no one whose faith is stronger than yours. Remember your Year of Reflection. Remember what it felt like to free yourself from the shackles of the world. Free from self-doubt."

Jude nodded, exhaling slowly. It was the same thing he'd been telling himself for weeks. Years, really. Because despite what Penrose thought, Jude had never really been able to free himself from doubt. Not during his Year of Reflection. Not when he became Keeper. Not even when he'd found Anton.

But doubt—doubt he could live with. Doubt was an old friend. Comfortable. But there was something far more dangerous to contend with, something that tripped wildly through his chest when he looked at Anton. Something that made him question not himself, but everything else he knew. The Order. The Prophets. Something he was beginning to think he would never be rid of.

Maybe something he didn't want to be rid of.

35

HASSAN

THE FIRST FEW NIGHTS WERE THE HARDEST. HASSAN DIDN'T KNOW EXACTLY where to go after leaving the Library. He wound up returning to the neighborhood where he and Khepri had been squatting before finding the Scarab's Wing and spent the next few nights staying in a variety of different abandoned homes, moving often because he knew Lethia's soldiers were patrolling. Maybe even searching for Hassan specifically.

Without the Scarab's Wing and without his own soldiers, who'd been subsumed by the rebels, Hassan had to think carefully about his next move.

Which was why, six nights after leaving the Great Library, Hassan marched up to the palace gates and announced himself to the guards.

"My name is Hassan Seif," he said to the two guards idling outside the gates.

He recalled what Lethia had told him back in the throne room when he'd first discovered her betrayal, about not wanting to spill his blood. He trusted that it had been true—after all, she'd had countless opportunities to get rid of him in Pallas Athos.

But then, she'd left him to die in the lighthouse that day.

The guard started laughing. "Nice try. But the prince is—"

"Dead?" Hassan asked. "Died in the fire that took down the lighthouse? Is that what they've been saying?"

The two guards looked at each other.

"My name is Hassan Seif," Hassan repeated. "And I have a message for Queen Lethia."

The soldiers dragged him to the throne room. Hassan still remembered the last time he'd been brought here as a prisoner, the shock and betrayal of seeing Lethia on the throne. It was just as infuriating now, and she looked more at home there than ever, lounging in a dark green and black kaftan studded with emeralds, her dark, gray-streaked hair arranged into an elaborate swirl of braids.

"Nephew," she greeted. "I'm surprised you've come to pay your respects. I thought you'd be hiding out with your little friends—the ones who tried to ruin my coronation."

"They're not my friends," Hassan replied.

She raised an eyebrow. It was an expression Hassan recognized well and it made a part of him suddenly miss her, a longing like a punch to his gut.

"You're working with them, aren't you?" she asked.

"I was," Hassan replied. "It turned out we didn't have quite as much in common as we thought."

"So what are you doing here?"

"I know they've been a thorn in your side," Hassan said. "Reminding everyone in this city how illegitimate your claim to the throne is. Showing people they can fight back."

"And?"

"And I can help you take them down."

This seemed to actually surprise Lethia, but she recovered quickly. "Why would I believe that? You are, after all, known as the Deceiver." A small smirk accompanied these words.

"Because their leader hates me," Hassan replied. "And I'm not terribly fond of him, either."

"You also hate me."

Hassan swallowed. He didn't want to show her how untrue that was. A part of him hated her. Another part of him still loved her, even knowing everything she'd done.

"Well, I'll consider your offer," Lethia said. "Obviously I can't let you leave here."

"Obviously," Hassan replied, and he saw that he'd surprised her again. "Can't allow the Crown Prince of Herat to go walking about when everyone thinks I died in the lighthouse."

"If it makes you feel any better, I actually did think you'd died in the lighthouse."

"Then consider me risen from the dead."

Lethia addressed the nearest soldier. "Take him upstairs."

The soldiers took Hassan up a familiar staircase and down a familiar hallway.

His chambers. For a moment he wondered if this was Lethia's way of being tender, allowing him to return somewhere that felt safe. But he knew she was only trying to hurt him more—make him a prisoner in his own palace, in his very own rooms.

He was brought dinner and even dessert by the servants. Some of whom Hassan even recognized. They clearly recognized him, too. He was treated well.

But he was still a prisoner.

When night fell, Hassan changed into the soft silks he'd once slept in and lay down on the bed, his chest tight. The room was just as he had left it, like he was fourteen years old and just returned from a trip down the river with his parents. He turned his face into the pillow, shoulders shaking with sobs.

After a few minutes, he calmed himself, rolling onto his back and staring up at the ceiling, shivering. The room was unbearably cold without Khepri beside him, too quiet without her laughter and soothing voice. Just over a week ago, he'd been reading poems aloud to her, pausing to explain the more obscure references as she laid her head in his lap and toyed teasingly with the tie on his shirt.

And then she'd betrayed him. Told him to go, like all her faith in him was suddenly gone. Was everything between them over? He didn't want to believe it, but she'd made her choice. And now it was time to make his.

The next morning he was summoned, but not by Lethia.

The Hierophant looked exactly as Hassan remembered from the lighthouse—dressed in pure white robes, his face hidden behind a glinting gold mask.

"Your Grace," he greeted softly as Hassan stepped inside the palace library. "So good of you to join me."

"I hope you're not expecting me to address you as the Immaculate One," Hassan returned.

The Hierophant made a sound almost like a laugh. "Of course not."

"Well, you wanted to talk to me," Hassan said. "Here I am."

"Yes, here you are. In the hands of the people you profess to hate most," the Hierophant said. "The queen told me about your offer. I must say I was very intrigued. What could have convinced you to turn on your comrades like that?"

"They aren't my comrades," Hassan said. "We want different things for this city."

"As do we," the Hierophant replied.

"You know," Hassan said, choosing his words carefully. "I still don't understand why you chose us. Nazirah. There are five other Prophetic Cities you could have taken. What do you want with this one?"

"Why have you walked into the belly of your enemy?" the Hierophant replied, deflecting Hassan's question.

"You know why," Hassan said. "Because I will do anything to ensure the safety of my people."

"Do you think it matters to me, whether it's you or your aunt sitting on that throne?" the Hierophant asked.

Lethia and the Hierophant had seemed closely aligned when he first returned to Nazirah. But maybe that was an illusion. Hassan had begun to suspect their alliance was fraying. The tension between the soldiers and the Witnesses the night he and Khepri had found the Scarab's Wing had hinted at it. And here was another hint. Hassan could find a way to use that to his advantage.

Careful not to give his hunch away, he replied, "She's loyal to you, so yes, I'm guessing you do."

"I let her take the throne because she gave me something I wanted."

Hassan remembered his aunt's words during his capture. "You wanted the Prophet. The real one." He swallowed, his breath coming more rapidly. "Because you want to start the Age of Darkness."

"You call it an Age of Darkness," the Hierophant replied. "We call it the Reckoning. A reckoning of light and dark that will bring us into a new era. But you see, I need help. Yours, in fact."

Because Hassan was the Deceiver. Because this darkness—this reckoning—was his destiny. "If I help you, you'll cause even more suffering than you already have."

"If you help me, you'll have what you want most when it's over. Nazirah."

Nazirah. He could protect his city. He could restore it to order. "What about my aunt?"

"I will deal with her," the Hierophant replied, and there was a note of something almost like anger in his tone. "I can see you are tempted by my offer."

Hassan didn't deny it. "Why don't you tell me what you need from me?"

"My people have been trying to get inside the Great Library for weeks," the Hierophant said. "But it seems it's under layers and layers of protection."

"I won't help you attack the rebels," Hassan said. Even if he had split with them, he wouldn't hurt them.

"I couldn't care less about the rebels. I thought that was clear. The matter of who rules this city is of little importance to me. I'm after something bigger."

"Bigger how?" Hassan asked. He knew he was treading a fine line here, trying to understand what the Hierophant was up to without arousing his suspicion. But if he played it right, he might be able to take his throne from Lethia, stop Arash, and drive out the Witnesses in one fell swoop.

"I'm afraid I have to keep that to myself for now," the Hierophant replied.

"Not sure I can help you if I don't know what you want," Hassan said. "Why are you trying to get inside the Great Library?"

"For the same reason we came to Nazirah," the Hierophant answered. "There is information in the Library . . . information that, in the right hands, can change the course of the world."

Hassan didn't have to ask if the Hierophant meant his own hands.

"So you want me to get inside the Library and get this information for you," Hassan said slowly.

"Yes," the Hierophant replied.

"I'll need a little more to work with," Hassan said. "What kind of information is this? A book? A map?"

"Are you agreeing?" the Hierophant asked.

"I didn't say that," Hassan replied. But he was thinking it. He could give the Hierophant a fake copy of whatever it was he wanted, and in return the Hierophant would make him king. He could reclaim his throne without spilling a single drop of blood. "You'll give me the crown if I get this for you? How can I trust you won't go back on your word? Or that your Witnesses won't just take it back from me?"

"Once I get what I want, I'll no longer have any reason to be in Nazirah," the Hierophant replied. "And I will take your dear aunt with me. Nazirah will be yours."

"I'm afraid that's not quite good enough," Hassan said.

"I've summoned a ship to take me and my most loyal followers away from Nazirah," the Hierophant said. "I can provide proof of this. I will make a public declaration that their calling is no longer in Nazirah."

In other words, he would set them on another city. Hassan didn't like that idea, but he would find a way to stop it from happening once the Hierophant was gone.

"All right," Hassan said slowly. "Just one problem. The rebels hate me now."

"Then I suggest, Your Grace, that you do what you do best," the Hierophant replied. "Lie."

36

BERU

BERU'S STRENGTH IMPROVED OVER THE NEXT FEW DAYS. THOUGH SHE COULD tell Hector was not pleased, he didn't raise the subject of leaving again. Beru did her best to keep busy, helping Azar with chores and exploring the oasis.

One morning, Hector intercepted her on the way back from breakfast.

"I want to show you something," he said. He took her down a path through the palms and up the side of a hill to the foot of a cave. The cavern was dark, but breaks in the ceiling gave way to shafts of sunlight that lanced down toward them. Beru spotted a bright triangle of light ahead. Hector led her toward it and they stepped out onto a rock ledge overlooking a pool of pure blue water, completely surrounded by rock. A hidden grotto within the oasis.

"It's beautiful." The air was so cool and crisp Beru could almost taste it.

"I found this place the other day," Hector told her. "I thought you'd like it."

Her heart seized in her chest, overwhelming her with the knowl-edge that Hector had come to this stunning place and thought of *her*. She recalled another day when Hector, then only twelve, had taken her down to see the tidal pools near their fishing village on Charis. They'd both been so innocent then. She was overcome with the weight of all that had happened between them since, and in the soft pleasure of this moment she ached with grief.

"What's wrong?" Hector asked, turning to her and brushing his fingers on the back of her hand.

Beru shivered, shaking her head. "Nothing."

She knew he wasn't fooled, that he could feel every emotion com-ing off her, but he didn't press her.

That night, she dreamed of Medea. She dreamed of her dead village, of every neighbor and friend Ephyra had killed. She walked through the village square, along the path that took her home. And when she entered her house, and went out to the back, she saw him. Hector, dead beneath the acacia. She dropped to her knees.

She opened her eyes and she was back in her room in the oasis.

"It's all right," a voice soothed. Hector. "It was just a dream."

He was sitting at the edge of her bed, rubbing a hand lightly over her shoulder. Still half asleep, Beru reached out to trace the side of his face. He let her.

"Did you see it, too?" she asked.

He nodded. She could feel the movement under her hand.

She was afraid if she opened her mouth to speak, she would cry—or worse, that she would tell him how she felt, that despite everything he was still the best person she knew, the most honest, the truest. It wouldn't matter, though, because the connection between them meant he already knew the truth in her heart.

"I don't know how you can look at me like that," she said, her voice shaking. She felt his surprise. "After all that I've done. All the pain I caused you."

Hector's jaw tightened. Beru suddenly felt a wave of emotion from him, something soft and fragile and *warm*.

It took her breath away.

"I forgive you," he said. "I—I don't want you to die."

Her eyes jolted up to meet his, and there she saw everything he did not say. That he'd grown to care for her, though he'd tried to fight it. That despite everything she was, he didn't want to let her go.

It didn't seem possible, that he could feel that way toward her. It *wasn't* possible. She was mistaken.

"I've lost everything," Hector replied. "My family. My place with the Order. Even my life. I can't lose you, too."

But since when had she been his to lose?

"It's you or me, Hector," Beru said softly. "It can't be both. You know that."

"Beru," he said, his voice taut with emotion. She hadn't known, until now, what her name sounded like on his lips.

He drew closer. Another wave of affection hit her, until she felt like she couldn't breathe. His hand cupped her elbow.

"You were willing to let me die once," Beru told him through uneven breaths.

"I know," he replied. "That was before."

"Before?"

He nodded. "My feelings changed."

His face was close to hers, his eyes fluttering shut. Beru longed to lean in and close the distance between them.

And then his words hit her and she pushed him back. His feelings had *changed*. Guilt turned her stomach. People didn't just go from loathing to love like that. Something had happened to Hector, something had made him feel this way.

"Beru, what—"

"I can't do this," she said in a rush, throwing off her covers and scrambling out of bed. "I can't—I just—I'm sorry."

She bolted through the door, leaving him in the room, alone.

Beru spent the night wandering the oasis, and in the morning she went to Azar's abode and found him puttering around the gardens.

"Good morning," he said without looking up.

"I need to ask you something," Beru said hesitantly.

"How wonderful," he said absently. "I love inquisitive minds."

"Well," Beru began. "Hector and I. The . . . connection between us. It's . . . more than just our *esha*. It seems like our emotions sometimes spill over."

And once, Beru had *purposely* let her emotions seep into Hector, letting him feel her pain and sadness to persuade him to come with her to Behezda. If she was capable of that, she was capable of worse.

Azar hummed. "When we die, our *esha* unbinds itself from us. *Esha* itself is just energy. It is only when it is bound to physical form that it becomes unique to the form it occupies. Nevertheless, if bound *esha* was taken from one form and put into another, it might still contain echoes of its first form, ties to the residual *esha* left behind. Those ties could manifest as a seepage between those forms."

Beru nodded. After leaving Charis, she and Ephyra had spent several months studying *esha* in whatever texts they could get their hands on in Tarsepolis. She understood the basic principles well enough, but this was something far outside of anyone's experience.

Beru hesitated. "Is it possible . . . could there be, uh, other . . . side effects from such a connection?"

"Side effects?" Azar asked, his brow wrinkling.

"Could it change the way those people felt? About each other?"

Azar seemed to think for a moment. "I suppose so, yes. If one had particularly strong feelings . . . feelings of hatred, or of love, those could bleed through to the other. It might become quite difficult to determine the origin of those feelings."

Beru looked down, feeling sick. It was all the confirmation she needed. Hector's feelings weren't real. They had been forced on him, his true feelings twisted beyond recognition because . . .

Because of Beru's feelings. *She* had forced this on him.

He didn't really want to save her. He only thought he did.

She had to tell him, she knew that much.

"I . . . I need to find him," Beru said, getting to her feet unsteadily.

Azar rose, too, and reached a hand to her wrist. "Are you all right?"

She wasn't. Beru's vision blotted out, her limbs weak. And then suddenly she was stumbling, falling against Azar's chest, clutching on to him as he lowered her to the floor.

Beru lay back and closed her eyes. A shadow fell over her.

"What did you do to her?" Hector's voice demanded.

Beru blinked her eyes open to find Hector's dark eyes staring into hers. "It's not—" she began weakly. She drew in a breath. "It's not his fault."

"What's happening?"

"Her *esha*," Azar said. "It's starting to fade again. I don't know how much longer she has."

"Then *do* something!" Hector demanded. "Heal her like you did last time. You can use my *esha* to do it."

Beru turned her head and saw Azar shaking his head slowly. "I'm afraid . . . that isn't an option this time. It would kill you."

Hector's whole body tensed. "There must be some other way."

"There is," Azar said. "The Chalice. If we knew where it was—"

"I'll find it," Hector said abruptly. "Whatever it takes, I'll find it. I'll go back to the Daughters, I'll make them tell me where it is. Just— don't let her die, all right? Keep her alive until I get back."

Beru tried to reach for him, but her arm felt heavy. Hector's attention refocused on her.

"It's not going to end like this," Hector said fiercely. "I won't let it."

"Hector," she said, trying to pull him down toward her. "I need to tell you something."

"What is it?" he asked, kneeling beside her, patient and warm in a way that made Beru's chest ache.

"It's not real," she said. "It's not . . ."

"You're not making any sense," Hector said. "It's all right. Just hold on. I promise I'll be back soon."

She felt so weak, as though she would black out at any moment. "No, Hector, listen. *Listen* to me, you . . . you can't . . ."

He stood, his eyes blazing at Azar. "Keep her safe until I get back, all right? I'm not losing another person I love."

Beru closed her eyes, wanting to cry. Hector thought he *loved* her. He was going to risk everything for her.

And it was a lie. But she had no strength left to explain the truth to him.

She could only watch as he walked away from her.

37

EPHYRA

IN THE HEIGHT OF SUMMER, BEHEZDA STANK.

The city sat on either side of a river that cut through a gorge of red rock. The water was shallow in the dry months, murky with silt and waste, perfuming the whole city with its stench. Ephyra had heard so many stories about Behezda, the City of Mercy, but the reality was a pale shadow of what she'd imagined.

Illya had set them up in a dark, creaky room inside one of the slouching buildings that lined the river. Ephyra didn't even remember how they'd gotten there or if Illya had paid for the room. None of it mattered.

She just remembered Illya steering her inside, telling her to sleep.

"I don't want to sleep," she'd said. "Come here."

When he'd hesitated, she'd sauntered toward him. "What? Are you scared of me?"

He hadn't moved as she stepped up to him, curling her hand around the back of his neck.

"Tell me this isn't what you want." She hadn't waited for his permission to seal their lips together.

"You don't," he'd said, breathing hard when they broke away. "You don't really want this."

She'd just kissed him harder, drowning her guilt and her grief in him. He took it all. She didn't want to feel anything but his hands on her, the heat and taste of him. The rest of the world had turned to ashes, and he was a fire she wanted to burn in.

"Right now, this is the only thing I want," she'd said, and then she'd pulled him down onto the bed with her.

In the morning, she woke to find him sitting on a stool beside the bed, staring out the door and toying with the metal cuff on his wrist, twisting it idly. Ephyra was suddenly, incomprehensibly furious.

"Go, then."

He glanced up at her. "What?"

She stalked toward him, standing over him so he had no choice but to look up at her.

"Leave," she said, clawing at the cuff on her wrist. She unlatched it and shoved it at his chest before walking away. "If you don't want to be here, then just go."

She looked at him, his expression confused, holding the cuff unsurely in his hand. Then he got up, and wordlessly walked through the door.

Ephyra watched him go, some broken piece of her shattering into dust. She still hated Illya, whatever had just happened between them didn't change that, but even a snake was better than having no one at all. The thought that she would *miss* him made her head go white with anger. It made something twist inside her gut to know that she had so little left in her life that to see Illya Aliyev walk away was a loss.

She stood there in the middle of the room, not knowing what to do, before she collapsed onto the bed and fell back asleep.

When she woke this time, it was to the smell of warm bread and grilled meat. Blearily, she rolled out of bed and stopped short. It took her a moment to process what she was seeing. Illya sat at the low table tucked into the far corner of the room, eating.

Ephyra took two steps toward him and then stopped.

"I got this from a street vendor around the corner," he said. "It's pretty good."

Hesitantly, Ephyra sat down at the table across from him.

"Here," he said, passing a jar of some sort of sauce to her. "You'll want that."

Ephyra watched him for a few more moments, uncomprehending, and then tore off a piece of warm flatbread and dipped it in the sauce. She ate it and Illya smiled up at her, like this was something normal, sharing a meal in a dingy little room. And it *was* normal. It was what normal people did, every single day. But not her.

After they ate, Illya cleaned up, almost fastidious, while Ephyra watched from the bed.

As he went to wipe down the table she rose and went to him, backing him against it. He turned to her and kissed her again. Ephyra lost herself in it, in him, the clawing creature inside her silent for now.

Heat scorched through her and she felt some part of her recoil in disgust while she pressed closer. It was both blessing and punishment, and each was a relief.

When she woke the next morning, Illya was still there.

Ephyra didn't know how long they'd been in Behezda. She slept through the days, waking only in the afternoon to choke down whatever food she could stomach. At night she haunted the city, keeping the Chalice close. Its power flowed through her, filling in her empty cracks and gnawing pain. She could feel its longing, its need for her to tap into its well of strength. She traced her fingers over it at night and imagined sucking the *esha* out of every person on the street.

She felt out of control in a way she never had before.

The only times she felt in control was in Illya's arms. They didn't talk about it. They didn't have to. Ephyra sought oblivion and Illya was happy to give it to her.

It didn't change anything between them. At least not in the ways she would expect. He was never soft with her—he'd taken what she said in the tomb to heart, and didn't try to win her over anymore. Every night they spent tangled in the sheets together only seemed to make her hate him more. And hating him made her want him more. And wanting him made her hate herself. He was the worst person she knew, the worst person she'd ever met who she hadn't killed, and finding release with him was easy, because she destroyed everything she touched and she didn't care if he was destroyed, too.

She *wanted* to destroy him. She wanted to burn everything down. She wanted to be the Pale Hand again, to punish everyone—herself most of all. She let Illya do it instead. She didn't know why he was still here, why he'd stayed with her, whether he wanted the Chalice for himself or just wanted to burn down everything the way she did.

It didn't matter. He had stayed, when no one else had, and if that didn't prove how awful she really was, she didn't know what would.

But that gnawing darkness would not let go, no matter how much she tried to drown it in Illya. And then there was the part of her she was afraid to even look at. Beyond the rage, beyond the grief. She couldn't even name it. But she knew what it was. Relief. Part of her was relieved that Beru was gone. And she hated herself for it.

She woke one night, after passing out beside Illya, and sat up in the dark. The Chalice was sitting on the bedside table. She remembered what it felt like to pull from its power, killing the Daughters of Mercy in the tomb of their dead queen.

She reached over and picked it up. She ran her fingers over the divots and engraved lines, mesmerized.

"I think it recognizes you," Illya said.

Ephyra startled, wrapping her hand around the stem of the Chalice. "What are you talking about?"

He sighed, rubbing a hand over his face and then kicking off the thin blanket. "I need to show you something."

He tapped on one of the incandescent lights and went over to the other side of the room, rifling through his things.

Ephyra sat perched at the edge of the bed, alarmed.

"You remember when you found me in the Thief King's hideout?"

Ephyra nodded.

"Well, I didn't just find the mirror and the other clue," he said, coming back to the bed. "I also found this."

He held an envelope out to her. It had clearly already been opened, the wax seal missing.

Ephyra took it with a shaking hand. She opened the letter hastily, pressing her fingers to her mouth when she saw that it was written in her father's unsteady scrawl.

"You read this?" she asked Illya.

He held his hands out and shrugged. "I was looking for clues about the Chalice."

Ephyra did not have the energy to be angry.

"I'm going to go for a walk," Illya said, heading toward the door. "I'll let you just—I'll be back."

Ephyra waited for the door to shut behind him before looking back down at the letter.

Dear Badis, she read, and then had to stop. This must be her father's letter to the Thief King, the one that had prompted Badis's brief warning.

> *If the Chalice exists, you don't want to go looking for it. The only thing you'll find is a quick death.*

Badis had been right, in the end. And it wasn't just her father who had found death.

Heart pounding, she read on.

> *Thank you for the gifts you sent last month, the girls loved them. I do regret that it's been so long since my last letter. The fact of the matter is that I have a favor to ask of you, and it's not exactly the usual kind.*

Ephyra wiped at her eyes. Her father's writing was so familiar, she could almost hear his voice, the gentle, hesitant way he spoke.

> *But first I should tell you about my daughter.*

Ephyra sucked in a bracing breath.

> *My eldest, Ephyra, did not have the most welcome start in life. When Cyrene was pregnant, she became very ill. It seemed impossible that she or the baby would survive. When we took her to a healer, they could not help her. But in my travels I had heard of a man, spoken of*

in hushed whispers. A powerful healer, more powerful than even the Daughters of Mercy. Eventually, I found someone who claimed to have met him. They told me where I could find him.

I returned home and packed up Cyrene, who was mere weeks away from giving birth. I knew that if we did not find this healer and persuade him to help us, the journey would kill her. But if we stayed home, she would die anyway. We went.

We found him out in the desert, in an oasis. We didn't know who he was, then. By the time we found him, it was almost too late. Cyrene was near death. The healer told us he would help us for a price. At that point I was desperate. He told me he wanted me to find Eleazar's Chalice. With no other choice, I agreed.

He healed Cyrene. Ephyra arrived two weeks later, perfectly healthy. We went on with our lives. We had another daughter. All was well, so we thought. And then the man who had told us where to find the healer came to me again. He told me he had lied to me, that the man he had led us to was not a healer—that he was a necromancer. That he'd kept himself alive for over five centuries. That he'd once been known as the Necromancer King. I didn't believe him at first. I had no reason to. I brushed him off.

Months later, Ephyra's Grace manifested. The Grace of Blood. Neither I nor Cyrene had any ancestors with

Grace. Of course, that is not so rare. But the things that our little girl could do with her power . . . it was like nothing I had ever seen.

Ephyra swallowed, eyes stinging. She remembered clearly the fear with which her parents had reacted when she'd begun using her powers for the first time. How once, she had accidentally killed a lizard in their yard just by touching it, and how her parents had looked at her afterward. Like they were afraid of her. She used to make plants grow out of seeds in the yard, just for the fun of it, until her parents caught her once and sharply told her to never do that again. Ephyra had cried herself to sleep that night, certain that her parents hated her, hated her Grace.

She had been right.

We have done our best to keep Ephyra's Grace hidden from the world. We fear that if anyone were to find out what she is, if word were to spread . . . the Necromancer King would find us. I fear he has already done so, and I fear what he will do to make sure we make good on the deal I made that desperate day. If I can find Eleazar's Chalice . . . I know it is much to ask you, to get involved in this. But please, my friend. I must protect my family.

Yours in desperation,
Aran

Ephyra closed her eyes, the tears falling freely as she clutched her father's letter in her hand. For the first time, she understood why her parents had seemed so afraid of her. They had feared only what her power would bring upon them. They had been disgusted only by the reminder of the choice they had made, to trust a man who called himself a healer.

But with this understanding came grief, deeper and more desolate than anything she'd ever felt. Her parents had been right to fear. Ephyra's power had brought death to their door. And this thing inside her, this darkness—it had a cause. The Necromancer King. It seemed impossible that he could still be alive after so many centuries—after Hadiza's story of how the Chalice had turned on him, the Daughters defeating him. But the yawning terror in her chest told her it was true. The worst villain in the history of the world had made Ephyra what she was—a monster.

Illya returned what must have been an hour later to find Ephyra still sitting on the bed, reading and rereading the letter.

"You're not afraid of me," Ephyra said, looking up at him.

He hesitated by the threshold. Perhaps her words were not entirely true. But then again, he'd come back.

"Do I need to be?"

Yes, the dark thing inside Ephyra answered. Everyone should be afraid of her. "You read the letter. You know what I am. Who made me this way."

He came closer, walking all the way over to the bed to sit beside her. "I don't believe anyone made you this way. The Necromancer King may have given you a piece of his power. Perhaps most of it. But that power is yours to wield."

And look at how she had chosen to wield it.

"The Daughters of Mercy knew," Ephyra said. "They must have. They were scared of me."

"Of course they were scared of you," Illya said. "They've spent their whole lives trying to uphold the rules. The natural law of life and death. But you're more powerful than they are. And you don't follow their rules. That's what separates the powerful from the weak. The powerful get to make the rules, and the weak have to follow them."

Ephyra didn't feel powerful right then, but she had while facing the Daughters. She'd lived on scraps for so long, killing because she had to and hiding in the rotten corners of the world because she was afraid. It had started with her parents' fear, with the guilt they'd thrust onto her because of what *they* had done.

And now, she had nothing. Nothing except all the power in the world. Power to face down the Daughters of Mercy and anyone else who tried to tell her how she ought to use it. Her parents, the Daughters of Mercy, the *world*—all of them feared her, and not because she had the power to kill but because her power meant she could break their rules.

She rolled out of bed. The Chalice was warm. It wanted her to use it.

"What are you doing?" Illya asked.

"Get up," Ephyra said. "You're going to help me."

"Help you do what, exactly?"

"Find me a victim."

The man's home was at the edge of the city. Ephyra found him there, alone.

He was a swindler, Illya had said. Taking advantage of the poorest and most vulnerable, promising them aid and then robbing them of everything they had.

Ephyra stepped through the front door.

The man jerked his head up. "What are you doing in my home?"

"What you do to those families," she began, "does it keep you up at night?"

He took a faltering step back. "W-what are you talking about?"

"I just want to know if you've ever once thought about the people you've cheated. The ones who have been left destitute because of you."

"H-how did you—"

"That's what I thought," Ephyra said, grabbing his throat.

The Chalice burned against her hip, where it was tucked among the folds of her makeshift cloak. Draining his *esha* was easier than ever. It felt *right*. Beru wasn't here anymore to make her feel guilty. And she didn't. These bastards got exactly what they deserved, and Ephyra was happy to be the vehicle of their comeuppance. It felt familiar.

This was her purpose. The Pale Hand was her destiny. She had the power to decide who lived and who died—not according to the laws of nature, not the tenets of right and wrong, but by *her* choice.

She was always meant to be the Pale Hand of Death. The Prophets had seen it, or so Beru had said. And now Ephyra did, too.

The man dropped to the ground, the pale handprint bright against his skin.

38

ANTON

ANTON HAD BARELY SLEPT A WHOLE NIGHT THROUGH SINCE THEY'D SET SAIL on *The Bellrose*. He dreamed of the lake, over and over, and every time, Jude was there. Anton supposed that he should count himself lucky to get to see Jude in his dreams—he certainly saw little of him while they were awake.

Since the night they'd kissed, things between them had been strained. Anton puzzled over it. Jude wanted him, he knew that—he'd told him as much, he'd kissed Anton back, and Anton could see it in how his gaze tracked him across rooms. But every time Anton wobbled too far into his orbit, Jude got this dark look in his eyes and a tightness in the bow of his mouth. Like wanting Anton was a punishment he had to endure.

So the days passed as they traveled north through the river gorge that cut between the Novogardian mountains. Anton spent his time making friends with the ship's crew, avoiding the Guard whenever he could, and trying to forget their destination. He grew more and more anxious as the days ticked by until even the Guard could tell something was wrong.

"You don't wish to go back there," Annuka said one night, when she was keeping watch over him.

"Not a lot of happy memories," he said.

"I'm sorry to hear that," Annuka said, and she did sound sorry. "It can be hard to return home."

"It's not really my home," he replied. "Nowhere is."

She nodded. "I understand. My home was not a place, either. It was people—my tribe. And when they disappeared, so did my home."

He could tell from the crack in her voice that this was painful to talk about, perhaps especially now that another home, Kerameikos, had also been taken away from her. He'd never known that kind of sadness. As far as he could tell, home was just whatever hurt most when you left it behind.

She looked at him, smiling but sad. "But we must never give up on finding a home. Sometimes you must make one for yourself."

"How?" he asked, before he could stop himself.

"You find something you want to come back to," Annuka replied. "And then you stay."

The next morning when Anton rose and went out to the deck, the air was freezing. They were close to his village, maybe a few hours away. Anton sidled over to one of the rails and leaned against it, looking out at the river and the surrounding mountains, capped with snow.

"There's ice in the river," said a deckhand named Adrien. He sounded offended. "*Ice*. In the middle of summer!"

"Welcome to the north," Anton said, stretching back against the rail.

"I can see why you left."

Anton laughed. "Yeah, that was the reason. I just can't stand the cold."

"Well, if you need help warming up," Adrien said lightly, flashing his teeth, "just let me know." He jogged off to help his crewmate secure the throw line.

Anton watched him walk away, amused. He turned back to go inside and saw Jude standing by the door that led into the main corridor. The look on his face made it clear he'd seen Anton's exchange with Adrien.

Jude turned abruptly on his heel, retreating into the corridor. Anton hesitated for a moment and then followed, cursing under his breath. He caught up to Jude halfway down the hallway, and looped his arm through Jude's elbow to drag him into the adjacent room.

"What are you doing?" Jude demanded.

"I thought we could talk," Anton offered. "You know. That thing we used to do." He glanced around and realized he'd dragged Jude into the Nameless Woman's private collection room, where they'd been caught sneaking around during her party.

Jude coolly stepped away from Anton. "Fine. What is it you want to talk about?"

"You could start by telling me how you are."

"I'm fine," Jude replied.

"Is that why you won't be in the same room as me?" Anton asked. "Why you can't even look at me sometimes?"

Jude tensed, and when he looked at Anton there was anger in his eyes. "And what should I be doing instead? Should I be flirting with the deckhands and pretending that you never—" He glanced around and lowered his voice to a hiss. "That you never kissed me?"

"You *wanted* us to pretend it didn't happen. To go back to normal."

Jude shook his head, looking at one of the glass walls and let out a hollow laugh. "You didn't need to make it seem so easy."

"You turned *me* down, so stop acting like I'm the one who hurt you," Anton said, an edge of anger creeping into his voice.

"It wasn't like that, and you know it," Jude said hotly.

"Then how was it?" Anton demanded, pushing into Jude's space.

"I saw how you were at the Hidden Spring. How you were with Evander and with—" He waved his hand to indicate the deckhand. "You flirt and you do whatever you want because it doesn't mean anything to you, but every time I look at you all I can I think about is that kiss and *I can't stand it.*"

Anton's breath caught in his throat and his gaze flickered from Jude's bright green eyes to the bow of his lips. Anton could still remember what those lips had felt like on his own. That kiss had been an impulse, a disastrous attempt to comfort Jude. But now, wanting to do it again—that was just selfish.

Jude seemed to realize their closeness and reeled back. "You don't get it. To you, that was just a stupid kiss. But to *me*? It could ruin everything."

His voice broke on the last word and Anton couldn't help but think of another argument, in the storeroom in Kerameikos. Jude's bitter defeat. The reckless request Anton had made, knowing it would change nothing. *Come with me.*

"I know what it meant to you," Anton said, forcing the words out. "I know what the Order demands of you, and I know it's not what you want, not really. But maybe that's easier for you. Maybe the only way you can want something is if you don't let yourself have it."

Jude swallowed roughly and Anton felt like the biggest fool in the world because for a moment he thought Jude would lean in and kiss him again.

Instead, Jude dropped his arm and turned away, leaving Anton with his back against the wall, breathing hard.

They docked in Lukivsk a few hours later. The small harbor was five miles from Anton's old home. They hiked through midmorning, Anton's breath coming out in puffs of fog. The chill settled into his bones like dread. He was about to face the past he'd been trying to run from for over six years.

Shame welled up inside Anton as they reached his home. The hut looked so much smaller than he remembered, leaning between two tall pines. It looked like it had been abandoned for years. And maybe it had. The last time Anton had set foot here was over six years ago. His brother Illya had left not long after that.

Father's probably drunk himself to death, Illya had said. *And as for our dear old grandmother . . . well, if you can survive on spite alone, I imagine she's right where we left her.*

He was about to find out if that was true. He paused at the bottom of the path, barely visible through layers of mud and weeds, and looked up at that dark, cramped space where he had spent so many nights huddling in fear, wishing he were anywhere, *anywhere* else.

The Paladin Guard stood behind him. He could feel Jude at his side. Even if he would barely look at him, Anton knew with more certainty than he'd ever known anything that Jude would keep him from harm.

Penrose fell to her knees and let out a sound. Anton started toward her, fear flooding his veins, wondering if somehow his grandmother had—

But a hand held him back. He glanced behind him, where Petrossian had a hand clamped over his wrist.

"This is a holy place," he told Anton. "The birthplace of the Last Prophet."

Something like anger roiled in Anton's chest. This place wasn't holy. It was a nightmare. One that he'd ripped himself from at the tender age of eleven, throwing himself to the mercy of the streets.

"Doesn't feel holy to me," Anton replied, shaking Petrossian's hand off.

Ahead of them, Penrose got to her feet. The other Paladin joined her at the top of the path. All except Jude. He hung back, watching Anton with wary eyes.

"What?" Anton demanded.

Jude averted his gaze. "You told me what happened here, remember? I just want to make sure you'll be all right."

Anton knew exactly how to read Jude, and the last few weeks had only made him better at it. He'd forgotten, however, that Jude knew how to read him right back. Even after their fight, even when they were both angry with each other, Jude was worried. It made him want to press himself into Jude's arms.

"I'll let you know if I start feeling like drowning myself in the lake."

Jude frowned and Anton suddenly couldn't stand to look at him anymore.

"Let's just go," he said, blustering ahead and leaving Jude to choose either to follow or get left behind.

"It's locked," Penrose informed him when he joined the rest of the Guard at the door. "No answer, either. We'll have to break it down."

Anton shook his head, stepping up to the door. He and Illya had gotten very good at unlatching the door from the outside so that they could let themselves back in when their grandmother locked them out. He braced one hand against the doorjamb, and with the other, twisted the knob, shoving the door up and back. It creaked open.

The sight of the drab, musty living room filled Anton with loathing and familiar dread. The same ratty gray carpet blanketed the scratched floors where he and Illya used to play card games. The same rotting wooden chairs slouched in front of the soot-covered hearth where they'd warmed their frostbitten toes in the winter. Moth-eaten drapes framed a grubby window that looked out onto the lake where Anton had almost drowned.

"Who are you?" a rasping voice demanded. "What are you doing in my house?"

Anton swung his gaze to the corner of the room where a figure stood.

"My . . . boy," the figure croaked. She let loose a hacking cough that went on for almost a full minute. "My sweet Anton. Is that really you?"

Anton couldn't move. He felt the expectant gazes of the Paladin. Jude shifted closer to his side. Anton stared at his grandmother. She looked crumpled and gaunt, far older than she had six years ago. She was bent over a gnarled cane, her legs much too frail and skinny to hold her up on their own.

"Are you Uliana, descendant of Vasili?" Jude asked.

His grandmother's eyes narrowed. "Who's asking?"

"Madame," Penrose said. "We are the Paladin Guard of the Order of the Last Light."

"Servants of the blasphemous Prophets," Anton's grandmother spat. "What are you doing with my Anton?"

Penrose glanced at Anton and then back to his grandmother. "We're in search of something. Perhaps you know where it is."

"Like I would give anything away to the servants of Vasili's greatest enemies!" his grandmother snarled.

"Babiya," Anton said, using the name he'd once called her. "These are my friends. Please, listen to them."

Her features softened and she shuffled closer to Anton. "My darling boy. I knew you'd come back to fulfill the destiny left to you by Vasili. I knew you wouldn't abandon me like that ungrateful, worthless brother of yours."

Anton had to force himself to step toward her, leaving the warmth of Jude's side. "That's right. I'm here to fulfill my destiny. But I need your help."

She hobbled to him, raising her dry, papery hands to touch his face. "At last," she crooned. "At last, at last."

Anton watched her features contort with ecstasy. Her eyes seemed too big for their sockets. He wondered how he had ever been afraid of her. She was old, and weak, and completely out of her mind.

"We need your help," Anton said again. "Is there anything you have of Vasili's?"

"Vasili?" his grandmother repeated. "Yes. Yes. Let me show you." She turned away and started shuffling to a corner of the room, where the books were kept. She plucked one from the shelf, shook off the dust, and began paging through it.

Anton went to her, gesturing at Jude to stay put.

"Here," she said, thrusting the opened book at him.

"His writings?" Anton asked. He looked down. "I thought these were all in Kerameikos."

"No," his grandmother replied with some disdain. "I salvaged some of them from the Prophets' minions. The most important ones. I had planned to give them to you when you were older. So that you would see."

"See what?"

She tapped the page. Anton squinted down at it.

I cannot see the future as the Prophets do, but now I have finally done what no one save for them has. I have seen into the past. Seen the legends of old with my own eyes.

"Vasili scried into the past?" Anton asked. "That's not possible, is it?"

"I suppose ... theoretically, it could be," Penrose said. "But it would take power, more than just the normal power of the Grace of Sight."

"You mean like the power of a Relic?" Anton asked.

Penrose didn't answer.

"What did he see?" Jude asked.

Anton looked down at the book. "'I search for the truth of where they began,'" Anton read aloud. "'How the holy Sight was first bestowed on them.' He wanted to know how the Prophets got their abilities. I think because he wanted them for himself."

"He did," his grandmother said. "But he found so much more than that."

"What do you mean?"

"He saw the beginnings of it all," his grandmother replied. Her eyes were glazed over, rapturous, as though she, like Vasili, could peer into the past. "He spoke to the one who created us all."

Anton remembered with a start the passage he'd read in the Kerameikos archives. *He wants to speak to me.*

This was what Vasili had done. By using the Relic of Sight to speak with the ancient god, he had broken the Four-Petal Seal.

"The ancient divinity spoke to him from the past," his grandmother went on. "He told him what was to come. And Vasili saw what the Prophets did to him. How they betrayed him and destroyed him."

"Enough!" Penrose cried. "Enough of these mad ramblings."

His grandmother swung around to fix Penrose with a stare. "Mad ramblings? Oh, yes, that is what they said about Vasili, too. That he was a madman, a raving king. And look where it got them."

"Babiya," Anton said. "Can you tell us where the Relic is? It would be a stone. Maybe Vasili used it to scry. Where is it?"

"Do you know how Vasili died?" she asked.

Anton nodded, but his grandmother pressed on anyway.

"He drowned himself," she said. "Walked into the lake, his wrists and ankles weighed down with stones."

Anton stood at the edge of the lake, watching the water slowly lap up toward his feet. Jude hovered a few paces away.

"Are you sure you'll be all right?" Jude asked.

"The Relic is somewhere in this lake," Anton replied. "We can't just dive down and search every stone. This is the only way to figure out where it is."

"That doesn't answer my question."

"I know."

Jude drew toward him, as if he wanted to embrace him, but then thought better of it and pulled back. "I'll be right here the whole time."

Anton felt the chill of the space between them, colder than the water at his ankles as he slowly waded in. He was already trembling. This was the place where he'd first had his vision, though his mind had pushed it down and sealed itself off from the trauma.

But now that he was back here, the false memory fell away and Anton remembered the cold bite of snow on his skin and that force, pulling him forward and forward into the lake.

"Anton?"

Jude's voice sounded hazy and indistinct behind him. Anton closed his eyes. He could feel the dark water of the lake pulling him down. He felt it press on his lungs.

"Anton!"

Jude's voice was much closer now, and there were hands on his shoulders, shaking him. Anton leaned into his warmth on instinct, wrapping one arm under Jude's. Jude just stood there, frozen.

Anton closed his eyes and fought the urge to cry. He pulled away from Jude.

"I'm fine," he said. He didn't look at Jude's face. "Sorry. I'm fine. I can do this."

He turned back to the lake. Taking a deep breath, he raised the smooth stone in his hand. It wasn't a real scrying stone, just one Jude had found at the lakeshore, but he figured it would work well enough. Closing his eyes, he dropped it into the water.

He felt the ripples it created and followed them out to each edge of the lake, reaching out with his Grace. He focused not on a name, not on the *esha* unique to a single person, but on his own Grace, letting it pull him through the sacred energy of the world to its origin. He felt it pulsing like a heart, warm and beating below the water.

He opened his eyes. He could feel the faint pulse of the Relic, drawing him toward the center of the lake. Jude was right beside him again, his hand on Anton's back. Anton realized he was shaking.

"Did you find it?" Jude asked softly.

Anton nodded, and Jude signaled to the rest of the Guard. They stood around a small watercraft, a boat that had once belonged to

Anton's father. They pushed it down the shore and it slid into the water. When they pulled up beside Anton and Jude, Petrossian and Osei held out their hands. Anton took Petrossian's, hoisting himself inside the boat.

"This way," Anton said, pointing toward where the Relic pulsed below the water. Jude lifted a paddle and threaded it through the water, angling the boat toward the Relic.

"Here," Anton said, when they reached the right spot on the lake. He could feel the Relic, pulsing stronger than ever.

Jude put down the paddle and shrugged out of his cloak. He set the Pinnacle Blade down and peeled off his shirt. With one last glance at Anton, he dove into the water.

Anton leaned over the edge of the boat and watched as the water rippled over Jude and then settled. He could feel Jude's Grace below the surface. The seconds ticked by excruciatingly slow.

And then Anton felt something tug from below. Like a dark, clawed shadow, taking hold of Jude and dragging him to the bottom of the lake.

The Relic. It had pulled Anton down all those years ago, and now it was going to trap Jude.

Without pausing to consider, Anton dove into the water. The cold of it bit into his skin. He gritted his teeth and pressed on, cutting through the water toward where he could feel Jude's Grace. The light at the surface of the lake faded as Anton kicked toward darkness.

He saw the bubbles first. Little pockets of air rising through the water. And then he saw Jude, floating in the blackness, his eyes closed and his face still.

Anton's heart stuttered in his chest at the sight, and he kicked with all his strength, propelling himself toward him. He looped his arms around Jude, pulling him back into Anton's chest, the panic overtaken by cold, deliberate calm. He had to get Jude to safety. It was the only thing that mattered. He looked up at the wavering light at the surface of the lake and kicked toward it.

Jude was lifeless in his arms as Anton dragged him toward the surface. At last, they burst out of the water. They bobbed there for a moment, Anton sucking in air and trying desperately to keep Jude afloat. He looked around, spotted the boat, and then dragged Jude toward it.

He felt someone grab hold of Jude, lifting his limp body into the boat.

Anton scrambled up after him, kneeling over him and cradling his face between his hands.

"Wake up, wake up," Anton pleaded, shaking him. "Please, Jude. Please!"

Someone was kneeling on Jude's other side. Anton glanced over and saw it was Osei, who had helped get Jude back into the boat. The other Paladin, he noted, were in the water around them. Evidently they'd all dived in when Anton had gone after Jude.

Anton didn't care. He leaned over Jude, pressing his cheek against his bare chest.

You can't do this to me, Anton thought furiously. *You can't leave me.* He could feel Jude's heart, beating faintly under his cheek. He wasn't sure when or how it had come to this, but Anton knew with frightening certainty that the idea of living without the swordsman was unfathomable.

Jude seized under Anton's hands, a wet gasp bursting from his chest. Anton flung himself backward, keeping his hands on Jude's arms as he turned to the side and coughed water onto the deck. Jude sucked in a breath and coughed even more, his whole body shuddering. Anton ran his hand through Jude's wet hair. At last, the coughing subsided, and Jude closed his eyes, leaning his head on its side against the floor of the boat.

"I got it," he said weakly.

"What?" Anton asked, still fussing over him.

Jude didn't answer, just uncurled one of his fists. A smooth, olive-sized stone, as black as onyx, slipped from it. It hung off a rusted silver chain, and there was a strange, shimmering glow around it. In his desperation to get to Jude, Anton hadn't spared the Relic a thought.

"Let's see it," Penrose said when they reached the shore.

Jude held out the Relic in his palm. Anton's hand shook as he reached for it. He dragged his gaze up to Jude's face, and Jude's eyes flickered up to meet it. They both held there for a moment.

This was it. The Relic of Sight, the thing that had caused Anton to have his vision here so many years ago. The catalyst that had started it all.

Anton squeezed his eyes shut and curled his fingers around the stone. And then he was falling, falling like he had from the top of the lighthouse, and when he landed it was in a familiar place.

A city of ruins. A red sky. A shadow over the sun. A colossal gate carved into the red canyon walls. Its shadow loomed over the maze of crumbling ruins. In the center stood one sagging wall of a broken tower. Beside it, Beru lay as still as a corpse, her eyes closed. Smoke twisted around her. He saw it billowing off four objects—a sword, a stone. A crown of gold. And a chalice.

Bright light, pale and cold like Godfire, streamed into Beru.

Flashes of destruction assaulted him. The falling of the Six Prophetic Cities.

And now he knew what would destroy them. Or rather *who*.

39

HASSAN

HASSAN STARED AT THE PASSAGE DOORWAY, UNCERTAINTY LURCHING IN HIS gut. Was he really going to do this? Lie to everyone he trusted? Lie to Khepri?

He would if it could set Nazirah free. He'd done it before.

The passage door creaked open, and Hassan stepped out. At first, no one seemed to notice him. Then he heard the smack of something hitting the ground, and saw a soldier had dropped a stack of books and was staring at him. Along with everyone else in the room.

"Uh," Hassan stuttered. "Hello. I'm back."

No one moved for a moment. And then Hassan saw Chike jab his brother in the gut. Sefu ran off, and Hassan realized with a sinking heart that he'd gone to get Khepri. She appeared beside him a moment later and froze in the entryway. Hassan felt frozen, too.

And then something snapped, and Khepri was marching toward him, her mouth set and her eyes hard, and Hassan didn't know whether she was about to punch him or kiss him. She just stood there, staring at him.

"Are you all right?" she asked after a long moment.

"Yes," he said. "I'm fine."

She nodded. "Good. That's—good."

She clearly didn't know what to say to him any more than he knew what to say to her. Their argument seemed to hang between them like a shadow.

"Does Arash know you're back?" she asked after a moment.

"I was about to go speak with him."

She nodded, still staring.

"I can take you to him," Chike offered, breaking the silence, which was beginning to grow awkward.

"Thank you," Hassan said, tearing his gaze from Khepri. He moved past her, following Chike through the door.

"Hassan, I—" Khepri began.

Hassan turned back, hope brimming in him that she was about to apologize, or throw her arms around him.

But she just said, "I'm glad you're back."

Hassan's gaze lingered on her for a moment before he replied, "Me too."

He followed Chike down the corridor, Khepri's barking voice behind him telling the others to get back to their business. People stared unabashedly as Hassan passed.

"She really lost it when you left," Chike said. "She was out most nights searching for you, actually. Sefu and I were worried she was getting reckless. Haven't seen her like that since the coup."

Hassan didn't think Chike intended to make him feel guilty, but he did nevertheless.

"Here we are," Chike said, clapping Hassan on the shoulder as they stopped in front of the door to Arash's office.

Hassan gave a faint smile in return and then took a deep breath and knocked on the door.

"Who is it?" Arash's weary voice inquired.

"It's Hassan," he said.

There was silence on the other side of the door. Hassan put a hand over his eyes, already regretting his decision.

A moment later, the door clicked open.

Hassan stood in the doorway, staring at Arash, who was still sitting at his desk. Arash waved some small object in his hand.

"This opens it," he said, gesturing at the door. "I invented it."

"Oh," Hassan replied. "You must be wondering why I came back."

"Not really."

"I overreacted the other day," Hasan said. "I was angry with you and with—with myself. But now I've had time to think. And while I was aboveground, I saw how horrifically our people are suffering at Lethia's hands. So I came to say that you're right. I've been playing it too safe. The Witnesses certainly aren't going to pull their punches and neither should we. I guess I lost sight of who the real enemy was and I just . . . I want to make amends."

"Do you?" Arash asked, unimpressed.

Hassan was beginning to get annoyed.

"You want to prove you're really on our side?" Arash asked.

"Yes," Hassan answered at once, but his stomach twisted. What would Arash ask him to do to prove his loyalty? Something worse than causing a crowd of innocent civilians to riot against their will?

"Then I want you to get it for me," he said.

"It?" Hassan echoed.

"The Crown," Arash answered.

"The Crown of . . . Herat?"

"No," Arash said impatiently, looking at Hassan like he was an idiot. "The Crown that was given to the first king of Herat by the Prophet Nazirah. The Crown that will turn the tide of this battle."

"Oh," Hassan said, relieved for a moment that Arash wasn't outright asking to rule the kingdom. "I told you that I don't know where it is."

"And I know you were lying about that."

"I wasn't," Hassan insisted, perhaps the first truthful thing he'd said. An idea suddenly glimmered to life in his mind. "But I can search for it. I know more about my family's history than anyone, so if there's some record of what happened to the Crown, I'll find it."

It would be the perfect cover for his real goal—finding the text that the Hierophant wanted. He could spend all the time he needed scouring the stacks of the Great Library.

Arash watched him with careful, disbelieving eyes. "Then I suppose you should get to work."

After three days Hassan had found nothing—neither the Crown nor the Hierophant's scroll. The Hierophant had given him very little information. All Hassan knew was that he was looking for some sort of covenant, older than the city itself, that was marked with the symbol of a compass rose. He'd scoured the ancient texts' vault. Twice.

On the fourth day, Khepri found him in the royal family's private collection wing. Glass cases displayed artefacts and documents that had been collected over the centuries and deemed noteworthy by the Seif line. When this was all over, Hassan would add his own selections to it.

"What are you doing here?" Hassan asked as Khepri entered.

She looked taken aback by his tone, which had been harsher than he'd intended.

"I just wanted to check on you," she said. "Now that you're not—I mean, we don't see each other as often."

Hassan had requested his own room when he'd returned to the Library. Partly to keep his search a secret, partly because he didn't know whether he'd be welcome in his old room with Khepri, and partly because he couldn't stand the thought of having to constantly lie to her.

"Well, you found me," Hassan said.

"You aren't really taking Arash's demand seriously are you? Proving yourself to him?" Khepri asked, running her finger along the edge of an ivory blade carved from an elephant's tusk.

This was why he'd been avoiding her. "It's not that I need to prove myself—I think he might be right about the Crown. Remember what you said about rebuilding? This could help us do that."

"You changed your mind, then," Khepri said. Hassan didn't say anything. "Let me help you."

The light streaming in from the high windows cast her in gold. It felt like a peace offering, and even though it would complicate matters, Hassan was too desperate to make things right between them to say no.

Hassan laughed, trying not to sound as nervous as he felt. "I think you're probably better suited to the action."

Khepri looked affronted. "Excuse you, just because I'm strong doesn't mean I don't know how to read."

"That's not what I meant," Hassan said, a smile breaking loose on his face. It felt nice to joke with her again. Like old times.

"Of course not." She picked up a knife, tossing it from one hand to the other.

"Be careful with this stuff," Hassan warned. "You don't know what it does."

Khepri grinned and spun the knife in her hand. "You really think your family is hiding the Crown down here?"

"No," Hassan admitted, examining a record his great-great grand-mother had evidently added to the collection. It declared the admittance of non-Herati scholars to the Great Library, a decision that had ushered in a golden age of innovation in Herat. "But there may be some evidence of it."

"Well, where's the oldest stuff in here? From the time of the first king?"

Hassan didn't answer. He couldn't keep the memories from surfacing. His father had taken him to this wing of the Library many times before. He knew it better than some of the rooms in the palace.

Legacy, his father had always said. *This is our legacy.*

This place connected Hassan to his past, to his future. And it connected him to his father. He could almost see him, standing in the room, his gentle smile as he talked to Hassan about the history of Nazirah. Their history.

He felt a touch at his elbow and turned to find Khepri standing beside him.

"Are you all right?" she asked.

"I don't know," he answered honestly.

He saw Khepri's tender expression, and had to look away. He spotted a familiar golden crocodile statue in the corner of the room. It brought on another memory—and a hunch.

Every time they visited this wing, without fail, his father would stop at the statue and touch the crocodile's snout. They weren't supposed to touch anything in the room, and his father always did it with a little wink, like he was getting away with something.

Hassan had asked him, once, the significance of the crocodile, who seemed out of place in this room of official documents and items of historical significance.

"He's the most important thing in this room," his father had replied. "The keeper of Nazirah's oldest secrets."

Hassan had never really known if his father was just teasing him. For all he knew, the crocodile was just a gift to the royal family from an important nobleman or something.

There was only one way to find out.

Hassan drifted over to the crocodile. The gold snout was cold under his fingers. The crocodile's eyes gleamed at him. Hassan stopped short. A symbol was carved into one of them. A circle with four points—a compass rose.

Hassan glanced at Khepri, waiting until she turned away before he leaned closer to inspect the crocodile. Curled within its mouth, what Hassan had at first assumed to be a tongue, was a piece of parchment. He ran his hand over the crocodile's teeth. He had the sudden, absurd impression that its jaw would snap shut on his fingers. He yanked his hand away.

The crocodile's eye peered at him. Without thinking, Hassan pressed a finger to it.

The crocodile's jaw snapped open. Hassan leapt back, heart pounding for a moment until he realized the crocodile had not, in fact, just come alive. But its jaw was now open wide enough for Hassan to reach in with shaking hands and pull out the parchment. It was sealed with wax, impressed with the same compass rose symbol as the crocodile.

This was it. This was what the Hierophant wanted. Hassan

unfurled it with shaking fingers. Like the Hierophant had said, it was a covenant, that looked to be signed in blood.

We, the Protectors of the Lost Rose, sign and seal this covenant, which serves as the first, and only, record of our existence, and the existence of the Four Sacred Relics:

The Crown of Herat, given to the first king by Nazirah the Wise. The first of the Four Relics, the source of the Grace of Mind.

The Crown? Was the Hierophant after it, too? And according to this, it wasn't just a powerful artefact, it was the *source* of the Grace of Mind. Did Arash know? And why did his father have this covenant?

Hassan kept reading.

The Pinnacle Blade, given to the first Keeper of the Word by Pallas the Faithful. The second of the Four Relics, the source of the Grace of Heart.

The Blood Chalice, given to the Sacrificed Queen by Behezda the Merciful. The third of the Four Relics, the source of the Grace of Blood.

The Oracle Stone, kept by the Wanderer, the last of the Four Relics and source of the Grace of Sight.

These Four Relics are the remains of the Great Deity, the Creator, the one who the Prophets slew. The powers bestowed by these Relics are the powers of the God, given to these mortals by the Prophets. Our duty is to protect them, to keep them from falling into the hands of those who might abuse their power.

Hassan almost dropped the scroll. The powers of an ancient god? That couldn't possibly be real.

What had his father been doing, hiding a text like this?

"Hassan?" Khepri said, her voice ringing through Hassan's whirling thoughts.

Hassan scrunched up the scroll and turned around swiftly.

She stepped close. "What is that? Did you find it?"

"No," Hassan said, too loud and too quick. "This is just some old list of court advisors."

"Well, I don't think we're going to find anything in here. Let's go to dinner and we can keep looking tomorrow."

Hassan waited until Khepri turned away to stuff the scroll into his pocket.

Whatever this text was, true or not, he was now fairly certain that Arash and the Hierophant were after the same thing—the Crown.

Hassan had to keep them both from getting it.

40

BERU

BERU GROANED, ROLLING ONTO HER SIDE. HER HEAD SWAM AS SHE OPENED her eyes against the glare of the sun.

"Hector," she mumbled. "Where's—Hector."

Someone gripped her arm, helping her sit up. "There's a dear. You're all right now."

Beru wiped at her eyes and turned to face Azar. His gaunt face swam before her.

The memory of Hector walking away came back to her. "Hector," she said again, jolting forward to grab Azar's shoulders. "You need to go after him. Please. I'm not strong enough, and I can't let him do this."

"If I go, we must both go," Azar said. "I cannot leave you here to die."

"Then I'll die out there," Beru said. "I'm too weak."

"Not if I restore you again."

"I thought you needed Hector for that," Beru said uncertainly.

"Not necessarily," Azar replied. "Not if I can take enough *esha* from somewhere else."

"No," Beru said. "I won't let another person die for me."

"Not a person," Azar said. "But a place."

Beru swallowed. "What . . . what do you mean?"

Azar gestured around them. "This oasis. There is so much *esha* contained here. Much more than the amount needed to fuel a single person's life. If I sucked all the *esha* from every living thing here—it would be enough."

"You would do that?" Beru asked. "Destroy your home for me?"

Azar's lips curled. "My dear girl. Haven't you figured it out yet?"

Beru's stomach dropped.

"This place isn't my home. It's my prison."

Beru reeled back. "What are you talking about? What prison?"

"The Daughters of Mercy put me here," Azar said, gazing out at the turquoise pools and the swaying palms. "They didn't know what else to do with me, you see. I was too powerful. Too powerful for them to kill. So they took the *esha* of everyone I'd brought back and used it to make this place. It became my prison—I needed its life to sustain me, for if I try to venture too far, I begin to fade. Much like you."

"Everyone you brought back?" Beru asked. "You mean—"

"Yes," Azar said, his eyes flashing. "Like your dear sister, I know how to raise the dead. In fact, you might say I mastered it."

"It was *you*," Beru realized. "You're the one who brought Hector back."

Azar smiled. "Thought you'd figure it out sooner."

"But *why?*"

"As a favor, to an old friend," Azar replied. "She brought him to me and asked me to resurrect him. So I did."

"Who are you?" she asked. Not just anyone could bring back the dead. Aside from Ephyra, Beru had only ever heard of one other person who could.

"I was a king, once," he said in a tone that was almost wistful. "Until they took that away from me and left me here to rot."

"You can't be him," she said, her voice shaking. "The Necromancer King lived almost five hundred years ago."

"I look rather good for my age, don't I?" he said, sweeping a hand down his arm. "As I told you when you arrived here, the oasis provides all I need. But now that you're here, I no longer require it."

"What do you want?" Beru demanded. Her voice shook. Hector was gone, and she was alone with one of the most dangerous men to ever live.

"I have been trapped in this oasis for almost five hundred years. All I want is my freedom. And you can give it to me."

"Your freedom," Beru echoed. "And then what?"

"And then my revenge."

"It's been five hundred years," Beru said. "Whoever did this to you is long since dead. The Daughters of Mercy—"

"Not the Daughters," the Necromancer King spat. "The ones they serve. The ones who foresaw my downfall."

"The Prophets?" Beru asked. "They're . . . they're gone. It's been over a hundred years since they disappeared."

"They are not gone," the Necromancer King said. "They simply don't want to be found."

"That's . . . impossible."

"And just a few moments ago, you believed it was impossible that the Necromancer King could still be alive."

"Why are you even telling me this?" Beru asked.

"Because we were meant to find each other, Beru of Medea," the

Necromancer King said, his fingers brushing the curls beside her ear tenderly. "We can help each other. Once I've filled you with the *esha* of this oasis, I can siphon it from you the way I have siphoned it from my prison these last few centuries. And once I have the Chalice, I can give you your life back."

"I won't help you," Beru said. "Whatever it is you're doing I—I won't be a part of it."

"My dear," the Necromancer King said. "It is charming that you think you have a choice."

His long fingers wrapped around her wrist and a surge of warm *esha* flowed through her. She gasped, watching as the copse of palm trees around them shriveled and died. The song of the birds above stopped abruptly and dozens of dark shapes plummeted to the ground. Sand overtook the grass. All around them the oasis withered and crumbled.

The Necromancer King released Beru's wrist and she fell to her knees in the sand. Wind swirled around her. Energy surged in her veins. She felt alight with it, every part of her tingling with life.

"The Chalice has been reawakened." The Necromancer King held out his hand. "It's time to go."

The *esha* swirling inside Beru felt like a roiling sea.

"I'm not going with you," she said. "You need me to leave this place, don't you? Well, I won't."

"That is rather unfortunate," the Necromancer King said. "I thought you wanted your swordsman to stay alive."

Beru looked up at him, realizing with horror what he meant. "You can't hurt him. He's gone."

"Your *esha* is connected to his," the Necromancer King replied. "I can pull it out through you."

"You're . . . you're lying," she said.

"Am I?"

Beru dug her fingers into the sand as the *esha* of the oasis shrieked inside her. She could let him kill her in this hollowed-out place. Let Hector die, too. Or she could go with the Necromancer King and hope to stop whatever he had planned.

She took his hand.

41

JUDE

JUDE PACED IN FRONT OF THE TENT IN THE CAMP THE PALADIN HAD SET UP about a league away from the lake. The air was growing cooler as the light faded in the sky. Annuka and Yarik were working on starting a fire.

Anton lay within the tent. Three hours had passed since he had collapsed after touching the Relic of Sight. Jude touched the Stone where it was tucked into his cloak pocket. It felt strangely cold, like it was forged from ice instead of stone.

"Any change?"

Jude glanced up and saw Osei standing a few feet away. Jude looked toward the entrance of the tent and shook his head.

"You should get some rest, too," Osei went on. "You nearly drowned."

"I'm fine," Jude replied, shaking his head. "I just wish I—"

"He'll be all right," Osei assured him. Then, after a moment, "He dove right in after you, you know."

There was something in Osei's tone that made Jude instantly wary.

"I think he cares about you."

Jude looked away. He could no longer guess at what Anton did or didn't feel toward him. And it didn't matter, anyway.

"He's the Prophet," he replied. The same thing he'd said to Anton. The same thing he'd been saying to himself over and over.

There was a sudden rustling sound and then Anton emerged from the tent, blinking out into the twilight. Osei was at his side at once, asking him how he was feeling. Jude just froze in place, watching as Osei explained what had happened after Anton touched the Relic.

Anton was silent for a moment. "I saw it again. My vision."

Jude's eyes widened.

"There was something about it that I didn't understand, the first time," Anton went on. "But I understand it now."

"What do you mean?" Jude asked.

Anton took a breath. "The ancient god. The one that Vasili believed spoke to him. The one they say the Prophets killed. He's real. And he's going to return, unless we stop him."

"This is impossible," Penrose said. It was not the first time she'd said it. No amount of explanation on Anton's part had gotten her to budge an inch. "The god *isn't real*. There's no way he's getting resurrected when he never existed in the first place."

"I'm just telling you what I saw," Anton replied. "You have to admit, no one knows where the Relics came from or how the Prophets got their powers. So isn't it possible—"

"No, it isn't," Penrose replied sharply. "Because what you're trying to tell me is that the Prophets were responsible for the slaying of a *god*.

And we know that to be a vicious lie invented to discredit and slander them."

"*Or it's the truth that the Prophets tried to bury,*" Anton shot back. "But you can't afford to believe it because it would mean that everything the Order stands for is a lie."

Penrose swallowed, flinching like she'd been struck.

"Jude," Anton said pleadingly. "You're the Keeper of the Word. You're the one who decides. Stop a god from being resurrected, or do nothing."

Jude closed his eyes. Anton was right about one thing. If what he'd seen in his vision was true, it meant that the Order of the Last Light was built on lies. Lies the Prophets had told them about where they had come from. Lies that meant that the Prophets—not the Witnesses, not the Hierophant—were responsible for the Age of Darkness.

He wasn't sure if he could accept that. And he *knew* Penrose couldn't. The Order of the Last Light meant everything to her. It had been her guiding light for her entire life.

With one stroke, Anton wanted to take that away from her. From all of them. If Jude couldn't believe in the Prophets, in the Order, what could he believe in?

"We all need to get some rest," Jude said. "We can talk about this in the morning."

He couldn't face the betrayal in Anton's eyes. Nor the fury in Penrose's. He turned to go back inside his tent.

Penrose pushed her way in after him. "I need to talk to you."

"It can wait until morning."

"It can't," she said. "It's about the Prophet."

"He's fine."

"But *you're* not." She took a breath. "I know you better than anyone, Jude. I know why you can't get your Grace back."

"Why is that?" Jude asked, his voice turning harsh.

"Because you can't detach yourself," Penrose replied. "Not from him. It's clouding your judgment."

"My judgment is fine."

"No, it isn't," Penrose said. "This is Hector all over again."

"This is nothing like Hector," Jude snapped.

"You loved him," Penrose said, voice hard. "Do you love the Prophet?"

"*What?*" Jude asked. He felt like all the air had been punched out of his lungs. "That's—"

"You can't have him," Penrose said. "Not the way you want."

"The way I *want?*" Jude said. "Since when are we allowed to want anything, Penrose?"

"We all swore the oath, Jude."

"But you *chose* this," Jude said. "You spent your whole life in search of the Order. You wanted this life and I—"

There was bald shock on Penrose's face. "You what?"

Jude had been about to say, *and I don't.* Those words had been ready to come out of his mouth, and he hadn't even realized they were true until this moment. He stood there, on the precipice of throwing away his legacy, his duty, his purpose not because he couldn't live up to them, but because he didn't believe in them anymore.

His faith had once been all he had. But that wasn't true anymore. It hadn't been true since the day Anton had stormed into the Tribunal Chambers. Since before then, maybe. Now, he had something else to believe in.

"It's late," he said to Penrose, instead of the truth. "Go get some sleep."

Penrose turned and whirled out of the tent, leaving Jude alone.

He laid the Pinnacle Blade and the Oracle Stone out in front of him. The Relic of Sight and the Relic of Heart. The origins of Grace. Anton said they were the key to stopping the Age of Darkness.

He gathered them again, putting the sword on his belt and the Stone in his pocket and then strode out of the tent and toward Anton's. Annuka stood on watch.

She nodded to him as he approached. "You're early."

"I couldn't sleep," Jude said. "I'll relieve you. One of us should get some rest."

Annuka left. Jude hesitated at the threshold of the tent and then bit down on his nerves and entered.

Anton was sitting up on the bedroll, his knees drawn toward his chest. He glanced up as Jude entered and for a moment they just stared at each other.

"How much longer until the next shift?" Anton said at last.

"A little over four hours," Jude replied. "Why?"

"We need to move fast if we're going to put enough distance between us and them," Anton said, pushing himself to his feet.

Jude froze. "What?"

"We have to go. I'm never going to convince the Guard that what I saw in my vision is true. You heard Penrose. The only option is to leave without them. We need to stop the Hierophant. We need to seal the Gate."

Jude's heart thudded. He had chosen to leave the Guard once before, but it had been a choice made out of desperation and fear. He'd been afraid of losing Hector, and afraid he would never be the leader the Order wanted him to be.

"Jude," Anton said, pleading. His dark eyes seemed to shine in the dim tent. "I can't do this without you. Please. Bet on me. You've done it before."

He had. He'd thrown his lot in with Anton at the Hidden Spring. It was one of the stupidest things he'd ever done but—

It had brought them both here. It had given him this boy, who put his life in Jude's hands and trusted him to keep it safe. Who kissed him and drove him mad and made him question everything he thought he knew. Who had slowly opened himself up to Jude, and who saw him like no one else ever had. Who had asked him once, to go with him. Jude had never given him an answer.

"That night in Kerameikos," Jude said haltingly. "When you found me in the storeroom."

"You mean when I found you drunk in the storeroom?" Anton asked, lips quirking into a smile.

"You told me that it must be hard to believe in something only to have it disappoint me."

He still remembered those words, and how they'd cut through the fog of his self-loathing like sunlight. He remembered how Anton had issued them, like a challenge. Daring Jude to say Anton wasn't the person who should have been Prophet.

"I should have told you, you never disappointed me," Jude said. "I was the one who failed you. And the Order . . . the Order failed us both. I was too blind to see it until you said that. You're always doing that—telling me the things I don't want to hear." His eyes caught on Anton's. "The things I need to hear most. Sometimes it feels like you know everything about me, even more than I know myself."

He didn't let himself look away from Anton. He felt laid bare, letting Anton see parts of him he'd never allowed anyone to see before. Not even Hector.

And even after seeing them, Anton still wanted Jude with him. He'd told him that, over and over, even when Jude couldn't protect him. Even when he let fear make him weak.

"I don't think I'll ever be what the Order wants me to be," Jude admitted. He had tortured himself with this thought, agonized over it, but he'd never allowed himself to say it aloud. Now that he had, it was a relief. "And maybe I don't need to be. Maybe I don't *want* to be."

Anton smiled at him again and Jude smiled back.

"Then," he said, taking Jude's hand, "what are we waiting for?"

42

EPHYRA

SOMEONE SHOOK EPHYRA AWAKE.

"Leave me alone, Beru," she groaned, rolling onto her side.

Her eyes flew open. And reality hit. Beru was gone. She shot up and found Illya crouched beside the bed.

"What is it?" she demanded.

He crossed his arms over his chest. "I thought you should know that the City Watch is looking for you. Apparently they think you've murdered several people."

"They can't know for certain it was me," Ephyra replied, pressing her palms into her eyes. "There were no witnesses. Besides, they don't even know who I am."

She paused, watching him closely as he stood. The morning light made his light brown hair look tawny, his eyes a honeyed gold. *He* was the only one who knew who she was. But what reason would he have to turn her in?

She dragged herself out of bed, taking the sheets with her.

"You've gotten reckless," he said, following her across the room.

"You've been out almost every night. You're barely sleeping. Do you *want* to get captured?"

"Why do you even care?"

Illya looked frustrated. "This thing between us—"

Ephyra laughed, loud and sharp. "*Thing* between us? You mean the one where you help me kill people and then we go to bed together? What are you even still doing here? Don't you work for the Witnesses?"

"I did. When it was convenient. I told you that."

She snorted. "Right. And that's what this is, too. Convenient." His expression flickered, like she'd actually wounded him, and for some reason it enraged her. "Who's the next target?"

"What?"

"Who is it?" she repeated.

"I—there isn't one," he answered. "It's been two weeks of this. You need to take a break."

But she couldn't. Beru was dead. If she stopped, she'd have nothing left.

"That's not your decision," she told him, pulling on her clothes.

"You look terrible," Illya said, coming up behind her. "You're running yourself ragged, and I think the Chalice is affecting you."

She tugged her tunic over her head. "Remind me why I allow you to speak to me?"

"Because," Illya said, drawing closer and winding an arm around her waist, "I'm very charming."

"If you're fond of that arm you'll remove it," Ephyra warned.

He withdrew it grudgingly. "I'm serious—you need to take a day off."

"Fine," she replied shortly, throwing on her cloak. "I'll find one myself."

"You're losing it," he called after her.

"I don't need moral judgment from a guy who kidnapped his own brother," Ephyra snapped, tying her mask in place.

"What would your sister think of you now?"

Ephyra raised her hand as if to strike him and pulled back at the last second. "Don't," she said in a quiet voice seething with rage. "Don't talk about her."

He leaned in and kissed her. It heated her blood and sent shivers through her.

Abruptly she broke away, pushing him hard against the wall by the throat. "Stay out of my way."

And before he could reply, she was gone.

It was late evening when she found her next victim. A merchant, who would be perfectly innocent if it weren't for the fact that he was clearly selling something besides carpets.

He was selling people. Specifically, fighters to provide entertainment in the sandpits. She tailed him through the early evening, and when night fell she made her move. He'd just stumbled out of a taverna and was shuffling down an alley.

Ephyra secured her mask and leapt down from her position on top of the opposite building. She didn't bother to make her landing light.

The man startled, whirling to face her. "W-who are you?"

"I'd rather talk about who you are." Ephyra drew closer.

The man looked confused.

"Actually," Ephyra went on, stopping a foot in front of him, "if it's all the same to you, let's not talk at all."

She leaned toward him and then stopped. She heard movement behind her. Someone else was in the alley.

The whistle of something flying through the air sounded behind her and Ephyra dodged left just as a crossbow bolt sailed past her, embedding itself in the wall next to her target's head.

She turned, eyes scanning the rooftops for her attacker.

The sound of footsteps echoed from the end of the alley and Ephyra turned to find a dozen members of the City Watch standing there. She took a step back.

The City Watch rushed at her.

"Get her hands!" one of them cried. "She's dangerous."

They swarmed her, and Ephyra fought them off as best she could, until one of them had her pinned to the wall face-first, twisting her arms behind her back.

"*Illya*," she cursed, thrashing against the hold. "Sold me out again." And she had trusted him, like an idiot.

"Actually, I did," a different voice said, and then Shara stepped into view. "I'm sorry, Ephyra, but what was I supposed to do? You disappeared with the Chalice and suddenly we're hearing all about murders in Behezda, and bodies turning up with a pale handprint. We knew it was you."

"You should have stayed out of it," Ephyra spat.

"That stopped being an option when you came looking for me in Tel Amot," Shara said. "And after you got Hadiza killed."

Ephyra struggled as one of the guards shoved her harder into the wall.

"Just give up, Ephyra," Shara said. "It'll be easier that way."

Ephyra closed her eyes, and reached for the Chalice. But before she'd even touched the empty folds of her cloak, she knew it wasn't there. In her rage she hadn't noticed the missing warmth and pull from it.

Illya. He must have taken it when he'd kissed her. He'd probably been waiting for an opportunity.

She went slack, all the fight going out of her at once, exhaustion burrowing into her bones.

"You didn't need to do this," she said to Shara.

Shara met her gaze evenly. "Yes, I did."

She was right. And maybe Illya had been right, too. Maybe she wanted to get caught. Maybe she wanted someone to stop her, because she knew she'd never stop on her own. Beru had died to stop Ephyra from becoming a monster, but she'd become one anyway.

She deserved whatever happened to her now.

43

HASSAN

IT TOOK HASSAN A DOZEN TRIES TO COPY THE TEXT. HE WASN'T SURE WHAT THE Hierophant knew of the contents of the scroll, other than the fact that it was some kind of agreement. To be safe, he retained most of the original text, and only changed a few key details that he hoped would throw off the Hierophant long enough for Hassan to form a plan.

When he was done, the real scroll tucked safely away, he lay in bed, reeling from the realization that his father had something to do with these Relics. Had he been trying to find them? Protect them? Was he part of the mysterious Protectors of the Lost Rose? Was that what the compass rose symbol meant?

He wished, for the thousandth time, that his father were still alive to tell him. He turned onto his side and grabbed a familiar object from the table beside him. The compass his father had given him.

He flipped it open out of habit, and watched the golden needle twitch on the etched lighthouse. The lighthouse no longer stood. But the compass still guided him there.

He squinted at it, suddenly focused on the compass rose. A moment later, he was rummaging through the drawers, looking for the scroll. Pulling it out, he looked at them side by side. The compass and the symbol of the compass rose.

Something deep in his gut told him it wasn't a coincidence. That the compass was a clue. His father had left it for him—he must have done it for a reason. Maybe for the same reason he had hidden the scroll. The compass was pointing Hassan not to the lighthouse, but to something that had been hidden within it.

Hassan left the Great Library a little after dawn, slipping out before anyone saw him. The streets of Nazirah were nearly empty at this hour, and the quiet felt almost like peace.

The Hierophant had instructed him to contact one of the Witnesses who was stationed near the marketplace. The Witness told him to take the text to a temple on Ozmandith Road. They had gutted all the temples along the road and had turned them into their own twisted places of worship.

Hassan didn't expect the Hierophant to actually be at the temple. He assumed he'd send his lackeys for this chore. So Hassan was surprised when he stepped inside and was greeted by that glinting gold mask.

"Do you have what I want?" the Hierophant asked.

Hassan withdrew the copied scroll and offered it freely. One of the Witnesses at the Hierophant's side took it, examined it, and then handed it to the Hierophant.

He held it and gestured with his other hand. From the back of the sanctum another Witness appeared holding a torch.

The flame was white.

Hassan held back a gasp. He thought that they'd destroyed all the remaining Godfire when they took down the tower.

The Witness brought the torch to the Hierophant, and without fanfare the masked man held the scroll to it. The flame chewed the edge of the scroll until it was just ashes as Hassan looked on in shock.

"This is a fake," the Hierophant said. He didn't sound angry, but that only made Hassan more afraid.

"I—"

"You thought you could trick me?" the Hierophant asked. "Is that it?"

Hassan swallowed.

"I think," the Hierophant said, "that the Prince of Herat needs to be taught a lesson."

The door opened, and Hassan turned. There in the doorway, limned in soft light, stood two Witnesses. And between them, Khepri, her arms bound behind her back by Godfire chains.

Horror and disbelief churned in Hassan's stomach. He caught Khepri's gaze and saw a mess of emotions on her face—betrayal, confusion, fear. His jaw clenched and he looked away. He hadn't wanted her involved in this, had hoped to leave her out of it. And part of him felt angered by her presence. She hadn't trusted him. She had followed him. Maybe she hadn't been trying to make things right between them at all—maybe she'd just been trying to spy on him.

"We found these two outside," one of the Witnesses said. On their other side, two new Witnesses appeared, dragging another captive along—Arash.

Hassan stared in disbelief, the knife in his heart twisting deeper. What was he doing there? Had Khepri brought him along?

The Hierophant waved the Witness with the torch forward.

The Godfire flickered as it drew closer to Khepri. Her eyes flashed with terror. As she struggled against the chains that bound her, something inside Hassan snapped.

"Wait," said Hassan, breathless. "Wait. I know where the Relic of Mind is. That's what you want, right? The Crown? I can get it for you."

The Hierophant held up a hand and the Witnesses stopped.

"You *traitor*!" Arash yelled. "You're just like the rest of them. You'd sell your own country, your own people, to that monster!"

"Either you or the Witnesses are going to destroy this country if I don't," Hassan said. "This is the only path to peace."

Arash opened his mouth to yell more, but one of the Witnesses covered it.

"Hassan," Khepri said, eyes pleading. He couldn't tell if she wanted him to go on or to stop. It didn't matter. There was only one way to save her.

"Let her go, and I'll get it for you," Hassan said. "The Crown for the girl."

"Very well, Prince Hassan," the Hierophant said. "But you do not want to disappoint me again."

The sky was gray and swollen with a summer storm as the Hierophant and ten of his Witnesses marched Khepri and Hassan to the site where the lighthouse had once stood.

"Hassan," Khepri muttered. "Please tell me you have some kind of plan."

He *had* one. But it had gone to shit.

He was cornered. The Witnesses had Khepri bound by Godfire

chains. He had only one play, and no guarantee that the Hierophant would honor the exchange.

And Arash . . . he cast a glance at him, only to find his eyes burning back at Hassan. He was plainly furious, and for once Hassan could not fault him for it. What he was about to do was unthinkable. But if they had any hope of making it out of this alive, it was his only choice.

They reached the ruins of the lighthouse. The sea crashed against the lonely rock where the tower had once stood.

"The Crown is here?" the Hierophant asked. "But the lighthouse was destroyed."

"It's underneath," Hassan said, trying to project confidence although he was going based only on his gut.

"Very well," the Hierophant said. "Lead the way."

Hassan nodded and they, along with two of the Witnesses, crossed to the ruins.

The Witness with the Godfire torch led them down a set of unbroken stairs, deep into the earth.

They descended into the darkness. Hassan took out his compass and used it to guide them through the dark chambers. Now that they were inside the lighthouse ruins, the needle had shifted, spinning slowly this way and that as they wound down the stairs.

"This way," Hassan said.

They reached a circular room of dark stone, which Hassan guessed was about three hundred feet below the surface of the rock. The compass needle wavered and started spinning wildly.

"It's here," he said. There was a round stone pillar in the center of the room that was about waist-high. Hassan went to it. The compass grew warm in Hassan's hand, the needle spinning faster. He put his other hand on the cold stone, and found a tiny circular indentation in the center of the pillar.

"Open it," the Hierophant commanded.

Hassan shook his head. "I don't know how."

The Hierophant didn't reply, but with a tilt of his head the Witness with the Godfire torch advanced on Khepri.

"Wait, wait!" Hassan cried. "Just give me a moment. Let me—"

The compass burned so hot that it scorched his skin and he dropped it. It fell to the stone ground, cracking open on impact. Hassan stared down in horror at the pieces of his father's compass on the ground. It was the last thing he had to remember him by.

And then something glimmered and caught his eye. Hassan knelt. Amid broken gears and shattered glass lay a golden disk the size of a coin, imprinted with the compass rose symbol. He picked it up and gazed from it to the pillar. With shaking hands, he pressed the disk into the stone.

At first nothing happened. Then with a great noise, the pillar began to grow, shooting up into the chamber's ceiling. As the pillar emerged from the ground, Hassan saw where part of it had been carved out, a stone platform upon which the Crown of Herat sat. The spiked points that arched above the twisted circlet looked almost like teeth, glimmering in the light of the Godfire.

"The Relic of Mind," the Hierophant murmured. He approached slowly.

Arash strained against his captors, staring covetously at the Crown as the Hierophant wrapped his hands around it.

A startled grunt drew Hassan's attention away from the Crown and to the chamber's threshold, where Khepri had one of the Witnesses pinned up against the wall, her chains wrapped around his throat. She kneed him between the legs and grabbed the Godfire torch out of his hands before he hit the ground. The other Witnesses moved to charge at her.

"Don't take another step," Khepri said.

The Hierophant froze and turned to her.

"It's not just the Crown you want," Khepri said. "You want all the other Relics, too."

She drew something from the folds of her shirt—the scroll. The *real* scroll. She must have found it in Hassan's drawers. Which meant she had come after Hassan, knowing what he was trying to do.

"Well, you're not going to get them," Khepri said. "This is what you wanted Hassan to find, right? Make another move and it'll be nothing but ashes." She nodded at the Witness who was holding Arash. "Release him."

The Witness looked at the Hierophant.

"Let us walk out of here," Khepri warned, moving the scroll closer to the flame.

"That won't be happening," the Hierophant said calmly.

Khepri lowered the scroll into the Godfire flame. It caught fire and she threw it to the ground.

Except the scroll didn't turn to ashes. Pale flame rippled over it, scorching the paper black. But it did not burn. The flames died away and Hassan dove for the scroll.

There was a new line of text on it.

The final secret of the Lost Rose, the secret that will not be passed on, is this: the Four Relics we protect contain the esha *of the ancient deity. It is from this that they derive their power. Together they formed the Four-Petal Seal, which has kept the* esha *of the ancient deity contained inside the Red Gate for over two millennia. All four Relics must be kept apart, for if they are reunited and used to unseal the Gate, the deity's* esha *will sow untold destruction upon the world.*

Hassan stared up from the scroll in shock. "This is . . ." he said.

"This is what you want, isn't it? To break the Four-Petal Seal. To unleash the god's *esha*."

Khepri's gaze snapped to him. "What?"

"There have been many mistakes made by the mortals of this world," the Hierophant said. "But the first and most costly was when they slew the ancient god. Everything since then has been a stain on the history of our world. The Prophets. The Graces. The kings and queens and heroes and villains. All of them existing in a world that never should have been. But we are going to remake it. To return the world to how it should be."

"*We?*" Hassan repeated.

"Yes, Prince Hassan," the Hierophant replied. "My most loyal Witnesses . . . and you."

Hassan stared at him. He'd assumed that the Hierophant had gotten everything he wanted from him. Why would he still need him?

Khepri pushed herself in front of Hassan. "There is no way you're taking him with you."

"We made a deal," Hassan said, looking at the Hierophant. "You said you'd be gone!"

"I will be," the Hierophant replied. "And you, with me."

"A *deal?*" Arash's voice dripped with fury.

"He's joking, right?" Khepri asked. "This was just part of your plan."

Hassan looked away from her.

"How *could* you?"

Hassan closed his eyes. He didn't have a way to explain to her that he'd been watching Nazirah slip through his fingers. Either he would lose it to Lethia, or to the chaos that Arash wanted to bring.

But he still needed her. He turned to her, facing the crushing disappointment and anger etched on her face. "Khepri, if what he's planning comes to pass, I can't keep Nazirah safe. No one can. The only way is to stop him. I need you to stay. Stay and protect this city while I'm gone."

He moved to touch her shoulder, but she pushed him away.

"I don't even recognize you right now," she said in a brittle voice. "But you're right—Nazirah doesn't need you. And neither do I."

Her words twisted in his gut like a knife. "I don't expect you to understand but I—I was trying to protect my people."

Khepri turned her face away. She wouldn't even look at him.

Grief and guilt rose in his throat and Hassan swallowed it down. He turned to the Hierophant.

"Deceiver," the Hierophant said, almost reverently. He reached a hand toward Hassan's brow and let his cold fingers brush against it. "You will come with me to witness the beginning of this new era."

Hassan stood there as two Witnesses flanked him, pinning his arms to his sides.

"Take him, too," the Hierophant said, and out of the corner of his eye Hassan saw them dragging Arash toward the exit.

Unlike Hassan, Arash struggled against his captors. "Where are you taking us?"

The Hierophant's fingers closed over Hassan's shoulder. "To the place where this all began."

44

ANTON

AFTER DAYS SPENT BANGING AROUND THE NAMELESS WOMAN'S SHIP, ANTON was glad to have his legs on solid ground again.

He sat across from Jude in the dining hall of a bustling taverna by the harbor, going over their plan one last time under the cover of the raucous chatter. They'd arrived in Tanais on the eve of their seventh day of journey. They would spend the night here, catch a train to Behezda in the morning, and arrive there the following day.

"Both the Chalice and the Crown are in Behezda," Anton said. "Or at least, according to my vision, they will be. And the Gate—the Red Gate of Mercy, that's where the Lost Rose sealed the rest of the god's *esha*. So once we get to Behezda all we have to do is get the other Relics and bring them there."

"And find someone to wield them," Jude added.

"You can wield the Relic of Heart."

"No, I can't," Jude said.

Anton looked at him in the low light. "You haven't tried. Not since Endarrion."

Jude looked away, off toward the crowd of other bored, hungry travelers, his expression pinched with displeasure. Something cold clenched in Anton's gut.

All of their interactions since leaving the Guard behind in Lukivsk had felt heavy with unspoken words. When they'd first arrived at the Nameless Woman's ship, Anton hadn't been able to stop himself from glancing over at Jude every few steps, opening his mouth to speak before quickly cutting himself off. Jude had left the Order with him. *For* him. He didn't know how to express what that meant to him. What he hoped it meant.

But on that first night, in the hallway between each of their rooms, they'd stopped and looked at each other for a long, stilted moment.

"Well," Jude had said at last. "Good night."

"Good night," Anton had replied.

And that had been it. Maybe Jude had turned away from the Order, but that didn't mean he'd changed his mind about anything else.

Now, sitting close in the taverna, Anton forced himself to speak. "It's all right, Jude."

"If Penrose were here, or the rest of the Guard—" Jude blew out a frustrated breath.

"You can tell me, you know," Anton said haltingly. "If you're upset about leaving the Guard."

He knew that Jude felt guilty about taking the Nameless Woman's ship, despite Anton's futile assurances that they hadn't stranded the others. Lukivsk was a small harbor, but ships passed through it every day. They'd find one to take them to Novogardia's capital, Osgard. The Order had acolytes there. They'd be safe—much safer than Anton and Jude.

But Anton didn't think that Jude's concern was just about the Guard's well-being.

He took a breath, meeting Jude's gaze. "Or if you regret it."

"I don't," Jude said, so easily it had to be the truth. "You were right. We weren't going to convince them, not in time to stop the Hierophant. It's just . . . I feel useless. You said you needed me but I can't even wield the Pinnacle Blade. I can't help you at all."

Anton wanted to tell him that it was more than enough that Jude was with him. But he knew if he did, it would open up the box of everything they weren't talking about. The box that had been shut tight since their fight on the Nameless Woman's ship.

"Let's play a hand of canbarra," Anton said instead.

"What?"

"I can teach you," Anton went on. "Look, it's late. Just for tonight, let's not talk about Behezda, or the Relics, or, you know, our impending doom. Let's play cards instead."

"But." Jude frowned, looking stymied. "We're supposed to be . . . lying low."

"Which is exactly what we'll be doing. Playing cards in the cardroom at a taverna? No one will look at us twice."

Which is how Anton found himself, thirty minutes later, sitting across from Jude in the taverna's noisy cardroom. As Anton had promised, no one came to bother them, or even seemed to notice them at all.

"See?" Anton said as Jude studied the cards in concentration. "I told you you'd pick it up."

"Stop distracting me," Jude replied.

Anton leaned his cheek into his palm. "Am I distracting you?"

He said it low and flirtatious, and watched the color rise in Jude's cheeks. He knew it was a stupid thing to do, but he couldn't stop himself.

Jude raised his eyes to meet Anton's, a hint of humor in them. He took his turn. Anton went next. The game ended a few turns later. Anton, of course, won.

"Don't worry," Anton assured Jude. "We'll keep practicing."

He almost suggested a rematch. He didn't want the night to end, not yet. Jude was light in a way he hadn't been since they'd left Endarrion. Since Anton had made the monumentally stupid decision to kiss him. Here, in the cozy light and warm bustle of the taverna, Anton couldn't keep his mind from wandering or his gaze from lingering.

They stumbled back to the room they'd rented and found it warmly lit by a fire in the hearth, with two beds canopied by cloth and laid out with furs.

"I am *very* glad to be off the ship," Jude said, leaning back against the cushions by the fire.

Anton stretched out beside him. The hearth's flame cast a golden glow on Jude's face, making his eyes look like seaglass.

"What?" Jude asked, and Anton realized he'd been staring.

He looked toward the flickering fire. "I know we said we weren't going to talk about it tonight, but I just wanted to say thank you, I guess."

"For playing cards with you?" Jude asked. Anton was pretty sure it was a joke.

"For coming with me," Anton replied, his voice steady even as his heart quickened. "If you weren't here . . . I don't know what I'd do."

Jude didn't answer for a moment. When Anton glanced back at him, he saw Jude's eyes were on the fire as well. "I left the Guard because you asked me to," he said finally. "But . . . I also wanted to. I think I've wanted to for a long time. Longer than I can admit. But I was afraid that without the Order . . . without their purpose and their rules I would . . ."

His voice petered out and Anton wished to pull him close, to take his face in his hands and kiss him. He didn't move.

"It's just that . . ." Jude looked down. "You were right."

Anton's heart pounded in his throat. "About what?"

Jude met his eyes. "That I won't let myself have the things I want. That it's easier this way."

Anton felt helpless in the heat of Jude's gaze, reckless hope soaring in his chest. "And what do you want?"

Jude looked at him, and looked at him, and just as Anton thought he was about to turn away, Jude leaned into him and pressed their lips together. It felt like something Anton had manifested out of his own longing as he yielded to Jude, clutching at his shoulders and letting him press him back against the cushions.

He could think only of how Jude had looked at him on the top of the lighthouse in Nazirah, the Godfire flame flickering behind them, the dark green sea churning below them. It had felt like something sliding into place.

Jude broke away abruptly, lifting himself up on one elbow, panting. "Anton." He sounded as terrified as he had the first time they'd kissed.

"You should have what you want, Jude," Anton said fervently, desperately. "You should have everything you want."

Jude's chest rose and fell with a labored breath. "I don't want to ask too much of you. I *can't.*"

"What are you talking about?" Anton asked, brushing his thumb along Jude's jaw. Jude shivered and caught his hand.

"I mean I will protect you," Jude said, his thumb pressing on the bones of Anton's wrist. "I will stay by your side until you ask me to leave. But I didn't defy the Order and abandon my Guard so that you'd—" He broke off, looking down at their joined hands. In a low voice he said, "I won't ask for more than you want to give."

Anton saw the hurt in Jude's eyes, the uncertainty, and understood suddenly what he was trying to say. He wanted to pull Jude down and kiss him again, to let it be that simple. But simple was a flirtation with a deckhand. Simple was kissing a boy who made eyes at you over a glass of magnolia wine. This wasn't simple—it was messy, and true, and sacred, because it was *theirs*.

"I told you that I knew what that kiss meant to you," Anton said, sitting up. "But I never told you what it meant to me, did I?"

Jude's eyes were somber in the low light. He shook his head.

"You know that I . . . didn't have the easiest childhood," Anton said, because it seemed like the place to begin. "When I was young, wanting things meant hurting when I never got them. So my whole life I just . . . tried to survive. Whenever someone tried to get close to me, I showed them what they wanted to see, gave them whatever it was they wanted from me and never asked for anything in return. It was easier that way."

Jude's hands twisted in the fur beneath them. Anton reached out to still them.

"But when I met you, you were . . . you tried so hard *not* to want anything. I didn't know what to do with that," he said with a helpless shrug. "But you still protected me, and I just—I *liked* you."

Jude was looking at him now, his fingers warm beneath Anton's.

"I like how serious you are and how funny you can be. I like the little crease you get between your eyebrows when you're worried." That very crease furrowed Jude's brow now, and fondness bloomed in Anton's chest. "You surprise me, all the time, and sometimes I think I'd do anything, absolutely anything, to make you smile. And when we kissed I finally admitted it to myself. What you made me realize that day on the lighthouse."

Jude had climbed up there with him. He'd faced down Anton's worst nightmare. He hadn't even hesitated. No one had ever done that for him before.

"I've been running for a long, long time," Anton said, touching his thumb to Jude's brow. "And you were the first thing that ever made me want to stay."

"Oh," Jude said faintly.

"Jude," Anton said, taking Jude's face between his hands, thumbs against his temples.

Jude leaned into him, closing the space between them until it disappeared completely. They kissed again, sweet and unhurried, Jude's hand a warm anchor on Anton's back.

"Your Grace called out to me," he murmured against Anton's cheek. "I found you."

Anton dipped to kiss his throat, beneath his jaw.

"That means," Jude said, brushing their lips together again, "I get to keep you."

Trembling, Anton shucked Jude's jacket off and untied the laces on his shirt until the soft fabric fell open, baring his chest. He felt Jude hold his breath as Anton pressed his palms there, fingers beginning to trace a familiar pattern over his collar.

The white Godfire scars stood out against his tan skin. Anton brushed his hand over one and Jude reached out to still his wrist. There was no shame in his eyes, just hunger, and something too tender to name. Anton leaned down, touching his lips to one thin, white scar that ran across Jude's collarbone. He offered the kiss like an apology, a benediction.

Jude brought Anton's wrist to his lips and pressed a kiss to his racing pulse, his eyes dark with the same intensity they'd held when he had promised to protect him. Anton caught Jude's hand, curling his thumb over one knuckle.

Whatever waited for them in Behezda, whatever nightmare crept in the edges of Anton's mind, he could face it. As long as Jude was with him. And in each touch and breath and kiss Anton found the thing that had eluded him his whole life.

Hope.

IV

DEATH AND RISING

45

JUDE

JUDE WOKE TO THE SIGHT OF AN UNTOUCHED BED ACROSS THE ROOM AND A
tuft of straw-blond hair sticking up from the blankets beside him.

He rolled onto his back and stared up at the ceiling in stunned
silence. He'd *kissed* Anton. Had, in fact, kissed him until the early
hours of the morning, stopping only when sleep started to claim them
both.

His chest warmed to think of it, but fear lurked at the edges of
his mind. Despite Anton's assurances last night, Jude could not forget
what had happened the last time he'd put his heart in someone else's
hands.

"Stop thinking." Anton emerged from the blankets.

Jude had seen him in the morning before but not quite like this.
He was mussed and warm from sleep, his dark eyes blinking. The
sight of him made the warmth in Jude's chest spread to his toes.
"What should I do instead?"

Anton gently combed his fingers through Jude's hair, pushing it
off his forehead. "I have some ideas."

The upturned corner of his mouth was begging to be kissed, so Jude did, pressing his thumb into the soft dip of Anton's waist where he had dreamed of touching him since the first night they'd met.

"Jude," Anton murmured. "*Jude*."

It was impossible that he could have this, after wanting it for so long. That he could have Anton warm beneath his hands, his pulse trembling against Jude's lips. That anything this precious could be his.

"We're going to miss our train."

Jude froze, his hand halfway up Anton's shirt. "What?"

"The train," Anton said, pushing himself up on one elbow. "To Behezda. We need to get going if we want to catch it."

He rolled off the bed, out of reach, and started tugging on his clothes while Jude stared, heat creeping up his neck. Reluctantly, he scooped his shirt off the floor and pulled it on and then reached for his boots.

At the train station, Anton volunteered to get their tickets, and then led Jude to the sleeper cars to board. Jude stowed their luggage in a compartment and then entered the private room that Anton had secured with the money the Nameless Woman had given them. There was a small table with a lamp on it, two chairs, and one bed that folded down from the wall.

One bed.

Jude looked at Anton.

"This was the only room they had," Anton said innocently.

An image from the night before appeared in Jude's head—Anton curled in Jude's arms, shadowed by the dying fire as he tilted his head up for one last kiss before he fell asleep. Jude, helpless to do anything but oblige.

"I'm sure it was," Jude said, smiling as he backed Anton into the room and kissed him to drown out the thought of what came next.

They disembarked the train at Behezda station the next afternoon. Like everything else in Behezda, the train station was carved out of the red rock face of the surrounding canyon. They walked beneath the shadow of the red cliffs above and out into the city square, a cobblestone plaza centered around a dribbling fountain, bordered by arched gates.

"Are you sure you don't need a scrying pool to use your Grace?" Jude asked, steering Anton into a side alley.

"I'm sure," Anton replied. He held the Relic of Sight in his hands and closed his eyes.

Jude had only seen Anton scry once before. At the lake, it had seemed like Anton had nearly been overwhelmed by his power, and it had taken all of Jude's strength to stop himself from grabbing Anton's hand and leading him out of that place.

Now, he just watched as Anton clutched the Stone, his lips forming wordless shapes. He was trembling, his face creased with pain. Abruptly, he jerked backward, dropping the Stone and stumbling back against the wall. Jude lunged toward him, catching him by the elbow.

"What is it?" Jude asked, steadying him.

Anton's eyes blinked open, his breath coming in quick puffs. "Sorry. It's . . . I felt the Chalice. But I also felt something else."

"Are you all right?" He placed a hand on Anton's back to soothe him.

Anton gulped in another deep breath, letting it out slowly. "I don't know. The Stone's power is . . . overwhelming."

411

Jude slipped Anton's hand in his and thought of the promise he'd made him, and with sudden clarity understood what it meant to Anton. That even without his Grace, without his power, he could still protect him. "I'll be right here, no matter what. Even if I have to dive into your nightmares after you."

Anton looked up at him with a shaky smile. Taking another breath, he curled his hand around the Stone again. It glowed softly against his palm as he closed his eyes, his whole body wracked with tension. Jude could only watch, completely helpless. They needed to do this, he reminded himself. They needed to find the other Relics. They needed to repair the seal on the Red Gate. It was only now, watching Anton, that Jude considered what this impossible task might cost him. Stopping the Age of Darkness could cost Anton his life.

With a sharp cry, Anton collapsed to the ground. The Stone pulsed with faint light against his collar.

"I saw it," Anton gasped as Jude knelt beside him. "I know where the Chalice is. But . . . it's impossible."

"What?"

Anton's dark eyes met his. There was horror in them, a deep terror that Jude felt in his bones.

"It's my brother," Anton said. "Illya has the Chalice."

46

EPHYRA

THEY GAVE HER FIVE DAYS TO DECIDE.

On the fifth day, the guard arrived. He was young, maybe even younger than her, with a baby face and eyes that had never seen violence.

"I'll face them," she said.

They didn't have prisons in Behezda. What they had was the amphitheater. They told her she had a choice. Face her crimes, or be sold into servitude without a trial.

She waited her turn in the amphitheater. There were other criminals who went before her—some that, if she were to meet them as the Pale Hand, she likely would have killed.

The accused stood in the middle of the pit, their hands bound to a pole behind them. In front of the pole was a table. On the table was a single knife.

Those that the accused had wronged could approach, one by one, and demand their retribution for what had been done to them. A finger. An arm. An eye. Sometimes they simply scarred their face, as a warning to the public of what the accused had done. And sometimes—sometimes they laid down the knife.

Mercy.

"You're going to have to face them," the guard said. "Everyone you wronged."

"That's going to be difficult," Ephyra replied coolly, "as they're all dead."

He shoved her forward roughly.

"Mercy," the woman at the edge of the pit claimed as they walked Ephyra to the center, "is not forgiveness. It is for those who were wronged to give, or not."

They tied Ephyra to the pole.

"The woman you see before you is known as the Pale Hand," the woman went on. "She has killed countless in this city and others. She has used the Grace of Blood—the Grace of our founders—to do it."

"She doesn't deserve mercy!" someone in the crowd shouted.

The woman cut a hand through the air to silence them. "Deserve? Mercy cannot be deserved. It cannot be earned. Only given. Who will give it to her?"

Silence fell over the crowd.

"Who has been wronged by her?"

No one's going to stand up, Ephyra thought. If no one came, would they let her go? Or would they kill her?

Someone emerged from the crowd.

"I have," said a voice. The voice was familiar, but it couldn't possibly belong to the person she thought it did.

Because that person was dead.

This was just a trick, like how she'd heard Beru's voice in the tomb of the Sacrificed Queen.

And yet somehow, impossibly, Hector Navarro was striding

toward her. He stopped by the table and picked up the knife. Gripping it in his hand, he locked eyes with her.

Ephyra could only stare at this specter of her greatest sin as it stared back at her.

"The Pale Hand killed my family," the specter said. "Took everything from me. And then she . . . she tried to take my life."

He stepped up to Ephyra, the knife flashing in his hand.

"For that," he said, "there is no forgiveness."

He raised the knife. Could a hallucination kill her?

The knife swung down and Ephyra squeezed her eyes shut. But the blade did not pierce her skin. Instead, she felt the ropes around her wrists give and fall away. A voice next to her ear whispered, "Beru needs your help."

Ephyra's eyes flew open. "Is . . . is this my punishment?"

His brows furrowed. "What?"

Ephyra slumped against the pole and looked away. "Beru's dead. So are you."

"Beru's alive," he said. "And I'm—you know what? We don't have time for this."

He grabbed her arm and dragged her away from the pole. Ephyra recoiled.

"You can't . . . you can't touch me." She was dreaming. This was all a dream and she'd wake up on the floor of that dingy cell, alone. Waiting for her punishment.

"You murdered me, so I think me grabbing your arm is a burden you'll have to bear," he replied drily.

"This isn't real," she said. "You're not real. You're dead."

"Not anymore," Hector replied. The crowd roared in Ephyra's ears.

Four members of the City Watch surrounded them. "This is not how mercy is given. Either you take retribution or you leave her."

Hector glanced quickly at Ephyra, shoving her behind him before turning to face the City Watch. Behind his back, he tossed the knife. Ephyra lunged to catch it.

The City Watch rushed at them. Hector kept his sword sheathed, using only his fists to defend them, but even Ephyra could see it would be more than enough. He moved so quickly she could barely parse his movements, dodging, blocking, sweeping, maintaining his position between Ephyra and the City Watch. Ephyra backed up, brandishing the knife, looking for any other attackers.

A moment later, Hector was back at her side, the members of the City Watch sprawled on the ground around him. The crowd above surged.

Ephyra stared at Hector. "Are you actually rescuing me right now?"

"Looks like it," Hector replied. In the distance, Ephyra saw more of the City Watch advancing from the edges of the pit. Hector grabbed her arm, pulling her toward the tunnel that would lead them out of the arena.

More members of the City Watch choked the exit of the tunnel. But the narrow quarters gave Hector an advantage—they were forced to face him one at a time.

In a flash, Hector had the first two on the ground, and a third pinned against the tunnel wall.

"Go!" he cried, heaving the City Watchman into the others so they were forced to retreat.

Ephyra didn't hesitate. She charged through the fray, ducking and sliding out of reach of the Watch, slashing their outstretched arms with her knife when she could not avoid them.

She emerged out into the sunlight, Hector at her heels.

They raced away from the arena, the shouts of the City Watch in their ears, and into the narrow, cobbled streets. They zagged down streets and alleys, up narrow stairways and through crumbling archways, losing whoever was left on their tail. Ducking into another alley, Ephyra suddenly pulled up short, grabbing Hector and shoving him against the wall, her hand at his throat.

"Were you lying in there?"

His eyes were wide with fear and she wondered, with some satisfaction, whether he was thinking about the last time they'd come face-to-face.

"Were you lying? About Beru?"

"She's alive," Hector said. "I swear she's alive."

She let go of his throat but kept him pinned, searching his face for the lie. Her heart hammered against her ribs. Beru was alive. She was alive. Ephyra felt even more like she was in a dream. Had the Daughters lied to her? Was Hector lying to her now?

"The Daughters of Mercy told me she was dead."

"The Daughters of Mercy tried to kill us," he said, breathing hard. "Abandoned us in the desert. But we lived."

Ephyra turned, covering her face with her hands. Beru. Alive.

"How are you alive?" she asked. "I *killed* you."

"Someone brought me back," Hector replied. "I don't know who."

There was only one other person Ephyra knew of who could raise the dead.

"Did you really find the Chalice?" he asked.

She looked at him sharply. "How do you know about that?"

"Because I'm looking for it, too," he replied. "That's how I found you. I heard that the Pale Hand had come to Behezda. I did some asking around. Eventually heard you'd been captured by the City Watch. And when I talked to the person who turned you in . . ."

"Shara."

"Took a little persuading, but eventually she told me everything.

How you had tracked down the Chalice. Killed the Daughters of Mercy for it."

"Why are you looking for it?" she asked, suspicion sharpening her tone.

"The same reason you were," he replied steadily. "Beru found me after you—after. There's some sort of . . . connection between us. Because of what you did. It restored her health for a little while. But it's not enough, so I left her and came here to try to find the Chalice. She's dying, Ephyra."

"What do you mean you left her?" she demanded. "Where?"

"Somewhere safe," Hector replied. "Somewhere no one could find her."

"*Where?*"

"There's a healer," Hector said. "He found us in the desert after the Daughters left us there. He took us to his oasis."

Ephyra's mind went white with fear. The blood drained from her face. All she could think about was her father's letter to Badis. *We found him out in the desert, in an oasis. We didn't know who he was, then.*

"Hector," she said, looking up to meet his eyes. "You left my sister with the Necromancer King."

47

BERU

THE NECROMANCER KING CURLED A HAND AROUND BERU'S ARM, DRAWING *esha* from her. Before he had turned her into his own personal energy source, she'd only ever had *esha* transferred *into* her. This felt very different—like being plunged into an ice bath. She was left cold and shaking afterward.

"Don't worry," the Necromancer King said, gently rolling her sleeve back down. "This is the last time."

Ephyra had said something similar to Beru once, after she'd taken the life of a priest to heal her. It hadn't been true then, either.

The Necromancer King stood in one smooth motion. He looked stronger than he had at the oasis, more robust. He was almost glowing. Beru, by contrast, was drawn and pallid. He had filled her with the *esha* of an entire oasis. An influx of that much *esha*, he told Beru, would have dire effects on anyone else. But not on her.

Revenants, he'd told her, were like a bottomless well. They could suck up any *esha* they were given. The Necromancer King was carefully siphoning off the font of *esha* he'd put in her. Unless he replenished the *esha* soon, he would suck her dry.

It had been eight days since they'd left the oasis, and they'd been searching Behezda for the Chalice ever since. The Necromancer King had said back in the oasis that it had been "reawakened" for the first time in nearly five hundred years. And over the days that followed, he'd felt it being used again and again. But then suddenly, it had stopped.

"Come," the Necromancer King said. "I feel another echo. This one is more recent than the others."

The Necromancer King had dragged Beru all over the city, behind temples and in dark alleyways where he said he could feel echoes of the Chalice. The echoes told him the person wielding the Chalice had used it only to take *esha*—never to heal, or to resurrect. And evidently they'd taken enough *esha* to kill, which meant there were half a dozen dead bodies out there marked by a pale handprint.

It didn't mean it was Ephyra. With the Chalice, anyone with the Grace of Blood could become powerful enough to kill. But in the pit of Beru's gut, she knew it wasn't someone else. She knew the Pale Hand was back.

Guilt clawed at her chest. She'd left Ephyra because she thought it was the only thing that would keep her from killing. But what if it had been a mistake? What had Ephyra become without Beru there to stop her?

The Necromancer King led her through the narrow streets of Behezda and finally stopped in an alleyway and closed his eyes, humming softly.

"This one is less than a week old," the Necromancer King said. "The echoes here are different. Stronger. Almost . . ." He paused, as if listening. "It's near."

Dread pitted in Beru's stomach as the Necromancer King led

them deeper into the heart of the city. All she could see when she closed her eyes was Ephyra's shattered expression when Beru had walked away from her in Medea.

She couldn't stand the thought of facing her again. But still she let the Necromancer King lead her on. If Ephyra was still out there, still killing, it was Beru's responsibility.

They stopped when they reached the edge of the river. A row of buildings lined it, crumbling and dingy with age.

The Necromancer King stepped up to one of the doors and grasped the handle, pushing it open.

"Who's there?" a voice called from within.

Beru blinked into the dimness of the room. A man stood inside, dressed in trim, Endarrion-style clothing. Ephyra was nowhere in sight.

The Necromancer King strode forward and Beru sucked in a breath, following.

"Don't come any closer," the man warned, backing up against a table.

"You have something of mine," the Necromancer King replied.

The man's golden gaze swept over the two of them, calculating. "Who are you?"

"Where's Ephyra?" Beru asked. Fear caught in her throat. "What did you do to my sister?"

His eyes widened. "You're her. The sister. The Daughters of Mercy said you were dead."

Beru froze. Ephyra wouldn't trust just anyone with knowledge about Beru. Who exactly was this man?

"How do you know Ephyra?" Beru demanded, stepping toward him. "What happened to her?"

"Now, Beru," the Necromancer King said fondly, patting her arm.

"You know we don't have time for this. We're here for the Chalice, remember?"

"Did the Hierophant send you?" the man demanded.

The Necromancer King tilted his head inquisitively. "The Hierophant?"

"What do you want with the Chalice?" the man asked.

"No one *sent* me," the Necromancer King replied. "I want the Chalice for myself. And I would like it now, if you please."

"Don't," Beru said before she could stop herself. She felt their eyes on her. "Don't give it to him. I know this sounds impossible, but he's the Necromancer King."

The Necromancer King flicked his gaze back to the golden-eyed man. "She's right," he said brightly. "Which must make you wonder— do you really want to stand between me and what I want?"

No one moved for the length of a heartbeat. Then slowly, the golden-eyed man reached down and drew something out of the bag at his feet. A silver chalice.

He turned it over in his hand. "This? Is this what you're looking for?"

Beru tensed at the sight of it, but the Necromancer King smiled.

"Perhaps we can come to some sort of arrangement," the man went on. "See, the Hierophant wants this, too. And he's going to be pretty mad when he realizes I've given it to someone else. So how about this—I'll hand over the Chalice willingly, and in exchange you kill the Hierophant."

"It would be my pleasure."

"No," Beru gasped as the Necromancer King approached the man.

The Necromancer King closed his long fingers around the stem of the Chalice. He shut his eyes and the Chalice seemed to glow for a moment in his hand.

"You have no idea what you've done," Beru said.

The golden-eyed man looked at her. "Your sister," he said finally. "If you do find her. Try not to judge her too harshly."

Something twisted in Beru's chest. This man *did* know Ephyra.

Beru stepped toward him, grabbing him firmly by the elbow. "Where is she?"

He shook her off. "Trust me. You're both better off." He turned to the Necromancer King. "Now, how about making good on our deal? Until the Hierophant is dead, I've got a target on my back."

The Necromancer King looked at the man like he was an especially interesting insect. "That sounds quite terrible."

"Are you—messing with me?" the man said unsurely. "You *are* going to do it, right?"

"Of course," the Necromancer King replied. "A deal is, as they say, a deal."

Beru stood there as the Necromancer King brushed past her.

"Come, Beru," he said over his shoulder.

Beru no longer knew if she could possibly stop him. But she was responsible for this, for him. It was because of her that he'd been let out of his cage. It seemed no matter what Beru did, she was destined to cause death and destruction. But this time, she wouldn't run from it.

She cast one last look at the golden-eyed man and then followed the Necromancer King.

48

HASSAN

THE HIEROPHANT HAD KEPT HASSAN CONFINED THROUGHOUT THEIR JOURNEY, which had taken them across the Pelagos and over the desert terrain to the City of Mercy. Now in Behezda, Hassan was kept in a small, dark room within a cave that appeared to house some sort of long-abandoned prisoner's work camp. A Witness was posted outside Hassan's room every moment of the day.

He had not actually seen the Hierophant himself since they'd left Nazirah, nor did he know what had happened to Arash. The only thing he did know for sure was that if there was any hope of stopping the Hierophant, he had to escape.

On the second day, a Witness entered with a bowl of soup on a tray.

"I won't eat this," Hassan said, crossing his arms and attempting to look the part of a petulant, spoiled prince. He made a show of shoving the tray away from him.

The Witness looked irritated.

"How do I know you haven't poisoned it?" Hassan demanded. "You taste it first."

The Witness heaved out a sigh and grabbed the spoon. He lifted it to his mouth and tipped it in.

And promptly dropped to the floor.

Paralytic powder. Zareen had gifted some to Hassan weeks ago, thinking it might come in handy at some point.

She'd been right.

After a few moments of terrified fumbling, Hassan slipped out of the room draped in the paralyzed Witness's robes. Listening for approaching footsteps, he crept down the darkened hallway until he reached an open door, firelight and low voices flickering through.

Hassan crept closer. He caught a glimpse inside, and immediately flattened himself against the door, heart hammering. Reaching inside one of his pockets, he withdrew a small spyglass, pilfered from the Library's collection of his father's old artefacts. He pressed it against the wall and looked inside, seeing the room as if through a window.

The Hierophant stood by the fireplace, surrounded by about a dozen Witnesses, one of whom was strangely covered head to toe, his face masked by cloth.

"The Chalice has at last been procured," the Hierophant said in his gentle voice. "I need one of you to meet with Illya Aliyev."

"He has the Chalice?" the masked Witness said in disbelief.

"Yes," the Hierophant said. "And he has made certain . . . demands of me in return for it. I am sending three of you to retrieve it from him."

Hassan's suspicion was correct. The Hierophant didn't just want the Crown—he was after all of the Relics. And if what the scroll said was true, he wanted to use them to unlock an ancient power.

"I will go," the masked Witness declared. "I will make Illya Aliyev fear your wrath and regret his own selfish deceit. He has given *nothing* to our cause. His loyalty is thin and sways with the lightest breeze."

"You will go nowhere," the Hierophant replied. "You shall remain here with me, to protect the Crown. Do not forget that you have failed me, not once, but twice. I expected better from you when I sent you to clean up Aliyev's mistakes."

The masked Witness stiffened. "Immaculate One, if you would just give me one more chance to prove myself—you know what I have given to this cause."

"Enough," the Hierophant said, the slightest edge to his voice, although he hadn't raised it. "Do you seek to question my judgment?"

The masked Witness fell to one knee. "No, of course not, Immaculate One. Never. I—I'll stay here, as you ordered."

The Hierophant sighed and looked away from the masked Witness. "You three. Go meet with Aliyev and bring the Chalice to the Red Gate. Here is the message he sent, and the address where you will find him."

The Witness at the Hierophant's elbow moved forward, holding out a folded piece of parchment. One of the other three Witnesses tasked with this mission stepped forward to receive it.

"You all have your orders," the Hierophant said, surveying his followers. "See it done."

As the Hierophant dismissed the Witnesses, Hassan slipped the spyglass back into his pocket and darted down the hall. He ducked into an alcove and waited for a few of the Witnesses to pass him. To his right, a low table displayed candlesticks of various heights. Hassan grabbed one of them, slipping it into the sleeve of his robe, and then melted into the group of Witnesses. He kept his sight on the three tasked with the Chalice's retrieval, hurrying through the cave's labyrinthine corridors after them.

49

ANTON

"WE'RE CLOSE."

Anton tugged on Jude's sleeve, reeling him back. They faced a row of dilapidated buildings at the edge of the murky river that cut through the center of the city. The feeling of Illya's *esha* scraped over him. It was ice, it was darkness, it was fear.

"He's in there," Anton said, pointing at one of the buildings.

Jude turned toward him, his brow furrowed in concern. Anton was accustomed to seeing the expression, but this time he didn't need to fight the urge to touch his thumb to Jude's temple. "Maybe I should go in alone. Last time you saw your brother, you didn't exactly come out unscathed."

The offer was tempting. Anton still sometimes saw Illya's laughing face in his nightmares. But the idea of Jude going alone, when they'd come so far together, was enough to make Anton refuse. "I'll be fine, Jude. I'll be with you."

On impulse, he leaned in to press their lips together. When he opened his eyes, Jude looked as though Anton had smacked him over the back of the head. The expression made something warm unfurl in Anton's chest.

Taking a breath, Anton stepped up to the entrance. Beside him, he could feel Jude shift into fighting stance, his muscles drawing taut, his eyes and ears focused and searching, his breath heightened but steady. Illya's *esha* rattled in Anton's ears.

Anton pushed open the door. Before he could take a step, Jude leapt forward.

There was a soft exhalation and a thump as Jude shoved Illya against the wall.

Illya looked at Anton, looked at Jude, and raised his hands in surrender. His expression was utterly calm.

"Well," he said blandly. "This is a surprise, brother."

"No," Jude said, his gaze hard. "You don't talk to him. You don't look at him. Your business is with me, or it's with the edge of my sword. Are we clear?"

Most of the time, Jude's soft features and gentle demeanor made it easy to forget he was deadly in combat. But then there were times like this, when there was ice in Jude's voice and fire in his gaze that made it impossible to do anything but heed him. Anton caught a hint of nervousness in Illya's gaze as he shifted it to Jude.

"All right then," Illya said. "What will it be, Keeper?"

"The Chalice," Jude said. "Where is it?"

"You're about five minutes too late," Illya replied. "Someone took it from me." He glanced down at Jude's fist, which was still clenched in the front of his shirt. "Do you mind?"

Jude flicked his gaze to Anton who gave a slight nod and Jude released Illya.

"Who took it?" Anton asked. "The Hierophant?"

Straightening his clothing primly, Illya said, "You're probably not going to believe this, but the Necromancer King took the Chalice from me. At least, that's who he said he was."

"The Necromancer King?" Anton echoed. "You're serious. Is he serious?"

"Deadly."

Jude moved between them. "Say we believe you. What does he want it for?"

Illya rolled his eyes. "What do you think? He wants what everyone in the entire world wants. Power. Everyone, that is, except you, little brother."

Anton reached into his shirt and drew out the Relic of Sight. Illya's eyes followed it, like a moth to a flame. "You know what this is, don't you? You want to know where I found it?"

"I'm sure you're about to tell me," Illya said smoothly, but Anton could see his hunger.

"I went back home. Saw our grandmother."

Illya's expression flashed with surprise.

"The Relic was in the lake, the one where you—where I almost drowned." In a low voice he added, "Where you saved me."

"The lake?" Illya echoed. "But—"

"Vasili had it," Anton went on. "And after he tore apart the Novogardian Empire, he took it into the lake and drowned himself. Just like I almost did. So no, Illya, I don't want power. Because as far as I can tell, power is madness."

"Then I guess we're all mad," Illya replied.

Before Anton could answer, the door cracked open behind them, revealing three robed figures. Witnesses. The tallest one stood in front, taking up the entire threshold. The two behind him were women, one with short, fair hair and freckles, the other tan with long, dark brown hair pulled into a tail behind her.

Jude pushed Anton behind him, his hand going to the hilt of the Pinnacle Blade.

"Ah," Illya said mildly. "You certainly took your time."

Jude's gaze narrowed in on Illya. "You were just stalling so that your backup could catch us off guard."

"Hand over the Chalice, Aliyev," the tall Witness said.

"Right," Illya said. "About that."

"The Chalice isn't here," Anton said. "You're too late."

The tall Witness's eyes widened. "You. You're the Prophet."

Anton shrank back as the other two Witnesses began to advance. Jude's hand tightened on the Pinnacle Blade.

A hooded figure, robed like the other Witnesses, appeared in the threshold, a metal rod in one hand. Before Anton could react, he swung the rod, catching the dark-haired Witness between the shoulders. She let out a bark of pain and collapsed. The other two turned back to face the rogue Witness in confusion.

In their moment of distraction, Illya lunged forward, a dagger gleaming in his hand. The blade slashed at the tall Witness, who fell forward with a deep groan, clutching at his stomach. Now defenseless, and the odds against her, the fair-haired Witness staggered away from the melee, backing out through the door.

Jude rushed toward the newest arrival, pinning him up against the wall with his own metal rod at his throat.

"Wait," the fourth Witness panted. "I'm not a Witness."

He reached up and tugged off his hood, revealing a handsome face, with warm brown eyes and dark curls.

Jude took a step back and let the metal rod clatter to his feet. "Prince Hassan?"

The boy's face slackened in relief. "Captain Weatherbourne. I didn't expect to see you here."

The dark-haired Witness grunted from the floor, clambering to her feet. Before she could so much as make a move, Jude and Hassan both spun toward her, grasping one arm each and shoving her back against the wall. She hissed in pain.

The tall Witness, still bleeding on the floor, let out a wet gasp and tried to crawl toward them.

"Please," the Witness pinned by Hassan and Jude said. "Let me take him to a healer. We'll go. We won't come back."

Jude glanced back at the bleeding Witness. "You'll tell the Hierophant where to find us."

"Please," the woman repeated. "He'll die if you don't let me take him."

"No healer is going to help you anyway," Hassan hissed. "And besides, isn't the Grace of Blood an abomination to you? Or now that you need a healer that doesn't matter anymore?"

The woman let out a whimper and Anton caught Jude's eyes, knowing what he was about to do.

Jude let go of the dark-haired Witness and nodded down at the one bleeding on the floor. "Go. Take him."

Prince Hassan gaped at Jude in disbelief, but a moment later he let go of the Witness, too.

She didn't thank them, didn't say a word as she stooped down and heaved the other Witness to his feet. They staggered out the door.

"What was that?" Anton demanded, rounding on Illya.

Illya turned away, flicking blood off the dagger. "Self-preservation. The Hierophant would have me killed if he knew I didn't have the Chalice anymore." He resheathed his blade.

"The Chalice isn't here?" Prince Hassan asked.

Jude glanced at him. "What do you know about the Chalice? And how did you find us?"

"I didn't," Hassan replied. "I was captured by the Hierophant. He took me here, to Behezda. He's searching for the Four Sacred Relics. He already has the Relic of Mind. And it's . . . it was my fault. A mistake. I'm here to make it right. I followed the Witnesses here to stop the Hierophant from getting the Chalice."

"How do you know about the Relics?" Anton asked.

Hassan squinted at him. "Who are you? And where's the rest of the Guard?"

Jude crossed the room toward Anton in a few short steps. "The Guard is . . . not here. Prince Hassan, this is Anton. He's the Last Prophet."

Prince Hassan stared at Anton, a complicated mix of emotions on his face. Anton felt the silence lengthen, growing awkward.

"He's also my brother," Illya added.

Anton ignored him. "We need to find the Hierophant. Can you help us do that?"

Hassan nodded. "I know he's heading to the Red Gate."

"So we go there. Stop him, get the Crown." Anton looked at Jude.

"And the Chalice?" Jude asked.

"I don't know," Anton said. "But I do know that everything is pointing me to the Gate."

"What about him?" Hassan asked, indicating Illya.

"I'll be getting out of this city as soon as possible."

Jude cast Anton an apologetic look and then grabbed Illya's arm before he could leave. "You're coming with us."

"What?" Anton demanded. "Why?"

"You know the Hierophant," Jude said to Illya. "You followed his orders. We need to know what we're walking into."

"I don't know him *that* well." Jude squeezed his arm tighter. "All right, all right!" Illya relented.

"One wrong move and you're dead," Jude warned. He let go of Illya, who flinched, and Anton couldn't help but feel a little smug.

Jude reached for Anton's hand. "You ready?"

"No," Anton answered, lacing their fingers together. "But that's not going to stop me this time."

50

EPHYRA

EPHYRA WANTED TO SCREAM. SHE WANTED TO RAGE AT HECTOR. THREATEN him. And she wanted to rejoice. To sob with relief.

Beru was alive.

But maybe not for long.

"How can the Necromancer King still be alive?" Hector asked. "He lived over five hundred years ago."

"He was powerful, even without the Chalice. My guess is he's been siphoning off *esha* in order to lengthen his life."

Hector closed his eyes. "It was him. It must have been. He's the one who brought me back."

"What does he want with you?" Ephyra asked. "With Beru?"

"I don't know," Hector replied. "He only told us he needed the Chalice to save her."

Of course. The Necromancer King would want the Chalice back, to restore himself to full power. And then what?

"We need to find it," Ephyra said, pushing herself to her feet.

Without the Chalice, the Necromancer King would overpower her. Even if they found Beru, it wouldn't matter.

"What happened to it?" Hector asked.

"Someone stole it from me," Ephyra replied. Illya. "But before that I used it. I . . . killed with it. I can still feel an echo of its power."

"So you can find it?" Hector asked.

"I think so." She glanced at him sharply. "Did you really come here to save Beru?"

Hector let out a breath and nodded.

"Why?"

"I just . . ." He pursed his lips. "It's a feeling. I don't know. I need to protect her."

The last time she'd seen Hector and Beru together, he had been waiting for her to die. His death was what had finally torn Ephyra and Beru apart. She felt unsettled to know that some sort of bond had formed between Beru and Hector after all that. She knew Beru had had a crush on Hector when they were kids—she'd once teased her for it until Beru got so mad she kicked her.

Ephyra was so used to being Beru's protector. It made her feel strange to think of someone else in that role. And not just anyone—Hector.

"If you're lying to me," she warned.

"I'm not."

Ephyra took a deep breath, her heart racing. Her palms tingled. She could feel the Chalice's pull best when she was using her Grace.

"Give me your hand," she said to Hector.

He glanced at her warily.

"If we want to find the Chalice, you need to trust me," she said impatiently.

"I'm not sure I can do that," he replied. "Considering, well . . . everything."

She didn't have time for this. She reached for him. He batted her hand away. She lunged again and before she could blink he had an arm curled around her neck.

"Don't touch me," he said.

She slipped her hand up, wrapping it around his wrist. She'd done this once before. Just once. Siphoning off a small, insignificant amount of *esha* from Illya to enter the tomb of the Sacrificed Queen. She breathed in, felt Hector's pulse tap against her hand and coaxed out a thread of his *esha*.

Hector withdrew his arm from around her abruptly, evidently realizing what she was doing. She broke away from him, the zing of his *esha* sparking through her.

It was enough. She felt the faint tug of the Chalice's power, whispering against the edges of her Grace.

Hector stared at her in horror.

"Come on," she said, ignoring his expression. "I know where the Chalice is."

They journeyed toward the edge of the city, toward the gate that traversed the mouth of the canyon.

"It's close," Ephyra said to Hector. What was Illya doing all the way out here?

Hector stopped suddenly, going tense at her side. Ephyra drew up beside him. She followed his intent gaze. In the shadow of the city gates stood a tall figure.

Ephyra glanced at Hector.

He took a halting step forward. "It's him."

Ephyra hesitantly followed. The man suddenly swiveled around, noticing her presence. He was tall and thin, with long dark hair and a hint of scruff on his chin. Tattoos covered every inch of skin that Ephyra could see.

"Well," the man said, smiling. "I'm having quite the lucky day. I finally get to meet the Pale Hand."

His genuine excitement disoriented Ephyra for a moment. Was this really the Necromancer King? He looked almost friendly. But that was definitely the Chalice, gleaming in his hand. And behind him, emerging from the shadows, was Beru.

Ephyra froze.

"Ephyra," Beru said, her eyes wide.

She was really alive. She was right in front of her.

"How did you get that?" Hector demanded, striding toward the Necromancer King.

He held up the Chalice, as if admiring it. His eyes flickered to Ephyra. "You want it, don't you?"

"Let her go," Ephyra said, her voice shaking with fury.

The Necromancer King raised one eyebrow. "I'd be happy to. Let's make a deal, shall we?"

"What kind of deal?" Ephyra asked, wary.

"A simple trade," the Necromancer King replied. "You, for your sister."

"Ephyra, you can't," Beru said. "He wants your power."

The Necromancer King's laugh was loud and booming. "She's right! Your sister's so wise, isn't she? I'll tell you the story if you like. It's a good one—very tragic."

"Spare me," Ephyra replied. "I already know you gave me some of your Grace."

"Yes, well," the Necromancer King sighed. "We all make mistakes."

"So now, what, you want it back?"

The Necromancer King tilted his head. "It's only fair." He looked down at the Chalice in his hand. "Last time I had possession of this Chalice, its power overwhelmed me. Turned on me. But with you . . . with you it will be different. With you, it won't resist me."

"Let her go," Ephyra said again. "And I'll give you anything you want."

The Necromancer King smiled. "Yes, you will."

Ephyra stepped toward him. He withdrew his hand from Beru, but she didn't move.

"Don't do this," she pleaded. "Please. Not for me."

Ephyra stepped toward her sister. Beru moved out of her reach. Ephyra let her hand fall.

Ephyra turned to Hector. "I'm trusting you. But if you hurt her—"

"I won't," he said. "I couldn't."

Ephyra nodded. "Then get her out of here."

The Necromancer King held out his hand. Ephyra took it.

He yanked her toward him and Ephyra stumbled as he gripped her wrist and pulled her arm out in front of him. She sucked in a harsh breath and heard Beru's gasp behind her.

With his other hand, the Necromancer King withdrew a knife. Ephyra cried out and tried to break away, certain he was about to kill her.

The knife slashed at her arm, just above her wrist. Calmly, he put the knife away and picked up the Chalice, holding it beneath the flow of Ephyra's blood.

"What are you doing?" Ephyra demanded.

He hummed gently, and then released her arm before swirling the blood inside the Chalice.

Ephyra watched in horror as he lifted the Chalice to his lips and drank. When he looked back up from the Chalice, his eyes were glowing.

"What did you just do?" she demanded.

The Necromancer King smiled, wiping a drop of blood from the corner of his mouth. Ephyra held her bleeding arm as he closed his eyes and raised one hand toward Hector.

Ephyra gasped, feeling her own Grace respond. Hector let out a grunt of pain and staggered, like he was fighting an invisible force. Then he grabbed Beru roughly by the shoulders.

Beru cried out, struggling against his hold. "Hector—what—"

"I'm sorry," he bit out, sounding like he had to fight to speak. "I'm not—this isn't me."

Ephyra's gaze went back to the Necromancer King, and she understood at once. The Necromancer King had commanded his revenant armies with the Chalice. He had *controlled* them. The same way he was controlling Hector now.

"This wasn't our deal," Ephyra raged. "You said you would let her go!"

The Necromancer King glanced at her. "I did, didn't I? I just never said I wouldn't take her back. You really should be more careful in the future."

He turned and swept away. Hector followed, dragging Beru with him.

"Ephyra!" Beru's panicked voice cried. "Ephyra, don't—don't let him—"

"Where are you taking them?" Ephyra asked.

"To get what I've lived for these last few centuries," he replied. "Revenge."

51

JUDE

THE RED GATE OF MERCY LOOMED BEFORE THEM, ITS SHADOW STRETCHING across the cracked earth as the sun sank over the desert. The ruins of Behezda's original city center spread out around them. The Hierophant and about thirty of his Witnesses stood in their shadow. Beside the Hierophant was an unfamiliar Herati man, bound by Godfire chains.

"Arash," Prince Hassan said. The chained man's gaze flickered toward him but he did not reply.

On the Hierophant's other side, a Witness clutched a glass box, inside of which sat a golden crown. The Relic of Mind.

The masked Witness who had attacked Jude and Anton in Kerameikos and Endarrion stepped out from the ranks, in front of the Hierophant.

"Illya Aliyev," the Hierophant said. "Where is the Chalice?"

Beside Jude, Illya tensed. "I had a run-in. Someone stole it."

"You let the Relic of Blood get stolen?" The Hierophant's tone sharpened.

"Didn't you do enough damage in Nazirah?" the masked Witness demanded. "When you let the Prophet go free? The Immaculate One had to send me to clean up after your mistake."

"And you've done such a wonderful job," Illya said drily. "Who was it who let the Prophet and the Keeper of the Word slip through their hands not once, but *twice*? And who is it who's standing here with not only the Prophet and the Keeper, but also two of the Relics?"

"Enough," Jude said. He faced the Hierophant, his hand on the hilt of his blade. "We know what you're planning. But if you unseal the Gate, you'll start the Age of Darkness."

"And you still think you can stop it," the Hierophant said.

"Why are you doing this?"

"Because we were *wrong*," the Hierophant said. "When the Prophets slew the god and took his power . . . they strayed from his plan. And we paid for it. So now we must set it right. We must open the Gate."

"You will bring ruin to the whole world," Anton said. "I've seen it. Is that really what you want?"

"When will you understand?" the Hierophant said. "It is not about what I *want*. Nor what you want. Our human desires do not matter. We are merely instruments to the will of the world."

Jude's faith had been broken before, but something had changed within him the night they'd left the Order behind. For the first time, he'd put his faith wholly in himself. No one, not even the Hierophant, could break it now.

"You think you have a choice?" the Hierophant asked. "That any of us do?"

"Yes," Jude said, staring into his bright blue eyes. "I do."

He undid his cloak, letting it fall from his shoulders. He folded it up neatly, walked calmly over to Anton, and then held it out to him. Anton took it hesitantly.

The masked Witness unsheathed his Godfire sword. The flames rippled brightly in the fading sunlight.

Jude gripped the hilt of the Pinnacle Blade. He could feel the surge of its power. He closed his eyes.

Please, he thought desperately.

The scarred Witness attacked. Jude tried to unsheathe his sword, summoning his Grace. It flickered to life and then sputtered out.

"You think you can still rely on that vile corruption?" the Witness spat.

He struck again, fast and hard to Jude's left. Jude turned, dodging the blow. The Witness slammed his fist into Jude's ribs.

"Jude!" He heard Anton's panicked voice behind him.

Jude choked out a gasp, air punching out of his lungs.

The Godfire sword swung down again and Jude barely had time to block it with his sheathed sword. Their swords crossed, bringing them face-to-face, and Jude stared into the Witness's eyes and the thin, pale scars around them.

Horror filled him, as it had the first time he had seen the evidence of what this man had done to himself. But with horror came something else, something he had tried not to see. Recognition. No matter how sickened he was at the thought that this man had burned his own Grace out, there was a part of him that understood it completely. Understood the overwhelming drive to prove himself worthy to a cause that wanted nothing less than his self-destruction.

They shared the same scars. And only now was Jude able to see the other ones, the invisible ones that the Order of the Last Light had left on him. The self-immolation that he had performed again and again, to deny the entirety of who he was, to burn away the parts that the Order did not want him to be. Reflected in the Witness's awful, senseless devotion was Jude's.

He did not want to see himself in this man, but he did.

"It will never be enough," Jude said. "You can devote every part of yourself to the Witnesses, to the Hierophant, and it will never be enough."

"You know nothing about me, about my devotion, or the Immaculate One!" The Witness lashed out with a roar, striking hard. Jude threw himself to the side to avoid it, and landed lightly on his toes.

He knew what he had to do.

The Witness charged at him again and Jude reached for the hilt of the Pinnacle Blade.

Stop fighting, the Nameless Woman had said.

He felt the weight of the sword in his hands.

He thought of drawing it in the Hidden Spring. Of Anton's fearful face in the window. Of that same face staring up at him in the cistern, the true north of his heart's compass. It had felt like being found.

And not because he was the Prophet, but because Jude had waited his whole life to find him, and when he had, it was nothing like he'd ever imagined. Anton was stubborn, and beautiful, and infuriating, and Jude had spent so much time pretending he wasn't set ablaze every time Anton so much as looked at him. He could not do it anymore. He would not.

He gathered his faith within him and moved through the koah. Breath. Movement. Intention.

He would let those feelings, the truth of his heart, take shape inside him. They would guide him, the way his faith in the Order once had, before that had shredded to pieces. Anton did not believe in the things Jude had believed in, but he believed in *Jude* and that was enough. It was more than enough, more than anything he'd ever been given. The seeds of Anton's faith made it possible for Jude's own faith to take root.

His Grace roared to life, echoing through his veins, flooding him with strength. A powerful storm raged inside him, unstoppable, undeniable. He was Jude Weatherbourne, Keeper of the Word. Captain of the Paladin Guard.

A boy with a heart in his chest and a sword in his hand.

Dust and sand swirled around him as he turned, drawing the Pinnacle Blade to block the Witness's attack. The strength of his parry pushed the Witness back. Jude went on the offensive, striking quickly. The Witness leaned away from the attack, the Pinnacle Blade passing over him by a hair.

The Witness stumbled, and Jude struck again, meeting the Godfire blade with a surge of strength. The combined power of the Pinnacle Blade and Jude's Grace blew the Witness off his feet, the Godfire sword flinging out of his hands.

He went down hard, sliding backward in the dirt and kicking up dust. His crumpled form let out a soft groan and he tried to crawl to his feet before giving up and collapsing back into the dirt.

Jude let him be. He wasn't the one they needed to stop. He advanced on the Hierophant. The Relic of Heart in his hand reverberated with power—so much power that Jude's body could not contain it alone. It spilled out into the air around him, kicking up dust and sand.

The Hierophant took a step back. His Witnesses closed ranks around him, but Jude barely paid them any mind. The Pinnacle Blade was alive in his hands as he whipped toward the Hierophant, felling any Witness who dared enter his path. Dozens fell in a matter of seconds.

In the length of a heartbeat he was on the Hierophant.

"Stop!" the Hierophant cried, flinging himself backward.

Jude stalked forward, raising his sword.

"Stop!" the Hierophant cried again. "Keeper. You know not who you seek to kill."

"I know you must be stopped," Jude replied. "And that is enough."

With shaking hands, the Hierophant reached behind his head and unhooked his mask, letting it fall. What Jude saw in its place made his blood freeze.

"You don't want to kill me," the Hierophant said. "You were born to serve me."

Jude stared down at the Hierophant.

The face of the Prophet Pallas stared back.

52

ANTON

THE STORM OF JUDE'S *ESHA* WAS LOUDER AND MORE POWERFUL THAN ANTON had ever felt it.

But even louder still was the silence that followed Jude's three uttered words: "Pallas the Faithful."

"Yes," the Hierophant—Pallas—said. "That was my name, once."

Anton watched horror and disbelief cloud Jude's eyes. His whole life had been devoted to serving the Prophets. Anton could not fathom how he felt now, facing the origin of his faith and hearing this man—Prophet—reject everything he had once stood for. To know that it wasn't just the Order that had let him down, but the Prophets themselves.

"It's not possible," Jude said. "This . . . it's a trick."

A wave of *esha* burst across Anton's senses. But it wasn't coming from Jude. This was one Anton had never felt before. It was hollow and deep, like an endless echo.

An unfamiliar voice rang through the air. "It is no trick."

Anton turned and saw a tall man with long dark hair standing at the edge of the ruins, holding what Anton knew at once to be the Relic of Blood. Beside him was Ephyra.

"Hello, Pallas," the man said, almost tenderly.

"Eleazar," Pallas replied sharply. "I never imagined I would see you again. I assumed you'd waste away in the desert."

Eleazar. The Necromancer King.

"Oh, well, I'm sorry to disappoint," the Necromancer King replied. "I, on the other hand, have imagined this moment many, many times. I'm delighted you survived to see it."

Anton studied Ephyra who stood rigidly beside the Necromancer King, her hand wrapped around her own bloody arm. She looked washed out, drained. What had led her to the Necromancer King's side? It didn't look like she was there by choice.

"All those years and you couldn't find anything better to do than nurse a centuries-old grudge," Pallas sneered.

"You did banish me to a desolate wasteland for over five hundred years," the Necromancer King said. "I found nursing my grudge to be a very productive use of that time."

"Behezda banished you," Pallas replied. "I wanted to kill you."

The Necromancer King smiled, gleeful. "Yes, you probably should have."

In the distance, Anton could see two more people approaching the Red Gate.

He knew when Jude had spotted them by his sharp intake of breath and the quietly uttered, "Hector?"

A stab of anger went through Anton. He remembered well what had transpired the last time Jude had seen Hector. That anyone could throw away Jude's friendship, his *love*, was unfathomable. Anton could see the raw pain on Jude's face and longed to cross toward him and comfort him.

But as his gaze went back to Hector, he saw that something was wrong. Hector went to the Necromancer King, pulling Beru with him, but he seemed to struggle with every step. As if he wasn't in control of himself.

Cold dread seeped through Anton's veins. Beru was here. This is what he'd seen in his vision. They were standing on the precipice of the Age of Darkness, and Anton didn't know how to stop it.

"You see, Pallas?" the Necromancer King said. "You aren't the only one with followers."

"You mean undead abominations you've enslaved," Pallas said.

Anton glanced back to Ephyra, who did not seem surprised by the appearance of Beru and Hector. He had to get her attention somehow. If she could steal the Chalice while the Necromancer King was distracted, they still had a chance to reseal the Gate. But her gaze was locked on Beru.

"Illya," Pallas said. "Since you let the Chalice slip through your fingers once, it falls to you to get it back."

Illya didn't move.

"Illya," Pallas said again, with less patience.

Jude turned toward Anton, catching his gaze. He glanced over to the Necromancer King, and then tilted his head back toward the Witness with the Crown.

Anton understood at once. He stepped toward Prince Hassan and nudged him discreetly. "The Crown," Anton said in a low voice. "We can get it while the Hierophant is distracted."

Hassan nodded. "What do we need to do to seal the Gate?"

"Someone to wield each of the Relics," Anton said. "And then I'll use my Grace to bind it."

"Is that something you've done before?"

"No," Anton admitted.

"Arash can wield the Relic of Mind," Hassan said, sounding pained by the idea. "We just need to get him out of the Godfire chains."

"All right," Anton said. "You get him. I'll get the Crown while Jude causes a diversion."

In front of them, the Necromancer King was holding the Chalice in one hand, his other outstretched to the Hierophant. The Hierophant sucked in a sharp breath and began to shake violently. The Necromancer King was draining his *esha*.

Jude ran for the Necromancer King, moving so quickly he was just a blur.

The clang of steel rang out and Jude skidded to a stop, the Pinnacle Blade locked with Hector's sword.

"*No*," Jude gasped. "Hector."

"I'm sorry," Hector cried out. "I can't stop myself!"

He attacked again and Jude did nothing more than parry the blow.

Anton bit his lip and forced himself to look away. He had to trust Jude. "*Now*," he hissed at Hassan.

The two of them took off, running at the Witnesses at the foot of the Gate. Anton flung himself at the Witness guarding the Crown, crying out as they toppled over. The box that held the Crown hit the ground beside them.

Anton dove for it. The Witness wrapped his arms around Anton's waist, holding him back. More Witnesses surrounded Anton, running for the Crown. Anton twisted and kicked the box as hard as he could away from them. It skipped across the rock and shattered open near where Hassan was fighting off another group of Witnesses, brandishing one of their Godfire chains.

The Witness leapt off Anton, following the others toward the Crown, but he was too late. Hassan picked it up and held it in his hands. Beside him, the other Herati man, Arash, was struggling to his feet, his Godfire chains coiled on the ground.

"Take it," Hassan said brusquely, thrusting the Crown at Arash.

Hesitantly, he reached for it.

"Anton, now!" Jude called. He was still battling Hector back. Behind him, the Hierophant was on his knees before the Necromancer King, who glowed with the Chalice's power.

"The Crown," Anton said to Arash. "You need to use it."

Arash looked down at the Crown and placed it on his head. Anton gripped the Relic of Sight, closing his eyes. He could feel the power of each of the Relics surging together, threading into one another. The Crown, the Blade, the Chalice, the Stone. Bright, cold light surrounded him. This was the god's *esha*, both the source of his power and the only thing powerful enough to contain him.

Through the Stone, Anton could see everything around him, although not with his eyes. All around him were concentrated, beating hearts of *esha*, each distinct. And where the Red Gate of Mercy stood, the threads of *esha* in each of the Relics knotted together, forming the seal that kept the god's energy trapped inside. Bursts of *esha* radiated out of it, making it look almost like a tiny sun, or a compass rose.

That was what Anton needed to repair.

He reached out and touched the Red Gate. He suddenly knew what he needed to do, by the same instinct that had caused his Grace to call out to Jude in the cistern in Nazirah. He breathed in and directed his own power toward the seal, his Grace reverberating out from him. He felt the smooth rock surface of the Gate and tried to bend the power of the combined Relics toward it. The Relics' *esha* resisted. They did not want to be controlled.

He dug his heels into the ground and pushed the Relics' *esha* with his Grace as hard as he could, shepherding it toward the Gate, into the broken seal.

His Grace strained inside of him. He was stretching it to its limits, even with the added power of the Stone. His knees hit the ground and still he held on, even as the white light screamed inside his head.

It was too much. The pain and the light would scorch his mind. That much power would overtake him. Drive him mad, just like Vasili. He would be nothing but a hollow shell. His grip on the Relics' *esha* began to slacken.

This was what his vision had been trying to tell him. This was what had scared him, paralyzed him. That bright, cold light—it was the god. And it was far, far too powerful for him.

He felt someone grab him and wrench him back from the Gate, severing his connection with the seal. Without a place to direct the *esha* of the Relic, it stormed through him, muting all of his senses. When the shock of it faded, Anton was on his back. Someone's hand closed around the Stone, ripping it from his neck.

"No!" Anton cried, opening his eyes and jerking upright. The world swam around him. All he saw was Pallas in front of him, holding the Stone. Somehow, he'd gotten free of the Necromancer King.

Anton could still feel the *esha* of the Relic, but there was nothing he could do as Pallas took up the combined power of the Relics' *esha*. It crashed through the Gate, shattering the seal.

Cold, bright light flooded out, bathing the world in its glow, whiting out everything around Anton until it was all he could see.

53

EPHYRA

EPHYRA HAD WATCHED THE SCARRED SWORDSMAN STRIKE THE NECROMANCER King with his Godfire blade. For a moment Ephyra had felt like it was burning her own skin.

The Necromancer King had had the Hierophant in his clutches, draining the *esha* from him—slowly, she assumed, because he wanted the Hierophant to fully comprehend his defeat.

But then the Witness's attack had set the Hierophant free, and Ephyra watched as he raced toward the Red Gate of Mercy.

In front of her, white flames danced on the Necromancer King's skin as he writhed in pain, the Chalice still clutched in his hand.

"*NO!*" he roared. The Chalice seemed to glow in his grip and Ephyra felt her own Grace reach out toward him. Somehow, impossibly, his burns began to heal.

A sharp cry of anguish rang through the air. Ephyra whirled, heart pounding. Beru lay sprawled in the dirt, in the shadow of a crumbling wall that must have once belonged to a great tower.

"Beru!" Ephyra cried, rushing toward her.

She reached Beru's side and dropped down in the rubble, cradling her sister in her arms. It took her a moment to understand what was happening. The Necromancer King was drawing Ephyra's Grace to strengthen his own, but it was Beru's *esha* that he needed to heal the Godfire burns.

She had to stop him.

He was pulling on her Grace, pulling on the Chalice to heal himself, but the Godfire persisted, trying to burn out his Grace even as he used it, as if the fire and his Grace were pushing against each other, neither one powerful enough to douse the other.

Ephyra closed her eyes, clutching Beru tighter, and focused on the *esha* draining out of her. She pushed with her Grace, grabbing hold of the *esha* to staunch the flow, but no matter how hard she pressed, Beru's *esha* spilled out of her like water in a cracked glass. She could feel it dwindling, Beru fading right under her hands.

"Ephyra?" Beru said faintly, looking up at Ephyra with unfocused eyes.

"I'm here," Ephyra said, pressing her palm to Beru's heart. "It's going to be all right."

"I'm scared," Beru said in a tiny voice.

In all their years together fighting and scrambling to keep Beru alive, Beru had never once let on how scared she was. No matter how weak she got or how awful she felt, Beru put on a brave face. Ephyra had always known it was an act, but to see that act finally shatter terrified her.

Ephyra wouldn't fail her. Not again. She let go of Beru's *esha*, even as it poured out of her. She could still feel the Necromancer King's Grace pulling at hers. Ephyra summoned all of her strength—all of her rage and her grief and even the nothingness that had consumed her when she'd thought Beru was dead—and pulled back.

The Necromancer King's Grace and the Chalice stuttered in her grip. Beru's heartbeat slowed under her palm.

No, Ephyra thought desperately. The Chalice called to her. Ephyra opened herself to it. Let it in. She was a conduit. She saw now what the Chalice wanted. Why it had turned on the Necromancer King. The Chalice did not want to be controlled.

Its power surged into Ephyra, breaking free from the Necromancer King's control. The Necromancer King let out an agonized scream as the Godfire overtook him, but it sounded far-off. Ephyra's Grace thrummed inside of her. It seeped out of her, too much for her body to contain.

It was not just the Chalice, she realized. Energy more powerful than anything Ephyra had ever felt flooded through her, burning hot and uncontrollable. Ephyra's hands were on Beru. Without knowing what she was doing or why, Ephyra guided the energy into her sister.

Whatever this was, it would save her, for good this time.

When she opened her eyes, four thick threads of *esha* were twisting around Beru like billowing smoke. She could *see* them. They spiraled around Beru and she began to glow from within, brighter and brighter. Fissures of light formed like cracks on her body.

Ephyra gasped through her tears. It was too late to stop the *esha* flowing into Beru. She could only hold on, swept inside its current, until it crested like a wave and *broke*.

It knocked Ephyra flat on her back, as if she'd been caught in a blast, with Beru at its origin. She crawled to her knees. Everything around her was still. The fighting had ceased. And there was Beru, lying on the ground, unmoving.

It felt like Ephyra's insides had been incinerated. A pitiful sound tore from her throat.

Beru stirred. Her eyes flew open.

Ephyra felt the air leave her lungs in a rush of relief. She had done it. She'd saved her. Nothing else mattered.

Beru got to her feet, smoothly, calmly, and then turned her head, surveying the scene before her. Her eyes landed on Ephyra, pinned there. Ephyra froze under her gaze.

That wasn't Beru.

She'd brought something *else* back.

54

BERU

BERU'S EYES OPENED. THAT'S WHAT IT FELT LIKE–NOT THAT *SHE* HAD OPENED her eyes, but that her eyes had opened on their own, upon some order that she herself had not given.

Her skin felt warm, tingling like a lightning storm raged beneath it. She felt herself rise to her feet, and again she knew it was not *her* doing it.

WHAT . . . IS THIS PLACE?

The thought. Again, not hers.

WHERE AM I?

And then.

WHAT AM I?

There were people around her. She saw Ephyra, on her knees in the dirt, as if bowing in supplication. Something about that felt right. Her eyes moved and she saw a tall, robed figure standing in the shadow of a red gate.

YOU. I KNOW YOU.

There was hatred in her gut. Betrayal. That man had done something to her. No, not to her. To *it*. The . . . presence inside her.

It wanted to crush him. But being in her body—that was new to it. It looked down at her hands. They were so small. What could hands like these do?

Her mouth opened. What came out was not a word. It was a sound like a sob, or a scream.

She watched Ephyra reel back.

The being inside her wanted to destroy. She could feel it building, this hunger, this need. Beru gathered her will. It was still confused. Hesitant. Unsure.

She opened her mouth once more. The sound came out again. She screamed, and screamed, and then her scream broke off and Beru pushed with everything she had and said, "*Get out of here. Get out of here now!*"

The being didn't want her to speak. It cut her off with a choke.

Get out of here get out of here get out of here, she thought. No sound came out.

The robed man moved toward them. He, too, bowed in supplication. This did not please the being. The man could not be trusted. The man—

The man had killed it.

The man had promised to serve it, but he had killed it.

"YOU," Beru's voice hissed, full of more hatred than she had ever felt in her life.

The man looked up at her, his blue eyes bright and glassy. There was fear on his face.

The being inside Beru writhed with fury. It remembered what it was now. It was a god. It had created all of this, the sand, the people, the sky. It had been the god of creation.

But it had been destroyed. And now remade. And it was something else now.

It was a god of destruction.

55

JUDE

THE GROUND TREMBLED BENEATH JUDE AS HE KNELT BESIDE ANTON'S STILL form.

"Anton," he pleaded, taking Anton's face in his hands. "Come on. Please. Wake up."

He wasn't dead, Jude knew that much. When his Grace had returned to him in full force, he had suddenly been able to sense Anton's—the way that he had in Nazirah. It was fainter than it had been then, a quiet undercurrent, but it was enough.

A high, frightened scream tore through the air. Jude looked up, and saw the girl—no, the creature—standing in the middle of the ruins, her face shadowed. She looked frayed, like she'd been ripped apart and put back together jaggedly. The power radiating off her was like nothing Jude had ever felt before. It was dark, chaotic, so potent he could hear it, a deep, bone-shaking roar.

The Hierophant was a blur of motion, tearing away from her.

Ephyra knelt at her sister's feet.

"*Go, Ephyra!*" Beru cried. "I can't hold it back any longer."

"No," Ephyra said fiercely. "I won't leave you!"

Another figure sprinted toward Ephyra's crumpled form. Illya. A loud crack startled Jude and he glanced up to see the Red Gate of Mercy beginning to crumble, the first pieces of debris crashing down just feet away from him. An even louder crash sounded as the arch of the Gate caved in.

Heart leaping in his throat, Jude wrapped his arms around Anton and heaved him to his feet.

Anton let out a soft groan and shifted. "Jude?"

Jude tucked himself under Anton's side. "We need to get out of here."

"The Gate," Anton said. "I couldn't—"

"Jude!" another voice called out. Hector sped toward them.

Jude gaped at him. He didn't understand why Hector had seemed to be under the Necromancer King's control, but he didn't appear to be anymore. There was no time to ask that or any other of the questions spinning through Jude's mind.

Hector reached them and without a word, slung an arm around Anton's other side, propping him up. "Come on."

The three of them careened away from the destruction, away from the god, as the cacophonous sound of the collapsing Gate rang around them. The sky flashed with bright, white light, like the biggest lightning storm Jude had ever witnessed.

They didn't stop until they reached the city walls, almost a mile from the Red Gate. Anton was still conscious, but not strong enough to stand on his own, so Jude and Hector helped him lean against the wall. Jude looped an arm around his waist for support.

"So, you've been keeping busy?" Hector asked mildly.

Jude huffed out a laugh. He didn't understand how Hector was here, what had brought them together again, but in the midst of the terror around them, it was something to cherish.

"You could say that," he answered. "Hector, what *was* that back there? With the Necromancer King?"

Hector sighed. "It'll be easier to show you."

Before Jude could question what that meant, Hector peeled off his shirt and turned around. Jude's eyes widened. A dark handprint stood out against Hector's tan skin.

"It was Ephyra. She killed me to save her sister."

Jude's next breath choked him. His heart plunged into his stomach. *Killed?*

"The Necromancer King brought me back," Hector continued, pulling his shirt back on. "It created a connection between me and Beru. Between our *esha*. I can feel what she feels. But right now . . . right now what I feel is the thing inside her. It's angry. It wants to destroy."

Jude suppressed a shiver. "I think I know what it is. I think . . . I think Ephyra resurrected an ancient god inside her sister's body."

It was exactly what Anton had seen in his vision.

"How—?" Hector cut himself off, staring at Jude. "Actually, you know what? I've heard and seen a lot of truly unbelievable things today, so I'm going to just go with you on that."

"Captain Weatherbourne," a voice said from behind them.

Jude turned to find Prince Hassan standing before them, looking scratched up but otherwise unharmed. He held the Crown of Herat in one hand.

"Prince Hassan," Jude said. "Are you all right?"

Hassan nodded, a haunted look in his eyes. "Arash, he . . . he didn't make it."

His countryman. "I'm sorry," Jude replied.

Hector was staring at Prince Hassan. "Aren't you the Prophet?"

Jude and Hassan exchanged a look.

Anton weakly raised his head from Jude's shoulder. "That would be me, actually."

Hector gaped at him, and then at Jude. "Is he joking?"

Before Jude could reply, the sky flashed bright with white light. The wall behind them began to shake, and it was a moment before Jude realized that it wasn't just the wall—it was the whole city.

"She's going to destroy Behezda," Hassan said faintly.

"It's still confused," Hector said. "I think it's just smashing things at random, trying to kill the Hierophant. It *hates* him."

"Then we should give him to it," Hassan said bitterly.

"The Hierophant might be the only one who knows how to stop it," Anton said. "Pallas, I mean. He's a Prophet. He's dealt with the god before."

Jude clenched his jaw at the reminder of the Hierophant's true identity. Pallas the Faithful. It filled him with horror and loathing to think what he had once worshipped had become this.

"We need to find him," Anton decided.

That broke through Jude's disgust. "No," he protested. "You're weak. You nearly *died*. And you don't have the Relic of Sight anymore."

"I failed," Anton said. "Let me do this."

Jude met Anton's eyes in grim acknowledgment. Trying to seal the Gate had almost killed Anton. But what it had unleashed might kill them all.

With a deep breath and a nod of assent, Jude curled his fingers around Anton's as if to say, *I'm here.* Anton closed his eyes and Jude felt him summon some deep reserve of energy, his Grace strengthening.

He swayed, eyes blinking open as he let his weight fall on Jude. "He's fleeing toward the mountain."

"I know where they're going," Hassan said. "There's a cave where the Hierophant and his Witnesses had me locked up."

Jude curled a hand around Anton's shoulder and looked up at Hector and Hassan. "You two, go find him. We'll wait for you here."

"What?" Anton demanded. "Why are they going?"

"Because you're about to collapse," Jude replied evenly. "So we're going to stay here while you recover your strength. Hector and Prince Hassan can handle it."

Anton did not look pleased, but he didn't try to move away from Jude, either.

Jude looked up to find Hector staring at them.

"Be safe," Jude said to him.

Hector just nodded and jogged after Hassan, who had already turned to go.

Another quake shook the ground and Jude turned to shield Anton between the wall and his own body as dust rained down. The shaking stopped but Jude stayed where he was, Anton's heart a steady pulse against his own.

"I couldn't do it," Anton said, his voice breaking. "We had the Relics. I was right there. And now the Age of Darkness is coming and—"

"We won't let it," Jude said fiercely, gripping Anton's hand. "We're going to make it out of here. I promise you. Whatever happens, I'll protect you, remember? Whatever happens."

Anton didn't say anything, just held Jude's hand tighter as the city crumbled around them.

56

EPHYRA

EPHYRA WOKE UP PINNED TO THE GROUND. SHE COUGHED OUT DUST AND raised her head weakly. Debris and rocks were piled high behind her.

There was no sign of Beru, but Ephyra wasn't alone. Someone lay beside her, half-covered by fallen rocks. She rolled the person over and saw it was Illya. His eyes were closed, and for a moment Ephyra thought he was dead. But his chest rose and fell.

She leaned over him, checking for injuries. His shirt was torn open, his whole left side wet with blood. Ephyra set her trembling hands on his ribs.

She had touched him like this before, skin-to-skin, but those nights felt a world away. She pressed down and focused on her own *esha*.

His lashes fluttered. "What are you doing?"

"Saving your life," Ephyra replied. She focused, but she couldn't seem to get her *esha* to flow into him.

"Come on," she whispered, gritting her teeth. The connection kept breaking. "Come *on*."

Illya opened his eyes.

"I'm not good at this," she said. "I haven't done it in so long. I'm . . . I'm better at killing than healing."

His hand came up to rest on hers. She met his gaze.

"You don't have to be what they say," he said. "The Pale Hand. The harbinger. You're not . . . you can be more than that."

"What if I can't?" she said, desperate. Tears soaked her voice. "What if I'm—"

"You're Ephyra," he said. "You can do this."

She shut her eyes and focused on the sound of his breath and her own, feeling the pressure of his hand on hers. The *esha* began to flow, seeping from her hands into him. The point at which they touched grew warm. Tears sprang to her eyes and relief rushed through her. She staunched the flow of *esha* before cutting it off altogether. She shuddered, light-headed, but Illya's wounds were healed.

He sat up, looking himself over in awe. "What happened?"

"My sister," she said, but that was all she could get out. "I need to find her . . . I need to stop that thing."

"I don't think you can."

"That's my *sister*," Ephyra said. "I need to get her back. Tell me what the Hierophant is planning."

"I have no idea what he's planning," Illya said, surprising her. "I knew he wanted the Chalice. That was it. What we need to do now is get out of the city before it's destroyed."

There was a great crash and the southernmost edge of the city seemed to buckle in on itself, the buildings collapsing into the breaking ground.

Illya was right. Going into the city would be suicide. But Ephyra had risked more for Beru every day for most of their lives.

She turned back to him. "Don't you need to go running back to your master now?"

He set his mouth in a tight line. "He's not exactly happy with me."

"Well, isn't that sad for you?" Ephyra sneered.

"He wants to rule the Six Prophetic Cities, not destroy them," Illya said. "Whatever he was planning, I think you screwed it up."

All of this was her fault. She destroyed everything she touched. Which now included an entire city.

"I didn't know this would happen," she said. She looked back at him. "Why did you stay? Why didn't you run?"

"The same reason you healed me," he answered, his eyes intent on hers. "I didn't want to see you die."

She didn't know what to make of that, only that she could no longer look at him. She got to her feet and began making her way toward the city. After a moment, she heard a soft curse and the sound of his footsteps behind her, quickening until he fell into step with her.

"What are you doing?" she demanded.

"I'm coming with you."

"Why? You just said you wanted to get out of this city."

"Well," he said. "There are a few things I want to take care of first."

Screams filled the air as Ephyra and Illya approached the city. Panicking crowds fled through the gates like a stream bursting through a dam. They had to push their way upstream through shrieking families and groaning carts.

"Look," Illya said.

Ephyra followed his gaze toward the city walls and spotted two familiar figures, one crouched over the other. Jude and Anton. Ephyra hurried over, Illya at her heels.

"Where is she?" Ephyra demanded the moment she was by their side.

Jude stood, glancing at Illya warily. "We don't know."

"What's going to happen to her?" Ephyra asked, too aware of the crack of desperation in her voice. She didn't ask the question she truly wanted to know: *What did I do to her?*

"When you brought her back, you brought something else back," Anton said. "A god. One that the Prophets slayed. It's . . . inhabiting her."

"But she's still in there," Ephyra said. "She spoke to me. There must be some way—"

"I don't know," Anton said. "But we need to stop her. However we can. Otherwise this city . . . this *world*, will be destroyed."

A chill crawled down Ephyra's spine. She had done this. *There's something dark inside of us.*

Beru had meant both of them, her and Ephyra. But it was Ephyra who'd unleashed it in them both. Ephyra, who had kept pushing, and pushing, even when Beru told her—*begged* her—to stop. And in the end, she hadn't been able to, not when she'd thought Beru was gone. Because losing Beru meant losing her faith in the world, losing her ability to see the good in people. In herself.

But it was still there, buried deep. She knew that now. She'd seen it when she'd healed Illya. There was something dark inside of her, but there was light, too.

"All right," she said.

Anton looked up at her, startled.

"I'm in," she said. She glanced over her shoulder at Illya. "So is he. What do you need us to do?"

57

HASSAN

HASSAN KEPT PACE WITH THE PALADIN HECTOR AS THEY CROSSED THE CANYON toward the Hierophant's hideout. They passed panicked Behezdans, rushing along the streets and crouching in alcoves to protect themselves from the violent quakes.

Hassan watched it all, helplessness and anger roiling within him. He could tell these people to get out of the city, to safety, but would they really be safe? The god would not stop, not until it had the one it wanted. The Hierophant.

They reached the entrance to the cave, where three Witnesses were standing guard.

"Stand back," Hector warned, and a moment later he was right in front of the Witnesses, his sword unsheathed. Then the Witnesses were on the ground. More rushed in toward them.

"Go on ahead," Hector said, jerking his head and facing off against the newcomers.

With the Witnesses occupied, Hassan darted into corridor and came face-to-face with the Hierophant. Flanked by more Witnesses, he watched Hassan's approach with icy blue eyes.

"*You,*" Hassan spat. "You did this. You brought that *thing* back, and now it's going to destroy this city while you're hiding out in here."

He was so furious, he barely registered the fact that he was charging toward the Hierophant. The Witnesses around him moved to hold Hassan back.

"Is this what you wanted?" Hassan yelled, struggling against them.

Another tremor shook the ground so violently it knocked several of the Witnesses off their feet. Hassan pulled away from them and seized the Hierophant's robes.

"It is, isn't it?" Hassan spat. "You wanted to open the Gate and unleash all that power. To cleanse the world of *your* mistakes. Well the god you brought back wants you dead. And *now* you want to stop it?"

The Hierophant met Hassan's gaze. "The god was never meant to return."

"It wants *you,*" Hassan growled. "Maybe if we hand you over, it will leave the rest of us alone."

"Prince Hassan, no!" Hector cried, and a moment later he felt arms hauling him back, away from the Hierophant.

Hassan whirled. "You think that just because he's a Prophet he's worth protecting? He *did* this. He doomed us all."

"You think a being such as a god will be satisfied with the death of one man?" the Hierophant asked. "No. It will not rest until everything we built is destroyed. This very world is an insult to it—it will wash it clean of any influence from me, from the other Prophets."

Hassan felt his skin prickle, and despite his hatred of the Hierophant he knew that he was telling the truth—or at the least, he believed his own words.

"We still need him," Hector said. "He's the only one who knows how to kill the god."

"Kill it?" the Hierophant said derisively. "It cannot be done. The first time the god was slain, it took seven Prophets. The best we can do is bind it."

"Bind it how?" Hector asked.

"The same way its *esha* was bound beyond the Red Gate," the Hierophant replied. "Only a Prophet can do it."

"We have a Prophet," Hassan replied. "So I guess we don't need you."

But even as he said it, he knew it wasn't completely true. Jude had said that trying to reseal the Red Gate had almost killed Anton. And when they'd left Anton at the city walls, he hadn't exactly looked like he was up for taking on a god. The Hierophant seemed to read the uncertainty in Hassan's eyes.

He smiled. "Even if your Prophet could do it, I have the Relic of Sight."

A loud boom shook the temple.

"We don't have time for this," Hector said. "The city is collapsing as we speak." He looked at the Hierophant. "You're coming with us."

"If you insist," the Hierophant sighed, managing to sound both put-upon and smug at the same time. "My Witnesses will accompany us."

Hassan, Hector, the Hierophant, and ten Witnesses marched out of the cave and back toward the city walls. The streets were flooded with even more people, fleeing out toward the city gates. The crush

470

of the crowd hemmed them in, making it difficult to navigate back to where Jude and Anton were waiting.

When they finally reached them, they were not alone.

Illya Aliyev stood with them, along with the girl—the one who had resurrected the god.

"You found him," Anton said, eyes locked on the Hierophant.

"And you brought Witnesses," Jude said, sounding none too happy about it.

The Witnesses eyed him with equal distaste.

"He's willing to help," Hector said. "Aren't you?"

The Hierophant swept his cold gaze over them. "I know how to stop the god. We need to bind it. But we'll need a place to trap it."

"I know a place," Illya said. "A tomb just outside the city."

"That will lead the god away from Behezda," Jude said approvingly. "But how do we draw it there?"

"I know how," Hassan said at once. He looked at the Hierophant. "We use him as bait."

Hassan couldn't help feeling somewhat victorious as displeasure spread over the Hierophant's stern face.

"Fine," he snapped. "But you all will protect me. And I will need the Relics—all of them, to seal the god away."

Jude nodded. "Once we get to the tomb, they're yours."

"Godfire chains will slow it down," the Hierophant went on. "We can use them to impede it temporarily."

Jude nodded. "All right. Then we all go to the tomb. Pallas will draw the god to us. We'll use the Godfire chains to disarm it, and then seal it inside the tomb."

"And what about Beru?" the girl beside Illya demanded. "We can't just lock her up."

"For now, we have to," Anton said. "Once it's contained, we'll find a way to expel the god from her."

The girl's gaze hardened.

"We'll find a way," Hector said. "We *will*."

"All right," Jude said. "We all know the plan. We all know what happens if we fail." He looked around at all of them. "Let's go capture a god."

58

BERU

THE GOD'S RAGE ONLY GREW, SHACKLING BERU WITHIN IT. SHE HAD MANAGED to hold on for those precious few minutes at the Red Gate, when the god was still confused. But now, the god's will was overpowering. It was like a cage penning her in, leaving her immobile, able only to see what the god was doing.

You are Beru of Medea, she told herself. *You are Ephyra's sister.*

The god's fury thrashed inside of her.

She thought of the oasis. She took herself back there, in the grotto that Hector had showed her the morning before everything had unraveled. That was the last time she'd felt peace. *That girl,* she told herself, as the world shook and broke around her, *that's who you are.* She wasn't this creature. She wasn't this wrath.

Something fluttered at the edge of her awareness. Something calling out to her—no, to *it,* the being inside her.

I'm here, it seemed to say. *Come and get me.*

The Hierophant, Beru understood at once. The god suddenly

halted its destruction, the trembling city going still. The Hierophant was calling to it from somewhere outside the city.

In a burst of bright light, the god transported them there.

The Hierophant stood before them, at the entrance of what appeared to be a tomb. A long courtyard lined with dead trees led to the stone steps of a mausoleum. The Hierophant was not alone. Everyone who'd been at the Red Gate stood with him—everyone except a few who must have either escaped or died when the Gate fell. Hector and Ephyra were among them, as were Anton, and Illya, the golden-eyed boy.

Don't hurt them, Beru pleaded. She did not expect the god to heed her, or even hear her.

The god let out an ear-shattering shriek and flew at the Hierophant. Illya and another boy Beru recognized but did not know dove in front of him, Godfire chains in their hands.

The god roared and thrust Beru's hands out. A burst of white light erupted from her palms, striking the two boys down. The two swordsmen—Hector and another Paladin—closed in on the Hierophant, standing between him and Beru.

"WHY DO YOU PROTECT PALLAS?" It was Beru's mouth that spoke, but it was not her voice. There was an echo of her voice within it, but it sounded ancient and terrible.

"If we give him to you, will you leave this city alone?" Anton asked.

The god's gaze found him on the Paladin's other side. "YOU DO NOT BARGAIN WITH A GOD, LITTLE PROPHET."

The god took a step toward Anton. The other Paladin stepped back, shielding him. The god tilted Beru's head. Something like recognition flashed bright in Beru's mind.

"YOU," the god said. "YOU SHOULD HAVE BEEN MINE."

The Paladin seemed to steel himself as she approached. He went still as she curled a hand beneath his chin, flinching when she lifted it gently.

"YOU WILL BE MINE."

"You can't have him," Anton growled over the Paladin's shoulder.

The god flicked Beru's hand and Anton went flying to the ground. The Paladin tried to whirl toward Anton, but the god held him firm.

"*Jude!*" Hector cried, leaping toward them.

The god waved Beru's hand and Hector collapsed to the ground. A bolt of pain shot through Beru. The god took a wheeling step back and froze, bewildered and incensed. In its distraction, the other Paladin darted off toward Anton.

The god's eyes locked onto Hector's. Beru watched understanding cross Hector's features. The connection between their *esha* remained, and it affected the god, too.

Someone pounced on her from behind. Without turning, the god slammed its attacker onto the ground, like it was swatting a fly.

"Beru," Ephyra's voice cried out, shaking. "Beru, you have to fight. You have to fight it."

The god turned toward the sound of her voice.

No, Beru thought desperately. *No, don't touch her. Don't hurt her.*

The god approached Ephyra, moving slowly, deliberately. Ephyra did not cower.

"It's me," she said softly. "Beru, it's me."

The god lifted a hand, and Ephyra rose a few inches off the ground.

"YOUR SISTER ISN'T HERE ANYMORE," the god said.

It's not true, Beru thought. *I'm right here, Ephyra.*

"YOU ARE THE ONE WHO BROUGHT ME BACK," the god went on. "GAVE ME THIS NEW FORM. PERHAPS, IN THANKS, I WILL NOT PURGE YOU FROM THIS WORLD."

Ephyra trembled, suspended in the air.

"THEN AGAIN," the god said, "I GAVE FORM TO THE BEINGS IN THIS WORLD, AND THAT DID NOT STOP THEM FROM KILLING ME."

The god tightened Beru's hand into a fist. Ephyra let out a broken gasp, and Beru realized what was happening. The god was squeezing her lungs, cutting off her air.

Beru felt like she was pounding her fists against a metal door, slamming against the walls of her mind, trying to tug at the god's will. But it was so much older, and so much more powerful than she.

She could only watch, despair clutching at her chest, as Ephyra's eyes fluttered shut.

"Prince Hassan, now!" Hector's voice bellowed.

Blinding pain ripped through her and Beru—the god—stumbled. Ephyra hit the ground.

The pain only worsened, screaming up her side until Beru collapsed. When she looked up, she saw Hector on his knees, blood seeping out of a wound in his side, his face contorted in pain. His other hand grasped the hilt of a knife, and it took Beru a moment to understand that he was not trying to pull the blade out—he was twisting it deeper. Using their connection to hurt the god.

The god roared in agony and Beru felt her own mind go white at the edges. When the world waved back into focus, she felt her body thrashing, fighting against someone, her chained hands pinned behind her back.

When she looked up, she saw Prince Hassan, Jude, and the Hierophant standing over her.

"YOU VILE CREATURES," the god howled. "YOU INSIGNIFICANT LITTLE *INSECTS!*"

Hassan and Jude hefted her to her feet easily, dragging her toward the entrance of the tomb while the god continued to spit curses at them. They deposited her inside the threshold and looped her chains around one of the pillars within.

The Hierophant stood in the doorway, a dark shadow blocking the light. He glanced at Hassan and held out a hand.

The prince hesitated, before finally handing him the Crown. Jude unclipped his sword from his belt and handed it to the Hierophant as well.

The Hierophant placed the two items on the ground, along with the Chalice.

The god watched him, restless with fury. The Blade, the Chalice, the Crown—they were all a part of it. Stolen from it. To see them in the Hierophant's possession enraged it.

"I have you now," the Hierophant said, not taunting, but simply a statement of fact.

"Wait!" Ephyra cried, appearing in the threshold. Beru slackened with relief. The god had not killed her. "Wait, just let me say goodbye to her, let me tell her that we're going to find a way to fix this. Let me at least—"

Jude stepped toward Ephyra, blocking her path. Beru could still hear Ephyra's pleading as the Hierophant stepped closer to her, gripping the last Relic—the Stone.

The other Relics began to glow faintly in the darkness of the tomb. Beru felt the Relics seize the god's *esha*.

The Hierophant strode forward, flanked by four of his Witnesses, crossing the threshold until he was standing over the god. He reached out and pressed his hand against Beru's forehead. His touch seared her skin, and she felt the god's *esha* pulse like a shock wave. The tomb shook with its power, trembling so violently it threatened to break apart. The god would bring the whole tomb down before it gave up control. It would bring the whole city down. The world.

She felt it build and build and then, like a breath being sucked from her lungs, the god's *esha* contracted. Beru gasped, the god's will suddenly giving way to her own. She was out of the cage, the god shut inside it. The mark on her forehead burned as the god's will rattled inside her, but the mark held. The god's will was confined within her own.

She stared up at the Hierophant, incredulous. What had he done?

"Beru!" Ephyra cried. She rushed forward, past Jude and the prince, and threw herself to her knees at Beru's side.

"It's you," she said, her voice close.

"It's me," Beru agreed, and Ephyra embraced her. Beru shut her eyes, just letting herself be held for a moment, safe. The god was still inside her, she could feel it, even now, prowling in its cage, but she was in control. Ephyra tugged at the Godfire chains, inhaling sharply when the metal touched her skin.

"Stop," Beru murmured. "Ephyra, don't."

Ephyra pulled away and Beru struggled out of the chains on her own.

"Wait," Jude said from behind them, looking wary. He looked over at the Hierophant. "I thought you were going to seal her in the tomb."

"Look at her," Ephyra said, spinning to glare at him. "She's in control. The god is bound."

Beru stood, leaning against the pillar for support. Ephyra reached for her.

The Hierophant moved, stepping behind Ephyra and seizing her arm with one hand. Before Beru could comprehend what was happening, he had the Godfire chains wrapped around Ephyra's wrist.

"You don't want your sister to get hurt," he said to Beru.

The swordsman and the prince started toward them, but Beru, fearing what the Hierophant would do to Ephyra, instinctively held up her hand. They were knocked back. The Witnesses, who had been standing by idly, now moved to restrain them.

Beru looked down at her hand, incredulous.

"The god's power still flows through you," the Hierophant said. "Although you are now the one in control. If you want to keep your sister safe, you will do as I say."

Beru stared at him, fury building in her chest. This anger was hers—but she felt the god's alongside it.

"Beru," Ephyra said, her voice steady. "You don't have to do this. *Don't* do this."

Beru met her gaze. She knew what Ephyra would do if their positions were reversed. What she had always done.

She flicked her gaze back to the Hierophant. "What do you want?"

The Hierophant smiled. "You will do my bidding. Use the god's power to serve me."

Beru felt the god's rage burn hotter. It felt like it would choke her. Whatever the Hierophant had done, it had put Beru in control of her own body again—but for a moment, she gave her voice over to the god.

"PALLAS THE FAITHFUL," it said. "YOU WERE MY MOST LOYAL SERVANT."

"And now," Pallas replied. "You are mine."

59

ANTON

THE WORLD WAS STILL SHAKING AS BERU STEPPED OUT OF THE TOMB, followed by the Hierophant and Ephyra, who was chained in front of him. Anton's breath caught in his chest. Jude was still inside.

He scrambled to his feet, his heart pounding and his head swimming. He could barely stand upright, still too weak to do anything but watch Beru and the Hierophant. And it *was* Beru again, not the ancient deity inhabiting her. He could see it in the way she let her gaze flicker over Ephyra, fear plain in her eyes.

There was no way to know what had happened inside the tomb, but Anton could guess. And it seemed Illya had guessed the same thing, because a moment later he was hurrying over to the Hierophant, kneeling at his feet.

"Immaculate One," he simpered.

The Hierophant paused, glancing down at Illya like he was a muddy footprint.

"You have failed me," the Hierophant said. "Disobeyed me. Why shouldn't I just kill you now?"

Illya's eyes flickered to Ephyra, and then back to the Hierophant. "Because I can be useful. I have been before."

"When you were loyal to our cause."

"I still am," Illya insisted.

The Hierophant actually laughed, low and rumbling like thunder. "Don't take me for a fool, Illya Aliyev. I know what you really are. You say you want power, but you don't even know how to claim it. So instead you seek out those of us who *do* have it, and lick their boots until they throw you a scrap."

Illya looked like he'd been punched. Anton felt a grim sort of satisfaction.

The Hierophant motioned toward Beru. She moved toward Illya and he flinched.

"But," the Hierophant said. "Your self-interest makes you predictable. And I suppose I may find a use for you."

Illya looked up, and stood at the Hierophant's wordless command. The Hierophant looked at Beru.

"Take us to Pallas Athos."

The air around them shivered with bright light, and then Beru, the Hierophant, Ephyra, and Illya disappeared.

The mausoleum was still shaking. Jude and Prince Hassan emerged from within, racing out onto the steps before the threshold of the tomb collapsed behind them.

"Anton!" Jude cried, running toward him.

"Where's the Hierophant?" Prince Hassan demanded.

Anton shook his head. "They're gone."

Jude reached his side and gripped his arm, pulling him over to where Hector was crouched in the dirt, still bleeding.

"We need to get out of here," Hector said grimly.

Jude helped him to his feet as the courtyard shook beneath them.

"Come on!"

The four of them ran over the trembling ground. Stones ripped up out of the path, like the seams of the earth were coming undone. A wall of blood-red water rose up from the lake beyond the tomb, rushing toward them.

Jude yanked Anton hard to the left, changing course. Anton stumbled, crying out as he hit the ground. Jude's hand slipped and he skidded to a stop.

And then the ground began to crack in two, a deep fissure forming beneath his feet, Anton on one side, Jude on the other.

"Anton!" he bellowed, as the ground shifted, the chasm widening between them.

Anton watched as Hector dove for Jude, wrenching him back before the abyss could swallow them. A great crash sounded as one of the huge stone pillars began to topple sideways.

Anton skidded to his feet and ran away from the falling debris, away from Jude. The pillar smashed into the ground in a cloud of dust and rubble.

A chunk of rock struck Anton in the back, knocking him to the ground. He closed his eyes and crawled forward.

He was on his own for the first time since that fateful day when he'd met Jude in a burned down shrine in Pallas Athos. He staggered to his feet. He had to keep going. If not for himself then at least for Jude, who would never forgive himself if Anton died.

He climbed through the rubble, his lungs heaving and his legs aching. And then through the dust he saw someone standing in front of him.

"Anton."

It was impossible. The Nameless Woman.

"What are you doing here?" he asked. "*How* are you here?"

"I came for you," she said. Even in the midst of this destruction she looked as unflappable as ever. The calm in the center of a storm.

"What do you mean you came for me?" Anton demanded, his throat hot with anger. "You left us in Endarrion!"

"I had to."

"Well, we failed," Anton spat. "*I* failed. I couldn't seal the Gate and now the god—"

"I know," she said simply.

Anton wanted to scream at her, to rage because somehow, all of this was her fault. She'd told him about the Relics, the god, the Gate. It all led back to her.

"You could have *helped* us," Anton pleaded. "Helped me."

She shook her head. "I could not enter the city of Behezda. Not while Pallas the Faithful was here."

"Why?" Anton demanded.

"Because I couldn't let Pallas get to me," she said. "If I let him kill me, it would have been over. The seal would have broken."

"Why would killing you break the seal?" he asked. "Who are you? Really." He'd asked himself that question every day since she'd shown up in that cardroom in Valletta. "You're not just a bounty hunter. Or a collector. Or a protector of the Relics. Tell me the truth."

"I thought you would have figured it out by now," she said. "Pallas the Faithful still lives. But he is not the only one."

The world, breaking around them, suddenly upended.

The Nameless Woman. The Prophet without a name. The Wanderer.

"Anton," she said, "I think it's time you learn the truth about where the Prophets came from, and how we killed the god who ruled us."

60

BERU

PALLAS ATHOS LOOKED JUST LIKE BERU REMEMBERED. WHITE MARBLE columns and austere streets gleamed in the moonlight. It was luminous at night, from their spot in the agora overlooking the city.

"This was my city, once," Pallas said. "It will be my city again. And the rest of the Prophetic Cities, too."

Beru turned her head to look at him. His face was pale, with sharp features and eyes so blue they put the Pelagos Sea to shame.

The god was restless inside of her. It was hungry. And it *hated*. It hated Pallas. It hated being captive. It even seemed to hate Beru, and her frail, mortal body.

Pallas turned toward the temple that stood on top of the hill in the agora. Its front portico and columns were blackened by fire. Pallas didn't need to command Beru to follow as he strode toward it. They had left Ephyra captive and bound by Godfire chains in one of the Witnesses' many hideouts in the city. But she was safe—as long as Beru didn't forget who she now served. They ascended the marble stairs and with a flick of her hand Beru blew open the doors.

484

Several acolytes stared at them from within. "You can't be in here."

Pallas strode into the sanctum. "I think you'll find that I can."

Beru watched the moment the acolytes took in his features. Recognized him as the very Prophet to whom they had dedicated themselves.

The first fell to his knees. "The Prophet Pallas has returned," he said, breathless.

The others followed suit, until Pallas was surrounded by supplicants.

"Go forth," Pallas said, waving them up. "And spread my message. Pallas has returned to the City of Faith. The people of Pallas Athos will bow to me again. And soon, the rest of the world."

The acolytes leapt to their feet, hurrying out into the night.

And then it was just Pallas and Beru. And the god who lurked inside her.

"Come," Pallas said, beckoning her toward the altar. "We have work to do."

ACKNOWLEDGMENTS

They often say that your second book is the most difficult to write. As it turned out, this one was an utter joy to write, thanks in large part to my amazing editor, Brian Geffen, who shepherded me safely through second-book woes with a deft hand, boundless enthusiasm, and judicious use of in-line emoji. To the incredible women who make up the marketing and publicity team at MCPG—Brittany Pearlman, Molly Ellis, Morgan Rath, Allison Verost, Johanna Allen, Allegra Green, Julia Gardiner, Gaby Salpeter, Cynthia Lliguichuzhca, Melissa Croce, Ashley Woodfolk, Mariel Dawson, and many more—this series, and my career, owes so much to your creativity and hard work. Mallory Grigg, Rich Deas, and Jim Tierney, thank you for making these books look as awesome on the outside as I hope they are inside. To Starr Baer, Erica Ferguson, and Ronnie Ambrose, thank you for your eagle-eyed diligence and your endless patience with my laissez-faire approach to capitalization. To Jean Feiwel, Christian Trimmer, and the rest of the team at Holt and Macmillan Children's: I feel incredibly lucky every single day to be one of your authors.

Thank you to my agents, Hillary Jacobson and Alexandra Machinist, for championing this series from the start, and special thanks to Ruth Landry, Lindsey Sanderson, and ICM. Thank you to Roxane Edouard, Savannah Wicks, and the Curtis Brown team for ferrying it around the world. Thank you also to Emily Byron, James Long, and the rest of the team at Little, Brown/Orbit UK.

To the cult: Meg RK, Amanda Foody, Janella Angeles, Kat Cho, Amanda Haas, Mara Fitzgerald, Ashley Burdin, Erin Bay, Christine Lynn Herman, Axie Oh, Ella Dyson, Melody Simpson, Madeline Colis, and Akshaya Raman—it is a gift to get to watch you all flourish, and to grow alongside you. (Get it, grow? Like trees???) Special thanks to Tara Sim for giving me the perfect emergency writing retreat, and to Alexis Castellanos and Claribel Ortega for not only being incredible friends but also lending your talent as graphic designers/gif-makers/trailer artists/all-around creative geniuses. Traci Chee, Swati Teerdhala, Patrice Cauldwell, Scott Hovdey, Chelsea Beam, and Laura Sebastian, I'm so grateful for your friendship, advice, rides to the airport, baked goods, Skype calls, and so much more. Special thanks to Sara Faring for letting me test out titles on you!

This book wouldn't be sitting in front of you without my family. Mom and Dad, thank you for always encouraging me and giving me space to become whoever I wanted to be. Sean and Julia, thank you for your unconditional support and for being my New York landing pad. Thank you to Kristin, for poetry and redwoods. To David, I miss you and I wish you could have read this one. Thank you, Riley, because what's a book without a signature cocktail (or five)? Thank you to Erica for basically everything, but especially sunset walks, desert nuns, and the medic scene. (You were right, of course, and I should never doubt you again.)

The biggest thank-you of all goes to the readers who make this all possible. Thank you for coming on this adventure with me.

extras

www.orbitbooks.net

about the author

Katy Rose Pool was born and raised in Los Angeles, California. After graduating from UC Berkeley with a degree in history, Katy spent a few years building websites by day and dreaming up prophecies by night. Currently, she resides in the San Francisco Bay Area, where she can be found eating breakfast sandwiches, rooting for the Golden State Warriors and reading books that set her on fire. *There Will Come a Darkness* is her first novel. Follow her on Twitter as @KatyPool.

Find out more about Katy Rose Pool and other Orbit authors by registering for the free monthly newsletter at www.orbitbooks.net.

if you enjoyed

AS THE SHADOW RISES

look out for

WE RIDE THE STORM
The Reborn Empire: Book One

by

Devin Madson

The kingdom of Kisia is divided, held together only by the will of the god-emperor. When an act of betrayal shatters an alliance with the neighbouring land of Chiltae, all that has been won comes crashing down.

Now, as the fires of war spread, a warrior, an assassin and a princess must chase their ambitions, no matter the cost.

1. MIKO

They tried to kill me four times before I could walk. Seven before I held any memory of the world. Every time thereafter I knew fear, but it was anger that chipped sharp edges into my soul.

I had done nothing but exist. Nothing but own the wrong face and the wrong eyes, the wrong ancestors and the wrong name. Nothing but be Princess Miko Ts'ai. Yet it was enough, and not a day passed in which I did not wonder whether today would be the day they finally succeeded.

Every night I slept with a blade beneath my pillow, and every morning I tucked it into the intricate folds of my sash, its presence a constant upon which I dared build dreams. And finally those dreams felt close enough to touch. We were travelling north with the imperial court. Emperor Kin was about to name his heir.

As was my custom on the road, I rose while the inn was still silent, only the imperial guards awake about their duties. In the palace they tended to colonise doorways, but here, without great gates and walls to protect the emperor, they filled every corner. They were in the main house and in the courtyard, outside the stables and the kitchens and servants' hall—two nodded in silent acknowledgement as I made my way toward the bathhouse, my dagger heavy in the folds of my dressing robe.

Back home in the palace, baths had to be taken in wooden tubs, but many northern inns had begun building Chiltaen-style bathhouses—deep stone pools into which one could sink one's whole body. I looked forward to them every year, and as I stepped into the empty building, a little of my tension left me. A trio of lacquered dressing screens provided the only places someone could hide, so I walked a slow lap through the steam to check them all.

Once sure I was alone, I abandoned my dressing robe and slid into the bath. Despite the steam dampening all it touched, the water was merely tepid, though the clatter of someone shovelling coals beneath the floor promised more warmth to come. I shivered and glanced back at my robe, the bulk of my knife beneath its folds, reassuring.

I closed my eyes only for quick steps to disturb my peace. No assassin would make so much noise, but my hand was still partway to the knife before Lady Sichi Manshin walked in. "Oh, Your Highness, I'm sorry. I didn't realise you were here. Shall I—?"

"No, don't go on my account, Sichi," I said, relaxing back into the water. "The bath is big enough for both of us, though I warn you, it's not as warm as it looks."

She screwed up her nose. "Big enough for the whole court, really."

"Yes, but I hope the whole court won't be joining us."

"Gods no. I do not wish to know what Lord Rasten looks like without his robe."

Sichi untied hers as she spoke, owning none of the embarrassment I would have felt had our positions been reversed. She took her time about it, seemingly in no hurry to get in the water and hide her fine curves, but eventually she slid in beside me with a dramatic shiver. "Oh, you weren't kidding about the temperature."

Letting out a sigh, she settled back against the stones with only her shoulders above the waterline. Damp threads of hair trailed down her long neck like dribbles of ink, the rest caught in a loose bun pinned atop her head with a golden comb. Lady Sichi was four years older than my twin and I, but her lifelong engagement to Tanaka had seen her trapped at court since our birth. If I was the caged dragon he laughingly called me, then she was a caged songbird, her beauty less in her features than in her habits, in the way she moved and laughed and spoke, in the turn of her head and the set of her hands, in the graceful way she danced through the world.

I envied her almost as much as I pitied her.

Her thoughts seemed to have followed mine, for heaving another sigh, Lady Sichi slid through the water toward me. "Koko." Her breath was warm against my skin as she drew close. "Prince Tanaka never talks to me about anything, but you—"

"My brother—"

Sichi's fingers closed on my shoulder. "I know, hush, listen to me, please. I just...I just need to know what you know before I leave today. Will His Majesty name him as his heir at the ceremony? Is he finally going to give his blessing to our marriage?"

I turned to find her gaze raking my face. Her grip on my

shoulder tightened, a desperate intensity in her digging fingers that jolted fear through my heart.

"Well?" she said, drawing closer still. "Please, Koko, tell me if you know. It's ... it's important."

"Have you heard something?" My question was hardly above a breath, though I was sure we were alone, the only sound of life the continued scraping of the coal shoveller beneath our feet.

"No, oh no, just the talk. That His Majesty is seeking a treaty with Chiltae, and they want the succession confirmed before they talk terms."

It was more than I had heard, but I nodded rather than let her know it.

"I leave for my yearly visit to my family today," she went on when I didn't answer. "I want—I *need* to know if there's been any hint, anything at all."

"Nothing," I said, that single word encompassing so many years of uncertainty and frustration, so many years of fear, of knowing Tana and I were watched everywhere we went, that the power our mother held at court was all that kept us safe. "Nothing at all."

Sichi sank back, letting the water rise above her shoulders as though it could shield her from her own uncertain position. "Nothing?" Her sigh rippled the surface of the water. "I thought maybe you'd heard something, but that he just wasn't telling me because he..." The words trailed off. She knew that I knew, that it wasn't only this caged life we shared but also the feeling we were both invisible.

I shook my head and forced a smile. "Say all that is proper to your family from us, won't you?" I said, heartache impelling me to change the subject. "It must be hard on your mother having both you and your father always at court."

Her lips parted and for a moment I thought she would ask more questions, but after a long silence, she just nodded and forced her own smile. "Yes," she said. "Mama says she lives for my letters because Father's are always full of military movements and notes to himself about new orders and pay calculations."

Her father was minister of the left, in command of the empire's military, and I'd often wondered if Sichi lived at court as much to ensure the loyalty of the emperor's most powerful minister as because she was to be my brother's wife.

Lady Sichi chattered on as though a stream of inconsequential talk could make me forget her first whispered entreaty. I could have reassured her that we had plans, that we were close, so close, to ensuring Tanaka got the throne, but I could not trust even Sichi. She was the closest I had ever come to a female friend, though if all went to plan, she would never be my sister.

Fearing to be drawn into saying more than was safe, I hurriedly washed and excused myself, climbing out of the water with none of Sichi's assurance. A lifetime of being told I was too tall and too shapeless, that my wrists were too thick and my shoulders too square, had me grab the towel with more speed than grace and wrap it around as much of my body as it would cover. Sichi watched me, something of a sad smile pressed between her lips.

Out in the courtyard the inn showed signs of waking. The clang of pots and pans spilled from the kitchens, and a gaggle of servants hung around the central well, holding a variety of bowls and jugs. They all stopped to bow as I passed, watched as ever by the imperial guards dotted around the compound. Normally I would not have lowered my caution even in their presence, but the farther I walked from the bathhouse, the more my thoughts slipped back to what Sichi had said. She had not just wanted to know, she had *needed* to know, and the ghost of her desperate grip still clung to my shoulder.

Back in my room, I found that Yin had laid out a travelling robe and was waiting for me with a comb and a stern reproof that I had gone to the bathhouse without her.

"I am quite capable of bathing without assistance," I said, kneeling on the matting before her.

"Yes, Your Highness, but your dignity and honour require attendance." She began to ply her comb to my wet hair and immediately tugged on tangles. "And I could have done a better job washing your hair."

A scuff sounded outside the door and I tensed. Yin did not seem to notice anything amiss and went on combing, but my attention had been caught, and while she imparted gossip gleaned from the inn's servants, I listened for the shuffle of another step or the rustle of cloth.

No further sounds disturbed us until other members of the court began to wake, filling the inn with footsteps. His Majesty never liked to linger in the mornings, so there was only a short time during which everyone had to eat and dress and prepare for another long day on the road.

While I picked at my breakfast, a shout for carriers rang through the courtyard, and I moved to the window in time to see Lady Sichi emerge from the inn's main doors. She had donned a fine robe for the occasion, its silk a shimmering weave that defied being labelled a single colour in the morning light. Within a few moments, she had climbed into the waiting palanquin with easy grace, leaving me prey to ever more niggling doubts. Now I would have to wait until the end of the summer to discover what had troubled her so much.

Before I could do more than consider running down into the yard to ask, her carriers moved off, making space for more palanquins and the emperor's horse, which meant it wouldn't be long until we were called to step into our carriage for another interminable day on the road. Tanaka would grumble. Edo would try to entertain him. And I would get so bored of them both I counted every mile.

Tanaka had not yet left his room, so when the gong sounded, I went to tap on his door. No answer came through the taut paper panes and I leant in closer. "Tana?"

My heart sped at the silence.

"Tana?"

I slid the door. In the centre of the shadowy room, Tanaka and Edo lay sprawled upon their mats, their covers twisted and their hands reaching across the channel toward one another. But they were not alone. A grey-clad figure crouched at my brother's head. A blade hovered. Small. Sharp. Easy to conceal. Air punched from my lungs in a silent cry as I realised I had come too late. I could have been carrying fifty daggers and it would have made no difference.

But the blade did not move. Didn't even tremble. The assassin looked right at me and from the hoarse depths of my first fear my cry rose to an audible scream. Yet still he just sat there, as all along the passage doors slid and footsteps came running. Tanaka woke with a start, and only then did the assassin lunge for the window. I darted forward, but my foot caught on Tanaka's leg as he tried to rise. Shutters clattered. Sunlight streamed in. Voices followed; every servant in the building suddenly seemed to be crammed into the doorway, along with half a dozen imperial guards shoving their way through.

"Your Highnesses, is everything all right?" the first demanded.

Sharp eyes hunted the room. One sneered as he looked me up and down. Another rolled his eyes. None of them had seen the man, or none of them had wanted to. Edo pushed himself into a sitting position with his arms wrapped around his legs, while Tanaka was still blinking blearily.

"Yes, we're fine," I said, drawing myself up and trying for disdain. "I stepped on a sharp reed in the matting is all. Go back about your work. We cannot leave His Majesty waiting."

"I hate being cooped up in this carriage; another day on the road will kill me more surely than any assassin," Tanaka said, stretching his foot onto the unoccupied seat beside me. "I hope His Majesty pushes through to Koi today. It's all right for him, getting to ride the whole way in the open air."

"Well, when you are emperor you can choose to ride wherever you go," I said. "You can be sure I will."

Tanaka folded his arms. "When? I wish I shared your confidence. This morning proves that His Majesty still wants me dead, and an emperor who wants me dead isn't likely to name me his heir."

It had been almost two years since the last attempt on

either of our lives, and this morning's assassin had shaken me more than I dared admit. The way forward had seemed clear, the plan simple—the Chiltaens were even pressing for an announcement. I had been so sure we had found a way to force His Majesty's hand, and yet...

Across from me, the look Edo gifted Tanaka could have melted ice, but when it was returned, they were my cheeks that reddened. Such a look of complete understanding and acceptance, of true affection. Another day on the road might kill me too, if it was really possible to die of a broken heart like the ladies in the poems.

Edo caught me looking and smiled, only half the smile he kept for Tanaka. Edo had the classical Kisian features of the finest sculpture, but it was not his nose or his cheekbones or his long-lashed eyes that made the maids fight over who would bring his washing water; it was the kind way he thanked them for every service as though he were not the eldest son of Kisia's most powerful duke.

I looked out the window rather than risk inspiring his apologetic smile, for however imperceptive Tanaka could be, Edo was not.

"His Majesty will name Grace Bachita his heir at the ceremony," Tanaka went on, scowling at his own sandal. "And make Sichi marry him instead. Not that Manshin will approve. He and Cousin Bachi have hated each other ever since Emperor Kin gave Manshin command of the army."

Edo hushed him, his expressive grimace the closest he ever came to treasonous words. He knew too well the danger. Like Sichi, he had come to court as a child and was called a guest, a member of the imperial household, to be envied such was the honour. The word *hostage* never passed any smiling courtier's lips.

Outside, four imperial guards rode alongside our carriage as they always did, rotating shifts at every stop. Sweat shone on the face of the closest, yet he maintained the faint smile I had rarely seen him without. "Captain Lassel is out there," I said, the words ending all conversation more surely than Edo's silent warning ever could.

In a moment, Tanaka was at my shoulder, peering out through the latticework. Captain Lassel could not know we were watching him, yet his ever-present little smirk made him appear conscious of it and I hated him all the more. The same smile had adorned his lips when he apologised for having let an assassin make it into my rooms on his watch. Three years had done nothing to lessen my distrust.

Tanaka shifted to the other window and, looking over Edo's shoulder, said, "Kia and Torono are on this side."

The newest and youngest members of the Imperial Guard, only sworn in the season before. "Small comfort," I said.

"I think Kia is loyal to Mama. Not sure about Torono."

Again Edo hushed him, and I went on staring at the proud figure of Captain Lassel upon his horse. He had found me standing over the assassin's body, one arm covered in blood from a wound slashed into my elbow. At fourteen I had been fully grown, yet with all the awkwardness and ill-assurance of a child, it had been impossible to hold back my tears. He had sent for my maid and removed the body and I had thanked him with a sob. The anger had come later.

The carriage began to slow. The captain rose in his stirrups, yet from the window I could see nothing but the advance procession of His Majesty's court. All horses and carriages and palanquins, flags and banners and silk.

"Why are we slowing?" Tanaka was still peering out the opposite window. "Don't tell me we're stopping for the night—it's only mid-afternoon."

"We can't be," Edo said. "There are no inns within three miles of Shami Fields. He's probably stopping to give thanks to the gods."

Removed as we were from the front of His Majesty's cavalcade, I had not realised where we were until Edo spoke, but even as the words left his lips, the first kanashimi blossoms came into view, their pale petals spreading from the roadside like sprinkled snow. A flower for every soldier who had died fighting for the last Otako emperor. Though more than thirty years had passed since Emperor Tianto Otako had been captured here and executed for treason, it was still a fearful sight, a reminder of what Emperor Kin Ts'ai was capable of—an emperor whose name we carried, but whose blood we did not.

Mama had whispered the truth into my ear as a child, and with new eyes I had seen the locked gates and the guards, the crowd of servants and tutors, and the lack of companions for what they were. Pretty prison bars.

The assassins hadn't been coming for Miko Ts'ai at all. They had been coming for Miko Otako.

"Shit, Miko, look," Tanaka said from the other side of the carriage. "Who is that? There are people in the fields. They're carrying white flags."

"There's one over here too," I said, pressing my cheek against the sun-warmed lattice. "No, two. Three! With prayer boards. And is that...?"

The carriage slowed still more and Captain Lassel manoeuvred his horse up the line and out of view. When the carriage at last drew to a halt, I pushed open the door, stepping out before any of our guards could object. Ignoring their advice that I remain inside, I wound my way through the halted cavalcade, between mounted guards and luggage carts, hovering servants and palanquins bearing ladies too busy fanning themselves and complaining of the oppressive heat to even note my passing.

"Your Highnesses!" someone called out behind me, and I turned to see Tanaka had followed, the gold threads of his robe glinting beneath the high sun. "Your Highnesses, I must beseech you to—"

"Some of those men are carrying the Otako flag," Tanaka said, jogging to draw level with me, all good humour leached from his expression.

"I know."

"Slow," he whispered as we drew near the front, and catching my hand, he squeezed it, gifting an instant of reassurance before he let go. I slowed my pace. Everywhere courtiers and councillors craned their necks to get a better view.

Some of the men blocking the road were dressed in the simple uniform of common soldiers, others the short woollen robes and pants of farmers and village folk. A few wore bright colours and finer weaves, but for the most part it was a sea of brown and blue and dirt. Their white flags fluttered from the ends of long work poles, and many of them carried prayer boards, some small, others large and covered in long lines of painted script.

Upon his dark horse, His Imperial Majesty Emperor Kin

Ts'ai sat watching the scene from some twenty paces away, letting a black-robed servant talk to the apparent leader of the blockade. The emperor was conversing with one of his councillors and Father Okomi, the court priest. They might have stopped to rest their horses, so little interest did they show in the proceedings, but behind His Majesty, his personal guards sat tense and watchful in their saddles.

In the middle of the road, Mama's palanquin sat like a jewelled box, her carriers having set it down to wipe their sweaty faces and rest their arms. As we drew close, her hand appeared between the curtains, its gesture a silent order to go no farther.

"But what is—?"

I pressed my foot upon Tanaka's and his mouth snapped shut. Too many watching eyes. Too many listening ears. Perhaps it had been foolish to leave the carriage, and yet to sit there and do nothing, to go unseen when His Majesty was mere days from announcing his heir...It was easy to get rid of people the empire had forgotten.

Only the snap and flutter of banners split the tense silence. A few guards shifted their feet. Servants set down their loads. And upon his horse, General Ryoji of the Imperial Guard made his way toward us, grim and tense.

"Your Highnesses," he said, disapproval in every line of his aging face. "Might I suggest you return to your carriage for safety. We do not yet know what these people want."

"For that very reason I will remain with my mother, General," Tanaka said, earning a reluctant nod. "Who are these people?"

"Soldiers. Farmers. Small landholders. A few very brave

Otako loyalists who feel they have nothing to fear expressing such ideas here. Nothing you need worry about, my prince."

My prince. It wasn't a common turn of phrase, but we had long ago learnt to listen for such things, to hear the messages hidden in everyday words. Tanaka nodded his understanding but stayed his ground, tall and lean and confident and drawing every eye.

"General?" A guard ran toward us. "General Ryoji, His Majesty demands you order these delinquent soldiers and their company out of his way immediately."

Ryoji did not stay to utter further warning but turned his horse about, and as he trotted toward the head of the procession, I followed. "Miko," Tanaka hissed. "We should stay here with—"

"Walk with me," I said, returning to grip his hand and pull him along. "Let's be seen like heirs to the Crimson Throne would be seen at such a time."

His weight dragged as Mother called a warning from behind her curtains, but I refused to be afraid and pulled him with me.

Ahead of our cavalcade, General Ryoji had dismounted to stand before the protestors on equal ground. "As the commander of the Imperial Guard, I must request that you remove yourselves from our path and make your grievances known through the proper channels," he said. "As peaceful as your protest is, continued obstruction of the emperor's roads will be seen as an act of treason."

"Proper channels? You mean complain to the southern bastards who have been given all our commands about the southern bastards who have been given all our commands?"

shouted a soldier near the front to a chorus of muttered agreement. "Or the southern administrators who have taken all the government positions?" More muttering, louder now as the rest of the blockade raised an angry cheer. "Or the Chiltaen raiders who charge into our towns and villages and burn our fields and our houses and murder our children while the border battalions do nothing?"

No sense of self-preservation could have stopped a man so consumed by anger, and he stepped forward, pointing a gnarled finger at his emperor. Emperor Kin broke off his conversation with Father Okomi and stared at the man as he railed on. "You would let the north be destroyed. You would see us all trampled into the dust because we once stood behind the Otako banner. You would—"

"General," His Majesty said, not raising his voice, and yet no one could mistake his words. "I would continue on my way now. Remove them."

I stared at him sitting there so calmly upon his grand horse, and the anger at his attempt on Tanaka's life flared hot. He would as easily do away with these protestors because they inconvenienced him with their truth.

Slipping free from Tanaka, I advanced into the open space between the travelling court and the angry blockade to stand at General Ryoji's side.

"No blood need be shed," I said, lifting my voice. "His Majesty has come north to renew his oath and hear your grievances, and if they are all indeed as you say, then by the dictates of duty something will be done to fix them. As a representative of both the Otako family through my mother's blood and the Ts'ai through my father's, I thank you for your loyalty and service to Kisia but must ask you to step aside now that your emperor may pass. The gods' representative cannot make wise decisions from the side of a road."

Tense laughter rattled through the watchers. They had lowered their prayer boards and stood shoulder to shoulder, commoners and soldiers together watching me with hungry eyes. Their leader licked his lips, looking to General Ryoji and then to Tanaka as my twin joined me. "You ask us this as a representative of your two families," the man said, speaking now to my brother rather than to me. "You would promise us fairness as a representative of your two families. But do you speak as His Majesty's heir?"

General Ryoji hissed. Someone behind me gasped. The man in the road stood stiff and proud in the wake of his bold question, but his gaze darted about, assessing risks in the manner of an old soldier.

"Your faith in me does me great honour," Tanaka said. "I hope one day to be able to stand before you as your heir, and as your emperor, but that is the gods' decision to make, not mine." He spread his arms. "If you want your voices heard, then raise your prayer boards and beseech them. I would walk with you in your troubles. I would fight your battles. I would love and care for all. If the gods, in their infinite wisdom, deem me worthy, I would be humbled to serve you all to the best of my ability."

His name rose upon a cheer, and I tried not to resent the ease with which he won their love as the crowd pressed forward, reaching out to touch him as though he were already a god. He looked like one, his tall figure garbed in gold as the people crowded in around him, some bowing to touch his feet and to thank him while others lifted their prayer boards to the sky.

We had been careful, had spoken no treason, yet the more the gathered crowd cried their love for their prince the more dangerous the scene became, and I lifted shaking hands. "Your love for my brother is overwhelming," I said to the noise of their prayers and their cheers. "But you must now disperse. Ask them to step aside, Tana, please."

"Isn't this what you wanted?" he whispered. "To let His Majesty see what he ought to do?"

"He has already seen enough. Please, ask them to disperse. Now."

"For you, dear sister."

"Listen now." He too lifted his arms, and where the crowd had ignored me, they descended into awed silence for him. "It is time to step aside now and make way for His Imperial Majesty, representative of the gods and the great shoulders upon which Kisia—"

While Tanaka spoke, I looked around to see the emperor's reaction, but a dark spot in the blue sky caught my eye. An arrow arced toward us, slicing through the air like a diving hawk.

"Watch out!"

Someone screamed. The crowd pushed and shoved in panic and Tanaka and I were trapped in the press of bodies. No guards. No shields. And my hands were empty. There was nothing I could—

Refusing the call of death, I snatched the first thing that came to hand—a prayer board from a screaming protestor—and thrust it up over our heads. The arrowhead splintered the wood. My arms buckled, but still vibrating, the arrow stuck. For a few long seconds, my ragged breath was all the sound left in the sultry afternoon.

"They attacked our prince under a flag of peace!"

The shout came from behind us, and the leader of the blockade lifted his arms as though in surrender. "We didn't! We wouldn't! We only ask that His Majesty name his heir and—"

An arrow pierced his throat, throwing him back into the men behind him, men who lifted their prayer boards and their white flags, begging to be heard, but imperial guards advanced, swords drawn. One slashed the throat of a kneeling man, another cut down someone trying to run. A few of the protesting soldiers had swords and knives, but most were common folk who had come unarmed.

"Stop. Stop!" Tanaka shouted as blood sprayed from the neck of the closest man. "If I do not—"

"Back to your carriage!" General Ryoji gripped Tanaka's arm. "Get out of here, now."

"But they did not—"

"No, but you did."

I followed as he dragged Tanaka away from the chaos and back to the cavalcade to be met with silent stares. Mama's hand had retreated back inside her curtained palanquin, but His Majesty watched us pass. Our eyes met. He said not a word and made no gesture, but for an instant before doubt set in, I was sure he had smiled, a grim little smile of respect. Wishful thinking. No more.

Edo stood waiting at the door of the carriage but slid out of sight as Ryoji marched Tanaka up to it and thrust him inside.

He held the door open for me to follow, and I took my seat, trembling from head to foot.

Still holding the door, the general leant in. "Do you have a death wish, boy?"

"I was the one trying to stop anyone getting killed, General, if you didn't notice."

"And painting a great big target on your back while you did it."

"They loved me!"

General Ryoji snarled an animal's anger. "You think it was you they were cheering for? They weren't even seeing you. That was Katashi Otako standing before them once more."

"And I'm proud to look—"

"Your father was a traitor. A monster. He killed thousands of people. You—"

Words seemed to fail him and he slammed the door. A shout to the driver and the carriage lurched into motion. Tanaka scowled, ignoring Edo's concerned questions, while outside, more people willing to die for the Otako name bled their last upon the Shami Fields.